OPERATION: MIDNIGHT

A THRILLER

Rick Simonds

RICK SIMONDS

"The thinking of a genius does not proceed logically. It leaps with great ellipses. It pulls knowledge from God knows where."

Dorothy Thompson

PROLOGUE

THE NIGHT WAS crisp and cool and the two homeless men moved closer to the barrel in which they had lit a small fire. Despite having a coat and gloves - both with holes in them - a chill ran through the middle-aged man's body. He spoke to the older man sitting beside him. "Ya' know Willie, I think we mighta' made a mistake not takin' that money like Harry did."

Willie rubbed his hands together. "Ya' think so huh?"

"Yeah, two thousand bucks to work in some lab. Why not?"

"Jake, look at me. Harry won't be working in some lab. Harry and that dog of his will be worked on in some lab. I've been here over a year and seen dozens of men like Harry being offered the same song and dance from the same people we saw tonight and ya' know what?"

"What?"

"Not one of those Harry types has ever come back, including their pets. Trust me, we did the right thing sayin' 'no'."

Jake reached into the bag of trash beside him and threw a milk carton onto the fire. "I guess we did," he said.

The night passed slowly as they stared into the flames.

CHAPTER 1

I HAD JUST approached a party of six when I saw the man walk into the dining room and be seated by the maitre'd. His face was gaunt as though his skin had been stretched over a skeleton. He had pitted, pock-marked cheeks. His sunken eyes hid behind thick glasses which rested on his hawk-like nose. His hair was sparse and a stringy white that lay across his head in a badly managed comb-over.

Once again he wore a tweed sport coat with suede patches on the elbows like a stereotypical college professor. Not that I would know. I just knew that he had been in earlier in the week and, although I hadn't been assigned to his table, he spent an inordinate amount of time staring at me. He gave me the creeps.

"Good evening, my name is Lonnie and I will be your server tonight," I said to the three couples seated around the table in front of me." Can I get you something to drink?" I know I'm supposed to ask them where they're from and encourage other folksy inter-actions but that just isn't my style. Besides, I've found everyone likes to get their drinks quickly anyway.

After several seconds, during which each of them looked around waiting for the other to go first, an attractive lady in a blue cocktail dress with a white pearl necklace said, "I'll have a Bloody Mary."

The man seated beside her with fleshy jowls and a red face addressed the table, "We're from Ohio and since we're in New Orleans, shouldn't we sample some of the local libations - being our first time and all."

He pronounced the city's name, like many tourists do, as if it rhymed with "your jeans" instead of the "Nawlins" as we locals do. The man looked up at me, slapped me on the back and continued. "Let's ask Ol' Lonnie here what the house specialities are or what he recommends."

I have been asked this question a multitude of times and, as usual, I gave my stock answer. "All of our drinks here are very good, but I'd be glad to mention several that have developed a loyal following here at *Bon Vivant* and in the city." I felt the eyes of "the professor" on me from across the room and when I looked up his eyes dropped into his menu. After going through the list of drinks and their ingredients, I said to the woman in the blue dress, "And ma'am, if you'd like a Bloody Mary, we offer what's called a Voodoo Bloody Mary down here which is not only quite spicy but also has a little extra kick."

"Sounds good, I'll have one," she replied.

"I'll take a hand grenade," said the woman to her right. "Say Lonnie, you have the most beautiful eyes - and they're different colors. How unusual."

Rather than tell her that I'm told that often or that six out of a thousand people have this condition, I said "thank you" and looked away.

The man sitting beside her said, "I'd like a sazerac and can you use Pernod in that please. I have a friend back home that told me that was the secret."

"Of course," I replied, pretending to write their orders on my notepad. "And for the rest of you?"

"I guess it would be almost criminal if someone didn't order a hurricane," said a man in a handle bar mustache and dark green cardigan sweater. "Let me have one of those." The well known rum drink originated in the 1940's because spirits were so rare in the city and bars had to purchase fifty or more cases of rum to get one case of whiskey. *Pat O' Brien's* is best known for that drink but we sell plenty of them here also.

A Ramos gin fizz and Pimm's Cup completed the order and as I turned to walk away the man with the fleshy jowls got a look at my notepad and said, "Hell, you ain't got nothin' on that pad of yours but lines and squiggles. Aren't you going to write those drinks down? How you goin' to keep that all straight?"

I chuckled to myself. If he only knew, I thought. It's not hard for me to remember, it's hard *not* to remember.

Antoine, the owner, had even instituted a special some nights when I was working, much to my embarrassment and against my wishes. "If Lonnie forgets, or makes an error in any of your orders, then it's 'on the house'," I have heard him say on multiple occasions. Pretty clever actually, I thought. It encourages the patrons to order more items in an attempt to "trick" me. It's not going to work though. If I can read a book and remember it verbatim… forever, then surely a couple more appetizers and a special request or two won't bother me. "I'll be all set," I said with a smile.

On the way to the bar I glanced at the mysterious man sitting alone and once again he looked away in what appeared to be an effort to not be caught staring. I recited my order to Carla, one of the bartenders, and watched as she frantically hit the buttons on the touch screen register; one of the negatives of having an order not handed in on a slip.

"Hey Lonnie, crazy busy tonight, huh?" said Fey, another server, who sidled up beside me and handed a slip to Alyssa, the other bartender.

"Yeah," I said, looking down at the dark floor beneath me lined with scratches from years of use.

Tall and thin with straight blonde hair in a ponytail and the owner of the whitest teeth I had ever seen, Fey had only started working at *Bon Vivant* a few weeks ago so I didn't know her well but she seemed nice enough. She looked like the All-American girl with an ever-present smile that was contagious. My guess is that she had been a cheerleader but I had never taken the time to ask. The truth is that even though this was my third year as a waiter, and fifth overall at the restaurant, I didn't really know any of the wait staff that well and that was the way I liked it.

In fact, I don't hang around with many people anywhere - with the exception of Dalton, who's not only my best friend and roommate - he's probably my only friend. I'm just not comfortable being around people, never have been. Although Dalton and I are about the same age, "barely legal," according to him, he has a more standardized job for someone our age in this tourist-driven city; he works as a busboy at *Brennan's,* one of the city's best known and most acclaimed establishments.

"Hey, are you waiting on the guy with suede patches on his sports jacket?" I asked Fey.

"Yeah, over on table 14."

"Have you spoken to him?"

"Just about his order. Why do you ask?"

"No reason, I was just curious. I've seen him before." *Last Wednesday from 8:30 to 9:23. Same sport jacket and shoes, darker pants, blue oxford shirt.*

"That's a good thing isn't it? Lots of people are repeat customers."

I didn't mention my feelings. Hell, I didn't know what it meant, but over the years I've come to trust my feelings and something about that guy just didn't sit right. He appeared to be antsy and with my peripheral vision I saw him looking at me an inordinate amount of time. I refused to acknowledge this and since my drinks were up, I headed back to my table.

Bon Vivant was hopping and the night passed quickly as I waited on my customers. At 9:32 "the professor" got up from his table and headed out of the restaurant. I felt his eyes on me as he left and when I saw that he was out the door I headed over to his table to see if he had paid with a credit card. I was disappointed, but not surprised, to see cash sitting on the table cloth. Fey came by and asked if anything was the matter but I assured her there wasn't and returned to my tables.

The Ohioans were just finishing their bread pudding and beignets for dessert and, after checking on the time, asked for their check at my earliest convenience. I removed the blank order pad from my vest, thought for a minute and wrote down the total.

Once again fleshy jowls weighed in after watching as I wrote down the total. "Hell's Bells boy, now don't go tellin' me ya' added that up in ya' head. We had drinks, appetizers, meals and desserts."

I shuffled my feet uncomfortably where I stood and purposely lowered my voice in response. "Yes sir, it's all accounted for."

"And it's all on one check like we asked?"

"Absolutely."

"Well then, let me see it."

I handed him the check which had blank lines with the number $437.63 written on the bottom. On nights that it was quiet I would go through the bother of actually writing down numbers, but on busy nights like this, I found it easier to just pantomime the task. Unfortunately, I knew what was coming.

He looked up at me incredulously and stood up, his napkin still fastened under his chin. "What is this shit?" he said with a bit of a slur, no doubt from the four Pimm's Cups he'd imbibed. "You expect us to pay whatever number you come up with in your head?"

"I assure you that it's accurate," I replied. "It's just that we're awfully busy tonight and you told me that you were in a bit of a hurry."

"That don't mean we wanna' be ripped off," he bellowed. "This is bull shit. Where's the owner?"

The attractive woman beside him lightly put her hand on his elbow. "Gerald, there's no need to make a scene. Perhaps Lonnie has it correct, and besides, we had a lot of drinks. Let's just pay it and go on."

"God damn it Becky, I ain't coming all the way to New Orleans to get snookered by some shaggy-haired kid pretendin' to have all the answers," said Gerald, eyes bugging out, his face now a bright red.

By now the large man had attracted the attention of all those dining in the room and several of whom, those who ate here regularly, were all smiles as the owner came to the table.

Antoine was dressed in a black tux with a black dress shirt and tie. A white carnation was carefully pinned on his left chest pocket. His black hair was heavily greased and combed straight back. Although *Bon Vivant* is not in the same category as *Brennan's* or *Arnaud's,* he always dresses in impeccable fashion and exudes class. "What seems to be the problem?" he asked the large man who stood towering over my six foot frame.

"This here waiter a' yours is tryin' to rip us off, that's what. He gives us this bill with nothin' but a number at the bottom and, not only didn't he write nothin' down but he didn't add it up either. He just looked at the paper for a few seconds and wrote down a number."

The locals leaned forward to hear Antoine's response having been treated to this spectacle before. "Sir, on nights when it's real busy I've given Lonnie permission to present the check on his own. You see, he has some special skills and it makes it a lot easier on our cashiers. I can assure you that it will be totally and completely accurate. He reached inside his jacket and produced a pocket calculator. But, if you'd like me to itemize the bill and check the total for you, then I'd be glad to do that."

"Ya' damn right I would," said the man, his jowls bouncing.

I proceeded to recite to my boss every item that had been ordered with the price of each accompanying the recitation. Antoine's fingers flew over the keys and when he was done he tipped the calculator so the customer could get a clear look. It read $437.63.

A group of nearby diners hooted with laughter as Gerald threw his napkin onto the table. Glaring at Lonnie he said, "I don't know how you did that kid, but I still think you're pullin' a fast one on us out a' towners."

Gerald's wife who, like the other two couples, was anxious to escape from the spotlight, reached into her purse and said, "Lonnie, I thought both the meal and the service were wonderful. What is twenty per cent of the total?"

I, too, was glad that this sideshow was over. "Thank you, ma'am, I'm glad you enjoyed it and thank you also for the tip. Twenty per cent is $87.53 making the total $525.16. I hope you'll come back and see us again." She handed Antoine a credit card and he hustled away to the front of the restaurant.

Several of the "regulars" gave me a round of applause and not wanting to further antagonize the group from Ohio I walked quickly back to the kitchen area out of the spotlight. Fey walked over to where I was standing. "That was great Lonnie," she said. "All the regular customers were waiting to see that big blowhard get put in his place. How do you do that anyway?"

I looked down at the floor as if I had dropped something. I really didn't feel much like talking about anything that has to do with me. I never have. "I don't know. It's really nothing special," I said.

She wouldn't let it rest. "Oh, but it is. You *are* special. Listen, we get off in a couple of hours. What do you say we grab a drink after work? Maybe some place on Bourbon?"

"Thanks Fey, maybe some other time," I said, shifting my weight from one foot to the other. "Besides, I really don't drink much."

She took a step closer which made me even more uncomfortable and said softly, her smile more radiant than ever, "It isn't about drinking. I just want to get to know you a little better."

I could feel my face getting red and didn't know what to say. I heard "Maybe another time," come out of my mouth. As I turned to go back into the dining room I looked over my shoulder. "But thanks," I added. She seemed genuinely nice but I've never found it easy to speak to girls. Most think of me as being a nerd, and always have, but that's alright by me. They're probably right.

CHAPTER 2

TWO HOURS LATER I finished setting up for tomorrow's luncheon and, as is my wont, I made sure the provisions were counted and put in order. The other wait-staff laugh at me and tell me that that isn't part of my job description but I know Antoine appreciates it and, besides, I don't mind doing it.

I also went in our walk-in freezer and packed up two large styrofoam containers of food that I will take to Holy Faith Baptist Church tomorrow to be handed out in their food pantry. This makes me happy and Antoine is totally onboard. I once read that 52 billion pounds of food are thrown out each year just by restaurants, manufacturers and grocery stores and felt this was a way that I could help in my community. This too, makes me happy and Antoine is totally onboard. We started this practice a couple of years ago when we weren't quite as busy and the irony is that by reaching out to help others it seems that we've become busier and there isn't as much food bordering on the edge to be given away. When Antoine realized this he pledged to donate so much each week regardless of spoilage and, as a result, the food pantries are guaranteed a set amount and the customers of *Bon Vivant* are getting nothing but fresh meat and produce.

After punching out and saying good night to those still working, I headed out into the humid night air. Some nights it seems so thick you can taste it but it's my favorite time of day and the smell of the Mississippi River, only a couple of hundred yards below, filled my nostrils. The city's unlike any other in the country and the sights and sounds of the working waterfront are often overlooked by those who consider it a tourist trap and never venture beyond Bourbon Street. Nicknamed "The Big Muddy" the river runs for over 2300 miles and it's been often said that it's "too dirty to drink, and too thin to plow."

Because I live just a few blocks from *Bon Vivant*, in the Warehouse District, I usually walk to work. I enjoy the atmosphere of New Orleans after dark and, since parking in the French Quarter can be nearly impossible, I leave my car at home. In fact, I walk pretty much everywhere I go in the city. The towing of cars, mostly tourist's rentals, is a major component of the city's income and I figure they're doing just fine without my assistance.

The quickest way to get to my condo on the corner of Gravier and Picayune Streets is to head west on Dauphine, where the restaurant is located, walk until it meets Canal Street, and then head south for four blocks turning right on Camp and then one more to the above mentioned corner. But I never go that way.

Tonight, like I've done hundreds of times, I head east until I hit Bienville, then on to Bourbon, which can be difficult navigating depending on the number of drunk tourists throwing beads up to topless women on balconies. Now I pick up Iberville, and could stay there until it intersects with Chartres, but then I would miss out on the beauty of Royal so I make a left turn, go another complete square in the opposite direction, and after twenty minutes I'm in front of my condo. Certainly not the most direct method of travel, but the one I find the most enjoyable. New Orleans has so much variety to offer and, despite having worked in the city for several years, I never get tired of the ambience.

Tonight I had just turned onto Bienville for the second time when I had a prickly sensation that there was someone following me. I stopped and glanced behind me but saw nothing. Nothing suspicious that is. There were assorted teens, tourists and transients but no one that drew my attention so I continued. I had crossed over Iberville on Chartres and in the distance I could hear the sounds of street musicians in Jackson Square. It sounded like Tank and The Bangas were on display.

I would often go out of my way when working the day shift to go through Jackson Square. Called the "Heart of New Orleans," this was where the Louisiana Purchase was celebrated and earned its name in honor of Andrew Jackson after the Battle of New Orleans. Remarkably, over two thousand British were killed in this two-hour battle which effectively won the War of 1812, yet resulted in only 21 Americans losing their lives.

I paused for a moment to listen as the soulful sounds wafted over me but it did not dispel the feeling that was slowly overtaking my every thought. Continuing on I picked up my pace and began to glance sideways with every stride. I felt my breathing becoming labored but at this point I didn't dare to stop again and look behind.

I knew that dashing across Canal Street in front of several oncoming cars was risky, but I threw caution to the wind and reached the opposite sidewalk to a cacophony of bleating horns. I walked on but was unnerved when a few seconds later I heard another series of blaring car horns.

As I approached my building on Picayune Street, I decided upon a strategy. I lived at #14 which was the fourth of eight buildings on the tiny street. These buildings were once all warehouses but were transformed into condos in the late 1990's. Originally there had been two good sized units upstairs but when I purchased the property four years ago, I had some walls removed to make one large unit which I now share with Dalton. It contains two bedrooms, two baths, a kitchen area, large living room with an office space at one end and, as a concession to the man-cave mentality, a space allotted for a theatre room complete with two large overstuffed recliners.

There had once been a freight elevator but I had a staircase put in to connect the second floor with the bottom section of my building. This was now being used for storage and as a garage for my Toyota Camry, in addition to the entrance to the building.

I stopped in front of unit #8 and made a great show, I hoped, of trying to find my keys which were nestled comfortably in my left pants pocket. Unable to "find"

them, I muttered a profanity out loud and then proceeded to knock loudly on the heavy wooden door. Since it was after midnight I knew no one would be up but I shouted, "Open up. I must have left my key at the restaurant." After a few moments and a second shouting, I said, loud enough for anyone near to hear, "Damn, I've got to go back and get my keys." Although there was a lock that Dalton used, I didn't need keys since

I had created a touch tone lock with a daily-changing seven digit code. A bit of overkill perhaps but I enjoy it.

I then headed back in the direction that I'd come, but instead of crossing over Canal, I circled around behind my building onto Camp Street and waited on a stone wall under a large oak covered in hanging moss. I hoped that my subterfuge would work.

From that location I couldn't see the front door of my condo but I could see the egress points on both sides of my building. If someone passed by on either side I would be able to spot them from my location under that tree. Sure enough, after waiting for about five minutes, a lone figure emerged from around the corner and moved slowly, pausing to look upward at the buildings on that street. As he passed under the street light I could see the gaunt figure had sparse white hair and a tweed sport coat. It was exactly who I expected it to be.

I slid back behind the stonewall refusing to move until he crossed Common Street and disappeared into the night. I looped around the other side, punched in the entrance code, and went upstairs to my condo. I was glad to be home but couldn't help but wonder, who was that man that was at the restaurant earlier and followed me to my home... and, more importantly, *what* did he want?

CHAPTER 3

I WAS ON my computer when my roommate Dalton came home shortly before 1:00 a.m. With reddish hair and a face full of freckles he tells me that he was teased by middle-school classmates who called him Howdy Doody. He is a bit shorter than me but more athletic and, as he is prone to say, 'better looking'.

The truth is that if I'm home it is a good bet that I will be on the computer. Like many "twenty-somethings", I spend much of my free time sitting in front of a computer. Not for social media, I couldn't care less about that, but in looking at news items, researching projects I'm currently working on, or playing whatever game I'm engrossed in at the time.

Dalton often stops off at one of the many bars on his way home from work in the hopes of finding a wayward feminine soul willing to engage in some form of carnal pleasure. Obviously he was, once again, unsuccessful on this night because he was alone.

"Hey Lonnie, you home?" he shouted as he came through the door.

"Strange but true," I replied. "No luck bagging the elusive miscreant tonight?"

He walked over to where I was sitting. "I'm not exactly sure what you're asking, but if bad luck refers to my attracting a young lady then I'm convinced that's exactly what it is. As the saying goes, if it wasn't for bad luck, I'd have no luck at all. Hell, it's their loss. They don't know what they're missing." He lifted both arms in a typical strong man position looking from one to another and then leaned toward his right arm to kiss that bicep. "I don't know how they can resist this." He lowered both arms and threw himself into the plush navy blue sofa situated beside my desk.

I smiled at his sophomoric attempt to display machismo. I couldn't comprehend the need for males to articulate either the venture, or vindication, of romantic conquest. I remember various boys back in high school bragging how they had "scored" and never understood the competitive nature of this activity. "How was work tonight?" I asked, hoping to change the topic.

"Busy as usual. There's a hardware convention in town and we had a couple hundred salesmen that reserved the entire upstairs. After a dozen rounds of drinks, several toasts and a countless number of off-color jokes, I had to deal with one plate of cajun crawfish that was knocked off the table and some guy from Detroit who threw up on the rug. Just another night at *Brennan's*. How 'bout you?"

"Like you, we were straight out most of the night...."

"And...."

"And what?"

" And, I can tell you want to tell me something else."

I turned in my chair and faced Dalton who was sprawled out with his fingers interlocked behind his head. "Do you remember one day last week I mentioned a man that came into *Bon Vivant* and struck me as suspicious, the way he kept staring at me."

"Yeah, was he there again tonight?"

"Yes, but that's not all. He followed me home after work. I sensed he was behind me so I pretended that I left my keys at work and circled around and hid. I saw him under the streetlight when he was leaving."

"Wow, that is weird. Any idea who he is or what he wants?"

"None, but I want to find out. It's not that he's said or done anything explicit but there's just something about him that creeps me out. I'm going to keep my eye out and I'd appreciate it if you do as well."

"Will do. What's he look like?"

"Old, thin, thick glasses, wrinkled, pock-marked face, and stringy white hair that he combs over."

"A real looker huh."

"Yeah, and both times I've seen him he was wearing a tweed sport jacket, the type a teacher in college would wear. In my mind I've nicknamed him 'the professor'. Ah well, enough about him," I said, straightening out at my desk. "Do you want to play a game of Starcraft?"

"No, and I don't want to play Steel Battalion, Fortnight, Braid, or any other of the most complex video games out there either because I cannot get to your level, I cannot beat you, and I cannot even compete with you. Doesn't it get boring, always knowing that with your intellect and memory, you're going to win at whatever you play?"

"I don't always win... plus, it's not always about winning. It's about competing, about being challenged. Besides, you've come close on several occasions."

"I'm sure that's only because you've let me. In fact, I'm not sure anyone can beat you in any game. Take chess for example. When was the last time you lost a game?"

I didn't want to get into the particulars of that question and, since I couldn't remember losing a match since my dad taught me when I was little, I thought it would be best to just ignore the question and get something from the refrigerator. The ability to be able to remember all of the moves from past world championships was certainly useful. "I'm going to grab a drink. Do you want anything?"

"Yeah, thanks. I'll take a beer if there's any left."

I walked toward the kitchen area, the overhead lights turning on and then off as I progressed through the spacious condo. I know it too was a bit of overkill but I have enjoyed "tricking out" my condo with as many modern forms of gadgetry as I could. I once read that Bill Gates' house had both lighting and music go off and on as movement was detected and I thought, what the hell, that can't be that hard to set up, so I did it.

I knew that there was no beer left in the refrigerator but I learned long ago that sometimes it was just easier to open the door of the fridge and make the announcement. "Hey Dalton, there is no beer in here. Do you want a soda?"

He looked at his watch and sat up quickly. "No thanks. I'll run out and get a 'sixer'. Do you want anything?" One advantage of living in NOLA - some places never close.

"I'll take an oyster po-boy if you don't mind. And get that dressed."

There are any number of varieties of this staple invented in 1929 during the streetcar strike in New Orleans but my favorite, with everything on it, or "dressed," is with shredded cabbage, pickle, mayo and a yellow Creole mustard. "Here take some money."

"I got it, catch me next time."

Since I was only charging Dalton $500 a month for rent and utilities, I was really catching most of the "next times" so by letting him pay for this, it accorded him a sense of equity.

"I'll be right back. Buzz me in." With that he was out the door and down the stairs.

As he stepped out onto the sidewalk a tall, young woman in blue jeans, light blue sweater and blonde hair caught the door before it closed. "Hi, is this where Lonnie lives?" she asked, looking inside.

"Yeah, I'm Dalton, his roommate. And you are?"

"My name is Fey. I work with him at *Bon Vivant*. Is he home?"

"Yeah upstairs." Dalton looked her up and down, noticed the white teeth and tight sweater and said, "Say, I was just going out to get some beer. Can I get you something?"

I'll just have what you're having, thanks. Do you think he'd mind if I went upstairs?"

"Hard to tell. If you work with him you know he's a little different, but hell, he needs more interactions with young women so I say, go for it. I'll be right back. Good luck." Dalton began walking away but not before glancing back over his shoulder at her backside.

Fay caught him looking, chuckled and waved. "I'll probably need it. See you soon."

I heard footsteps coming up the stairs and assumed it was Dalton returning for something he must have forgotten, but when I looked up from my computer it was Fey who entered my condo. I am not sure if I was more surprised that she hadn't knocked before entering or that she was here at all. Since we never have company, being the gracious host was not, and never has been, my strong suit. I saw no reason to begin now. "Fey, how did you get in here?" I asked.

CHAPTER 4

"I WALKED UP the stairs - and hello to you, too, Lonnie."

"You know what I mean. That lock has eight pin, bump- resistant cylinders and a dual-locking system that can withstand up to eight thousand pounds."

"I'm sure it is wonderful and could hold back the Hulk, but the door was open. I arrived as your roommate was leaving, and he told me to come on up. He even asked me what I'd like to drink, which is more than I can say for you. Aren't you glad to see me?"

I got up from my desk and walked toward her. Her blonde hair, which she often wore up at work, was now hanging around her shoulders, iridescent in the recessed lighting. I had never noticed how truly attractive she was. "Sure... I guess. How did you know where I live?"

Fey sat down on the black leather couch and pulled one leg up under the other as if she intended to stay awhile. "I looked at your file at the restaurant. All of our contact info is there, you know, for tax purposes. I know you said you didn't want to go out so I thought I'd come to you." She surveyed the spacious surroundings. "This is a lovely home, Lonnie. I had no idea."

"Actually it's a condo and since you're the only person to have ever been in here besides some contractors and Dalton, no one has any idea. And that's the way I like it." I recognized that that came across as a little curt and that decorum dictated that I offer her something to drink, so I did so.

"Why thank you. Since I know you don't have any beer, at least until your roommate returns, I'll take a glass of water if it's not too much trouble."

I thought better of responding and headed for the kitchen. When I returned, Fey was looking at a painting I had hanging in the living room. It was titled, *Cathedral Plaza*, and was a typical street scene by local artist Dianne Parks, who was one of my favorites. I have several of her works, but because she had become so well known, it was the only actual painting of hers that I owned. The rest were all prints.

I handed her the glass of water. "This is beautiful," she offered, her gaze sweeping over the stately interior brick walls that I left when renovating. "How about giving me a little tour of your condo? It looks wonderful."

I couldn't think of a thing I'd less rather do but said, "Sure."

As we walked from room to room the lights ebbed and flowed and the music switched from a sultry Preservation Hall jazz to the pulsating techno sound of The Prodigy. Fey, duly impressed, glanced upward but was unable to see any of the speakers that I had recessed or how the music could change on its own. "How did you do that," she asked.

"It was not really all that difficult," I replied. "I enjoy playing with electronics and different devices to make my life easier and more fun. I simply ran Cat six cable to create a multi-zone control system with a speaker switcher. I use my computer to distribute audio over wire home network in the form of digital audio files."

She looked at me with her mouth open. "Oh," was all she said.

We continued through the kitchen, by the bathroom, and into the far end of the condo where I had converted two small bedrooms into a home theater. The large screen covered most of one wall with two large fabric-covered recliners facing in that direction.

"I can see you have all the comforts of home," she said, "except maybe the touches a woman can bring," a twinkle in her eye. "Has your mother been here to see what you've done to this place? Do you have a sister."

I thought these to be rather odd questions but didn't really want to go down that path, so I headed back toward the main room. "No, they live a ways away in the country, so neither of my parents have been here since I've made my renovations, and I don't have a sister - or any siblings for that matter."

I sat back down on the black couch, expecting Fey to sit opposite me in an arm chair, but instead, she sat next to me, forcing me to move closer to the arm. She noticed this and slid closer, looking me directly in the eye. "Lonnie, is there something about me that upsets you? You seem to want to avoid me."

"N-no," I stammered. "I just haven't had a lot of contact with girls. Please don't take it personally. I kind of like just staying to myself."

She put her hand on my wrist. "That doesn't sound like much fun."

Just then the sound of "When the Saints Go Marching In" resonated through the condo, so I stood up and took out my smart phone to buzz my roommate in. *Thank god for Dalton*, I thought. Moments later the door opened and he stepped inside n holding a brown bag in his arms. Behind him was "The Professor," brief case in hand.

CHAPTER 5

DALTON WALKED IN, put his bag down on a table, and sputtered, "I'm sorry Lonnie. He was waiting for me as I arrived at the door and I had no choice but to ring the bell."

"The Professor" forced his way past Dalton and walked up to me until we stood face to face. I was unnerved and didn't know whether I should run or reach for my cell phone to call for help. Although I had a good six inches on the man, I am not one to engage in confrontation. "Who are you and what do you want," I asked in a tone that I hoped was assertive.

"Are you Lonnie Clifford?" the be-speckled intruder asked.

"You know I am or else you wouldn't be here. I'll ask again, who are you and what do you want?"

"Do you mind if I sit down? I will try to answer your questions." Without waiting for a response the man moved across the room and sat down on the oversized sofa, knees together, his leather brief case in his lap. Unsure where this was headed, I sat in one of the two chairs facing the man. Dalton sat in the other and reached into the bag extracting a beer.

I had lost my appetite but decided to go on the offensive. "Twice you've come to *Bon Vivant* and I sensed you watching me. What is it that you want?"

"I'm not exactly sure, but I believe that I've been looking for you for years. If you're who I think you are, then you're in a great deal of danger. He looked directly into my eyes. "I see that you have heterochromia iridis."

"Danger, what kind of danger… and from whom - and what does having different colored eyes matter?"

"Before I answer that, do you mind if I ask you a few questions first?"

I was certainly not in a position of control and although the man now appeared to be non-threatening, I was anxious to hear what he had to say. "Go ahead," I replied.

He began. "What can you tell me about your parents?"

"They Live in Leesville, a couple hours west of here."

"What are their names?"

I was becoming uncomfortable with this line of questioning. "Just exactly what is this about? Did I win a prize from Publisher's Clearing House?"

"The Professor" did not take his eyes off of me, nor did he smile. "Please humor me."

"Their names are Bob and Martha. My dad is a farmer and my mother teaches third grade at Leesville Elementary."

"How old are you and how long have you been on your own?"

"I'm almost twenty two and have lived in New Orleans since I was seventeen. As you obviously know, I work at *Bon Vivant* and have for over five years."

"Ever since you graduated from high school?"

"Yes, something like that." There was no reason to tell him that I had never graduated from high school. I saw no sense in it. Once I realized that I didn't need teachers to learn, I found being in school was a waste of time. If I wanted to know something I just went on line and read about it. If you remember everything that you read, it's pretty easy to learn. I dropped out of school as a sophomore, stayed at home for a year and have been here ever since. I only do that which I enjoy and have a happy life… until tonight anyway."

"Lonnie… is it okay if I call you Lonnie?"

I looked at Dalton who had finished his beer and was taking another out of the plastic holder. "Since it's my name, I guess so." I realized that this was rather rude of me but I was growing frustrated with his interrogation.

"Do you mind me asking where you got the money to purchase this property? You do own it I expect. It's pretty nice for someone your age, don't you think?"

"First of all, that's really none of your business," I said, sitting forward in my chair, "and secondly, you haven't told us your name either."

"My name is not important," he replied, "and as I told you, I will tell you the reason that I'm here in just a minute but please, answer *my* questions first."

I sat back in my chair and decided to play along in the hopes of getting to the bottom of this. Fey, who was sitting quietly beside the man, finished her beer and was handed another by Dalton. I thought momentarily about the po-boy I had ordered but continued. "My parents gave me the money to buy this place. They told me that they had saved up money for my college education and when I decided not to go to college they gave me that money for this instead."

"I've heard that you have quite a memory. Is that true?"

I had no interest in getting into this topic but Fey had other ideas. "Lonnie is amazing. He never forgets anything. He can remember every order without writing it down and can do all of the math in his head."

I was relieved that Dalton didn't chime in with his opinions of my relative abilities but then I saw the man reach into his brief case. "Whoa, what are you doing?" I asked.

Rather than remove a weapon of some sort as I feared, he took a Rubik's cube out of his case and held it in his hand. I looked at the multi-colored toy, its patterns in typical disarray. "Would you be willing to try solving this problem, you know, matching all of the colors up?"

I, of course, knew what the goal was but never found the game to be either interesting... or challenging. This particular version was a simple 3x3 format. I much preferred the more difficult varieties such as Master Pyramophinx or cuboctahedron. "What is the reason for having me do this?" I asked.

"It's nothing more than a social experiment," he replied. "Do you think you can solve it?"

It wasn't a question of whether I could "solve" it, it was if I wanted to be judged as a lab rat and demonstrate my innate abilities. I chose not to and instead slowly moved the colored tiles into the prescribed positions.

After a couple of minutes I was done and handed it back to the man. I had hoped that that would serve to alleviate the need for any further demonstrations but then Dalton had to pipe up with the verbal parry that I had used on him.

"I thought you said earlier tonight it's about competing, Lonnie, about being challenged. That's not the best that you can do. I know you better than that. I've seen you solve three dimensional cubes faster than that."

"The Professor" began to rearrange the tiles while Dalton was talking and once again they were jumbled in a random pattern. "Look," I said. "You still haven't provided me with any answers. If I play this silly little parlor game can we then dispense with any more exhibitions?"

"Fair enough," the man replied. "But this time do the best that you can do. I will time you."

He removed a stop watch from his jacket pocket and once again handed me the plastic cube. "Ready... set... Go!"

My fingers flew over the plastic tiles setting and locking them in place. "Stop," I said when the last colors matched. I looked at Fey and Dalton who were staring at each other in astonishment.

The man looked down at his watch and said, "5.7 seconds. Only one in a thousand people can even do it in less than a minute. Your time is less than a second off the world record!"

CHAPTER 6

I WASN'T SURE what I was supposed to do or say so I just handed the cube back to the man on the couch.

"Jesus Christ, Lonnie!" said Fey, "that was unbelievable."

I didn't share Fey's sense of adulation and was, quite frankly, disappointed that I hadn't gone a second faster. However, I sure as hell wasn't going to say that now, especially in front of this man who not only didn't I know, but also didn't have an understanding of why he was here.

The man put the Rubik's cube back in his briefcase and removed a handkerchief from his pocket. He dabbed at his brow which was noticeably marked with beads of sweat. "Would you mind if I had a glass of water?" he asked as he removed his glasses and wiped the perspiration from both sides of his nose.

"I'll get it," said Dalton rising. "I need to use the bathroom anyway."

I decided it was now my time to go on the offensive. "Okay, now that you've had your fun, it's time for some answers on your part. First of all, what is your name and what exactly do you want from me?"

The man moved forward on the couch and put his handkerchief back in his pocket. "All right, I'll tell you why I'm here but please understand that what I'm about to say might be hard for you to understand... or believe."

"Leave that up to me."

"Of course. My name is Gordon Wormwood and I came here to find out more about you and, as I said earlier, to warn you that your life may be in danger."

Dalton returned with a glass of water, handed it to the man and sat back down. "Why would anyone want to hurt Lonnie? He sure as hell hasn't hurt anyone working as a waiter at *Bon Vivant*."

"No, of course not. It is much deeper than that. It goes back long before he began working at the restaurant."

"Before that I was just a kid in Leesville, Louisiana. I had few friends, did little beside go to school, come home, do a few chores on the farm, and mind my own business. Who on earth would care about me?"

"Lonnie," began the man who identified himself as Gordon Wormwood," how many foreign languages can you speak?"

I thought back to my high school years when I would lie on my bed and play Berlitz tapes that I got from the school library. I would listen for several hours, commit the conversational vocabulary and grammar to memory, and effectively learn a language in a couple of days. Since I could remember everything that I heard, I found it quite easy. I have never actually spoken German or Chinese Mandarin, I never found the need to, but speaking and understanding French, Russian, Italian and Japanese has come in handy on several occasions when waiting on the many tourists we attract at *Bon Vivant*. "A few," I responded.

Fey was taking all of this in with a wide-eyed innocence. I had almost forgotten that she was in the room... almost. "A few? How many is a few?" she asked.

"I don't know, several I guess. I went through a period where I thought it would be fun to know how to speak different languages."

"That's funny 'cause I've never heard you speak anything but English," said Dalton.

"No, and you probably never will. I never felt the need to speak Arabic around the condo."

"But," said the man, "you could if you wanted to. As a hyper polyglot you possess yet another special skill that many would find highly valuable."

"What's a hyper polyglot?" asked Fey.

"It is generally defined as an individual who can speak six or more languages," replied Wormwood. "Noah Webster, famous for creating a dictionary, is said to have mastered twenty-three languages, but there are others who can speak far more."

"And why is this important to Lonnie?" asked Dalton.

"It isn't really," said the man, "but what *is* important is that he has the capacity to learn, *and remember*, as many languages as he wants to learn."

Fey ran her hand through her blonde hair as she leaned forward. "Do your parents speak a lot of languages, Lonnie? Do they have a fantastic memory like you do?"

It didn't take a long time for me to respond as I recalled my Dad working on the farm and my Mom creating lesson plans or correcting papers. "No, neither of them can speak anything but English and their memories are nothing like mine."

Wormwood paused and looked directly into my eyes. "That's because, if I'm correct, they are not your real parents, Lonnie."

CHAPTER 7

I STOOD INSTANTLY and got in the man's face. "What do you mean they aren't really my parents?"

The man slowly rose, turned away from me, and walked behind the couch. "I told you when I arrived that there is much you may not be able to understand or want to believe. What makes what I have to say so difficult is that I have no proof. It's just a feeling that I have, an educated guess if you will."

"You come into my home, make ridiculous statements, and then tell me that they're based on a hunch or guesses?"

By way of answer the man asked me yet another question. "Lonnie, haven't you ever thought it strange that you have so many skills, so many unique abilities, and yet your parents possess none of them?"

"I, of course, have thought many times about the abilities that I have, but I never really stopped to consider whether they were genetic inheritances or whether I am just one of the 'lucky' ones. Obviously we all have different strengths and weaknesses and mine deal with memory."

"You're whacked. You are also superior when it comes to games, computer skills, technology, and online, real-time competitions," said Dalton pretending to count on his fingers.

"And math, and the spatial reasoning needed to solve a Rubik's cube, and who knows what else," said Fey.

I glanced at her as if to say, "Whose side are you on anyway," but then realized that I hardly knew her and wasn't sure why she was here, especially on *this* night.

"Have you ever taken an IQ test?" asked Wormwood.

"No, my guidance counselor tried to get me to take one my sopho-more year in high school but then I dropped out and nothing ever came of it. Why do you ask?"

"It might answer a lot of questions, that's all," said the man who was now slowly pacing behind the couch. "It may show that you are a bright young man, or then again, it might show that you are a whole lot more than that."

I looked at Dalton who was now eating the po-boy that I had asked him to get for me. He had pieces of cabbage and Creole mustard on the sides of his mouth. Our eyes met and he extended the sandwich toward me as if in offering. I shook my head. I was in no mood to eat but saw Fey reach out and grasp the wrapper. I looked back at the man behind Fey. "Why is that important to know - and I still don't see what any of this has to do with my life being in danger."

"Don't you see, there is a great deal here that doesn't add up. You have an intellect that is seemingly off the charts yet your parents are just common, average people. It doesn't work like that. Of course, there are child prodigies, but typically their parents are highly gifted or else..."

"Or else, what?"

"Or else the child has had a rich, varied and highly challenging early childhood. Studies have shown that gifted children are not so much prod-ucts of their genetics, but rather their upbringing. Mozart, who composed his first symphony at the age of eight, was born into a family of musicians. Julius Caesar, one of the world's greatest military strategists, rode horse-back into battle behind his uncle - at the age of three!"

"What does that have to do with me?"

"That's just it, it doesn't. My guess, Lonnie, is that you would register as a genius on any of the intelligence quotient tests commonly given, yet there seems to be no reason for such an occurrence. Do you remember any special stimuli as a baby or even as a toddler?"

"As good as my memory is now, I don't remember my early childhood. I think I was five or six before I started to realize that I was 'different' from other kids. I'm sure my Mom read to me when I was a little but they never went out of their way to provide any special learning skills. I had, what I would consider, to be a 'normal' childhood."

"Having an excellent memory is very different than having an eidetic or photographic memory. Actually, these two terms are often used interchangeably but are quite different," he said. Plus, there are even different types of memory excellence. Hyperthymesia is where an individual has superior autobiographical memory, they can remember everything they did every day of their lives while other so called savants can remember certain items. A man named Tom Morton knew over 16,000 phone numbers in England. Andries Slyusarchuk could memorize 5,100 numbers in two minutes and Akita Haraguchi could recite pi to 100,000 decimal places."

Fey wiped mayonnaise from the corner of her mouth. "Have you ever tried doing any of those things, Lonnie?"

"No, I never had any interest in drawing even more attention to myself. Kids in school thought I was weird enough as it was."

The man stopped pacing and walked out from around the couch to once again come close to where I was standing. "From what I am surmising, and have heard here tonight, you are different, *very* different. Yes, there are people who have eidetic memories, it is generally considered that between two and ten per cent of children may have this, but you have other skills as well; the abilities to reason, relate and create. These do not come commonly to persons with eidetic memories. When one is blessed with such a memory, as well as these other skills, then that individual is considered to be truly special - *gifted.*"

CHAPTER 8

"BE THAT AS it may, Mr. Wormwood, it doesn't explain why my life may be in danger."

"Actually, it is Dr. Wormwood and therein lies the rub. As I said earlier, I have no real proof that you are a genius or that your parents are not your biological parents, but when I heard about you and your incredible memory I had to come speak to you and hopefully get some answers."

Fey was taking the last bite of the po-boy, *my* po-boy, and wiped her mouth with the back of her hand before speaking. "How did you hear about Lonnie's memory?"

"And even so," said Dalton interrupting, "you said yourself, there are lots of people with eidetic memories."

"That's true, there are, but as I also said, there are but a handful of truly gifted individuals. And as to how I heard about Lonnie, it was actually more about where. For a long time I have searched off and on for two individuals who may possess unique talents and ironically, I came to New Orleans for a short stay and was having dinner at *Le Pavillon*, where I am staying, when I overheard some tourists talking about a waiter at *Bon Vivant* with an amazing memory. I decided to check it out for myself."

"That's when you came in last week?" I asked.

"Yes, but I was trying to not be obtrusive and really couldn't determine anything so I came back."

"Why not just speak to me? I didn't even wait on you either time. What's with all the cloak and dagger stuff?"

Wormwood sat back down. I looked at the clock on the bookshelf to his right and saw that it was getting very late but it didn't appear that anyone was in a rush to be going anywhere. Because I still had plenty of questions, I settled back in my chair.

"I intended to but I had a nagging feeling that I was being watched so I decided that I would lay low for a few days before stopping in at your restaurant again. And rather than speak with you there, in public, I decided to follow you home. I must admit that your little subterfuge almost worked. If I hadn't recognized this young lady who waited on me then we might not have connected."

I looked over at Fey. Recognizing my annoyance, she stood and announced her intention of using the bathroom. "I had no idea about any of this, Lonnie. I know that you are shy so I just figured that I would visit you. You know... get to know you a little bit."

I simply nodded. I was more interested in what Wormwood had to say than Fey. "You had a feeling that *you* were being watched. By whom, and more importantly, *why?*"

"As I said, my title is Doctor. I have doctoral degrees in both Genomics and Bioinformatics and have spent much of my life working on governmental projects."

"What type of government projects?" I asked.

"They have dealt with the study of DNA, artificial intelligence and various forms of biological data. Most of this is classified so I can't go into it but suffice it to say that it is complex and very much under the radar."

"Suffice it to say that I have no freaking idea what those subjects even are," said Dalton as Fey returned from the bathroom and grabbed the last beer from the six pack before sitting back down.

Although I also knew little of what the man was speaking of, I ignored Dalton's comment. "Why would anyone be watching you and what does that have to do with me?"

"The government doesn't like to have loose ends and at the end of my employment I was unhappy with the direction we were headed. So, I told them that I would no longer be involved in their projects."

"What happened next?" I asked.

"They tried to convince me to stay on, first by offering me more money and, when that didn't work, they threatened me. They said that because of my involvement and knowledge of their work that I could be a governmental risk if I left at this stage."

"So what did you do?" asked Dalton.

I felt it was not Dalton's place to be involved in the conversation as it related to Wormwood, but since he and Fey had been involved from the beginning, I said nothing. The man didn't seem to take offense to the question.

"I quit. I packed up all of my belongings, cleared out of my office, took all of my files and walked out the door. That was two months ago and I haven't been back since. They weren't happy."

I still wasn't satisfied with the information being given. "But you haven't told me why they would be watching you, and again, how does any of this have anything to do with me?"

"I told you that according to the heads of the project that I was working on, there are two individuals who were determined to be inordinately talented. They were recognized as 'special' at a very early age and were to be nurtured, trained, and 'programmed' as part of the project."

"So, what happened?" asked Fey.

"Both of these 'super' babies reportedly went missing at an early age. Although it happened before I began working in the program, it seems that their parents understood what lie ahead and removed them from the safe house in which they were living."

"And they've never been found?" asked Fey.

"No, not as far as I know. I'm not privy to all the inner workings of personnel and I was not housed in the same location as others, but Lord knows they've tried."

"What does the government want with these two now? You said it's been almost twenty years," she continued.

"Because of their innate abilities and incredible capability to remember, some components of the government hope to bring them back into the fold. You can certainly understand how learning a foreign language in one day, instantly memorizing pages of files, or having the ability to decipher codes could be a tremendous asset."

"Like to the CIA," said Dalton.

"Yes, or to Homeland Security, NSA, or any of the seventeen agencies under the government security umbrella. And while that may be alright for some people, I was hoping to protect them from being harassed. I'm sure that my bosses recognize my interest in the two subjects, especially since I quit, and have been having me watched in case I was able to find either of them."

"And you think that I may be one of the two?"

"I don't know whether you are or not but what I do know, is that if you are, and they find you, they will make your life a living hell. They will force you to work for the government and your life, as you now know it, will be over. My interest is in warning you."

"How can they do that?" asked Dalton. "This is America for Christ sakes. How can they make you do something against your will?"

"All in the name of national security. Since the Patriot Act was passed in 2001 Uncle Sam has virtually unlimited powers."

"But you have no idea if Lonnie is one of those individuals that you refer to as 'special' or 'gifted'?" said Fey.

"That's just it, I don't. Listen, it's very late and I have thrown a great deal at you tonight. As I mentioned, it is easy to check whether your parents are your biological parents; simply take samples of each person's DNA. Did they ever mention anything to you about being adopted?"

"No, absolutely not, but how would knowing about my parents affect any particular attributes that I might have inherited?"

"As I explained, geniuses are not accidental and do not come from normal, common place parents or from those with no intent of developing a special child. Lonnie, I may be bothering you for no reason but we can get answers very easily. Simply get DNA samples from both of your parents and bring them to me. I can do the test myself. Wouldn't you like to put this to rest once and for all?"

Actually, I was pretty much blown away by all of what I'd just heard but simply nodded my affirmation.

He reached into his briefcase, removed a small plastic bag and from that took a cotton swab. "Here, put this in your mouth, rub it against your cheek and then put it back in here," he said, holding out the plastic bag.

I did as he instructed.

"Also, I will administer an IQ test as well and all of your questions will be answered. You will not have to wonder, or worry, ever again. You can continue to wait on tables without thinking about me or my fears. Can you get away to visit your parents?"

I told him that I thought I could but before I did that I needed to process all that he had said. He was not having any of that.

"I'm staying in room 433 at *Le Pavillon* under the name Franklin Claremont. Stop in when you're back from your trip. I'll be down here for a few more days." He rose to leave.

"Do you have a cell phone? I can call you when I'm back."

"Absolutely not. Those are nothing more than glorified tracking devices."

I thought about all that he had said and decided to proceed. "Okay, I'll talk to Antoine, my boss, and shoot for the day after next. It takes awhile to get to Leesville, but if I head up there in the morning I'll have enough time to do what is necessary and I'll stop by your hotel room later that night."

I shook hands with Wormwood as I saw him to the door. When he had departed I went back up the stairs where Fey and Dalton were engaged in conversation.

"What do you make of all this, Lonnie?" asked Fey. "It all seems so strange."

"Yeah," agreed Dalton, "it's like something you'd see on TV."

"I really don't know what to make of it," I replied, "but it's too late now to do anything. I'll deal with it in the morning." I walked over to a closet and removed a blanket and pillow and handed them to Fey. "As late as it is, you might as well spend the night on the couch."

"Thanks Lonnie, I'd like that."

Amazing, I thought as I headed up to my bed, and I'm not sure what was more so; that I had just been told that my parents were not really mine, or that I have a girl sleeping in my condo.

CHAPTER 9

GORDON WORMWOOD RETURNED to his room at *Le Pavillon* and checked behind each door, the broom closet and the bathroom where the shower curtain was pulled back all of the way to guarantee there was no one in his room.

He made sure his briefcase was locked before putting it under his bed on the far side. He carried it with him, manacled to his wrist, wherever he went because he didn't dare leave it behind or utilize a hotel safe. He didn't trust any of the staff.

He had taken a huge risk going out to *Bon Vivant* and then going to Lonnie's condo. Wormwood realized that he was confronted with a no-win proposition since he preferred to order room service for meals yet knew if he was going to find either of the "super babies" he had to leave the confines of his room.

He hung up his sport coat and removed his trousers and dress shirt before lying down on his bed. His mind raced because he truly believed that Lonnie was one of the individuals he'd been looking for. From what Lonnie's two friends said he has exceptional aptitude in many areas and his memory is undeniable. Plus, when he actually tried to solve the Rubik's cube, he demonstrated world-class spatial reasoning and dexterity.

I should have the answer very soon whether or not the pair that Lonnie believes to be his parents truly are. I will administer an IQ test to him and then run DNA tests on him as well as Bob and Martha Clifford when he returns.

Wormwood wanted badly to call one of his former work associates but knew that wouldn't be wise as they might be listening - not to him since he'd make the call from a pay phone - but on his friend's line. They would know that he is in New Orleans. So far he felt he'd been able to avoid the net that Cricket and his men were casting.

Perhaps I should go to the authorities, he thought, but who would I contact? I trust no one and the mere fact that those projects are continuing unscathed gives credence to the fact that persons in the government must be willing to look the other way.

Wormwood made sure his curtains were tight, his door locks were secure and his briefcase was indeed under the bed before attempting to fall asleep.

CHAPTER 10

THE DRIVE WEST to my parent's home in Leesville is supposed to take four hours from New Orleans but since I was in somewhat of a hurry I expected it to take much less. My intent was to drive there, ask some questions about my upbringing, get DNA samples, and return tonight so that I could go to Dr. Wormwood and get some answers. I'm not as eager to take an IQ test. It's not that I'm concerned with the outcome, it's just that I have never enjoyed being a lab rat.

There are major highways that run west through Baton Rouge and on into Lafayette, the unofficial capital of Cajun Country, and then up to Alexandria. The traffic was light and I made good time on these turnpikes. From there I headed south on the Lake Charles Highway to Leesville. I drove with the windows down letting the warm morning air energize me. The blazing foliage of the Sourwood and Ginkgo trees provided framework on both sides of the highway. A sense of deja vu swept over me as I went by the entrance to the Fort Polk Army base and soon after passed the familiar sign: Welcome to Leesville: "The Best Home Town in the Army."

I know I could have asked my mother what the story concerning being my parents was when I spoke to her on the phone yesterday and informed her that I was coming to visit, but I figured a topic so serious needed to be tended to in person. It had been a long time since I had been home and Mom said she would call in sick so she could be there when I arrived. I guess her third graders would just have to terrorize a substitute teacher today. She tried to get me to tell her "what the occasion" was for my unexpected visit but I thought it prudent to say nothing over the phone.

I had rigged up a Bose speaker system in my 2009 Toyota Camry and the sounds of *Dysylm* reverberated throughout. My parents live on a 46 acre farm near Billy Goat Hill and as I drove up the circular driveway to the house I was greeted by Sammi, the black lab that I had received as a present on my eighth birthday. She was now almost fourteen and while she once would have jumped up on me in an exuberant greeting, she now was restricted to wagging her tail. I bent down to her level so I could rub her ears.

"Hey Lonnie," shouted my mother as she walked out onto the porch that ran in front of the house. I stepped up to meet her and threw my arms around her in a bear hug.

"Hi Mom, how've you been?"

"Just great thanks, but how about you?"

I stepped back and got a good look at the woman who brought me into this world, at least I think. She had a few more wrinkles on her face than the last time I saw her and a few strains of white hair were competing for prominence in her short dark hair, but her warm smile, which seemingly came from her heart, dominated her face.

"Where's Dad?"

He's out back in the barn tinkering with something or another. Go on out. He'll be thrilled to see you. I just made some fresh lemonade, can I get you a glass? Are you hungry?"

" No thanks, Mom. I'm a little bit thirsty, but after I see Dad I think I'll make a quick run into town. I have a couple of errands to run and I might just make a stop at Flavor Shakes while I'm there. You know how much I love their coffee frappes."

"You always did. I remember how you always wanted us to take you there after your Little League games.

I thought back to the only organized sporting event I ever participated in and realized that I enjoyed the post-game visits to Flavor Shakes more than I did the games themselves. I'm sure the fact that I struck out more often than Joey Tribbiani in *Friends* had something to do with it.

"You are going to stay for dinner, aren't you? I know you said on the phone that you couldn't stay long but I have a roast being cooked - prime rib - your favorite kind. Why is it again that you made a special trip?"

Her rapid-fire questioning, which was so typical of her, made me smile. Since I had never mentioned why I was coming, I wasn't sure why she used the word "again," but I wanted to wait until I had both parents together before I explained the reason for my trip. "To see you, Mom," I replied. "It's been too long. And no, I can't stay for dinner but I'll have a sandwich when I get back."

She stepped closer, put a hand on each of my shoulders, and looked deeply into my eyes. It *has* been too long. You go see Dad and then hurry back from town so we can talk. I'll mix up some tuna fish. Do you have a girl friend yet?"

I smiled, shook my head and went out the back door, Sammi close behind. "It's good to see that Mom hasn't changed," I said to the lab who wagged her tail in reply.

As I walked across the dirt driveway behind the house, I heard a clanging sound from inside the barn and found my father leaning under the hood of a rusted Ford pickup. He heard Sammi and I approaching and straightened up, Allen wrench in hand. "Lonnie!"

"Hey Dad, working on Rusty?" We wrapped our arms around each other and squeezed. I had forgotten how strong he was. He had worked on a farm since he was a boy and was the hardest working man I knew. There was no such thing as a weekend off when you live on a farm and I don't know that he'd ever taken a vacation.

He rubbed his forehead with his forearm. "Absolutely. When I heard you were coming home I decided to check the ol' truck out. You know, in case you wanted to take her for a spin around the property." A deep chuckle rose from within. "You always did like driving Rusty."

I laughed along with the gentle giant. I had learned to drive using this rusty old beauty and although it hadn't qualified for a sticker for years, it was perfect for cruising around the dirt roads on the farm.

"I sure did, Dad. Still do actually, but I think I'll take a raincheck for now. I need to run into town for a couple of minutes and Mom's making tuna fish sandwiches. How are you feeling?"

He lifted both arms in a body builder's pose and tightened his fists.

"If I felt any better there'd be an investigation," he said, a smile engulfing his face. "How's everything in the big city? How's Dalton doing?"

"Everything's fine. We're both real busy... you know, with tourists and all."

"When isn't New Orleans busy? I'm surprised that Antoine gave you the time off to come here."

Again I wasn't ready to begin the conversation that I so desperately wanted to have. "I know, he said to say hi to both of you." I thought back to the time he helped me celebrate their 25th anniversary at *Bon Vivant* and charged us nothing for what was a fabulous meal.

My Dad walked over to a work bench and picked up a rag to wipe his hands. "It's been awhile, Lonnie. I miss seeing you, we both do. I loved having you here, you know, helping around the farm and all."

"I miss you guys too, but I don't know how much help I was. I was probably in the way most of the time or in my room on the computer."

"You were never in the way. Whatta ya' need in town?"

"I just have to run a couple of errands and then I thought I'd make a quick stop at Flavor Shakes. Want anything?" I didn't think that telling either of them that I was going to stop at the city hall for a copy of my birth certificate was in my best interest.

"Nah, your mother made some fresh lemonade so I'll have some of that. She and I are going to make a quick run to the bank in a minute? You want to take Sammi with you?"

I looked over at the black Lab lying contentedly on the barn floor. At the mention of her name she looked up. "Sure, I know how much she loves going for rides." We started walking.

Mom was hanging laundry on the clothesline as I reached the house. "Do you want a rocky road sundae with whipped cream and nuts?" I asked, knowing what the response would be.

"My goodness no. I'm trying to keep this girlish figure." She ran her hands down the apron stretched across her front. "You have fun." She headed back into the house.

I opened the passenger side door to my Camry and Sammi climbed gingerly onto the front seat. I remembered when she would have run and got her leash at the mere thought of going for a ride but the years had crept up on her and I knew by her measured methodical movements that a leash was no longer necessary.

Before I got in the car I stopped to look at the family farm. The white house with dark green shutters was badly in need of paint and many of the shingles on the roof were torn or missing. The large red barn, too, had a tired roof and one corner had collapsed several years ago in a hurricane. Some might fret over what needed to be done but I had never seen my parents upset about what they had or didn't have or heard them complain about their lot in life. I obviously had inherited that love of a simple life and I wanted to hurry back and get to the bottom of this. I wondered, was getting a coffee frappe a defense mechanism?

CHAPTER 11

THE RIDE INTO town was both quick and uneventful but for some reason I felt nostalgic as I drove past the library and then the high school. I didn't expect that since I had never considered those to be my "glory days" like so many teens since I had only spent two years at LHS.

I chuckled at the high school sign heralding "The Home of the Wampus Cats". This half-dog, half-cat creature, part of Appalachian lore, has been the mascot for almost a century. Described by many sources as having six legs and in some instances walking upright, Leesville adapted it to look more like a mountain lion or wildcat and uses its image as the name of the yearbook and on their athletic uniforms, none of which I ever bought or wore.

The city hall was just as I remembered it, a two story brick building that houses government agencies and public services. I went to the second floor to the City Clerk's office and was greeted by a frail white-haired lady in horn-rimmed glasses that reminded me of Granny in the Beverly Hillbilly re-runs I had seen.

"And how may I help you, young man?"

"Hi, my name is Lonnie Clifford and I would like to get a copy of my birth certificate please."

"Certainly. It's nice to meet you Lonnie, my name is Claire. Clifford huh, are you Bob and Martha's son?"

I'd forgotten how provincial small towns can be. "Yes, those are my parents. I'm guessing you know them."

"Oh heavens, yes. They are the nicest people. We go to the same

church. Give me a couple of minutes. I need to go into the back office."
She disappeared and was gone for several minutes. When she finally
returned she had a glum look on her face. "Lonnie, I'm afraid that I
couldn't find your certificate. Were you born here at Byrd? A lot of people
living here in Leesville were born at Doctors Hospital at Deer Creek.
Could that have been the case? What was the date?"

She was referring to the regional hospitals in town and I, of course,
couldn't be sure of that but I gave her the date. Once again she retreated
to the back office.

Claire returned minutes later but had no different results. "I don't
understand it, there's nothing in the files either alphabetically or by date.
Your parents don't have a copy?"

"We must have misplaced it. I'll look again when I go home." I wasn't
about to go into the reasons for my being here but after hearing this I
was even more mystified. I had lived in this town all my life and as far as
I knew I was born here also. I thanked Claire for her efforts, promised
to say hi to my parents for her and headed out. I was even more looking
forward to speaking with my parents now.

I arrived at Flavor Shakes with a myriad of thoughts racing through
my head. Ah yes, the giant frozen yogurt painting on the wall in their
signature blue and orange colors was still there and although the special
of the day, a Banana Bomb, was inviting, I went with my go-to drink, a
coffee frappe. As usual the service was quick and I was preparing to leave
when Tim Harkins pulled up in a Chevy Silverado. We had not really
been friends in high school - I'm not sure I had any - but he would have
probably passed as the closest thing to it.

"Lonnie Clifford. Well, for Christ sakes, what the hell brings you
back to Hicksville?" He put his arms around me, squeezed, and only let
go when he noted that I didn't return the fervor.

"Hey Tim, just came back to visit my parents. How're you doing?"

" Busier 'n a ATM in a whore house," he said slapping my back. "I
just bought me this new Chevy, workin' full time at Jackson Brother's
Garage, and fixin' on getting married this summer to Becky Guerrette.
Life is good, Bro."

By now I was more than ready to head back but he would have none of that so I went back in and took a seat in a booth and waited while he ordered. For the next fifteen minutes he regaled me with stories about people who I didn't really care about. It wasn't that I didn't know them, it's just that I was in a hurry and could probably have gotten along without knowing that Dusty Morgan was cheating on his girlfriend with Nicole Rideout who had breast implants or that Lance and Barb Preaux were getting a divorce. Besides, I wanted to get back to my parents. I was done with my frappe and afraid that I was doomed to spend my afternoon here when Sammi, sitting up in the driver's seat, began to bark.

I stood instantly. "Geez, I'm sorry Tim, but I forgot that I had Sammi with me and as hot as it is, I need to get her back home." I extended my hand. "It's been great catching up on everything."

He ignored my hand, stood, and once again wrapped his arms around me. "Lonnie, it has been great hasn't it. How 'bout stoppin' over later and throwin' down a few Lone Stars?"

"I'd love to Tim, but I'm heading back to New Orleans tonight. I've got to work tomorrow." I saw no purpose in telling him the real reason I was in town and I sure as hell had no interest in drinking beers with him and Becky Guerrette. "Thanks, though. Say hi to Becky for me."

I was in my car with the motor running before he had a chance to object. I patted Sammi on the head as I drove out of the parking lot. "You know, you may not be a Saint Bernard, but you sure saved my life back there." She had no idea what I was saying but she was sure it was important and licked my right arm.

As I drove back to the farm I thought about how happy I was to be living and working in New Orleans. Small towns can be great places to say you're from, but not so great in which to live. "It's a big world out there," my Dad used to say to me when I was about ten, "and you owe it to yourself to see it." I wasn't sure just how much of this big world I intended to see since traveling wasn't my favorite cup of tea, but I knew that I now only wanted to visit Leesville, and not live there.

I pulled into our driveway and opened the door for Sammi. She went ahead as usual but was forced to wait on the porch as I walked toward the house. I noticed that my Dad's truck was missing but then remembered that they had planned to go to the bank.

I went in, sat down in the living room and turned on the TV set. As I surfed through the channels I remembered how few options they had on the "basic" package. Ah well, Judge Judy would have to suffice.

It wasn't until the end of the show that I realized how long they had been gone. That wasn't like them, especially since they knew I was home. After trying both parents cell phones and having them go to voice messages I decided that I would call the bank to see how long ago they had been there and if they were on their way home.

I found the number, dialed, and a female voice responded pleasantly, "Leesville Bank and Trust, how may I help you?"

I identified myself and asked if my parents were still in the bank. The voice on the other end replied hesitatingly, "Please wait one minute."

A man's voice came on the line a couple of minutes later and said, "Lonnie, you may want to come into town. I'm afraid there's been a terrible accident."

CHAPTER 12

I RAN TOWARDS my car, Sammi following behind me in a labored jog. I didn't intend to take her but when I opened my door she jumped in and then moved over and up onto the passenger seat.

My heart was pounding in my chest as I sped out of the driveway sending dirt flying onto the porch. It was not a long ride but it seemed interminable despite my breaking the speed limit the entire way into town. I fought back tears as I thought about what might have happened to my parents - it had to be my parents - why else would the man state that it was "a terrible accident?" What could be more terrible?

When I arrived in town I saw police cars and an ambulance parked at the corner of 5th Street and Port Arthur Avenue, their red and blue lights piercing the tranquility of the placid town. Because traffic was being blocked off, I pulled over and parked a couple hundred feet from the activity. I got out, slammed the door and ran toward the police cars.

As I reached the intersection, I saw my father's red Ford truck twisted and gnarled, the driver's side demolished and caved in. The truck was partly on the sidewalk, the glass in the windshield shattered. A stream of smoke rose from beneath the hood which had been forced away from the chassis and like much of the front end was crumpled.

The paramedics were breaking down a gurney into the back of the ambulance, a sheet covering the body. I tried to cross over to the side of the accident but I was stopped by a young policeman in uniform with short cropped brown hair and a somber look. His name tag read "Evans" and I vaguely remembered him from school years ago but I was in no mood to re-establish a relationship. His arms engulfed me in a bear hug. "I'm sorry, I can't let you go over there."

I was also in no mood for conversation. "Those are my parents," I said breaking free from his grasp and running across the street before he could stop me. I got to the back of the ambulance as the paramedics were sitting down one on each side of the two bodies draped in white. The driver held the door but was unable to close it as I leaned inside the vehicle.

I felt an arm on my shoulder and turned. It was Glen Bell, the Chief of Police of Leesville. Although I had never met the man, I knew who he was. Hell, we all knew just about everyone in town. That was the nature of small rural towns, it seemed like no one ever moved into town. It always seemed it was the desire, especially of young people, to move out. His rock jaw and military haircut were just as I remembered it. I doubted that he had gained a pound since I last saw him.

"Lonnie, right? I'm Chief Bell. I'm terribly sorry. You can see their truck… they were in a terrible automobile accident." He paused and took a deep breath. "I'm afraid they didn't make it."

I dropped to my knees on the road behind the ambulance. "No, this can't have happened," I wailed, tears running down my cheeks. "I just saw them. We were going to have lunch."

Bell helped me to my feet. He put his arm under mine around my back and steadied me, directing me toward his car. "Here, have a seat for a minute," he said, opening the passenger side door for me.

"I need to go see them," I cried.

Bell leaned in to me and spoke in a soft tone that was almost a whisper. "There's nothin' you can do for 'em now Lonnie and you don't want to see 'em like that."

Tears continued to fall from my face and I simply nodded at his suggestion. Everything seemed surreal and I had no idea what to say or do. The small group of people who had gathered at the scene of the accident began to disperse as the ambulance drove off.

I slumped down into the seat as I watched it pull away, its lights flashing and saw a tow truck with MORGAN'S GARAGE emblazoned on the driver's door pull up next to my Dad's truck which was still smoking. It was at that point that I realized that there was not another car on the side of the road. I sat up. "Chief Bell, where is the other vehicle? The other car that was in the accident?"

"I'm 'fraid that right this minute we don't know where it is or who was driving. We have an all-points-bulletin out across the county so we'll find him but as for now it looks like a hit and run. Trust me, he can't get far with the damage that he must have sustained in the accident."

"What about the cameras. Aren't there cameras on the outside of the buildings or traffic cams?"

"I'm sure that them big cities have 'em on every corner but we never installed 'em. As you know, there ain't a lot of crime here in Leesville and truth is, we never felt the need."

"Didn't anybody see the accident?"

"We're not sure yet, but you know how this town is Lonnie. If anyone saw something they'll come forward. We'll find out who's involved."

I stepped out onto the sidewalk and looked back at my car. Bell knew what I was thinking and said, "Would you like somebody to give you a ride home Lonnie, or stay with you awhile?"

I wasn't sure what I wanted or needed but said "no," thanked him, and headed back to Sammi waiting in my car.

CHAPTER 13

I FELT UNCOMFORTABLE returning to the house where I grew up. Although I had many happy memories of my time on the farm, for evermore it would be my parents house; the house and farm that they loved so much and the place they had spent their entire adult lives.

As I walked into the kitchen the redolent smell of both roasting meat and fish filled my nostrils. I took the tuna fish out of the refrigerator, the tuna fish that my mother had lovingly prepared for me, and once again I broke down in tears. Knowing that I would never share another meal, never see them again, seemed so surreal. I didn't feel like eating but grabbed the loaf of bread and made a sandwich. It was more of an homage than a meal. I also turned off the stove, took out the roast Mom was cooking, covered it and put it in the fridge.

Before leaving I took some time to look around my childhood home. In the living room there were framed photos of me in a Little League uniform, holding a trophy when I had won the spelling bee, holding Sammi when she was a puppy and others. I had never realized that there were so many pictures of me on their walls and virtually no others.

I remember my father telling me that he had lost all of his photos from high school and the service when the roof leaked one spring and my mother never wanted anyone to take a picture of her. The only picture of both of them on the wall was their wedding photo. I took it down and looked carefully at the two people who meant so much to me. I would take that with me and cherish it forever. As I took one last look around the room my many childhood photos further proved to me how much I was loved.

I couldn't get myself to spend the night there so I rented a room at the Spring Gardens Motel on the outskirts of town. It seemed so odd, staying in a motel in my own hometown. There would, no doubt, be a great deal more things that seemed odd. Spring Gardens typically didn't allow pets but since they had, of course, heard what had happened to my parents, they made an exception. It had been a long time since I had slept with Sammi on the bed beside me, but tonight I was glad for the company. Knowing that something was dreadfully wrong, she laid beside me, her head facing the pillow. I hugged her face, tears falling from my eyes. The morning light was visible around the curtains before I fell asleep.

Later that morning I awoke to a truck pulling out of the motel parking lot and cursed the annoyance. I glanced out the window, saw the sun shining through the dust-stained glass, and felt further annoyed that the day was going to be a pleasant one. Foolishly perhaps, I felt the day should be as sullen and morose as I felt. I took Sammi outside and contemplated the tasks that were being thrust upon me.

I remembered that I came to Leesville with a purpose, and although I certainly didn't need to go to the morgue to identify the body like they make people do on TV, I did want to get a swab for DNA. I also knew that while I was in town I needed to make arrangements for my parent's funerals and take care of other business as well. I'm sure some would feel that I was acting impetuously, but I really didn't want to hang around town. After a lengthy walk, which was probably more therapeutic for me than Sammi, I took an equally long shower and headed out.

Morrison's Funeral Parlor was a family run business in the center of town that had served the Leesville area for two generations. I had attended a couple of funerals there when I was younger but did not expect to plan one - at least not this soon.

After meeting with the owner, Kyle Morrison, and making arrangements for a weekend service, I headed to a nearby real estate office and then to the Leesville Bank & Trust in an attempt to put the necessary affairs in order. I decided to inquire about putting the farm on the market but had my doubts that it would sell since there were so few people moving into town. Besides, who wanted to take on the work involved in running a large farm. I just knew that I did not want to live there. Again, I knew there would be some that would say that I was acting way too quickly in making this decision but I knew, for me, it was the right thing to do.

Bill Donovan was the manager of the bank and he took me into his office to offer his condolences and his assistance. He was a tall, handsome man with curly dark hair, expressive eyes that seemed to be perpetually smiling and was wearing a suit that appeared to be custom fitted. "I will gladly transfer the funds from your parent's bank account into yours, Lonnie, or, if you prefer, you can simply withdraw what's in it." He reached for a folder. "Let me look up their account number."

"Thank you Mr. Donovan, and it's 4087163295."

Donovan smiled as he wrote down the number. "I'd heard you were a bit special."

I ignored the comment. "Since I'm now living in New Orleans, if you don't mind, I would prefer to close the account and rather than do it now I will stop in when I come back for the funeral." This all seemed so overwhelming that I just wanted to get out of there. He understood and promised me that everything would be in order when I returned. I had no idea how much money was in their account but assumed it wasn't much and truthfully, I didn't care.

Finally, I headed to Byrd Regional Hospital where the bodies would be held until they would be cleared by the Medical Examiner and then picked up by Morrison's. I had put this off as long as I could and dreaded the thought of having to look at my parents in that condition. I walked into the lobby, identified myself to a woman at the front desk who served as a receptionist behind a glass window, and asked to see my parents.

She went online to confirm that Bob and Martha Clifford were being held and after obtaining affirmation directed me to the basement where a makeshift morgue was set up to hold bodies until custody was transferred. After signing my name along with my address and phone number on a lined sheet, I followed the person in charge, whose name tag read Myron, to a room at the end of the hall. "Are you sure that you want to do this?" he asked. "Would you not be better off remembering them as you knew them?"

I assured him that I would be alright even though I had no idea if that was true. He unlocked the door and switched on the light and there, on two metal tables, were my parents seemingly asleep with sheets pulled up to their heads. "Most of the damage was done internally," Myron explained. "So, other than that cut on your father's forehead, they don't look too bad."

I felt a chill run through my body and wasn't sure if it was from the temperature, which was obviously much lower than the air outside, or from the stark realization of where I was and what I was looking at. I rubbed my arms with my palms and moved closer to the tables. I bent over and kissed my mother's forehead, tears once again forming in my eyes. "Would you mind giving me a couple of minutes alone?" I asked Myron.

He saw that I was struggling to maintain my composure and took a step toward the door. "I ain't supposed to leave anyone alone in here but considering the circumstances, I think it'll be alright." He closed the door quietly behind him.

For a minute I just stared at the bodies of the two people who had raised me and provided me with so many happy memories. I kissed them both and then took the cotton swabs inside the plastic containers from my pocket. After dabbing them inside their cheeks and replacing them in the tubes I kissed them once again and walked out.

Myron was standing in the hall as I exited. He reached in, turned off the lights and checked to make sure the door was locked. "Is there anything else you'd like Lonnie?" he asked.

Just to see them one more time and tell them that I love them, I thought. "No thank you," I said.

CHAPTER 14

THE RIDE BACK to New Orleans took more time than ever before. With Sammi sitting beside me, her head out the window and the wind blowing on her face, I retraced my earlier travel route. Despite having a myriad of thoughts and ideas racing through my mind I saw scenery that I had never noticed. The bromide, "stop and smell the flowers" for most is a mantra rather than a message but I had begun to focus… focus on things that I was oblivious to prior to the death of my parents.

I was driving through Pineville when I first smelled and then saw a brush fire being tended to on the side of the road. The acrid stench of burning tires filled the air and I closed the window to escape the malodorous fumes. It was then that I remembered the roast that Mom had hastily thrown in the oven for my visit. I had taken it with me figuring that Dylan and I could eat it when I got back home. Sammi certainly hoped that she could be included in that equation as she could no doubt smell it in the trunk.

As I went to turn down the radio my cell phone rang. The number came through as "blocked." "Hello."

"Hey Lonnie, it's Chief Bell. Ya' gotta minute?"

"Sure. What's up?"

"First of all, let me again say how truly sorry I am. I thought a lot of both of 'em. They were the salt of the earth."

"Thanks Chief. But there must be more to this call than that."

"Well, actually there is," he said, seeming to pause as if he wasn't sure just where to go next. "As I told ya yesterday, I knew that somebody, if they saw sumpthin', would come forward and I was right. Orville Foster from New Llano was in town picking up some things from the dry cleaners and said he saw a black SUV drive into the side of your father's truck and force him off the road. He said he didn't even think to look at a license plate and was astounded when the SUV drove off. He did notice that the windows were tinted so he has no idea who, or how many, were in the vehicle."

"Was there much damage done to the SUV? Have you found it yet?"

"No, we ain't been able to locate the vehicle but Lord knows, we got enough people lookin'. We got a BOLO out all over the region. I'm sure we'll find it soon, where can they hide? As for damage, Orville said he couldn't tell 'cause they drove off so quickly, but he didn't think there was much. It was one of them big ol' boats if ya' know what I mean. He didn't come forward 'til today 'cause he figured plenty a people saw the incident."

I patted Sammi sleeping on the passenger seat. "Well, thanks Chief. I appreciate all you're trying to do. I'm sure you'll keep me posted."

"No problem Lonnie, but there's just one more thing. Do you know if your parents had any enemies? Orville said it didn't seem all that accidental. He said after the initial contact that SUV kept pushin' that truck right into the light post."

I thought for a few seconds about his inquiry. "Please understand Chief Bell, that I'm living in New Orleans and know virtually nothing about what's been going on back here. This is the first time I've been back in almost a year. It's hard for me to believe that they would have any enemies though."

Chief Bell raised his voice. "That's the way I figured it too. Lonnie, I've known your parents for over thirty years. Your dad and I were in the same grade in school and played football together." A pause came over the phone. "I got no idea who'd want to hurt such nice God-fearin' people, but I promise you this. We'll catch the sumbitch who did this. You can bank on it." Another pause and I heard a garbled voice in the background. "I gotta go Lonnie but I'll keep ya' posted. Have a good 'un."

I thought that was an odd comment considering but didn't dwell on it. That seemed to be the standard sign-off for most people in today's society without thought or meaning. My next task was to text Dalton to let him know that I was en route and the approximate time that I should arrive home. Since he was working, and I didn't want to leave Sammi alone in my condo, my plan was to drive directly to *Le Pavillon* and see Wormwood. Now that they were dead, I was even more determined to find out if Bob and Martha were my real parents.

The sun was beginning to set as I pulled into the street level of the parking garage that served several businesses including the hotel. I lowered both front windows down half way, locked the car door and walked toward the hotel. Since I knew that they wouldn't allow pets inside, I hoped to make my visit a brief one.

Large marble pillars supported the narrow white building that resembled the binding of a book when viewed from the end. I entered *Le Pavillon* and as always, was taken by its beauty. Nicknamed "The Belle of New Orleans," it was radiant with its marble floors. The magnificent Czechoslovakian crystal chandeliers overhead screamed of Parisienne opulence and the ornate moulding and deep navy hanging tapestries provided a sense of warmth to the setting. Several large gold framed paintings and oversized mirrors hung from the walls. It was a throwback, like so many of the exquisite hotels and restaurants, to a more grandiose time in New Orleans. It had been completely restored and it's 226 rooms and overall charm had earned it its distinction on the list of Historic Hotels of America.

I recognized the concierge dressed in a black tux with a red carnation tucked into his lapel who strolled toward me as I walked across the lobby. A giant of a man with dark black skin and an infectious laugh, he had eaten at *Bon Vivant* on several occasions.

"Hey Clarence, how are you tonight? Busy?"

A contagious smile full of shining white teeth were displayed as he responded. " Wuzzup Lonnie, what brings you by?"

"Just visiting a friend," I said as I kept walking. As much as I enjoyed Clarence's personality, I didn't want to engage in a lengthy conversation.

"If ya can't remember how to get home, stop back down an' I'll help ya." His laughter filled the room.

I headed for the elevator and pushed the button for the fourth floor.

The door swung open and I waited as a desk clerk and a couple of older ladies exited. I stepped inside and was joined by a couple who were engaged in an argument. The woman was upset that the man, who I'm guessing was her husband, had been encouraging women on Bourbon Street to bare their breasts. I chuckled to myself. It's not the first such argument in this city. They're definitely not in Kansas any more.

I got off and walked down a long corridor until I found room 433. I had thought of calling ahead to the hotel to let him know that I would be stopping by, but since I still wasn't sure how much to trust him, or anyone else for that matter, I'd decided that I would just stop in and hope that I caught him in his room.

I knocked on the door and heard movement. "Who is it?" came from the other side.

"It's me, Lonnie," I replied. He opened the door a crack, confirmed that it was me, and then poked his head out and looked both ways down the hotel corridor before ushering me in.

"I was worried about you," he said. "I expected you yesterday."

I sat down on the plush jade-green upholstered couch and took a deep breath before answering. "My parents are dead."

CHAPTER 15

"WHAT THE HELL did you just say?"

"I said that my parents were killed in an automobile accident - a hit and run actually - when I went out to Leesville to see them. That's why I couldn't stop by yesterday. I'm sorry. But here," I said, reaching into my pocket and withdrawing two plastic bottles used for prescriptions that held Q-tips with the saliva of my parents on them.

"Oh Lonnie, it's me that should be sorry." He sat down beside me and put his hand on my shoulder. "It's just what I was afraid of. It's what I was trying to warn you about when I came to your condo. I will test the DNA on those for you in a minute. I have a "testing-lab-on-a-chip" and just need to mix a few chemicals and warm it up. It will take about four hours before I have the results but then you'll know."

"Actually, you said *my* life was in danger. There's no proof that my parent's deaths were anything but an automobile accident. But it seems so suspicious, the timing and all. Why would anyone want to kill my parents? Do you think this is related?" I realized that I must have sounded like a fool rambling on but I had so many questions.

"I'd be surprised if it wasn't. I do think it's highly suspicious that your parents just happened to get in a fatal automobile accident at the same time that you attempt to get answers to serious questions. It just shows you how serious these people are… how deadly. I don't think you realize what, or with whom, you are dealing."

It was unfathomable how two innocent people could have died for seemingly no reason at all. He was right, I didn't understand any of this and it was time that I got some answers. "The police think that it was an accident but a witness saw the car that hit them drive off. Those things don't happen in Leesville."

Wormwood rose and walked slowly toward the bedroom. He paused to switch on a lamp "That would be something they could… and would, do. Make it seem like some type of an accident to deflect the real motive of their actions. This group will stop at nothing."

I had heard enough of this. I stood and shouted into the bedroom where he had headed. "This is bullshit. You show up unannounced with a ridiculous story about government projects, artificial intelligence, and biological experimentation and now my parents are dead. What is going on?" I glanced out at the office building opposite and the red-purple streaks above that structure stretched across the sky. Because it had been such a warm day the windows were open. The curtains fluttered softly in the late afternoon breeze coming off the Mississippi.

Wormwood returned from the bedroom with a black leather briefcase in hand. Once again he sat down on the couch facing the fireplace in the elegantly furnished room. I sat down beside him.

"Lonnie, what I am about to tell you is highly classified. I told you at your condo that I had taken my files when I quit but, in actuality, I removed many of their files dealing with experimentation that was to have been ceased many years ago. These files were to have been destroyed much like most of the information from the Edgewood Arsenal Experiments in 1975 and today all of the documentation is digitalized. I have obviously put myself in harm's way by taking these but I was willing to take that risk if it can bring an end to these practices."

"You stole these from the lab?" I asked incredulously. "No wonder you're afraid that they may be after you."

"Of course, but I felt that I needed to. I figured that nobody would believe me if I didn't have some type of evidence outlining how horrific this experimentation was… and still is. Typically all of these TS, or top secret, projects are compartmentalized so we only know what we are working on and not any others but I took all of the files I could find so as to provide proof.

I'm sure he wanted me to sit quietly and listen but I was tired of playing this cloak and dagger game. "If it's so secretive, then why are you telling me?"

"Because you need to know. You need to know the truth about your parents, yourself, and why I believe you are in grave danger. Earlier I told you that I have spent my life working on government projects related to artificial intelligence and various studies of biological data but what I didn't tell you is that many of these projects have been going on for years, unbeknownst to not only the general populace, but to Congress and the Executive Branch as well."

Beads of sweat were forming on his upper lip but I could tell that he had no intention of stopping so I leaned back in the couch.

"For years the Department of Defense, the CIA, and DARPA have performed illegal testing and human experimentation on soldiers in an attempt to create 'the perfect soldier' and on unsuspecting citizens as well."

"What is DARPA? I've never heard of that."

"Most people haven't although it has become somewhat better known recently. It stands for Defense Advanced Research Projects Agency and it is in this agency that I have worked for the past twenty plus years. It was first created under Eisenhower in 1958 as a response to the Soviet launching of Sputnik 1. The original mission was to avoid being surprised by any technological advancements of our enemies. It morphed into our creating surprises for our enemies and other advancements. This is where the Internet was first created. It has become a monstrous part of our nation's defense and this year's budget alone is almost $3 billion."

"I don't see how that impacts me or why that is so dangerous."

Wormwood punched a code into his briefcase lock, opened it, and removed a handful of files. "For the past fifty years the government has conducted a multitude of experiments on its own citizens, its own soldiers, without their knowledge. Usually these projects are conducted by small research teams and run from three to five years, often in conjunction with university studies and government grants, but not always. Have you ever heard of the Edgewood Arsenal, Project MK ULTRA, Bluebird, or the Monarch Project?"

" No, but am I to guess that I should have?"

"Not necessarily. Most of what DARPA does is secretive but it at least comes under the auspices of the Department of Defense and is monitored by a Director. There have been a few leaks over the years and a couple of congressional reports that attempted to provide some answers, but in actuality, they never scratched the surface of what was done... or is being done."

"One of the advantages of this agency is that it is both small and flexible and avoids hierarchy which allows for a rapid transferral of information and ideas. They seek to hire creative people, empower them, and encourage them to produce radical rather than incremental innovation. There are only 240 employees and over half of these are technical. In fact, they have been called '100 geniuses connected by a travel agent.'"

"According to DARPA it doesn't own or operate any laboratories or facilities but I know that to not be the case. There is research being done in over 80 institutions. These include colleges, hospitals, prisons and pharmaceutical labs. There are always several projects going on simultaneously by various offices and for the most part are somewhat transparent, at least to those in charge. But, one such group, under the Biological Technologies Office (BTO), is referred to as 'Blackout'.

While there has been experimentation for many years, a scientist decided to pull away from Blackout and BTO and conduct his own work in what he calls OPERATION: MIDNIGHT.

This has been in existence for only about six years and is off the grid. The DARPA headquarters has been in Arlington, Virginia since 2009 but a couple of segments of MIDNIGHT operate in underground labs in the mountains outside of Asheville, North Carolina. That is where they have engaged in dozens of heinous experiments and sadly, in one of those is where I worked until I decided that I'd had enough."

"What type of experiments?"

"Experiments that are designed to manipulate gene expressions, brain washing, mind control. We have attempted to enhance a human's natural abilities through genetic engineering. Imagine having soldiers that kill without remorse, are immune to fatigue, are incapable of feeling fear and perhaps even have the ability to regrow limbs that are lost or destroyed in battle."

While I was fascinated by what Wormwood was saying, I still wasn't sure of the relevance to me.

Wormwood answered that question without any more prodding. "Lonnie, I might be dead wrong but I think that your father, your real father, may have been involved in this experimentation as a soldier, perhaps without his knowledge or approval. In addition to all that I mentioned above, they also have conducted tests to artificially develop muscle mass, increase a person's hearing and eyesight and even change the color of an individual's eyes, which can lead to heterochromia. Much of that goes back to the work of Josef Mengele and the Nazis."

"Another aspect of their work is injecting brain cells into animals. This chimera manipulation was supposedly banned but I assure you that it continues."

"You mention all of these tests that are being conducted. Who's in charge of this? If the government outlawed all of this, how is it able to go on? I can't believe that in this day and age this would be allowed."

Wormwood shook one of the files in front of me. "Exactly. That's what they expect everyone to think, that this couldn't still be going on. Much of what had gone on was brought to light by a Congressional Committee chaired by Frank Church in 1975. They published six books of findings the following year after investigating several government agencies and it was supposed to put an end to these activities. But," his voice began to rise, "it *is* still going on. There are any number of people working on advancing AI or artificial intelligence with robots and continuing experimentation on what's called the Active Denial System (ADS) which is a heat ray that works like a microwave. This has actually been sent to the Middle East and supposedly returned without being used yet but many doubt that... and there is so much more."

"Why would our leaders, our government, begin this in the first place?"

"As I said, it began as a defensive or reactionary effort. There were studies to determine how much nuclear fallout would be required to make the planet uninhabitable. There were several tests such as Bluebird that used military personnel as guinea pigs with over 7000 military personnel being given LSD and other experiments attempting to simulate a biological warfare attack that sprayed our own citizens with various forms of bacteria, so that we would be ready if just such an attack took place."

"Wow. Who was in charge of this?"

"The head of the CIA, Allen Dulles. He had complained that there were not enough human guinea pigs so Project Artichoke in 1951 led to MK Ultra which was sanctioned in 1953. There were actually 149 separate projects under that heading. There has been some backlash over the years and in 1977 a great many documents were released under the Freedom of Information Act. Congress is convinced that these experiments are no longer being done but, again, that is NOT the case."

"In 1978 the CDC conducted experimental Hepatitis B vaccine trials on promiscuous homosexual men in New York, San Francisco and Los Angeles. Is it a coincidence that the first cases of AIDS in this country were reported in those cities less than three years later?"

"In 1987 the Department of Defense admitted, that despite a treaty banning research and development of biological weapons, there were over 120 research facilities still in operation. As recently as 1997 eighty-eight members of Congress demanded an investigation into the use of bio weapons. Regardless, it's still going on."

I couldn't believe what I was hearing. "Unbelievable. Who's responsible for these?"

As I said, the man in charge of doing much of the illegal experimentation for OPERATION: MIDNIGHT is known as Derek Spillbane. He began in the program years ago, and has risen through the ranks to the point where he is now in control. Typically DARPA rotates Program Managers every five or six years to insure an infusion of fresh thinking but Spillbane has managed to hang on. He has refused to accept that his work will be for naught if it's shut down so he went rogue. He went underground literally and figuratively. Like many a scientist, their work is their life. Frankly, I think he is a bit mad and that's why I made the decision to get out of that program after all these years. I think he would stop at nothing in order to maintain his secrecy and that of his work. You need to avoid him at all costs."

"I don't even know who or what I'm trying to avoid. What does he look like?"

"That's the hardest part. No one is sure, at least no one that I know. Word got out that because of the secrecy of the program, and his desire to maintain anonymity, he had plastic surgery to conceal his looks. I'm not even sure if that's his real name. As I said, although we started at about the same time we were never together. We were assigned to different projects working in different locations. Now that he is working in one of the secret labs in Asheville most of his communicating comes through texts and emails to those who work under him. I'm not sure that there is anyone that is in direct contact with him and that's the way he wants it. I'm afraid that if he is indeed after you, or finds the whereabouts of the two individuals missing from what he believes is "his" program, then it may be too late."

"Terrific, I'm to avoid a man who I don't know what he looks like but may be after me for a reason I'm not sure of. This shouldn't be difficult," I said sarcastically.

"He generally has an assistant who reportedly does his dirty work. He's not a physically imposing man, he's only about 5'7", but word is that he's extremely dangerous. He used to show up every once in awhile at the lab where I was working to check up on us. I don't know his real name either - he just goes by 'Cricket.'"

"Cricket?"

"I'm told it comes from Shakespeare's Macbeth. Crickets cries were omens of death in Elizabethan times according to legend. He is a bald man and has a scar over his left eye. And, oh yes, he has a tattoo of a cricket on his right forearm. We all tried to ignore him when he was around. We weren't privy to what he has done but the stories of his ruthlessness were rampant. I'm sure there are others involved in doing the dirty work and he has helpers working with him, but he is the one people talked about."

I didn't know what to believe, but I knew that I had Sammi waiting in the car and I needed to push him along. "I'm not sure what my next step is but how about you run the DNA tests that you talked about and let me get the results of those before I hear any more. I have my dog with me and need to get home but I can come back."

"Of course, I'd be glad to. I want to help you get to the bottom of this." He rose from the couch, picked up the two plastic containers that

I had given him and turned to walk back toward the bathroom. As he
_ _ed in front of the windows, I heard an explosion and saw Wormwood
_ ked down from the impact of what must have been a high-caliber
_ Blood seeped from his chest and was splattered over the blue uphol-
_ d chair and onto the maroon oriental rug. His body lay twisted, his
_ es sat skewed on his face, his eyes were open and vacant.

_ My first reaction was to duck or hide but then I realized that the
_ must have come from one of the high rise office buildings facing the
_ . I scooped up the files sitting on the couch and threw them into
_ nwood's briefcase along side the others. I thought about grabbing
_ lastic containers with the DNA swabs but they had rolled across the
_ under chairs and I didn't dare take the time. I bolted for the door.

CHAPTER 16

I OPENED THE door, checked in both directions and headed left toward the stairs. As I reached the door to the stairs I looked behind me and saw a short man in dark jeans and a black tee shirt get off the elevator and head in the direction of Wormwood's room. Since whoever did the shooting wouldn't have had the time to get to his room, I knew there had to be at least two people involved. I didn't look back as I headed for the parking garage, the leather briefcase bouncing against my thigh.

When driving out of the garage, I turned and drove slowly in front of the hotel trying not to cause suspicion. As I passed *Le Pavillon* a tall man with dark hair in a leather jacket ran across the street toward the hotel. I watched in my rear view mirror as he hurried toward the parking garage. I couldn't get a look at his face as he was back to but I had a feeling that he, too, was somehow involved in Wormwood being shot.

Sammi, sitting on the seat beside me, had no idea of my predicament as I headed for my condo. I'm sure that she recognized the difference in scenery between The Big Easy and sleepy little Leesville, but to her it was just nice to take another ride.

I checked the rear view mirror continually and, although I saw nothing suspicious, I took several extra turns before arriving on Picayune Street. After parking in the garage below my condo, I dashed up the stairs and called *Bon Vivant* asking to speak to Antoine.

It was Fey that answered the phone and she recognized my voice. "Lonnie, is that you? Where are you?"

I had no interest in re-enacting the day's events and just wanted to speak to Antoine and get off the phone. I still had no idea with what, or whom, I was dealing with but I knew that they meant business and I needed to keep a low profile until I knew what was going on. "I'm home. I just got here and need to speak to Antoine."

"Are you all right? Are you coming in?"

"I'm fine, but no. I need to take a few days to sort this out," I replied, becoming exasperated. "Please put me through."

"Okay, just a minute, I'll get him."

A couple of minutes later Antoine came to the phone and as briefly as I could, I told him about the death of my parents in an automobile accident and that I really needed a few days off to deal with the funeral arrangements. I conveniently neglected to mention both the circumstances surrounding my parent's accident and the death of Wormwood and all that he had shared with me.

As expected, Antoine was sympathetic and couldn't have been nicer. "Oh my god, Lonnie, that is horrible. I am so sorry. You take all the time you need. I'll get someone to take your place."

I thought of Dalton and how he wanted to move up from a busboy to a waiter at Brennan's but hadn't been there nearly long enough. "Say Antoine, my roommate Dalton, who has worked at Brennan's for almost three years, would be interested in making the move. Do you think you could use him? He's a hard worker and a nice person. I know you've met him when he's stopped in to meet me after work."

"I remember meeting him," said Antoine. "Ya know, we're probably alright. I have a couple of people who I have used part time, but have him stop by and I'll speak to him... and Lonnie, let me know if there is anything you need. I'll make sure that your check goes out tomorrow. Stay in touch."

My next call was to Kyle Morrison who had given me his cell phone number when I was in town. He informed me that the wake would be Friday night and the funeral the following morning if that was alright with me since he had received the go-ahead from Chief Bell. That gave me a couple of days to deal with that which I needed to determine, so I assured him that that was fine and we discussed various arrangements. He guaranteed me that everything would be taken care of and would be tastefully done.

I thanked him, hung up, and turned to Sammi who I could tell needed to go out. We went across the street to a small triangle of grass that served as a buffer at an intersection. She wasn't used to such a small area since growing up on a farm allowed her the run of the land. While she did her business, I glanced continually in all directions fully expecting to see a car full of killers pull up next to the curb.

Thankfully, I saw nothing out of the ordinary and when I returned to my condo, I realized how tired I was suddenly feeling and went to my bed to lie down. Sammi hopped up on the bed and laid her head beside me on the pillow, an idiosyncrasy she had enjoyed when she was a pup but hadn't been able to do since I had moved away.

I awoke when I heard voices and, after glancing at the clock beside my bed, I realized that I had been asleep for several hours. My not-so-vigilant "watch" dog slid off the bed and went to greet Dalton and Fey. They were both down on their knees patting the black Lab as I came in. They rose and both put their arms around me in a group hug. "I am so sorry to hear about your parents," said Fey. "It's absolutely awful."

"It's unbelievable," echoed Dalton. "I can't believe this has happened. I feel so bad for you."

"I appreciate your concern, and yes, it really has been an unbelievable series of events."

"Oh, and thanks a lot for hooking me up at *Bon Vivant* I stopped in there after work and Antoine said he could use me as a waiter. It'll be full time while you're gone and then he said we'd see after that. As much as I'd like to do that at Brennan's, it could be years."

Fey walked over to me and handed me an envelope. "Speaking of that, this is your check from work. Antoine asked me to give it to you and said there was a couple of extra dollars in there - to put towards the funeral. He also gave me this for you. He said you could probably use something decent to eat." It was a styrofoam container, the type we used at the restaurant if a customer was unable to finish their meal.

I stuffed the envelope into my pocket and sat down on the couch. I realized how long it had been since I'd eaten and the styrofoam container was a welcome sight. Sammi too, was thrilled with the container of veal Parmesan which I shared. After finishing my meal and a bottle of Abita

Amber, I decided that it was time to catch the pair up on what had transpired this afternoon. The reaction was as expected.

"Oh my God, Lonnie," said Fey after hearing my story, "What are you going to do?"

Dalton was equally as concerned. "You need to go to the police. I can't believe you just left and are sitting here calmly eating when there are killers out there that are searching for you. Wormwood was right."

I understood their concern. Hell, I was petrified actually. I looked at the two of them who were now sitting across from me. "First of all, I may be sitting, but I'm anything but calm. I'm scared, but quite frankly, I'm not sure what to do."

Dalton rose again and began to pace. "What do you mean, you don't know what to do? You need to get your ass to the police. Christ O' Mighty Lonnie, you've had three people that have been connected to you die in the past few days. We might've thought that Wormwood was making shit up but all that he's predicted has come true. You need some help."

Fey chimed in. " Dalton's right. You need to go to the authorities. You need someone on your side, besides us, that you can trust."

"That's just it Fey," I replied, "I don't know who I can trust." I got up from the couch. "Who am I going to go to… the New Orleans police, the FBI? And what am I going to tell them - that a man I never saw before this week, thinks my parents aren't really mine, yet they're all now dead. That I'm being hunted by a maniacal mystery man who runs OPERATION: MIDNIGHT and, along with his assistant, Cricket, wants to engage me in some horrific experimentation."

Sammi, who obviously could sense that I was upset about something, got up and came over to rub up against my leg. "What I *am* going to do, at least until I have figured out the rest, is go through the files in Wormwood's briefcase. Hopefully, that will provide some answers."

CHAPTER 17

"MYSTERY MAN, CRICKET, OPERATION: MIDNIGHT. What is this all about?" asked Dalton. "It sounds like something out of *Criminal Minds*."

"I know, but this is what Wormwood told me earlier today. He said there was this secretive organization called Blackout that Congress doesn't even realize is still in operation and that it's run by a mysterious guy named Derek Spillbane."

"Is that's who's looking for you?" asked Fey.

"I can't imagine that he is. After all, he's a scientist in charge of multiple projects but Wormwood said that Spillbane has an associate who goes by the nickname of 'Cricket' and, though small in stature, is coldblooded. He has a tattoo on his forearm and a scar over his left eye. He's worked with Spillbane for awhile and does whatever is necessary to keep the experimentation secret and projects running. Supposedly virtually no one knows what Spillbane looks like because he has had plastic surgery and has chosen to micro manage clandestinely."

"The whole thing sounds creepy," she added. "What else have you been told?"

"I don't know a lot more than that but hopefully, after going through these files, I'll have a better understanding of what's going on."

"Can we look with you?" asked Fey, leaning in as I opened the case.

I didn't have any reason for them not to look at the files but I felt queasy about it. In all probability Wormwood was killed, at least in part, because of what was inside these files, so I felt there was danger involved for anyone who had knowledge of Blackout's activities.

"Are you sure you want to? Obviously these are people who will stop at nothing to get these back. I'm afraid I'd be putting you in danger. You might be better off not knowing what's in these files."

Fey took the file that was on top of the pile that I had removed from the briefcase. "I'm not worried," she said. "Wormwood was the one who stole the files and knew all about what was going on. They certainly can't view me as a threat."

Dalton also took a file. "Besides, I'm assuming these are just his notes."

"Actually, from what he told me this afternoon before he was killed, these are not just his notes, but files that he stole from OPERATION: MIDNIGHT. I'm not sure what we're going to find but its a safe bet that they didn't want him, or us, to have them."

All three of us settled back and began to read but it wasn't long before Dalton broke the silence. "Jesus Christ Lonnie, this is unbelievable. I can't believe the United States Government did some of this shit. I mean, I'd heard that there were tests done trying to manipulate behavior through the use of LSD and other drugs, but purposely dropping bacteria in light bulbs throughout the New York City subway system or injecting chemicals into the water supply in Washington, D.C.. Are you fucking kidding me?"

"That's nothing, how about this," said Fey. "Biological agents contaminated such places as San Francisco, Minneapolis and St. Louis and our Senate knew about it? This is our government experimenting on its own people. They knowingly infected people with cancer cells, allowed hundreds to die from syphilis even though they could have been treated, and in Chicago infected prisoners with malaria. This *is* unbelievable!"

I had gone through several files by now and was equally as stunned by what I had read. With the assimilation of each bit of information I was more aghast at the thought of what was being done without the knowledge of the American people. And what was most startling is that this was not back some 50-60 years ago. In 1990 some 1500 babies in Los Angeles, mostly black and Hispanic, were given an experimental measles vaccine without the consent, or even knowledge, of their parents. In America?"

Fey stated what by now was clearly obvious. "I can understand why the people running these operations wouldn't want this information to get out. If people knew this was going on there'd be hell to pay."

"Ya think," said Dalton. "And with taxpayer's money."

We seemingly lost track of time and it wasn't until Sammi whined to go out that we realized how late it was. "Do you mind taking Sammi out, Dalton," I asked. "If you're going to watch her for a couple of days while I go back to Leesville for the funeral it might be good to let her get acquainted with you."

"No problem. Watching a dog take a shit under a street light in New Orleans after midnight sounds like a good time to me." Smiling, he grabbed the leash, fastened it to Sammi's collar, and headed down the stairs.

Although I was exhausted and ready for bed, I figured that I would keep reading and turn in when Dalton returned. Fortunately for me I can read very quickly. Unfortunately, I can't forget what I've read and lord knows, there was plenty in these files that I wished I *could* forget.

CHAPTER 18

WHEN I WOKE up I was surprised to find that it was almost 9:30. The three of us had read files until the middle of the night and continued to shock one another with the depth and breadth of governmental experiments. Each one seemingly more reprehensible than the one before.

I now understood why Wormwood was so worried about Spillbane tracking him to get back the stolen files. I wondered if they knew where Wormwood was and could have killed him sooner but had allowed him to live until he had found me and/or the other individual that was supposedly being searched for. It couldn't be coincidental that both he and my parents died shortly after our meeting. But, if my parents were killed, then why was I being allowed to live... or was I?

With these and countless more questions reverberating in my head, I headed out of my bedroom with Sammi. On the couch, where Fey had once again crashed, there was a pillow and a blanket neatly folded. I was surprised to see that she was already up and gone since I knew that she didn't have to work until later that afternoon.

A moment later Dalton appeared. "I thought I heard you," he said. "What time is it anyway?"

"It's about 9:30. I guess we needed the sleep after our nocturnal read-a-thon."

Dalton opened the refrigerator door and removed a half-gallon of milk. "Not surprising. I don't know about you, but I had trouble getting to sleep. I couldn't get some of those images out of my head."

I poured some dry food that I had taken from my parent's house into

Sammi's dog bowl and filled a small Tupperware container with water. "I know exactly what you mean but I guess I'm more concerned with what it all means for me."

"That's totally understandable," said Dalton grabbing a box of Raisin Bran from the cupboard and sitting down at the kitchen table. "What are you going to do about Wormwood's death? Are you going to tell someone that you were there?"

"I don't think so. I'm really not sure who to go to and I really need some time to process all of this. Besides, I need to leave pretty soon to go to my parent's wake. That's tomorrow tonight and I have a couple of people I need to see before that. Are you going to be okay with Sammi for a couple of days?"

"Hell, yes. By the time you get back we'll be the best of buddies. I need to let the people at *Brennan's* know I'm getting through but I don't work today and not until the night shift tomorrow at *Bon Vivant.* It will be my first shift as a waiter so Antoine wants me to come in a little early to get acclimated. I hope he doesn't expect me to remember all the orders without writing them down."

"Ha, I don't think so, but you'll do fine. I really appreciate you helping me out with this. I didn't expect to have a dog here anytime soon but then,"… I let the obvious conclusion to that statement hang in the air.

Despite the fact that we had read deep into the night, there were dozens of more files that had not been examined. Also, although Dalton or Fey had read the contents of some, I felt it necessary to read every file for myself and I wanted desperately to understand what might have been the cause for Wormwood's death. Was there some particular project that he was working on that Spillbane didn't want discovered?

In mid-afternoon our doorbell rang and Fey bounded up the stairs after being buzzed in. "I only had to work the lunch shift today and I couldn't wait to get back here to read more about Blackout," she said, heading directly to the living room sofa where the files were spread out. "It's all I could think about all day. Have you learned a lot more since I've been gone?"

Dalton and I agreed that we had but neither of us wanted to stop to talk about it absorbed as we were in our reading.

A couple of hours later we were still deeply engrossed in what we were doing when Dalton broke the silence. "Holy shit! Listen to this. DARPA has a $2 billion plus budget researching the creation of a 'super soldier' capable of re-growing limbs lost in battle, and who could be genetically engineered to kill without remorse, be void of fear and demonstrate no fatigue. They are also injecting human brain cells into animals which could cause thought consciousness or human memory."

He continued, "In 2015 the Journal of Medical Ethics acknowledged that animals in these experiments could potentially develop human physical or mental features such as human limb or neuronal development. In 2005 Senator Samuel Brownback of Kansas tried to ban this "chimera" research but was unsuccessful."

I had no response to this as I had heard some of this from Wormwood and had just finished reading about the 2045 Program designed for cybernetic immortality. My life had gone from: who's responsible for waiting on table 12 to modifying the human genome. Once again we read well into the night stopping only to eat pizza that we had delivered and to take bathroom breaks. Finally, we decided to call it a night.

Fey verbalized what was on all our minds as she stood to stretch. "I can't imagine what would happen if the American people knew what was going on."

"This reads like some science fiction movie," agreed Dalton. "Christ, I understand now where ideas like the Manchurian Candidate come from. What do you think Lonnie, after reading all of this?"

"I'm blown away like both of you are, but truthfully, I'm more concerned with how this all impacts me. Am I wrong to worry about that rather than what soldiers will look like in the 22nd century or whether our kid's kids will live to be 150?" I rose from the couch.

Fey put her hand on my shoulder, her incredible eyes boring into mine. "You are not wrong. You have every reason to worry about what's going on in your life, especially with what has taken place recently. Hopefully you can find some answers in all of this."

CHAPTER 19

AFTER ANOTHER NIGHT of restless sleep I got up early and decided to take Sammi for a walk. She had no idea what was going through my mind but appreciated the chance to walk along the bank of the Mississippi. We strolled along a paved walkway next to the river known as the Moonwalk. Tourists think the boardwalk must have a connection to Michael Jackson but those of us living in NOLA know it refers to a former mayor, Maurice "Moon" Landrieu who approved its construction in the 1970's.

Because of the overriding fear I was dealing with, I cut the walk short much to Sammi's disappointment. I spent the next couple of hours doing things around the condo and then packed and prepared for my trip. I purposely didn't read any more of the file entries because I knew once I began, I would want to keep going and I wanted to stay on schedule. My intent was to make a couple of stops before going to the funeral home. I was not looking forward to this trip but it needed to be done and I would feel a lot better if there was closure - on many fronts. I was getting ready to take Wormwood's briefcase and my one overnight bag down to the car when my cell phone rang.

"Hey Lonnie, it's Fey. I'll be right over. I'm going to go with you today. I thought you might like some support... and company."

"You're... what?" I wasn't sure that I was hearing correctly.

"I'm gonna' go with you. I'm worried about you and want to help. You've had a brutal week and you could use someone to talk to. Plus, you said yourself that there's some mystery man who might be looking for you. Who knows, another pair of eyes might come in handy."

I thought about the ride, the visits to different businesses, the fact that I wasn't coming back until tomorrow and what people might think but I said, "What about your job?"

"Oh, I've already cleared it with Antoine. In fact he encouraged me to go. And Lonnie, I know you're staying over night but that doesn't have to be any different than when I've stayed over at your condo and slept on the couch. I'm not trying to hit on you."

I didn't know if that was meant as a statement of fact or as a joke but I did know that I wasn't sure how to respond so, I simply told her I would wait a few minutes until she got here. After I hung up I thought about how my life had become so complicated. Here was a girl that I had only known for a short time planning an overnight trip with me to help bury my parents.

I told Dalton what was going on and he could see how confused and conflicted I was by this turn of events. He didn't help when he said, "She's pretty, she seems nice enough, and she obviously likes you, but how much do you really know about her?"

"Not a great deal, obviously."

"Be careful then. That's all I can say."

CHAPTER 20

FEY AND I arrived in Leesville in mid-afternoon and went directly to the Funeral Home to make sure that all of the arrangements had been made for that evenings wake.

As we entered, I noticed that there were two workers attaching tiny devices on the walls. Since I was pretty familiar with electronic equipment, I assumed they were cameras of some sort. Kyle Morrison, a bit reluctantly, affirmed my suspicion.

"Yes, Chief Bell asked if I minded if they inconspicuously fastened a couple of these in the entry and viewing rooms. He said that in certain cases it can be valuable to know who is in attendance at wakes and funerals. I'm sorry that you had to see that."

I understood what it was that Bell was hoping for and I was assured by Kyle that everything was ready to go and the visiting hours would be from 7:00-9:00. He asked if I wanted to see my parents and I hesitated, not sure if I was ready for such a viewing. Is anyone ever ready, I thought. I purposely had not looked at their bodies under the sheets when I saw them at the police station. Simply seeing their faces there was tough enough.

We walked out back to the preparation room where they were in light brown caskets with white interiors. "I used laminate with a polyester interior," Kyle said. "These are inexpensive but still nice. You'll note that we are using what's called a full couch so that a full view of the bodies can be enjoyed. Fortunately, their faces were not harmed other than a cut on your father's face and we were able to conceal that pretty well."

The temperature in this room was noticeably cooler than the rest of the house and when the top half of their caskets were opened I was taken by how peaceful they both looked. For a moment I had a sense that they were simply asleep and would sit up at any time. Oh, how I wish that was the case.

"I hope you don't mind," said Kyle. "I went to your home with Chief Bell and got a suit and a dress from your parent's closet. I wanted to make sure they looked good but I didn't want to bother you."

"They look wonderful, so alive," said Fey, who I had momentarily forgotten was standing beside me.

"Yes," I agreed. "You did a wonderful job and no, I don't mind that you went to get their clothes." The truth was that I didn't know my father owned a suit. Since I never graduated from high school, I had never seen him wear one. Could that be the same one he wore when he got married, the one in the photo?

I picked out a book for visitors to sign, approved of some flowers that would be delivered later that day and then left my address in New Orleans so Morrison's could bill me. I turned and looked at them once more as I headed out. Tears filled my eyes but I didn't want Fey to notice.

"Are you okay?" Fey asked as we walked back to the car.

"Yeah, but I gotta admit this was tougher than I expected. I saw them lying there and memories of my youth came rushing back. I can't believe they're dead." I was no longer concerned if she saw tears dripping down my face.

"I remember one day in school when I was in the third grade and the kids in Mrs. Spracklin's class had been making fun of me yet again so I pushed one of the kids at recess and was told that I'd lost my recess privileges for a week. When I got home and told my parents I expected to be scolded but instead, they asked if I had started it and when I said 'no' they took me back to school and told the principal they were tired of hearing about me being bullied just because I was different from the other kids." The tears fell freely. "They always looked out for me and stood up for me."

Fey stepped toward me and wrapped her arms around me. She pulled my head down onto her shoulder and we stood in the parking lot as tears wracked my body. I felt her hand rub the back of my head and I didn't want her to stop.

CHAPTER 21

I STOPPED BRIEFLY at the police station to pick up death certificates and our next visit was to Magnolia Realty where I was to sign some papers putting the family homestead on the market. Perhaps I should have been sentimental but frankly, my memories were no longer of when I learned to drive by taking "Rusty" on the roads around the farm or the warm summer nights endlessly throwing tennis balls to Sammi, but instead, were of the image of my parents lying in Morrison's caskets.

The owner, Dan Sargent, a thirty-something native of Leesville who once had my mom as a teacher, assured me that he would have no difficulty selling such a beautiful piece of real estate. I had my doubts.

"Lonnie, I guess the question is how much you want to ask for the property," he said, as we sat across from his large mahogany desk covered with golf trophies and photos. He wore light colored chino pants, a pink polo shirt with a crest and tassel loafers. He looked like he was as prepared for a club championship match as he was to take a listing.

"I really have no idea of what it's worth, " I replied. "Have you sold anything recently of comparable value?"

A smile broke across his handsome tanned face. "Well, as you know, we don't have a flourishing market here in Leesville, especially for homesteads. Most of the people moving into the area are affiliated with Fort Polk."

"So how do we proceed?"

"The real value, especially to someone local, is in the land. It's listed as having almost forty-six acres and it's good farm land. The house, while

I'm sure it's nice, doesn't have a lot of value. It's really about the real estate. It really matters how aggressive you want to be and how quickly you hope to sell it."

I leaned forward and put my elbows on his desk. "Dan, I really have no idea what to ask but I do want to sell it quickly. So, why don't you do your market research or whatever is needed, put a fair price on it and get it sold. I have no desire to own it. I'm going to stay there tonight which will be the last time."

"Sounds good to me." He slid some papers across the desk. I saw that one was an Exclusive Right to Sell form and a couple other forms that the Real Estate Commission must have required. "Just put your John Hancock on a couple of these and I'll get right on it. I'll have a sign on it later today and will get it on the MLS today as well. I have gone to the town office and have all that I need to complete the disclosures. I'll text you with the suggested price. Fair enough?"

"Sounds good Dan." I stood and shook his hand. "I appreciate your help." The receptionist offered her good byes as we walked across polished hardwood floors and out into the bright sunlight. Azalea bushes filled the carefully manicured stone walkway on each side of the door, their bright red blossoms in full bloom. I wondered why I hadn't noticed them on my way in.

"I'm glad we're staying at your house tonight," said Fey as we walked out of the real estate office. "I kinda figured you wouldn't want to go there but I'd like to see where you grew up."

"I'm not real excited about going there but I figured that I would grab a few things that may have sentimental value since I don't expect there'll be any reason to go back. But first, I need to stop at the bank." I looked at the time on my cell phone. "I need to hurry if I'm going to shower and change before the wake."

Bill Donovan greeted me at the Leesville Bank and Trust and ushered me into his office. Looking at Fey he said, "I'm sorry ma'am but I'm going to have to ask you to wait out here while I go over some things with Lonnie."

He nestled into his chair and removed a file from one of his desk drawers. "I wasn't sure whether you were going to stop by today or after the funeral tomorrow morning, but it will take me just a couple of minutes to transfer everything from your parents account into yours."

I glanced up at the wall clock in his office. "That would be great Mr. Donovan. I'm obviously in a bit of a hurry since I need to get to Morrison's pretty soon."

He got up from his desk and walked out of his office returning with several papers a short while later. "Since you are already on their account as their beneficiary, I will only need copies of their death certificates in order to complete the transaction."

I had picked those up earlier and handed those to Donovan. He slid across a printout that showed the current balance.

I glanced at the bank statement that showed my parents had $304,386 in their account. I looked incredulously at Donovan. "Are you sure this is right? How can this possibly be? I mean, my mom was a school teacher and according to Dad, the farm was more a labor of love than anything else. Plus, they already gave me money to buy my condo."

"I really can't answer that," he said, looking down on the account history. As you probably are aware, ever since Nine-Eleven and the introduction of the Patriot Act, it is difficult to make large deposits or withdrawals without filling out forms. Our records on hand don't go back far enough to show when any large deposits were made but it looks like there's been quite a bit of money in there for awhile. With your signatures on this transfer slip the money will all be transferred into your account now Lonnie."

I signed the necessary form and walked out of the bank still reeling from this discovery. Fey didn't notice that anything was different and I wasn't ready to disclose any information.

Since it was past five when we left the bank, I hurried home to get prepared for what I knew would be a difficult and tiring night. I was sure there would be a fair amount of people show up, most of whom I didn't know, or hadn't seen in years.

"Oh Lonnie, this is so nice," Fey said as we pulled into the driveway of the family farm." It's so much bigger than I imagined."

I looked at the hammock in the side yard, the flowering bushes my mom took such pride in growing, and then beyond the house into the open fields and the big oak tree behind the barn that held both a dilapidated tree house and a rope swing. Fey's eyes followed mine and she knew that I was looking at the property through the eyes of a young boy. "You must have had so much fun growing up here. There's so much to see and do."

I nodded in agreement and turned my attention to the house. It was nice to see that there was no major evidence of disrepair to the house other than some peeling paint. As I entered the kitchen I noticed some dust on the tables and counter but overall it didn't look too bad. I know that "staging" homes for sale was all the rage on TV, but I had neither the time nor inclination. If someone was interested in the property, especially in the land as Dan Sargent suggested, then I'm sure they would overlook the cosmetic flaws. I paused and slowly glanced around the kitchen. On the wall heading into the living room were those pictures of me as a young boy that I had noticed earlier and others of the three of us. I took those down and stared long and hard at my loving parents who just a short time ago I had hugged. It seemed surreal that two caring, loving people would no longer reside in this comfortable home.

CHAPTER 22

I HAD DECIDED that the funeral tomorrow was going to be a private graveside service and because both of my parents were the only child in their respective families, there would be no family members in attendance. The wake tonight would be the last opportunity for friends and neighbors to pay their final respects. When we drove up to the funeral home there was already a line that went out the door and snaked around the house into the parking lot. I had no idea they had so many friends.

"Oh my God Lonnie, look at the people." Did you have any idea there would be this many?"

"No, but they lived in Leesville all of their lives and remember, my mom taught a lot of kids who are now adults - as well as their parents."

"What would you like me to do? Do you want me to stand beside you in the receiving line?"

I thought for a moment about how many times I would have to introduce her - to people who I didn't know - and thought that that would be incredibly complicated. And more importantly, what would I introduce her as? Hell, I didn't even know myself why she was here. "I don't think so. That will just make it longer than it needs to be. As you must know, I'm not looking forward to this at all. I'm just doing it out of respect for my parents. I'm sure they would have wanted it. I appreciate your offering though."

"Okay, I'll just kind of mill around and sit in one of the chairs provided. Let me know if you need anything."

I thanked her, walked in the side door that Kyle had shown me earlier in the day, and prepared to shake the hand of several dozen well intentioned semi-strangers. Perhaps this might have been easier if I had actually finished school or been more involved in community activities, but I knew that that just wasn't me. Although my parents had spent all of their lives in Leesville, my time there was much shorter. Actually, in the past five years I had only been back a handful of times.

I looked at my parents silently reposing in the caskets and marveled at how good they looked and how much at peace they were. I knelt between the two caskets, placed a hand on both, and said a silent prayer thanking them for all they had done for me. It is so true that we don't know what we have until it's gone and I'm not sure why, but at this moment, I thought of Dad trying to teach me to hit a baseball out behind the barn and Mom cooking baked stuffed shrimp for all of my birthdays because she knew it was my favorite. Tears again rolled down my cheeks and Kyle Morrison handed me a Kleenex. I hadn't heard him come in.

"Lonnie, I know this is a difficult time, especially with the way they died. Death is such a final thing but rest assured that your parents will long be remembered. They were very well liked and respected in this community." All I could do was nod my head. "There's a lot of people waiting, I think we'd better begin."

A couple of hours later the line had begun to thin out and I was emotionally and physically drained from all the hugs, handshakes and well-wishes. This was one of the most difficult days of my life. Not only because I was preparing to bury my parents, but because I was required to smile and make small talk with people who I hardly knew.

Several of my former teachers came through the line and asked what I was doing with my life. I detected a sense of disappointment when I told them that I was waiting on tables in New Orleans. Perhaps they expected that by now I would have written a Broadway play or discovered a cure for cancer. I guess that I should have felt flattered that they expected big things from the "boy with the magical mind," as Mr. Zucchi, the guidance counselor, once called me. All I wanted was this night to be over with so I could return my life to normal… at least as normal as it could be with no parents and a maniacal mad man searching for me.

It was at this point that I saw Fey walking toward me seemingly in a state of anxiety. I excused myself from the couple in front of me and asked what was the matter.

"I got kind of bored just sitting in the chair watching you greet people so I decided to take a walk outside."

"Yeah, so what." I couldn't believe she interrupted the service to tell me that.

"While I was out there I saw a short man standing beside a black SUV. And Lonnie, I never saw that man you described yesterday and couldn't tell from the distance if he had a scar, but this guy was bald."

CHAPTER 23

"ARE YOU SURE? What was he doing"

"I don't know. I stepped outside to get a little fresh air and was just looking around. I couldn't see him that well and honestly, it didn't even register until I'd come back inside. I thought he looked kind of strange and then I remembered what you had told us."

I had no idea what to do. I had no desire to go outside and see if he was there. I'd already seen what his people were capable of. They had undoubtedly shot Wormwood. Were they responsible for the death of my parents?"

I decided that I would give Chief Bell a call and stepped away from the receiving line for a moment. He had been in Leesville for many years so there was not the consternation that I felt in New Orleans regarding law enforcement. As I waited for Bell to answer his phone he walked into the viewing room in a light blue Oxford shirt and gray trousers,

"What is it Lonnie? What's wrong.?"

"What... how?" My thoughts were jumbled.

"I've been over by the door. I wanted to pay my respects, but thought I'd also keep an eye out on the proceedings. Wouldn't be the first time a person of interest made an appearance at a wake or funeral. Why'd you call?"

I explained to him that Fey had seen someone suspicious in the parking lot. I really didn't think it was the time or place to go into detail.

"Suspicious? How so? What's he doing?"

Fey responded. "I saw someone standing beside a black SUV and since I knew that a similar type of vehicle ran into Lonnie's parents, I thought I should let him know."

I was pleased that Fey didn't say anything about the death of Wormwood or Cricket and a clandestine government agency.

"I'll go out and take me a look around. You two stay in here. There's only a few more people in line and we don't need to spook 'em any more than they already are. When you headin' back to N'awlins?"

"Tomorrow morning some time. There's the funeral service early on and then I need to do a few things around the house before it goes on the market."

"How 'bout you stop in and see me for you go back. I'd like to hear what you got to say." He headed outside.

I returned to stand a few feet from my parent's caskets to speak with the last of the visitors. One of the last to go through was Bill Donovan from the bank.

"Lonnie, I am so sorry for your loss. Your parents were the nicest people. This is just a horrible thing that happened."

I thanked him for his kind words and once again for his help with the transition of my parent's account into mine.

"Not a problem and one more thing. You were in a hurry this afternoon and I forgot to tell you this. In addition to the account they had, there is a safety deposit box in their name that they took out several years ago. I, of course, have no idea what's in it, but I thought you might want to take a look while you were in town. You'll need my help to open this - every box needs two keys for the safety of our patrons. I don't know if you'll be able to find their key at home somewhere but I'll be in tomorrow morning and if we have to I can get a locksmith and we can have it drilled."

"Thank you again, Bill. I will look for the key tonight and absolutely stop in before I head back." My head was spinning... a bank account with $300,000 in it and now a safety deposit box? What other surprises were in store?"

CHAPTER 24

I AWOKE, WHAT I considered prematurely, as the sun's rays pierced the dusty windows. I contemplated going back to sleep but reconsidered when I heard movement down stairs. I had slept in what once had been "my" bedroom when I was younger but now, in addition to still housing my bed, it had been transformed into a sewing/storage room. I've always been amazed at how people collect so much stuff that they're convinced they can't live without.

The sounds that I heard below were those of Fey who was scurrying about. I could hear her humming a Beatles song which amazed me. Not that she could hum or that she knew a Beatles song, but that she was doing it in my parent's home. The smell of bacon permeated the house. I put on a clean tee shirt and the same jeans that I had worn yesterday on the drive and headed downstairs. I had a white shirt and dress pants in the car that I would change into before going to the cemetery.

"Hey sleepyhead, I thought you were never going to get up."

I looked at the clock in the living room as I came down the stairs. "Excuse me. It's 6:45."

"I know, almost lunch time. But for now you'll have to settle for breakfast. I found a bunch of food in the fridge and thought I'd make you a meal. How do you like your eggs?"

I had to admit her smile was infectious and who doesn't like having a country breakfast prepared for them even if it is 6:45. "Over easy if that's okay. Did you find what you were looking for?"

"I did. I've been up for awhile actually. I didn't sleep very well."

"The couch isn't that comfortable?"

"It's not that. It's just knowing what's happened. I couldn't make myself sleep in your parents bed and then, after thinking about that guy that I saw in the parking lot last night, I had trouble falling asleep."

I poured myself a glass of orange juice. "I know what you mean. Was the guy you saw wearing a leather jacket? Was there anyone with him? Are you sure you saw someone suspicious or could it just have been your imagination?" My mind was once again racing.

"I'm sure of what I saw. He was on the other side of the hood of a black SUV. I didn't see any thing or anyone else, the windows were tinted, but I assume that there was someone with him who was driving."

I thought back to both what Wormwood had told me before he was shot and what I had seen when leaving that hotel. It seemed like Cricket had somehow tracked me down. It didn't surprise me that they could find me but I still didn't understand *why* they would want to find me.

"I've got to see Chief Bell this morning before I go to the bank. I may open up to him about being in the room when Wormwood was shot."

"That seems like a good idea. You need to confide in someone. What do you want to do before you go see him?"

"I want to go through all of the rooms just to see if there is anything of importance that I want to keep. I doubt there is, I believe I took everything that I wanted when I moved out a few years ago."

"What about the food in the freezer and canned goods and things like that?"

"I'll ask Bell about local food banks, Goodwill, and agencies like that. I'm sure they'll be glad to go through the house and take the furniture, clothing etc. I'll also let them have the vehicles. They're not real new but they should be worth something."

"Would you like me to pack things up while you go to the police station. If you don't mind I'd like to go with you when you go to the bank."

"That would be great if you would. There are some empty boxes in the pantry that should work. I really don't want to spend any more time here than I need to."

After breakfast we walked around the house looking in all of the rooms as well as closets and cupboards. Fey asked me many questions, most of which I was reticent to talk about. We then walked out back and into the barn where my pickup sat up on blocks. I patted the driver's side hood.

"Why does this truck mean so much to you Lonnie?"

"To me, old Rusty here isn't just a truck," I began. "This hunk of metal wasn't just a form of transportation. It's well, you know, a remembrance of how I am a bit... different."

"You mean with your memory and your intellect and all."

I looked down. "Yeah, do you understand how difficult that is as a kid? I'm sure to some it seems cool to be able to remember everything but, trust me, it's no fun when everywhere you go you get pointed at or made fun of. I can't tell you how many times I came home from school crying because I'd been beaten up or bullied. When my parents complained they were told that 'kids will be kids.'"

"No, I have no idea what that must have been like, but what's that have to do with Rusty?"

"In Louisiana there are no laws against driving on farm roads on your own property so my father taught me to drive when I was about twelve. That way, when I came home from school, home from being called names like "geek," "teachers pet," or "nerd," I would climb into the truck and drive around the fields on the farm and not give a damn what others thought of me... at least, for a short while. So you can see, Rusty was more of an oasis than a pickup truck. It was a metaphor for freedom, at least to me."

"Wow, that's sad. Lonnie. I had no idea you went through that. I just assumed, especially living in the country, that everyone would think your being smart was cool."

"Yeah well, I guess kids are the same everywhere. I also helped Dad put in a used transmission one year when it went and did several other jobs on Rusty as well. I figure he assisted me in my mechanical training and he never even complained once." My attempt at humor went unacknowledged so I stopped talking.

I had spent enough time traveling down nostalgia lane and wasn't sure why I had confided in Fey but I couldn't take it back now. I could, however, take care of the business I had to attend to and get back to New Orleans. I gave Rusty a final rub and headed back out of the barn. As I slid the large double doors closed and turned to walk back toward the house a vehicle pulled into the driveway… a black SUV.

CHAPTER 25

I SAW THE look of terror on Fey's face and turned to look for a place to hide when the realtor, Dan Sargent, walked around the corner of the farmhouse.

"Hey Lonnie, I thought I saw you out here when I drove in. I was hoping to catch you before you left." Seeing the look on our faces, "Is there something wrong?"

"Not at all Dan," I said, walking towards him. And this is Fey." I just realized that I didn't even know her last name. "What's up?"

"I wanted you to know that after speaking with the designated broker in our office and doing some research, I came up with what I feel is the fair market value and asking price for this property."

"Sounds good. What'd you come up with?"

"As I said earlier, I think the real value is in the land whether it be as farmland, the way it has been used, or sadly, as happens sometimes, if it's divided someday into house lots. So the price I arrived at is $349,000. That is a fair price for perspective buyers and one that you should be able to get. How does that sound?"

"Whatever you say is good by me. Do you need me to do anything else?"

"Yeah, that's why I stopped out. I have one more document for you to sign. Plus, I wanted to take a look around and go through the house so I can get a better sense of what I'm selling. I based the price more on the land value and comps as it relates to living space, bedrooms and bathrooms but I really need to see it."

"Understandable. Here, let me sign what you need. The house is open so help yourself." I looked down on the document where he had inked an X, signed the necessary paper, then reached into my pocket and handed Dan a key. He headed out toward the barn as I walked out front with Fey.

"That was scary Lonnie," said Fey. "Do you think we're going to be spooked every time we see a black SUV? And furthermore, how many of them are there anyway?"

"I don't know on either count but I'll be a lot happier when we get to the bottom of this. As I said earlier, I think I need to say something to Chief Bell. He may not be able to do anything but at least I trust him."

"Good idea, but he can't possibly know anything about secret government projects, can he?"

I stopped walking. "I don't know but, speaking of not knowing, I went to introduce you earlier today and realized that I don't know anything about you. I don't even know your last name." I stared into her crystal blue eyes.

"You've never asked me anything or shown any interest in finding out about me. Let's sit on the porch for a minute and I'll tell you what you want to know." A slight mist fell from a sky that was darkening.

"If you don't mind, I'd like to take care of business first. I need to get to the cemetery. We can talk on the way back to New Orleans."

"Okay, you get going and I'll do what I can to pick up around here. Oh, and Lonnie, it's Chadwick."

"Excuse me?"

"My last name, it's Chadwick."

"Oh, okay." I wasn't sure that I wanted her going through my parent's things, a lot of which might be personal, but then, I wanted to be by myself at the cemetery. Plus, I wanted to get going and I appreciated the fact that she was trying to pack some items up for me. "I'll come back and get you before I go to the bank. The funeral service won't take long so I should be back in a couple of hours."

Due to my father's military service my parents were eligible to be buried in the Central Louisiana Veteran's Cemetery. The service was performed by Walter Corcoran, a long-time minister at the First Union Baptist Church where my parents attended. He spoke with reverence and personal experience having known them for years. Although it had been a long time since I had attended a funeral, and never one for a relative, I found it strange being all by myself. I appreciated how heartfelt his words were.

Following the service I headed into town. I was told that Chief Bell was in when I walked into the police station. By now I knew where his office was located so I headed straight back. I knocked on the door jam of the open door and saw that he was on the phone. He waved me in and remained seated behind his desk as I entered.

When he completed his conversation he rose and walked over to shut the door to his office. "Hey Lonnie, I been 'specting you. Whatta ya' say we make some progress here today. I got me an idea you haven't been exactly forthcomin' with all you know." He sat back down, leaned back and put his feet up on his desk.

I spent the next half hour telling him about Wormwood's visit, warning and subsequent death. I explained the reason for my visit to see my parents and the disbelief that I harbored about them not being my biological parents. As I expected, Bell was incredulous.

"So you're tellin' me that you think someone killed your parents and now's after you. Is that what I'm hearin'?"

"I know how crazy it sounds, I felt the same way. But think about it. I've had three people die in my life in the last week."

Bell dropped his legs and sat up. "And you feel these are the dealings of a secret government agency?"

"Honestly, I don't know what to believe. All I want is to live in New Orleans, work in a restaurant, and be happy. I know nothing about these government agencies and can't imagine why they would want me... dead or alive."

"What about the guy your girl friend saw last night, and incidentally, when I went out there to have a look-see, 'twas no black SUV in the parking lot. I ain't sayin' she didn't see sumpthin', I'm just sayin' it weren't there when I went out." Bell picked up an old football that was sitting on the corner of his desk.

"She isn't my girlfriend, she's just a... she works with me." I changed the subject. "I was told that the person in charge of this operation called

OPERATION MIDNIGHT, is a man named Derek Spillbane who no one knows much about. He has an associate who supposedly is short and ruthless. That may have been him with the SUV." Bell had put the football back down and was writing in a notebook.

"And who told you this - that Wormwood fella' that was killed?"

"Yes, in fact, just before he was shot."

"And what have the authorities determined about his murder?"

I knew this track of questioning was bound to happen and got up from my chair. "That's just it, nobody has contacted me. I grabbed Wormwood's brief case and got out of there before anyone came."

"Good golly, you're tellin' me that a man got shot in broad daylight right in front of you in one of N'awlins fancier hotels and they haven't contacted you?"

"That's what I'm saying. I know it sounds weird."

"So, how do you know that Spillbane was involved in the killing?"

"I don't. I just know that as I was driving out of the parking garage at *Le Pavillon* I saw a man fitting the description of his associate, at least from what Wormwood told me - a man who calls himself 'Cricket.'"

"Cricket? This is definitely gettin' weirder. Do you still have the briefcase? Have you looked to see what's inside?"

"I do and I have."

Bell ran his hand through his hair, an idiosyncrasy that I noted was common with the Chief. "Lonnie, I obviously have no jurisdiction in N'awlins and quite frankly, want no part of a government investigation, but I got me a friend in the FBI and know a couple more at Fort Polk who I'll talk to. I want to find out who killed your parents and see if it was on purpose. And, as to whether they're really yours, I wouldn't put no stock in that." He once again picked up the football. "As I said, I played high school ball with your Daddy and he was a good man. We'll get to the bottom of this."

I could tell that Bell was ready to move on from this conversation. I was actually relieved that he hadn't asked me to go into the contents of the briefcase. I shook his hand and walked out of the station not sure if I had done the right thing in telling him all that I did. I expected it wouldn't take long to find out.

CHAPTER 26

AFTER LEAVING THE police station I went and picked up Fey and then headed to the Leesville Bank & Trust. Built in the early 1900's it was a typical Southern structure made of brick with white columns reminiscent of bygone days.

As promised, Bill Donovan was in his office and was more than eager to help. I was fortunate enough to have found my parents security box key in my father's bedside bureau. After exchanging greetings he unlocked the door to a small room off the lobby of the bank which was actually part of a large vault and which contained hundreds of safety deposit boxes all with numbers on the outside. There were several different sizes but the one that matched the number on my key - 207 - was about the size of a Number 10 envelope. Fey and I walked in to the room and Mr. Donovan walked over to the desired box.

I had always thought that these rooms were situated deep in the bowels of a bank but I guess I've seen too many movies. That must be why Spike Lee and Denzel Washington didn't shoot *Inside Man* in Leesville.

He held up a key and said, "It takes two keys to get into a box, Lonnie. For the safety of the customer. Also, it's not customary to have anyone else inside when opening a box but if you're sure it's alright with you then I'm okay." After I nodded he inserted his key and stepped back.

I placed my key into the box and turned. It slid out as I pulled. Donovan removed his key, turned and headed for the door. "Let me know if you need anything."

In the middle of the room, outside the vault itself, there was a small island on which people could place their boxes when removing them from their location.

Fey watched as I lifted the cover. "Are you excited, Lonnie? What do you expect to find? Could there be a lot of money?"

"I really have no idea what could be in here," I said, as I removed the box from its outer sheath. "Its not big enough to hold much of anything and besides, my parents didn't have a lot of money." I didn't let on that Mr. Donovan had already transferred a 'lot of money' from their account into mine. There was an envelope in the box with my name hand written on the outside. I opened it and took out the letter which had been folded in thirds. Fey moved in close to me as I held it in my hands. We both read silently.

Dear Lonnie,

If you are reading this letter then I'm afraid that something has happened to me, or God forbid, my wife and I. You'll note that I wrote 'my wife and I', rather than 'your mother and I', because sadly, Lonnie, I'm afraid that I must tell you that we are not your true parents.

Please note that we have thought of you as our own and loved you as if you were our child, but the truth is that you were given to us to take care of by your biological parents when you were a young boy.

Your Dad and I were in the service together and developed an amazing friendship, which often happens, during that time. In fact, he saved my life by carrying me back to safety after I was hit by the shrapnel of a land mine.

After he returned back from a second tour, he was taken, due to his extreme intelligence, into a special unit. He was excited about this because he was led to believe that he would be working with counter- intelligence.

I lost track of him at this point but three years later he showed up at my home, your home, in Leesville, and although he said he couldn't talk about it, he said his assignment was very different than what he had thought - or hoped for. He also said that it was extremely secretive and dangerous!

He had with him a small baby. You! He asked me, no begged me, and Martha to take you in and raise you as our own. He said that he feared for his life and more importantly, he feared for your life. He said that he was living in a "safe" house that was anything but, and had nowhere else to turn. What could I say, we were brothers. The man saved my life. It was the least that I could do. He also told me that I was not to use or tell you what your real name was because he wanted you to have no connection to the two of them.

I never met your real mother. He said that she had some health issues but that she understood what had to be done. Martha and I told anyone who asked that we adopted you but it wasn't an issue because people around here keep their noses out of other peoples business. We never brought it up because we thought of you as our own.

Your father handed me an envelope with a good deal of money in it, and said that it should be enough to see that

you were well taken care of. I put the money in the stock market, made some good investments and that which he gave me became a lot more. And Lonnie, I never touched a penny of your money for the farm or our use. My wife and I had all that we needed and felt blessed to have you in our lives. We were glad to be able to help you with your condo and whatever is left will be in our account and will go to you.

I stopped reading and looked away. Tears came to my eyes as I thought of some of the tough times that my "father" had endured on the farm. One year there was a terrible drought and he had to take out a big loan in order to plant crops the following year. He even took a job working weekends at the Agway store to pay off the loan. I wiped the tears away from my eyes with the back of my hand.

"Are you okay," Fey asked.

"Yeah, I just had no idea about any of this. I feel so bad because they struggled all of their lives to make ends meet and all they would've had to do was use some of the money that my real father gave them to hold.

They never took vacations, drove old vehicles, and you saw the house. It needs a new roof and any number of other upgrades."

"It just shows you what good people they were. You are lucky to have been raised by them."

I nodded in agreement and turned back to the letter.

Your real Dad didn't want us to tell you that you were not our own. He said that it would be too dangerous for you even after the passage of many years. As I am writing this I have no idea where he is or if he or your mother are even alive. I would only ask that you look after my wife (your mom) if she is still alive and if not, please see that we are buried in Evergreen Cemetery.

I stopped reading for a minute and looked away from the letter. Fey could see that I was upset and once again asked if I was alright.

"I couldn't even bury them right. I had them buried in the Central Louisiana Veteran's Cemetery because he was a veteran. I thought I was doing something nice for them."

Fey put her hand on my jaw and softly pulled my face toward her. "Lonnie, I'm sure they would be very proud to be buried there. You need to stop beating yourself up. You did a wonderful job in very difficult circumstances." I nodded and turned back to the letter.

Lonnie, I hope you know how much we love you. You are truly a special young man and I hope you have a long, prosperous and happy life. You have made our lives so very much richer by being part of them.

Love, Dad

ps. I have no idea what this means but this message that I have included, was left at our house in an unmarked, unstamped, envelope several years after we took you in. Your name was not on the note or the envelope but I didn't think it was too difficult to figure out that it was intended for you. It simply said on a separate sheet: "If he becomes as gifted as I expect, he'll figure it out."

There in the safety box was a small piece of white-lined paper folded in half.

CHAPTER 27

I UNFOLDED THE paper and laid it down on the island table then took my hand and rubbed it several times in an attempt to remove the wrinkles. Fey, who had read the previous letter over my shoulder, now leaned in closer to get a look at this note. The message was hand written and so light that it was almost illegible. It was a seven-pointed star much like pieces of pie. In four of the sections were the following words: dolphin, Horton, Myrtle, Munin. The other three sections were blank.

I read the note for the second time and then looked at Fey who was seemingly in a trance, her mouth open. "What in hell does this mean?" she asked, looking up from the mysterious note.

"You got me," I admitted. "Obviously, it's some type of cryptic message but without spending some time examining it, I have no idea. A seven-pointed star is called a septagram but beyond that it is clearly a mystery. I wonder if it is intended to be a series of clues. And why are there not words in each of the seven points?"

"Who's it from?"

"I don't know but the letter says that it arrived several years after they took me in. I have no idea when I arrived at their house, if that's what really happened."

Fey realized then what the letter had stated and put her arms around me. "Oh Lonnie, I'm so sorry. I can't imagine what you're feeling right now."

"How could I have lived this long and not known that those were not my real parents. I have so many different thoughts. I feel stupid, I feel angry, I feel confused."

"That is understandable but I'm sure a lot of these questions will be answered. There's no reason to feel stupid. How could you have known? And most importantly, regardless of what you just read, don't lose sight of how much they loved you."

The images of my parents being laid to rest this morning came to me and once again tears came to my eyes. It seems like I have been doing a lot of crying lately. "It also appears that Wormwood was right, these weren't my real parents. And what the hell could have been happening to my real parents that was so dangerous that they couldn't raise their own child?" I stepped away from Fey, folded the papers and put them in my pocket and then slid the deposit box back into its slot. There were so many questions that I needed answers to and I wasn't sure where to turn.

"The letter said that your real father was afraid because his mission was 'secretive and dangerous.' Do you suppose, like Wormwood surmised, that he was involved in any of those projects that those files describe?"

The thought had crossed my mind and it seemed to make sense but I had no way of knowing. What I did know was that I needed to get out of here… out of this bank, out of this town.

"The letter also said that your father had 'extreme intelligence.' Maybe that explains why you're so smart. Do you remember when Wormwood was asking you questions about the couple you thought were your parents and whether they could speak multiple languages or had special memory skills?"

I looked at her and was forced to grin. "Yes, I remember."

CHAPTER 28

MY MIND WAS racing as I navigated my car back on the highway toward New Orleans. I had stopped at the farmhouse for one last time, thrown a few items in the trunk that I thought I might want to have as keepsakes, and saw that Fey had stacked several boxes of house items and canned goods in the hall to be donated.

I then went outside and took one last walk around the yard glancing in all directions. I now had second thoughts about keeping anything as I realized that my life, as I had known it, was a sham. What other mysteries was I to discover?

What had started as a drizzle had now become a steady rain and the windshield wipers beat a pattern across the glass. For a long time the two of us said nothing as we looked through the windshield at the desolate landscape and miles of Southern Yellow Pine and Baldcypress, each of us lost in our own thoughts.

Fey finally broke the spell. "Lonnie, I'm not sure what to say. With all that has gone on, it just seems so overwhelming."

I looked into her crystal clear eyes, typically so radiant, which were solemn and sad. "There really isn't a lot to say. I'm afraid that I have spent two decades living on this planet and it's all been a lie. The sad thing is that I don't know what is the truth. Not only don't I know what, but I think more importantly, I don't know why."

She nodded as if to share my sense of frustration and bewilderment. "I can't begin to know how you feel," she said. "But it must be painful reading that note from the people you thought were your parents."

"It's more painful that they're dead. I still consider them my parents even if I didn't share their genes. They're all I ever knew. I don't know the circumstances surrounding their accident. Was it tied in to anything that I'm dealing with or was it simply a random automobile accident; the type that happens thousands of times every year? We may never know, but it doesn't hurt any less."

"What are you going to do about finding your real family?"

"I'm going to examine the note that was stored in the security box and see if it offers any clues to my past. I have no idea what the words in the star mean but I'm intrigued by the post script to my father's note where it says, 'if he becomes as gifted as I expect, he'll solve it.'"

"Do you think that that post script is from your real father?"

"I don't know what to think. But speaking of 'real fathers', I think it's time that you tell me something about yourself. As I said earlier, when I went to introduce you I realized that I don't know anything about you."

Fey sat back in the passenger seat, her hands resting on her thighs. "My story pales in comparison with yours, Lonnie. I'm a northern girl who grew up in a small town in Connecticut, went to college for two years and then dropped out and came to New Orleans looking for employment. Since I had waitressed summers during college I had some experience and was able to hook on at *Bon Vivant*."

That sure doesn't tell me a great deal about her I thought to myself. "What about your family?"

"My father and mother were divorced when I was young and I don't remember him at all. My mother got re-married to a guy named Joe Chadwick and I was adopted by him so my last name is the same as his. He is basically an asshole who treated my mother like dirt and me worse."

"One night when my mother was visiting a relative I woke up with him sitting on my bed feeling me up. I could smell liquor on his breath and he tried to get me to kiss him. He called me a cock-tease and said I really wanted it. I screamed and dragged my finger nails across his face and finally he left. I tried to tell my mother the next day but she didn't believe me. She works in an office for a real estate company and tries to do her best but when she refused to hear my side of the story I knew that I needed to get out of there so I came south."

"Wow, that's terrible. I'm sorry you had to go through that and it's easy to see why you'd want to get away from him."

"Thanks. It certainly hasn't been a glamorous life that I've led. Other than trying to avoid that jerk it's been pretty boring... that is, until I met you." Her smile lit up her face and seemed to transport her from remembering what must have been a difficult childhood.

"Have you heard from them since you moved down here?" I asked.

"I called my mother to tell her that I was working in New Orleans and was safe but I didn't get through so I left her a message and asked her to call me. She never bothered to call back so I gave up on both of them. I don't expect to see her anytime soon and I hope I never see her bastard of a husband."

"Do you have any brothers and sisters?"

"Nope, just a cat named Sawyer. You know, after the character in *Lost*."

I didn't know but chose not to pursue that line of questioning any more. There was a myriad of questions that I could have asked but I felt uncomfortable asking anything more personal and figured it really wasn't any of my business. At least I now knew her name.

The rain continued to pelt the country side and we were soon once again absorbed in our thoughts as the miles disappeared behind us. Finally, as we pulled into the outskirts of New Orleans, Fey asked what I intended to do next.

I had been running that through my mind most of the trip and really wasn't sure how to best deal with the threat from a surreptitious government agency. After burying my parents earlier today, I felt that I had no one to turn to. Although I hadn't interacted with them for quite awhile, I hadn't needed to, but I always felt the security of knowing they were there if necessary. I suddenly felt very alone.

CHAPTER 29

THE NEXT DAY I made the decision to deal with some of the issues that were troubling me. While I wasn't sure who to trust, I knew that by avoiding my responsibilities I was prolonging the stress that I was under. The first item on my agenda was to notify the police that I had been witness to a murder. I couldn't believe that they still hadn't contacted me since I was seen by employees both arriving at and departing *Le Pavillon*. Plus, by now surely the police must have watched the security tapes.

The city of New Orleans is divided into eight police districts and because *Le Pavillon* is on Poydras Street adjacent to the French Quarter, it falls under the jurisdiction of the Central Business District. I went to the headquarters on North Rampart Street and was met at the reception desk by a middle-aged black woman with short-cropped black hair and a neatly starched uniform fighting to keep her midriff behind the confines of her belt. The name tag on her chest read 'Montgomery.' "And how may I help you honey?" she said with a deep southern accent and a mouth full of gum.

I decided that I had better tread carefully. "Who should I speak to if I saw a crime?" I said softly.

"What type a' crime?"

I looked around to see if anyone was listening in on our conversation. "A death."

The woman's jaw was working overtime on what looked like multiple pieces of gum. "Honey, yo gonna' have to give me more n'at if yo wanna' see some'un."

"I'd heard that there was a death recently at the *Le Pavillon* Hotel and I wondered if I might be able to speak to the detective who is working on that case."

"And who might you be?"

I didn't want to give my name but sensed that I was getting no further unless I played along. "Lonnie," I said quietly. "Lonnie Clifford."

"Well, Lonnie Clifford. You wait right 'der and I see what I can do fo' you." She disappeared into the office complex. A couple of minutes later she returned and buzzed me inside.

A short man in a light blue sports jacket, khaki pants, and a bald pate walked me over to a cubicle, moved a stack of files from the chair beside his desk, and extended his palm. He looked around the room as he shook my hand. "Have a seat. I'm Detective Colucci."

After taking my name and contact information he asked, "How can I help you?" The air conditioner was obviously not working in the office so beads of sweat had formed on his forehead, several of which dropped onto the blotter on his desk as he leaned forward.

For some reason I didn't feel comfortable sharing what I had witnessed, or had been told, with this detective so I offered up what I hoped was a possible, yet peripheral, response. "I have relatives coming into town this weekend and they had planned on staying at the *Le Pavillon* Hotel." I paused.

"Really, where they coming from?"

I hadn't expected that response and was forced to think quickly. I remembered what Fey had said. "A small town in Connecticut," I responded. "Outside of Hartford."

"So, what's the problem?"

"Nothing I guess, but I heard there was a death there earlier this week and I know that that might make my relatives uneasy so I was checking in for them, that's all."

"A death. What type of death?"

"Some type of shooting, I think." This wasn't going at all like I had hoped.

"And where did you hear about this shooting, Lonnie? I thought you told Sgt. Montgomery that you saw a crime being committed."

"I work as a waiter at *Bon Vivant* so we hear stuff all the time. You know, overhearing customers and all." I hoped that would satisfy him as being a plausible explanation. "I told Sgt. Montgomery that so I could get a little more information."

He reached across his desk and took a business card from a metal holder and handed it to me. "Well Lonnie, you can go ahead and assure your relatives that it's safe to stay at *Le Pavillon,* or any other hotel for that matter. There have been no shootings that I have been notified of and, if there had been, I would have heard."

He chuckled, "I have been told, however, that there have been sightings of ghosts at that hotel so I guess there have been some deaths there. Call me if you see any of them or if you have any further questions."

The reference to ghost sightings in that hotel was widely known as a superstition in the city but had no bearing on my visit today and I found his attitude towards my concerns condescending. I shook his hand, thanked him for his time and headed out of the police headquarters more bewildered than ever. Why would he bring up ghost sightings at this hotel? More importantly, why didn't he ask if I knew more than what I was letting on and, more importantly, why were the police covering up the death of an individual in a hotel room?"

CHAPTER 30

AFTER STOPPING AT the Winn Dixie to pick up some groceries and dog treats for Sammi, I decided that I'd better check in with Antoine at *Bon Vivant*. He had been very patient with me and I knew that he would continue to be so, but I felt that I owed him an explanation. The trouble was that I had no idea how long I would be out or what I could use now as an excuse. I had no reason to tell Antoine about Wormwood or any of his intimations.

When I arrived at the restaurant the staff was cleaning up after the luncheon shift. Antoine was in his office sitting at his desk in front of an adding machine, the sleeves of his white shirt rolled neatly up his arm. He rose as I walked in, came around from behind his desk and wrapped his arms around me.

"Lonnie, I am so sorry for what you've had to go through. Have the police found out any more about your parents accident?"

"Thanks Antoine. No, at least I haven't heard any more. I'm sure I will if they come up with something."

Antoine went back to his office chair. "It's good to see you. Is there anything I can do for you?"

"You've done a great deal already Antoine, but that's why I stopped by, to see if you minded if I took a little more time off."

"Mind - I insist. You take all the time you need, Lonnie. Things are going pretty well here, actually. I'm happy with Dalton. He has done a good job filling in for you. He doesn't have your memory - who does - but he works hard and the customers seem to like him."

"I'm glad to hear that. He's a good person and I know how excited he is to be waiting tables instead of bussing. Are there any other changes?"

Antoine thought for a minute. "The only other change is I hired a new dishwasher this week. He goes by 'Bud'. He's a middle-aged man, rugged as hell, and seems to be doing a great job.

"That's good. I knew that you needed someone else in the dish room. Where'd he come from?"

"I'm not really sure. He just showed up unannounced one day and asked if I had any openings. Said he'd served in the Army special forces and could use a job. I told him the only thing we had was in the dish room on the night shift and he said that was fine with him. Other than that, everything's the same."

I could see how busy he was so I thought I'd better move on. "Sounds good, Antoine. I'll keep you informed and again, I really appreciate it." I headed out of the office into the dining room but saw neither Fey nor Dalton and figured it was either their day off or they were scheduled to work later on the dinner shift. Several others of the waitstaff came up to me to offer their condolences but I felt uncomfortable and left quickly.

I intended to return to the condo but as I got in my car I made up my mind what had to be done. I would return to *Le Pavillon* to try and determine what was going on. I hoped that Clarence was working today.

The sun was setting over the Mississippi as I traversed the short distance to the hotel. Like many cities dependent upon the tourist trade, the traffic makes travel difficult at best. As I pulled into the parking garage I was engulfed by a feeling of déjà vu. It had not been that long ago that I was exiting from this garage in fear of being seen - or shot!

When I walked into the hotel lobby I went to the concierge counter and asked a young black man with cornrows if Clarence was working. "He's around here somewhere," he said. "He may be takin' bags up to a room."

I thanked him and decided I would wait for him here in the lobby. I didn't feel right asking a stranger about the shooting so I grabbed a couple of peanut butter and jelly sandwiches and sat down. *Le Pavillon* was known for their complimentary PB&J sandwiches and hot cocoa or cold milk. I remember reading that this tradition began in 1988 after a guest asked for this as a snack. Like so many traditions in this city, it's unique perhaps, but delicious just the same.

Several minutes later I saw Clarence coming out of the elevator, a trademark smile covering his face. I walked towards him and asked if he would join me in a corner of the lobby, a small alcove with four maroon upholstered chairs, two on each side facing one another. He lowered his large body into the chair and leaned forward, his massive thighs spread wide.

"What's up Lonnie? How can I help you?" His legs bounced with his weight resting on his toes.

I wasn't sure what to say because, while I wanted information, I didn't want to implicate myself in a murder. I leaned forward to shorten the distance between us and caught Clarence off guard by speaking softly. "Do you remember when I was here about a week ago?"

He understood by my actions that I wanted a low key conversation and responded in kind. "Yeah, I remember. I may not have the memory that you have but I can clearly recall seeing you walking through the lobby. Visitin' with a friend wasn't ya?"

"Yes, I was there for a few minutes and that's what I want to ask you about. I heard later that there was a shooting here that day."

"A shooting?"

"Yes, a shooting. Are you telling me that you don't know anything about a shooting here that evening?"

Clarence got up off the chair and stepped nearer. "Lonnie, I got no idea what you be talkin' about. There weren't no shootin' here. Where you gettin' your infomation?"

The time for dancing around this topic was done. I needed to get to the bottom of this. "Clarence, I haven't been totally upfront with you because I'm not really sure what went on that day. All I know is that I was witness to a shooting. Have you got your master key? I'd like to take a look in room 433." I got up and headed toward the elevator hoping that he'd see my level of seriousness.

He put his arms out, fingers pointing upward as if to signal a stop. "Wait Lonnie, I do have a key but I can't just let you in. "Sposin' there's someone in there." He walked toward his concierge desk. "Let me take a look."

After a couple of minutes he pointed to the screen. "It's open. There's no one in there tonight - at least not yet. I can let ya' look but course I gotta come with ya.'"

We went up to the fourth floor and Clarence opened the door to the room in which I saw Dr. Wormwood get shot. When I left he was slumped against the wall of the room with his eyes glazed open and blood pooling on his shirt. I went directly to the spot where I left the body and looked to see if there were any signs of blood.

Clarence bent over beside me. "What you looking for?"

I finished running my fingers along the baseboard and stood up. "Clarence, when I was in this room last week visiting a man that I had just recently met, I saw him get shot. I heard the gunshot and saw him get knocked down with blood pouring out from his chest."

"What did you do?"

"I was petrified so I ran. I went down the stairs, ran outside and drove off."

I now had Clarence's attention. "Did you see who did it?"

I saw no reason to go into Wormwood's story with this amiable hotel worker. "No, nor did I want to. I just wanted to get outa' there." I walked over toward the window and looked out. "The shot had to have come from that building over there," I said pointing to the office building across the street.

Clarence stood beside me and looked out to where I was pointing, dwarfing my thin frame. "But that doesn't answer your question does it Lonnie. I swear we'd have heard if there was a murder in one of our rooms. And more importantly, what happened to the body?"

"I have no idea. That's what's driving me crazy. It makes no sense."

"I tell ya' what. Lucille is in charge a house keeping. I'll look her up and ask on the down low if she knows anything 'bout what yer askin'. Ya wanna' give me ya' phone number and I'll get back to ya'?"

I thought about it and replied. "If you don't mind Clarence, you give me yours and I'll call you tomorrow."

I figured that with all that was going on in my life, I didn't need my number out there any more than it was.

CHAPTER 31

FEY WENT TO the grocery store to pick up some much-needed items. Like most of the waitstaff, many of her meals were eaten at *Bon Vivant* at a reduced rate and as she stood in front of her full length bathroom mirror she noted that she had put on a couple of pounds. One of the dangers of working at a quality restaurant she figured.

She decided to allocate much of the day for cleaning her apartment since she had neglected it of late. It was 1200 square feet and had two small bedrooms, a living area with kitchen nook and bath. She used one of the bedrooms and called the other her office although there was really no need for such. Between spending two days in Leesville and the nights poring over the governmental files, she had not slept in her bed much recently. She smiled as she thought of recent developments.

After sweeping, vacuuming, wiping and washing she decided that she would jump in the shower. She was scheduled to work the night shift which she preferred. Although it cut into her social life the tips were much better than either of the other two shifts and, because it was typically so busy, the time flew by.

As she was preparing to get undressed her cell phone rang. She looked and saw that it was her mother. "Hey Mom, how are you doing today?"

"Better honey. I know you said that you would do the calling but I haven't heard from you for a few days and thought I'd give you a ring. Been busy?"

"Yeah, sorry. I went to Lonnie's home town to attend to some things.

I told you that his parents were killed in what appears to be a hit and run and we went there for the wake and then the funeral."

"That must have been difficult for you."

"It was. He understandably took it very hard but guess what. He found out that those weren't his real parents."

"What? How could that be?"

"He was dropped off at that home by his real parents and raised by the Cliffords all these years. It turns out that his father was afraid for him due to his job with government experimentation. I can't go into it but Lonnie has been left clues in a letter that he assumes was from his father and this could be important."

"Sounds exciting."

"Yeah. Listen I've got to take a shower and get ready for work but I'll call you again in a couple of days. Like I told you earlier, let me do the calling."

"Sounds good. Take care of yourself. I love you honey."

"I love you too, Mom. Bye."

CHAPTER 32

FOR THE NEXT two days I stayed home with an expressed interest in laying low and seeing what might develop from any of the circumstances I was dealing with - if anything. I felt a bit guilty for not going to work but, having been assured by Antoine that everything was under control, I resisted the urge to return.

Much of the time I spent studying the sheet of paper that I had gotten in the safety deposit box but had no success in determining the solution of the cryptic message. I was perplexed by the "clues" but found myself being more disappointed due to the words of the later note, supposedly from my "father." "If he becomes as gifted as I expect, he will figure it out." I took this as a challenge and since I loved participating in games and brain teasers, I fully expected to be able to solve this puzzle.

Taking a break from the paper, I decided to call Clarence and see if he had learned anything about Wormwood's body disappearing from room 433 of *Le Pavillon*. I dialed the cell phone number I had been given.

"Hello," came from the other end.

"Clarence, it's Lonnie. I'm calling like I said I would, to see if you found out anything about room 433?" I found myself struggling to avoid using the words, "dead body."

"Z'up Lonnie. I spoke to Lucille like I said I would but I'm 'fraid I don't have a whole lot to be tellin' ya'. She didn't know nothin' 'bout no dead body but she did go talk to a person named Chamiqua whose job it is to clean that room. Chamiqua told Lucille that she found nothin' in that room that weren't sposed to be there."

" There was no body lying up against the wall? No blood on the floor?"

"She said there was nothin' outa place, nothin' unusual. She did say though that there was a bit of a smell in the room."

"A smell? What kind of smell?"

"She said it kinda smelled like ammonia or vinegar or somethin' like that. It was strong enough so she had to open a window," she said.

"Wait. She had to open a window? There wasn't a window already open?"

"That's what she said. Is any of this makin' sense to ya'? I can't tell if this be helpin' or not. I can probably get them to call ya if ya want me to."

"Are there security cameras on each floor? If we can get a look at that we can figure out who was in there and how they removed the body."

"Ain't no cameras on any of the floors inside the hotel, or any hotel in the city, for that matter. Privacy rights ya' know. Outside's a different story of course but ain't been no reports of anybody seein' anything spicious."

"How could they have removed a dead body without anybody seeing it?"

"Spose they coulda' put it in a suitcase like they do in them movies."

I didn't feel like going down that path. "What time would Chamiqua have cleaned the room?"

"Sometime in the late mornin' probably. Check out is at 11:00 so dependin' on what time she got to that room. You want me to go ask her to be mo' specific?"

"No, I don't think that's necessary. I decided that there was nothing more to be gained by speaking with Clarence and I had no interest in dragging either of those cleaning ladies into this. I had no desire to go into any depth on the disappearance of what I assumed to be a dead body. How could someone get into that room without anyone knowing about it… and then remove the body of a grown man without making a scene was beyond me. Never mind who had done the shooting or why they wanted Wormwood dead. "You've been a lot of help Clarence. I'm not sure either what this means but I thank you for your help and I'd appreciate your not making a big thing out of this."

"Hell's bells Lonnie, I ain't gonna say nothin' to nobody. I don't wanna' be involved and it sure ain't good for business."

"Makes sense, and again, thanks a lot." I hung up and thought about what I'd just heard. I know there was an open window when I left and I saw Wormwood crumpled on the floor with a bullet wound and blood seeping through his shirt. I saw a short man in jeans and black tee shirt heading towards the room as I was leaving and a tall man in a leather coat heading to the parking garage a short while later. I left there in late afternoon and the cleaning lady was supposedly there before noon so that left an eighteen hour gap of time. By the report of the smell it sounds like someone got in there to remove the body and clean up but I had no answers to my many questions. Of one thing I was certain, however, Wormwood had warned me that my life could be in danger. I now had no doubt that he was right.

CHAPTER 33

I TURNED AGAIN to the "clues" that were left on the piece of paper in the safety deposit box. Because I didn't want to damage the original, I typed the words on another piece of paper in case there were fingerprints on the paper that could provide information. I smiled thinking maybe I have watched too many cop shows since I didn't intend to take this paper to the police station. I sat down in front of my computer with the intent of researching online for what I hoped were answers.

dolphin, Horton, Myrtle, Munin

Overall there were 4 words in 4 divisions comprised of 29 letters. I felt the first order of business was to determine if these were intended to be viewed as a whole, or whether they should be examined individually. The latter seemed to make more sense since it was hard to imagine how the four words had any relationship with one another. Three of the four words began with capital letters, they were not in alphabetical order, and the last word, Munin, was totally unfamiliar to me. Was it even a word?

I knew that I would have to go online to examine that word but I could not imagine how to proceed with the others. Were they truly "words" as we know them or could they have been some form of code using only certain letters within each word. Most importantly, what was I looking for? It's pretty daunting to try and decipher something that makes no sense, in a pattern that you don't recognize, in order to find something that you don't know. And yet, I kept coming back to the phrase, "If he becomes as gifted as I expect, he'll figure it out." God, I love challenges.

The other concern that I had was why were these words arranged in the manner they were? Why have them divided into pie pieces in a seven-pointed star and not listed either in a row or with one on top of another. And why were some points of the star left blank?

Before I could type in the words on my keyboard I heard the "Saints are Marching" refrain indicating that I had company. I looked at the small monitor at the top of my desk which was connected to an exterior camera I had installed, and saw a dark complected man in a dark suit standing in front of my door. He was not only tall with stylishly long black hair but was wide and compact like a wrestler or football lineman. He appeared to be a Latino.

"Can I help you?" I said into the monitor.

The man glanced upward at the camera and said, "Actually, I hope I can help you. Are you Lonnie Clifford?"

"I don't know a Lonnie Clifford," I lied. I certainly didn't want to let any other strangers into my home. I'd already seen how that turned out.

He continued to stare into the camera above the door. "Look Lonnie, I'm a friend of a friend of Greg Bell of Leesville. I'm an FBI agent and was told that you might need some answers. Let me come in."

After I had him produce his badge, I buzzed him in and went down to meet him as he came up the stairs. He shook my hand and introduced himself as Hector Montero.

"How do you know Chief Bell?" I asked.

"I don't actually. I know who he is but we've never met. As I said, I got a call from a friend of mine who works at Fort Polk. He was contacted by Bell and I was told that you have had some strange occurrences in your life in the last few days. Tell me what's going on." He unbuttoned his suit jacket and made himself comfortable on my sofa.

I proceeded to explain some of what had occurred purposely leaving out the part about the files that I had in my possession and the note from my father. I made a point to tell him about Wormwood's accusations about my parents accident, the government agency Blackout, and his being shot in my presence only to have no one know a thing about it.

"So you're saying that he was killed right in front of you yet there was no report of the murder."

"That's exactly what I'm saying. When I ran out of that room he was bleeding from the chest and his eyes were glazed over yet open. I didn't wait around, but he sure looked dead to me. But later, when I checked with both the police and people that work at the hotel, they said there had been no report of a murder."

"You went to the police? Why would you want them involved if you didn't have to?"

I thought that was an odd comment coming from a FBI agent but continued. "I wanted to do the right thing. Anyways, it doesn't matter. The homicide detective told me there had been no report of a murder."

"So what do you think happened?"

"Whoever shot Wormwood must have come and taken care of it. Somehow they got into the room, cleaned up the mess and removed the body. The woman who cleans that room, Chamiqua, told Clarence, a friend of mine who works there as a concierge, that she opened the window to get some fresh air later when she was cleaning but when I left that room the window was open."

Montero removed a small comb from his breast pocket and ran it through his wavy black hair. "I suppose I could nose around and see if the NOPD actually had a homicide and are sitting on it but maybe we'd be better off not rattling their cage. I'm more concerned with this experimentation that Wormwood said was still being done - this Operation Blackout. Did you get anything from him that can prove that it exists?"

I decided to let down my guard - a little. "I really don't know anything but I took some files from Wormwood when I left. He said that he had stolen them from his work."

"I'm guessing that's why he got shot," said Montero. "Let me see those files Lonnie. Maybe there's some clues there."

I thought quickly about what my next move should be and decided that I wasn't ready to give those files up. "I don't have them here. I was afraid that somebody might come to try and steal them back so I put them in a safety box at my bank."

The man looked at his watch as he got to his feet. "I'll need to see those right away. I'll do a little investigating for you too. See if I can't get to the bottom of this. I'm out of town tomorrow but I'll come back in a couple a days and we'll talk again. And Lonnie, I'd keep my door locked and not venture outside. At least until we can get some answers." He shook my hand and was down the stairs and out the door before I could ask another question.

I thought about what he had said. 'Get some answers'. Hell, all that I had were unanswered questions. And now I had another man who I didn't know, and didn't know if he could be trusted, offering to provide "help."

CHAPTER 34

I WOKE TO the sensation of a wet tongue lapping my cheek. Sammi had decided that either she had to go outside to do her business or that it was time that I got up and got going - or perhaps both. I grabbed her leash and headed out into the sunlit morning. The air already felt muggy as I strolled down toward the banks of the Mississippi. I thought about taking her for a long walk but then remembered what Montero had said about not venturing outside. Besides, I wanted to begin doing research on the clues in my lockbox note so as soon as Sammi did 'her business' I returned to the condo.

When I got home I saw that Dalton had already gone out. He was either working the early shift or perhaps golfing, something that he enjoyed doing whenever he had the time and money. In either event, I was glad because it would provide me with the quiet time that I needed to study. I filled Sammi's bowl with food, leftover chicken from an earlier meal, made myself a cup of dark roasted coffee in the Keurig and settled in at my office desk.

I laid the note down on the desk beside my computer and googled "Munin." It was a word that I wasn't familiar with though, after looking at the screen, perhaps I should have been because among the options was both a video game and a type of computer software described as a network monitoring application.

Since I had no idea what I was looking for, I recognized that I would have to delve deeper into all of the potentialities. The video game of that name was of the puzzle platformer variety and was created in Portugal in 2014. It referenced Norse gods and monsters. The software company titled "Munin" was basically used to analyze resource trends and potential bottlenecks.

I saw no relevance in either of these and since neither seemed significant, at least to this point, I continued reading. There were ships in the Swedish Navy named Munin and a satellite launched from Vandenberg Air Force Base in 2000 also with that name.

Lastly, there was a reference to a Muninn in Norse mythology; a raven, who along with Huginn, served the Germanic god Odin. In a work, *Prose Edda,* written by Snorri Sturluson in the 13th century, he details the two birds as flying each day all over the world (Midgard) and returning each evening with information to pass on to Odin. For this reason Odin was known as the raven-god and was revered for his wisdom.

I wasn't sure of this connection either but continued to read about Odin who often would dress in disguise and travel about as a wanderer. Because of his reliance upon the ravens for information he gave them the ability to speak.

I paused when I came to the passage that explained that their names were later anglicized and changed to Hugin and Munin, the word I was looking for. But, what was really fascinating was the meaning of their names in Old Norse. The word huginn meant "thought" while muninn meant "mind or memory."

I pushed my chair back from my desk and stared at the screen. Considering my ability to remember everything that I saw or read, the correlation to me seemed far too obvious. Certainly it couldn't be coincidental, could it? As one who doesn't believe in the randomness of coincidence I found this to be strange but then again, everything in my life now seemed strange.

CHAPTER 35

WHILE THE NAME Munin might have been referencing the raven whose name meant mind or memory, it didn't explain why it was included in this group of words inside a seven-pointed star on the note I was given. Interestingly, the software company of that name used a raven as their logo so it seemed there might have been a connection, for marketing purposes if nothing else.

I turned my attention to the other words - clues? dolphin, Horton, Myrtle. Were they in a particular order? Did it matter? Two of them were capitalized while the other - dolphin - was lower case so I decided to put some time in trying to decipher how a dolphin might be connected to a Old Norse raven.

I was examining the multitude of types, varieties, scientific differences and references to dolphins in literature and mythology when my phone rang. The number appeared on my phone as "unknown caller" which gave me pause but I answered it with trepidation.

"Lonnie, it's Agent Montero. I did some subtle digging into the murder you say you witnessed a few days ago. I actually had a friend of mine in the bureau make a couple of calls but he told me that Homicide has heard nothing about this, other than you walking in and asking about it. I guess, after your visit, they followed up and visited the *Le Pavillon* Hotel but were told by the manager that there was no report of anything resembling what you say you witnessed."

I didn't know how to respond to Montero but what he told me didn't surprise me. Whoever was involved obviously knew how to cover their tracks. I was concerned that by making further inquiries we would stir up the police department and I would be dragged deeper into the investigation. At this point I just wanted it all to go away. Who knew whether or not someone in the NOPD might be involved in the cover up. "Doesn't surprise me," I said.

"Did you have a chance to grab those files you mentioned yesterday? I'd like to stop over and take a look at those."

"I didn't. I haven't had a chance to do much of anything I've been so busy."

"I didn't think you were working?"

I didn't want him to know what I was, or wasn't, doing. "I'm not but, as you know, my parents were killed recently and I'm still trying to come to grips with that. How about you give me your number and I'll call you when I've got them."

"I'll call you back. When's a good time?" His tone had changed from cordial to business-like.

I wasn't surprised that he wouldn't give me his number, nor was I upset. I figured that that should give me enough time to figure out what I wanted to share.

As I hung up the phone I heard Dalton walking up the stairs his golf bag slung over his shoulder. "How'd you play?" I asked.

"Not bad but I was paired up with a couple on vacation from Minnesota or Michigan or some other god forsaken northern state and they were awful, at least he was. Plus, he was so freaking slow. If you suck, at least suck quickly." He took his clubs into his bedroom, dropped them on the floor with a thud and then re-emerged.

"Why do you play that game if it's so frustrating for you?" I asked.

"I love the game, it's the people who I play with that are frustrating. My dad, who taught me how to play, played in the same foursome every week and he always told me how great it was. Not just the enjoyment of playing the game, but playing with friends. When you go as a single and get paired up it's the luck of the draw. And then, probably because they've watched Tiger Woods on TV, they adjust their clothing before every shot, measure the wind and take four practice swings before shanking it into a sand trap. I need a beer."

When Dalton returned from the kitchen he stopped beside my desk and looked at the notes I had spread out in front of me. "What are you working on?" he asked.

"I'm trying to solve what I think is a riddle of some sort. I had a note left in my safety deposit box with words on it that don't seem to make sense... at least to me."

He stared at the notebook pages then turned to walk away. "As the saying goes, it all looks Greek to me. I think I'll go watch some television." He headed down the hall towards the theater room leaving me to my research.

I hadn't realized how late it had become until darkness enveloped my area. I had spent a great deal of time trying to decipher the clues I had been given and while learning much about the many species of dolphins, I could find nothing to tie them in with a raven or Germanic God. As Dalton had so succinctly stated earlier that day, and Cicero hundreds of years before, it truly did look like Greek to me also.

CHAPTER 36

THE DAYS SEEMED to be flying by considering that I hadn't worked in awhile and yesterday, other than for taking Sammi out for a walk and to do her business, I hadn't left the condo.

I decided to make copies of several pages of Wormwood's notes hoping that it would mollify Montero. I somehow doubted that it would. After running a half-dozen sheets through my printer/copier I put them in a folder and decided that I would contact the FBI to leave a message for Montero. I had no interest in having him show up again and hoped that I wouldn't have to share all of the notes that were in the bag belonging to Wormwood. Perhaps I could just fax these few. Although he had refused to give me his cell number I figured by speaking with him at his office, or at least leaving a message if he wasn't in, I could circumvent the need to get together.

I googled the FBI office in New Orleans which was on Leon Simon Boulevard looking for the phone number. The website showed that it was one of 56 field offices in the United States along with 380 other regional satellite offices in smaller cities around the country. Although the agency was created in 1908, according to the homepage, the primary goal since the attack on 9/11 has been to prevent another terrorist attack. *What about attacks by the government on its own people,* I thought.

A female voice came on the line. "Federal Bureau of Investigation, how may I direct your call?"

"I'd like to speak with Agent Montero please."

"I'm sorry, what was the name of that agent?"

"Montero, Hector Montero." I waited to be re-directed when her voice returned a few moments later.

"I'm sorry. There is no agent here in the New Orleans office by that name. Could he possibly be assigned to one of the satellite offices? We have six of those here in Louisiana."

"I guess. I'm not sure. Do you have a directory of the agents in those offices?"

"I do. If you'll give me a little time I'd be glad to check for you."

"Great. Thank you. "

A couple of minutes later the receptionist returned on the line, her voice resigned. "I'm afraid that I could not find an Agent Montero on the roster of any of the Louisiana satellite offices. I'm sorry, can I direct you to another agent? Can I ask what this is about?"

I was momentarily astounded. I didn't know what to think but I knew that I didn't want to speak to anyone else, nor did I want to discus the reason for my call. "No thank you. Perhaps I got the name wrong. I appreciate your time. "

After hanging up I walked around my condo finally sitting down on the couch in the living room a multitude of thoughts racing through my mind. Sammi, seemingly sensing a change in my personality, jumped up onto the couch and leaned up against me. I pulled her close to me, kissed her on her head and rubbed her ears. I felt the need to draw her close to have a bond with another living being.

I knew what I had to do next so I took my cell phone out of my pocket and punched in Chief Bell's phone number. The fact that the FBI had no record of an Agent Montero terrified me. Perhaps Chief Bell could provide an explanation. He had earlier given me his direct cell number and answered on the third ring.

"Hey Lonnie," he answered. "Funny you should call. I intended to call you later today. What's up?"

I got right to the point. "You remember earlier when I told you about the potential government conspiracy and you told me that you would get in touch with a friend of yours in the FBI?"

"Yes, course I remember."

"Do you mind telling me what his name is?"

"Not t'all, it's Wes Mathewson."

"Did you talk to him about what we discussed?"

He paused before responding. "Lonnie, I'm really sorry but I haven't had a chance to. It's not that I haven't thought about it, I told you I would, it's just that things around here have been crazy busy. Why'd you ask?"

I told him about my visit from Montero and my subsequent phone call.

His response was immediate. "Lonnie, let me hang up. I'll call him right now and see if he knows Hector Montero. I'll shout right back at ya'."

I walked around my condo picking up items of clothing, putting dishes in the dishwasher and pretending to clean when really I was just anxiously biding time waiting for my phone to ring. I weighed my options. If there truly was an Agent Montero I needed to find out a great deal more about him and where he was assigned. If there was no such person I didn't know what I should do but I was certain that I'd be in more trouble than I'd bargained for.

My cell phone rang and I picked it up expecting it to be Chief Bell but when I looked I saw that it was Fey. I didn't want to answer and tie up the phone but figured that I would make it quick. Strangely, a small part of me missed seeing her since it had been awhile since we'd returned from Leesville. "Hey Fey, what's up?"

"Hey Lonnie, I'm just checking in on you. I haven't spoken to you recently and was thinking about stopping over after work. Are you going to be home? And have you made any progress in solving the clues in that note?"

"Yes I will be home, and no, I don't know that I have." I didn't mean to be rude but wanted to not engage in a conversation. "Look, I can't talk right now but Ill see you later. Okay?"

"Okay, bye."

I had no sooner hung up with Fey then my phone rang again. This time it was Bell. "Lonnie, I finally got through to Mathewson. He says he's never heard of an FBI agent name of Montero."

"How can that possibly be," I asked. "Or more importantly, if you didn't talk to your friend in the FBI, Mathewson, how could this alleged agent, who identified himself as a friend of your friend, know what's going on with me?"

CHAPTER 37

AFTER THE PHONE call from Bell I was even more perplexed, and yes scared, than I'd been. What made matters worse was that I felt that I really had no one to turn to, no one who I could trust in helping me solve all of the questions and mysterious events that had recently come into my life.

I thought back to just a couple of weeks ago and how happy I was working as a waiter and living my life comfortably in my own tricked-out condo with a sophomoric roommate. Since then I had been told that my parents weren't my own, had them die in a car crash, witnessed a murder that no one corroborated, inherited $300,000, was given a mysterious note that may impact me but that I haven't been able to decipher, and been visited by an FBI agent that no one's heard of.

I was once again going through the information on my desk trying to make sense of the note left in my parent's safety deposit box when Fey appeared on my outside camera. I buzzed her in and met her in the living room. She was wearing cutoff jean shorts with tears in them, a low cut yellow shirt with tennis shoes and white socks with yellow tassels on the back. As usual she was her ebullient self which I actually found reassuring. A little positivity in my life couldn't hurt.

"How's everything at *Bon Vivant?*"

"Everything's good. We've been real busy but Dalton's filled in nicely and Antoine asks constantly how you're doing. He keeps telling Dalton and I to assure you that your job will be waiting whenever you're ready to come back."

"He has been so patient but I just don't know when that'll be. I don't feel that I've made much progress in solving any of the mysteries in my life."

She started walking toward the office end of my bedroom. "You said that you haven't had much success yet with solving your note? Can I see it?"

"I have materials laid out on my desk. I don't know if it will make much sense but you can take a look if you want."

Fey pulled up a chair and sat down on the side of the desk. I sat down beside her. The original note had been copied and placed in a plastic Zip-Lock bag. Pages of information littered the top of the surface. "What have you discovered so far?"

"I started with the word Munin because I was not familiar with that word and it seemed different than the others."

"What did you find?"

"Nothing definitive but a raven from Germanic mythology and the definition of Munin from Old Norse meaning 'mind and memory' seems to have the most relevance. I've been trying to examine the word 'dolphin' most recently."

Fey turned the copy towards her and studied its contents.

"It sounds like you are spending time on the words inside the star figure. Have you thought perhaps that examining the star itself might lend itself to clues. After all, there are only four words and three blank spaces."

"No, I haven't given that any thought but that might make sense. I know that a seven-pointed star, a septagram, which is sometimes referred to as an Elven star, has many magical traditions tied into the number 7. The septagram has significance to the seven days of the week, seven planets, seven magical metals and seven pillars of wisdom."

She nodded as she listened intently. "I haven't heard of a septagram. I've heard of a pentagram because that's sometimes used with the occult."

"Right, and those two stars have something in common. They both can be drawn without removing your pen from the paper. Perhaps more importantly, the Elven star is considered to be a protective symbol designed to 'defend secrets from the outside world.'"

"If that's true then that may relate to what Wormwood was saying.

You know, that the federal government has been keeping secrets from the public."

"Or that my father, if that's who it was, has defended his secrets by encrypting a message inside random words and a star... steganography."

"Steganography? What does that mean, Lonnie?" asked Fey

"It goes all the way back to the Greeks and literally means 'covered writing.' It is the hiding of a message within a message and generally was used to hide significant items behind those that were meaningless. If the Greeks wanted to send a critical message they would write it on a bald messengers head and then let his hair grow out. When he later arrived at his prescribed destination they would shave his head in order to read it."

Fey exuberantly slid her chair over closer towards me and put a hand on my shoulder. "This is exciting."

I wasn't in a position to share her enthusiasm but respectfully didn't pull away. I hadn't had time it seemed, with all that had happened, to consider what my feelings toward Fey were. I couldn't very well compare her to other "relationships" that I'd had, since I'd never had one. With her hand on my shoulder I wasn't really sure where my eyes should be. It didn't feel right looking into her eyes but then when I dropped my head and looked down I saw her breasts struggling to escape her yellow shirt and felt even more awkward.

Fey sensed my discomfort and gracefully withdrew from her embrace. "I have no doubt that you'll discover what is intended for you. You not only have an amazing memory, you also have a fabulous mind. It's incredible really that your father would know this even though he hardly got to know you."

"Actually, we're just assuming that the note came from my real father. It was not signed."

"He probably was afraid that it would get in the wrong hands."

"That's just it. Afraid *what* would get in the wrong hands?"

"Whatever's in the note. Let's keep looking."

CHAPTER 38

I AGREED THAT more work was needed. After having examined the note for hours I recognized that it wasn't simply going to take research, but also a sense of intuition. The use of the Elven star appeared to be significant because both possibilities included defending secrets either from me or from the general populous. It also provided as many questions as answers. Why were only four of the seven points of the star filled with words?

Fey moved several sheets around that I had printed relative to dolphins. While remembering what I'd read was not difficult, I thought by having them laid out in front of me it might trigger a response or give me a visual clue. I continued to read about the different varieties but then decided that perhaps I should examine the etymology of the species. "Dolphins are aquatic mammals in an informal grouping within the order Cetacea which excludes whales and porpoises. Zoologists use the term paraphyletic because the descendants of that subgroup come from the same ancestors."

"And why is that important?"

"I'm not sure it is. Here in the U.S. there is some misunderstanding where dolphins are considered to be porpoises. Also, there are six species of dolphins commonly thought of as whales and are collectively known as 'blackfish' so as you can see, it's pretty confusing."

"That is fascinating but does it help you solve the mystery of the note?"

I wasn't sure that it did but what I read next triggered a wakeup call.

"Fey, look. The word dolphin is originally from the Greek delphis which was related to the Greek delphus meaning 'womb.' Could that possibly be what I think?

"You're way over my head. I don't understand what you're suggesting. What is it that you think?"

"That somehow this reference to womb relates to my mother."

Fey looked at me with a sense of disbelief. "Neither Wormwood nor your parents have said virtually anything about your biological mother. What could this mean?"

I rose from my chair. This time I put my hands on Fey's shoulders... for support. "Think about it. What if the word Munin refers to me, the Elven star, as defined, refers to secrets that are being kept, and dolphin refers to the womb or more succinctly, *my* mother."

"What are you, what is *he* trying to say?"

"Recognize that this note was dropped off years ago and therefore anything that is included could have a very different meaning today. So much may have changed but if we take it at face value, at least when written, could it be that my mother was... or better yet, *is,* still alive?"

My excitement spilled over to Fey. "Holy shit, that would be awesome. Especially, as I said, there has been no indication or discussion of that by anyone. Throughout this entire time there's been virtually nothing said about your mother. This could be huge, what's the next step?"

"First of all, there's no guarantee of this. I'm just trying to piece together clues that I may or may not be reading correctly at all. This really is a reach. We don't know if my biological father is still alive, if my parents are together, or even if that note is from him."

"Could it be from your mother? As your father, er step-father, said, your biological father was involved in dangerous activities. Perhaps he died and the note was sent by your real mother."

"Real, biological, it's so complicated and, as you suggest, that certainly could have happened. That's just it, I have no idea."

"So what do you intend to do?"

"The only thing I can do, the only thing that makes any sense, is to keep trying to decipher the words on this note. While the words don't seem to make a lot of sense, the comment, 'If he becomes as gifted as I think, he'll figure it out' gives me hope. That wouldn't have been written if the words in this star didn't carry some meaning to me regardless of who it's from."

Fey leaned forward in her chair. "So, for the sake of discussion, let's assume that what you've conjectured is accurate and it refers to your mother. Does that mean that the next two words, Horton and Myrtle, are stating that she is still alive or, better yet, are clues to where she, or they, are located?"

"I only wish that I had solid responses to your questions but I don't. But, at this point, my intention is to go along with that premise and keep searching for answers."

CHAPTER 39

I SAT BACK down with the intent of going back on the computer to look up those two words when my cell phone buzzed. It was Chief Bell.

"Hello Chief, anything new on our imaginary FBI agent?"

"No, but member when we spoke earlier today I said I'd intended to call you."

I chuckled into the phone.

"Never mind, course you remember. Anyway, we got talkin' and I forgot to tell you that we may have a lead on who's responsible for killing your parents."

My mind raced. I didn't know if I was more amazed that they 'may have a lead' or that a police chief, could forget to tell someone something that important. "A lead?" I said.

"Yeah. One of my deputies spotted a car that resembled the one that ran into your parents. It was a big black SUV and it had damage to the front of the vehicle."

"Did they pull them over? Do they know who was driving?"

"No on both counts. The deputy was parked on Main Street facing north when he saw the SUV drive by him headin' in the opposite direction. He intended to follow the vehicle but, as you know, that can be a busy intersection."

I thought to myself how the traffic in New Orleans, and especially in the French Quarter, can be busy compared to that of *downtown* Leesville but of course said nothing.

Bell continued, "By the time he was able to turn around and get into traffic he was a fer piece behind. He turned on his blues and floored the cruiser but was never able to catch the SUV. But, even though he didn't catch up to him, this is a good thing."

"How is not catching up to him a good thing?"

"The fact that he was unable to catch up means that sumbitch musta been flyin' and you don't go that fast unless you're purposely running from someone or something. Plus, it also shows that the perp, if he's the individual responsible, musta pulled off somewhere before the deputy could catch up to him; he must still be in the area. The fact that the SUV ain't been repaired probably means they haven't dared to take it to a body shop."

"What's the next step?"

"We're going to have a flyover. We have us an FBI aircraft and intend to fly the length of Main Street in a southerly direction and over all of the roads that run into Main in any direction. As you know, many of the properties are set back and can't be seen from the main road. With this aircraft we can see if that black SUV is in anybody's yard. We have coordinated it with both state and federal authorities so if it's spotted we can pounce immediately. We'll get that bastard."

CHAPTER 40

DALTON SHOWED UP with two large pizzas and he, Fey and I took Pepsis out of the fridge and sat down in the living room to eat and discuss the day's events.

"Since when are you bringing home dinner out of the goodness of your heart," I said, as I tore off a couple of pieces to put on a paper plate.

"Since I started making mega bucks in tips," chuckled Dalton. "No wonder you guys love working at *Bon Vivant,* I made over $300 tonight. That's more than I used to make in a week."

"That's because you were a busboy," said Fey. "If you'd been a waiter at Brennan's you'd be making more than Lonnie and I do. It's more expensive to eat there."

"Yeah," said Dalton reaching for another piece, "I'd have gotten to that just in time to purchase a cashmere coffin. Do you know that some of the busboys have worked there over forty years."

"Speaking of working, I need to get back in to see Antoine. I feel so guilty having taken so much time off," I said.

"Also speaking of working, I say we get back to work trying to solve that mystery note," said Fey. "Are you going to help us Dalton? What's the next word?"

"I'm going to finish this last piece of pizza and watch a little TV. You guys don't need me and besides, what you don't understand is that waiting on tables is tiring work." Dalton tried not to smile as he walked down the hall.

"The next word is either Horton or Myrtle," I replied.

Fey headed for the bathroom, turned and looked back at me. "Could it be a Dr. Seuss reference? He wrote both *Horton Hears a Who* and *Myrtle the Turtle.*"

I looked up at Fey. "You're kidding right?"

"No, why? It was just a suggestion."

"No reason. It's just that it's Yertle the Turtle."

"Oh yeah, that's right," she chuckled. "Yet another reason why nobody has ever written 'If she's as smart as I think, she'll be able to solve it,' about me."

She returned and we sat down in front of the desk and looked at the last two words. "For the sake of moving forward, let's go with the assumption that this note is from my biological father. And, if this note is from him, then he must want to warn me about someone or inform me about something. All I know about my "real" father is what I read in the note that I received and I know virtually nothing about my mother. Since I don't know if either of them are still alive, I need to try to solve the next two clues and then, if I am correct with the dolphin "womb" clue, perhaps we will know more."

Fey's face lit up, her blue eyes sparkling. "What have you learned so far about Horton? Do I need to remind you of Horton Hears a Who?"

I joined her in laughter. "Is the extent of your literary background that which has been written by Dr. Seuss? Let me guess, your go-to cooking specialty is green eggs and ham?"

"Don't knock it 'til you've tried it. No, it's not the extent, but you gotta' admit that he's helped a lot of kids enjoy reading, or at least, being read to." She finally stopped laughing. "Okay, I'll move on? What else have you got for that name?"

I leaned back in my chair. "The name Horton derives from the Old English which translates to 'farm on muddy soil.' It is the leading manufacturing company of engine cooling components, D.R. Horton has been the number one builder of homes in America since 2002, Tim Horton has over 4,000 coffee shops and then you've got celebrities, or former celebrities, like Lester Horton, Willie Horton and Johnny Horton."

"Sounds like you've done your research. Does anything stick out from that?"

"Nothing yet, I'm just beginning to look in depth."

"I've never heard of Lester Horton, or Willie for that matter. Wasn't Johnny a singer?"

"Willie was a murderer who was let out on furlough in Massachusetts in 1986 by Michael Dukakis then Governor of that state. He proceeded to rape and murder again which played a role in the presidential election of 1988 when Dukakis ran and was defeated by George Bush."

"Doesn't sound very pleasant."

"No, and I can't imagine that being part of the message. Lester was a dancer and choreographer from a half-century ago who created a training technique still used today."

"It just came to me," said Fey. "I do remember who Johnny Horton was and Lonnie, one of the big hits he sang was the *Battle of New Orleans*. My mother used to listen to 50's and 60's music all the time. Maybe there's a correlation there seeing as how we live and work in that city."

"I thought of that and, just to be safe, I looked up the names of his greatest hits." I hit the print button on my computer and the following 12 titles appeared on a sheet. Fey removed the sheet and read the list.

North to Alaska

Whispering Pines

Johnny Reb

The Mansion You Stole

I'm Ready If You're Willing

When It's Springtime in Alaska

The Battle of New Orleans

All for the Love of a Girl

Sink the Bismarck

Comanche

Jim Bridger

Johnny Freedom

She stared at the list for several minutes and then placed it back down in front of me. "Other than the reference to New Orleans nothing jumps at me," she said. "I recognize 2-3 others but don't know anything more about him or these songs. It just seems to make sense that it would be The Battle of New Orleans since we live here."

"Yes, but remember, when that note was delivered I was living in Leesville. Whoever dropped off that note would have had no idea that I was going to move to New Orleans.",

"Oh yeah, good point."

I felt it was time to move on and didn't feel the need to recite that which I'd read about Horton or his songs so I chose instead to bring out the sheet with Myrtle typed on the top. Listed were different references to the word MYRTLE

- a shade of green
- an Italian fairy tale written in 1634 by Giambattista Basile
- several ships commissioned by the Navy and named the USS Myrtle
- two steamboats built in Oregon in 1908 and then in 1909
- a flowering shrub used for ornamental purposes - sacred to Venus, is the symbol of love and the Hebrew symbol of marriage
- Moaning Myrtle - a ghost haunting the girls bathrooms in Hogwarts castle
- in the Urban Dictionary a hired gun who works for the thrill of the kill.

Once again Fey took the list and studied it while I went back to looking at the Horton references.

"Does the symbolism of Venus and love tie in here do you suppose? I don't get the shrub connection but maybe I'm missing something."

"I've struggled there as well. I also examined to see if there was a connection between any items listed including the building of steamboats or naval ships - remember there was a Swedish ship with the name of Munin. Could there be a correlation there? And then there's the song, *Sink the Bismarck.*"

"Plus, dolphins live in the water. Three of the words relate to ships and all four are in the water. Do you suppose that the clues are pointing you toward a boat or going onto the ocean?"

Dalton walked in at the end of Fey's comment and chuckled. "Haven't you solved this yet Lonnie? I thought by now you and Nancy Drew would have this all figured out."

"Ha, not yet. We've made some progress but haven't been able to put it all together. I'm trying now to determine out how the word 'Myrtle' figures into the equation. Any thoughts?"

"That's easy. I love golf, as you know, so when I see Myrtle I think of Myrtle Beach, the golf capitol of the world. That's their marketing slogan in fact."

"But it's Myrtle, not Myrtle Beach," said Fey.

"True, but perhaps that's part of the challenge," I said. "Maybe he wanted to have the clues be a bit obtuse. Since I've already examined the other forms of Myrtle I might as well give this a shot. How many courses are there in Myrtle Beach?"

"I've only played 3-4 but there are dozens."

I assumed that Dalton was right but for my purposes I needed to have the specifics so I Googled that destination. After wading through all the golf packages being offered, I came to a list that I printed to lay out on the table.

- Golf courses in and around Myrtle Beach, South Carolina:
- Aberdeen. Magnolia Greens
- Arcadian Shores. Man O War
- Arrowhead. MBN
- Azalea Sands. Meadowlands
- Bald Head. Myrtlewood
- Barefoot. Oyster Bay
- Beachwood. Panthers Run
- Black Bear. Pawleys Plantation
- Blackmoor. Pearl
- Brick Landing. Pine Lakes
- Brunswick Plantation. Possum Trot
- Burning Ridge. Prestwick
- Caledonia. River Club
- Crow Creek. River Hills
- Crown Park. River Oaks
- Diamondback. Rivers Edge
- Eagle Nest. Sandpiper Bay
- Farmstead. Sea Trail
- Founders. Shaftesbury Glen
- Gen. Hackler. Thistle
- Glen Dornuch. Tidewater
- Grande Dunes. Tigers Eye
- Heather Glen. TPC of Myrtle Beach
- Heritage. Tradition Club
- Indian Wells. True Blue
- Indigo Creek. Wachesaw East
- International. Wild Wing
- Legends. Willbrook
- Leopards Chase. Witch
- Lions Paw. Wizard
- Litchfield. Whispering Pines
- Long Bay. World Tour

Dalton pointed out the courses that he had played as we went down through the list and then it caught my eye. I stood up excitedly, "Oh my god, I've just spotted something that might either be a remarkable coincidence or else it could be the clue that I've been looking for... and you guys know my feelings about coincidences."

CHAPTER 41

I LAID THE lists I had compiled from both Horton and Myrtle beside the long list of golf courses in Myrtle Beach. "Look carefully at the lists and see if you can see anything unusual," I said to both Fey and Dalton who were now straining to see what I had spotted.

They both looked at the lists for a couple of minutes but neither was able to recognize what I had seen. I then took the two lists and lined them up in a particular order with the bottom of the Myrtle Beach courses aligned with the top of Horton's songs.

"Christ Lonnie, can that be? Both lists have Whispering Pines on them," said Dalton. "What the hell do you suppose that means?"

"I have no idea but doesn't it seem rather odd that there would be two exact matches?"

"I think it's almost creepy," said Fey.

A smile came across my face. "What, that Dalton might have provided some help. Yeah, it's terrifying."

"I resemble that remark," said Dalton. "But seriously, you have no way of knowing whether the song is a clue, that golf course is a clue, or whether, as you suggested, it's just a huge coincidence."

"We studied some works back in high school of a writer named Emery Allen who once wrote that, 'some things are too strange and strong to be coincidences.' I agree with that, especially when it comes in a note left for me with the expectation that this note was someday to be discovered."

"You remember that from high school?" said Dalton incredulously. "I forgot what I had for lunch."

I ignored Dalton's comment and said instead what was now on my mind. "What concerns me is that, as I just said, this note was meant to be discovered at some point but not until Bob and Martha died. No one could have predicted when that would occur and what if they had lived thirty more years?"

Fey rose from her chair. "I see what you're saying. It might have been a moot point. It could have made the message meaningless if it was discovered long after your real parents were dead."

"Exactly, and perhaps that's what's happened. So we're trying to find a needle in a haystack when there's no longer a haystack. It might all be for naught."

"What are you going to do next Lonnie?" asked Dalton, "Put more time into studying the songwriter and the golf course?"

"Actually, I had another thought. Let's assume that it is no coincidence and not really the solution to this puzzle but rather, a means to an end."

Fey seemed to understand where I was going with this. "Are you saying that it isn't about either of those two items - the song or the golf course?"

"Exactly. What if my father wanted me to come to a solution through a rather convoluted path. It seems that he has given me a series of clues and expected me to not just discover them, but also to determine how to best interpret them."

"So it isn't necessarily that the clues by themselves that are so difficult," said Fey, "but trying to determine how to put them into context that's the real challenge."

"That's what I'm suggesting. We now believe that Whispering Pines is significant but what if it's the words themselves that are meaningful rather than the lyrics of a song or the name of a public golf course in South Carolina."

"What else could it be?" asked Fey

"It sure sounds like a golf course to me," said Dalton. "They often have names that are symbolic of nature and tranquility." He turned the paper towards him that had the course names on it. "See here; Heather

Glen, Magnolia Greens, River Oaks- they all seem to equate to peace and serenity."

"You're right," said Fey, but those names also sound like cemeteries. You know, peaceful, tranquil, serene. Is it possible that the note is giving you the name of the cemetery where your mother, father, or both are buried?"

I nodded my agreement. "Definitely a possibility. I am going to do some searching to see if there is a cemetery by the name of Whispering Pines. Sadly, I think there is a much better chance that they're in a cemetery than at a golf course." I sat back down in front of my computer and typed in Whispering Pines. As expected, a plethora of options were presented including a brand of tea, campgrounds, a catalogue selling items for rustic cabins, and a category that immediately piqued my interest when I saw it - nursing homes.

"What if my mother is still alive and is being cared for in a nursing home by the name of Whispering Pines?" I offered. "Like Dalton said, those too are often given names that connote serenity." For the first time I felt a sense of progress even though I had no way of knowing whether I was on the right track.

Fey shared in my enthusiasm. "Lonnie this is so exciting. That's a great idea. You've done a fabulous job narrowing this down. Which of those two options are you going to try first? You need to find out if you're right."

I was forced to chuckle at her exuberance. "Whoa there young lady. Being an optimist it makes sense to research nursing homes first in the hope that she's still alive but remember, not only don't I know if I'm correct, but even if I am right and she's being cared for in a nursing home there's a couple of small problems. I don't know which Whispering Pines she might be staying at, what she looks like, or even what her last name is. Remember, my last name - Clifford - was my step parent's surname. I never knew that I actually had a different name."

CHAPTER 42

I REALIZED THAT there was no way that I could discover if my mother was staying at a nursing home by the name of Whispering Pines without actually visiting such a location. After all, I couldn't very well call up and ask the receptionist if there was an old woman staying there that had given birth to a son who she had given away. I had no idea what she looked like or what her name was. I didn't even know if she was alive. This seemed like a herculean task.

"What's our next move?" asked Fey.

I noticed the obvious use of the possessive pronoun but chose not to make a big deal about it. I was more concerned with how to find my mother. "Since I can't call, I guess I'll need to determine if there are any Whispering Pines nursing homes nearby and figure out if it's worth my while to visit. There is no proof that my theory is correct so I might be just whistling in the wind."

"True, but that may be better than whispering in the pines," said Dalton.

I ignored that and typed in Whispering Pines nursing homes on my computer. I found multiple options as I surmised considering how tranquil that name sounded. Five locations popped up including Ripon, Wisconsin, Longview, Texas, Frostproof Florida, Fayetteville, North Carolina, and lo and behold: Plain Dealing, Louisiana.

"That seems almost too good to be true," said Fey. "Plain Dealing can't be more than a couple of hours away."

"And, as I said earlier, they wouldn't know that I was living in New Orleans. The message was delivered to my parents in Leesville."

"Either way, Plain Dealing is a hell of a lot easier to get to than going to Wisconsin," echoed Dalton.

"No question about that but let me remind you that there's no guarantee that our supposition is correct and, even if it is, and she's actually living there, I'm not sure how I could recognize her or discover which resident is the correct one, But, the good news as Fey suggested, is that it's within a couple hours, one hour and thirty-six minutes to be exact according to the GPS. I can drive there, ask questions, and still be home the same day."

"But if you find her you're going to want to spend some time there," said Fey.

"That's true. I may need to change my attitude because it seems that I'm going into this with a negative outlook."

"What's your second option?" asked Dalton. "You know, if she's not there."

"I'd rather not think about that - at least not now. If I leave first thing in the morning I can be there before lunch and hopefully get some answers."

"I wish that I could go with you," said Dalton, "but I'm working a double shift tomorrow. Can you spell Mega-bucks boys and girls?"

I smiled at Dalton's newfound penchant for making money.

"I, on the other hand, am off tomorrow so I call shotgun," said Fey. "I brought a change of clothes with me so if you don't mind I'll turn in on the couch." She removed a toothbrush from her purse and headed for the bathroom. I looked at Dalton who was rolling his eyes.

CHAPTER 43

THE SUN WAS just beginning to rise when the task force congregated at the Leesville Police Station on West Lee Street. In addition to the dozen officers from that office, including patrol officers and several from the Special Reaction Team, there were another dozen from the Vernon Parish Sheriff's Office. The SRT officers were highly skilled and trained for high risk tactical situations including crowd control and rural searches.

Greg Bell, as chief of that department, was in charge of this task force and was assisted by Monty McLean from the Sheriff's office. They had received cooperation from the FBI's field office in Alexandria which was providing the use of a Cessna for their surveillance. The task force was in the meeting room gathered around the coffee pots when Bell walked in.

"Men, I know you've been briefed on what we're looking to do today but I want you to realize the seriousness of the assignment and encourage you to take every precaution. As y'all know, Bob and Martha Clifford were killed in an automobile crash with a black SUV a short while back in what was determined to be a hit and run. What ya' don't know is that there's been a report of that vehicle being linked with the commission of another murder. We don't know if there's any correlation but until we can prove otherwise, let's assume they're linked."

"Who filed that report Chief," asked Frank Morton, a patrol officer from the Sheriff's Department. "When did that happen?"

"I don't have that info yet Frank - it's through the Feds - but there may be credence to it so it's important to know what we're up against." Bell nodded toward a man in the front row. "Joe Truax, from our department, saw a black SUV two days ago with what appeared to be damage to the front of that vehicle."

"Where was it seen?" came from the back of the room.

"Joe was parked in town and the vehicle sped away down South Main Street. He pursued for several miles but lost him so today we're gonna' try to determine if this vehicle's owner is living in the immediate area by placin' a unit at every access point off a Main Street which, cordin' to city maps, numbers twenty-three. As you probably know, these run alla way to Rosepine. Monty will hand out your assignment sheets."

"How do we know he's still in the area?" asked one of the sheriff's deputies.

"We don't but, since the vehicle was spotted just a couple a days ago, we think he may live, or be stayin' somewhere near. The Feds have agreed to provide a Cessna Skylane with a trained pilot. That plane can provide persistent wide-area surveillance over a twenty-five square mile area so if the vehicle's parked well off'n the road or behind a barn or garage we can spot it."

"Will that allow us to spot individuals within a home or other structure if we see the vehicle we're looking for?" asked Steve Lacognata.

Bell responded, "No, the signal is updated only one time per second, slow by video standards, but good 'nuff to follow vehicles should they be movin'."

Monty McLean stopped while passing out papers. "Let me add something to the previous response Greg. If the vehicle's actually parked inside a structure, we may not be able to see it, but that's where other technology comes in. The Cessna will utilize a Dirtbox which may assist us in driving out the perp and can also tie in others if we can spot him."

Rick Crawford, a recent addition to the VPSD asked, "Sheriff, as you know I'm new. What's a Dirtbox?"

Several in the room smiled as McLean continued. "It stands for Digital Receiver Technology and it's a device that masquerades as a cell tower so all mobile phones within range will automatically connect to it thinking it's a tower. This fake tower records all calls made from a cell phone and can break encryption and retrieve data from thousands of phones during a flight. It's a helluva tool."

"Isn't a search warrant required for something like that?" continued Crawford.

"No, it's not required. The courts have determined since 9/11 that this "trap and trace" system can be used by law enforcement agencies along with the DNR or Dialed Number Recorder which records all numbers dialed in or out to particular phones. We have some technology on our side but the rest is up to us. If we spot the vehicle from the air then we'll tighten the noose by moving everyone in closer and send the SRT team in to capture."

Bell once again took control. "I've already met with those members to go over protocol and I'll remain here at the command post and coordinate actions with each of you and our 'eye in the sky.' Do not... let me say that again, DO NOT attempt to apprehend on your own. As I said, they could be very dangerous and we don't want nobody getting hurt. Monty'll be with the pilot in the Cessna. Be sure y'all get your vests and helmets, we head out at oh seven hundred. If y'all have any individual questions see me."

CHAPTER 44

THE TWO DOZEN members of the task force were divided into two-person teams with each team being assigned a series of roads they were responsible for clearing. Because many of the driveways off the main roads were lengthy, and the homes were unable to be seen by the officers in patrol cars on the side streets, it was determined that they would have to drive slowly up each driveway.

The hope was that they could spot the SUV and then radio it in to Bell and McLean before they were spotted. If there was no SUV in the driveway and no garage or out-building in which to hide a vehicle, they could check it off their list and move on. They had all been instructed to not confront anyone if they did spot the vehicle but call the location into headquarters and then everyone would be notified.

In Louisiana, since there is little fear of harsh winter weather, the number of people who have garages is minimal. On the other hand, because farming plays a major role in the economy, there are many properties that have barns in which to store livestock as well as farm equipment - and an occasional black SUV. It was determined that the task force would not enter any barn that was closed, but instead, make note of it and, if the SUV was not found, then they would make a list and stop by again with back up. After the initial investigation was completed, which took several hours, a total of nineteen of these were reported.

After doubling up patrols it was determined to knock on the door of those nineteen houses and ask permission to look in their barn. If there was no answer then they would look in any out buildings before moving on. It seemed simple since people with nothing to hide would not object to the police looking in their barn. In each instance one set of officers would be assigned to remain in their patrol car while the other pair would go to the house and then on to the barn.

Roger Pierson, a member of the Sheriff's department, walked slowly up to the door of 32 Flying Ridge Road. They were several miles from town and this was his last stop. His partner, Tim Crossman, stayed a few steps behind, his eyes scanning in all directions. Behind them in the driveway was their back up, both members of the Leesville Police Department. The house was not unlike dozens of others in the town. Painted white with a roof in need of repairs, it had two stories with multiple bedrooms and a wrap-around porch. Out back was a large red barn with a wrought iron horse weather vane on top. Beside it was a smaller gray out-building that looked as if it was much newer than the barn and had been affixed midway down the side. It had a small door and two windows facing the driveway that were covered with shades.

Pierson was met at the door by an older man wearing jeans and an Atlanta Braves tee shirt with coffee stains down the front. His hair was uncombed, a several-day stubble covered his face. "What can I do ya fer," he said.

"Good morning. Officer Pierson of the Sheriffs Department doing a routine check and we'd like to take a quick look in your barn if you don't mind."

"Don't sound routine to me. Whatcha lookin' fer?"

Pierson noticed that the curtain in the window on the second floor directly above the door was slid to the side and he could see a bright red shirt but couldn't see a face. "We're looking for a black SUV that may have recently been involved in an automobile accident. What is your name, sir?"

"My name ain't important and furthermore, I don't own no SUV so you can go 'bout ya' business." He spit a wad of tobacco juice on the dirt beside Pierson's feet.

"Okay, we'll take a quick look inside and then be on our way. How many other people live in this house?"

"None a ya' goddamn business and I ain't givin' ya' permission to be snoopin' round my barn so get the hell off my property." He slammed the door in Pierson's face.

Tim Crossman shrugged his shoulders as if to say, "what should we do," and took several steps in the direction of the barn. Suddenly, the upstairs window was opened by the man in the red shirt. The barrel of a rifle was now visible and a shot rang out. Pierson saw his partner fall to the ground, blood spurting from his neck.

CHAPTER 45

PIERSON LOOKED TO his right where he saw another man coming around the corner of the house onto the porch. He sprinted to his vehicle and dove behind the front as bullets ricocheted off the hood. The officers in the backup patrol car radioed Bell announcing that shots had been fired and an officer was down and were now returning fire. The man on the porch blew out the windows of the cruiser with a shotgun but was then hit by return fire and fell backwards into the side of the house.

In the background sirens could be heard screaming from several directions. "You will soon be surrounded," yelled Pierson. "Your only chance to save your lives is to come out with your hands up." This was met with another round of shots being fired from the man in the upstairs window and another shooter now became visible in the barn shooting from an opening in the large sliding doors.

Two police cars sped into the driveway spewing dust as their cars fishtailed alongside the other patrol cars. The officers exited the vehicle and dove to the ground behind what was now a metal wall. "What do we have?" asked one of the cops.

"At least two shooters. One in the upstairs window, one in the barn. A third was hit and is on the porch. I have no idea how many more are inside the house - or barn, for that matter," said Pierson. Shots continued to be fired. One of the backup officers, unable to use the car radio, was on his cell phone with Bell apprising him of what was occurring. They could hear more vehicles stopping at the end of the driveway their occupants moving stealthily on the opposite side of the house. Momentarily the shooting stopped and they could no longer see the man in the upstairs window.

An eerie silence permeated the property and then from behind the house a man in a red shirt sprinted toward the barn. Shots were fired from the barn in an attempt to cover the man who squeezed in between the barn doors. In the background to the right Pierson could see SRT officers moving behind the barn their weapons drawn. More vehicles could be heard pulling up to the end of the driveway.

Suddenly, the barn doors were opened on both sides and the men on either side jumped into a black SUV that was parked inside. With the roar of the engine the vehicle sprang forward, avoided the two cruisers in the yard and headed straight at the police cars parked across the end of the driveway.

"THEY'RE MAKING A RUN FOR IT," screamed Roger Pierson.

At the last second the SUV veered to the right in an attempt to reach the main road. Two of the patrol cars that were just arriving positioned their vehicles on the main road behind the front two for just such a circumstance and the driver of the SUV, seeing this, tried to avoid the imminent contact. But when he did he went off the driveway into a drainage ditch that ran alongside the road separating it from the property.

The vehicle went nose first into the bank of the ditch, its rear wheels now off the ground spinning silently. Smoke was emanating out from under the hood of the vehicle, a burning smell filled the air. Officers quickly rushed to surround the SUV. The driver appeared to be unconscious, the man in the passenger seat with multiple weapons pointed at him opened the door and stepped out with his hands up. He was grabbed and thrown to the ground. His arms were pulled behind his back and handcuffs quickly administered.

Pierson had watched this from his position in the driveway and he and others now turned their attention back to the house. SRT officers could be seen walking around and through the barn after having checked to make sure there was no one else inside. Greg Bell, who had just arrived, stood behind Pierson's patrol car with a megaphone pointed toward the house.

"Whoever's in the house come out with your hands up. This is your last chance. The house is completely surrounded. I'm going to count to five and then gas canisters will be fired into the house... five... four..."

There was movement at the door which was then pushed open. Out stepped the man in the Braves tee shirt. Behind him came a woman carrying a toddler who was crying and holding the hand of a young girl. The woman was barefoot with worn jeans and a white tee shirt with stains on the front, Her hair was stringy and unkempt. The little girl clung to the leg of the woman and she, too, began to cry. Police officers from all directions surrounded the four.

CHAPTER 46

THE DRIVE TO Plain Dealing was uneventful and, as advertised, took slightly under two hours. We didn't get away as early as I would have liked. I took all of the files to the bank and, after stopping for gas and along the way for lunch, we pulled into the town a bit before four. We found the Whispering Pines Nursing Home with no problem and, as expected, it was nestled among majestic southern pines towering over the facility.

As I was getting out of the car my cell phone rang. I didn't want to answer it but looked down and saw it was Greg Bell. "Chief, what's up?"

"Lonnie, I got some news for ya'. Yesterday I told you that we were going to go house to house today to find that black SUV."

"Did you find him?"

"We sure as shit did but I gotta tell ya' it's been a helluva day here. We found where the vehicle was and wound up in a shoot-out. One of our men was killed as were two of theirs, but Lonnie, we got 'em."

"And they admitted to killing my parents?"

"Yes and no. The guy that was actually driving the SUV was killed in the shootout along with his brother. He had a rap sheet a mile long. He lived there with his brother, father, two friends, plus his girlfriend and two little kids. Can you imagine having your kids around those characters - eight of 'em living under one roof. What the hell's the world coming to?"

"So how do you know that it was these guys that killed my parents - and why would they do that?"

"Once we got 'em at the station the old man talked. He said his son was offered ten grand to take out your parents by some bald guy. He didn't know his name. They'd been watching Bob and Martha and were going to shoot them at their home but when they saw 'em drive into town they figured they might be able to get away with it being an automobile accident and all. He said none of the rest of 'em had anything to do with it."

I pictured my parents being loaded onto the gurney recently and thought of the repercussions of what I'd been told. "I'm glad you got them Chief but it won't bring my parents back."

"No, but I knew you'd want to know. Rest assured these guys won't be hurtin' nobody else for a long time."

I hung up with Bell and repeated what he'd told me to Fey. I know that Bell had intended to ease my mind with his call but I didn't feel any better after having been given that information. Fey, sensing this, brought my mind back to the purpose of our trip.

"I'm sorry Lonnie that you've had to go through so much but today might turn out a lot better. How are you going to find out if your Mom is here?"

I shut the car door and headed for the facility. "I'm really not sure. My only hope is that although I don't know my real last name, that my first name was given to me by my real parents and someone will recognize that if I ask around."

"That makes sense. Let's hope there aren't several women in here that named their son Lonnie." A smile covered her face.

As is often the case, I failed to see the humor in her statement. "I don't see that being a problem but let's hope there is *one* in here who named *me* Lonnie."

It appeared to be a charming place and as we approached the main building we saw several people outside sitting in chairs reading books or conversing in small groups. When we entered the building we were directed to "command central" which was a desk in the middle of the facility. Behind the counter sat a middle-aged lady wearing a turquoise sweater and glasses that hung on her ample chest from a chain around her neck. Her name tag told me she was Lucinda.

"How may I help you?" she asked in a nasally voice.

"Hi, my name is Lonnie Clifford and I have an unusual request. You see, I was adopted when I was very young and don't remember my mother. I have reason to believe that she may be a resident here but since we've not seen each other in almost twenty years, I'm not sure where to begin."

She lifted her glasses on to her face and looked down at her computer. Several seconds later she looked up. "I'm sorry. I'm afraid we have no one staying here whose last name is Clifford."

"Oh, no, her last name wouldn't be Clifford. That was the name of the parents who raised me."

"And you don't know her last name?"

"No, I'm sorry."

"Then how do you know she's here?"

"I don't but… it's too complicated to go into but here's what I was wondering. Is there any way that I could get everyone together and ask them if any of them gave birth to a 'Lonnie?'"

She looked down at her watch. "We will be serving dinner in about fifteen minutes so everyone will be coming to the dining hall." She smiled, "We tend to eat a little earlier than some… you know, the age and all. That would be a good opportunity for you to get everyone's attention and make your request."

"That would be terrific. You don't mind my doing that?"

"Oh heavens no. I think it will be quite fun and I'm sure the ladies will find it fascinating. If your mother is here it could make for a wonderful day."

Fey, who had been remarkably quiet to this point asked, "How many residents do you have living here? How many are women?"

"Currently we have 78 residents, 52 of which are women. They range in age from 53 to 97 and most have chronic health conditions. We have 24/7 availability of doctors, nurses, physical therapists and health care aides so we're very proud of our five-star rating. We consider this to be a big extended family. Would you like a short tour?"

Since we had a few minutes to kill, and since she was being so helpful, we agreed to that and were shown around the premises including all of the amenities to help elder citizens enjoy their later years. It was pretty impressive but I wanted to get on in my quest. "Lucinda, if you don't mind I'd like to speak to the residents. You have been wonderful but I'm sure you can understand my interest."

We walked into the dining hall and our tour guide picked up a spoon and a glass and proceeded to bang one against the other. The room turned silent. "If y'all could give this nice young man a minute of your time he's got something that could be right interesting. This here's Lonnie Clifford." She extended her left arm palm up as if she was introducing royalty.

I had forgotten how little I liked speaking in front of people and felt my throat go dry. Fey reached down to the table in front of her and poured me a glass of water. I took a long drink and began. "As Lucinda stated, my name is Lonnie Clifford and I've come here today to try and find my real mother. I was adopted as a baby and really have never seen or known who my mother is. I don't even know her name but I believe she may be here in Whispering Pines. So, my question to all of you is: Did any of you ever give birth to a boy named Lonnie about 22 years ago?"

I watched as all of the residents rustled in their seats and looked around at one another with expectation. Fey, too, was looking across the room like a spotter in an auction waiting for a sign or twitch. Unfortunately, there was none coming. After another minute, which seemed like an hour, I thanked everyone for their time and said,"I'm going to leave my phone number with Lucinda so if any of you need to get in touch with me please call."

Fey and I walked slowly back to "command central" and I couldn't remember being so disappointed or embarrassed since my freshman year in high school when I slipped and fell down in the cafeteria. At least no one here was laughing at me. Lucinda looked despondent. "Lonnie, I'm so sorry it didn't work our for you. I was really hoping."

We took a few steps toward the door. "Yeah, me too. But again, I thank you for being so helpful." I turned to go.

Fey didn't follow my lead but instead walked up to the matronly lady. "Lucinda, I was just wondering. You told us earlier that there were 78 residents including 52 women living here. Isn't that correct?"

"Yes, that's right. We're allowed a maximum of 84 but we're down a few now. Why do you ask?"

"Because, I counted all the women in the dining room and I only counted 49. Where are the other three?"

CHAPTER 47

LUCINDA STOPPED, THOUGHT for a minute, and then brought her hand to her forehead. "Of course, I never even thought of the other three. They're all in the Perkins Wing... that's for residents that are unable to come to the dining hall or, in some instances, even feed themselves." She started to walk towards the other end of the building. "Follow me," she said, "while you're here we don't want to leave any stone unturned."

I was taken back by this turn of events and once again felt a ray of hope after being so discouraged in the dining hall. We went down a long hall and through a door into a separate unit. A large brass plaque was on the wall in appreciation of Walter and Emily Perkins' contribution.

In the first room an elderly woman was in bed with a tube connected to the back of her hand. Her head was propped up against a pillow, her eyes bright in contrast to the wrinkles that covered her face. She smiled as we moved closer to her bedside. "Ethel, how are you doing today?" asked Lucinda.

"I'm doing just great," came the weak reply. "How are you doing Lucinda, and who are these nice people?"

"I'm having a great day too and they have come to ask if you ever gave birth to a boy who you named Lonnie?"

"Well isn't that an interesting question, but no, I was only blessed with two beautiful girls; Lisa and Sarah."

We thanked her for her time and moved on. The next room we came to was empty. We were told by a nurse assigned to this wing, named Jackie, that her health had worsened and had been taken by ambulance that morning to a local hospital. We told Jackie, a young black lady with a mint green uniform and a head full of braids with gold beads on the end, what we were attempting to do.

She said there was one more resident in this wing, a Dorothy Rawlings. "But," she warned, "Dorothy is not in great health and it may be difficult to speak to her. She lapses in and out of consciousness and we never know what we're going to get on any given day. She can be very pleasant and talkative some days and morose or unresponsive on others.

"What are her health issues?" I asked.

She deals with extreme bouts of anxiety, has nervous breakdowns and also suffers from respiratory ailments and has a weak heart. She has been with us for many years, long before I was hired, and has steadily declined. Frankly, we're surprised that she's made it this long."

"How old a woman is she?"

"Mid to late fifties. She's not really that old but is in tough shape. I've been told by others that work here that she's been through a lot."

Fey looked at me and said, "with all that we've heard and read about, she could be the one."

I said nothing but followed Jackie into the room. Lucinda's cell phone vibrated and she excused herself wishing me "good luck." The woman was sitting in a wheel chair staring out the window at a garden in full bloom. Despite what I thought was a warm day, she had both a shawl over her shoulders and a blanket in her lap.

She turned as we entered but said nothing. Her face showed no recognition nor emotion. She stared blankly at Jackie who pulled up a chair from the kitchen nook and sat in front of her. Fey and I stood to the side.

"Dorothy, this young man has come to ask you a question. Are you doing okay today?"

"What is it?"

Jackie rose from her chair and beckoned me over to replace her. The woman across from me stared at me, a stream of saliva escaped from the corner of her mouth. Her head sagged slightly to one side.

"Dorothy," I began. "I've come to ask you what you may consider to be a strange and personal question. You see, many years ago I was adopted and have never known my real father or mother. Like many people who have gone through this, I'm on a mission to find the woman who gave birth to me. Dorothy, did you ever give birth to a boy named Lonnie?"

There was no response from the woman in the wheel chair but tears pooled in her eyes and then slid down onto her cheeks. Fey took a Kleenex from the box on the kitchen table and dabbed at her cheek and wiped the spittle from her mouth. Dorothy took the tissue from Fey's hand and dropped her head into her hands, the tears flowing freely, her frail body beginning to shake. We watched not knowing what to do or say but then she raised her head and extended her thin, pale arms toward me.

"Lonnie," she cried.

CHAPTER 48

I STOOD, LEANED into the wheel chair, and gently wrapped my arms around the woman. She nestled into my shoulder and I felt her tears drop onto my neck. Fey, who had pulled a chair over beside me, was squeezing my arm.

Dorothy slowly broke out of our embrace and wiped her eyes. A smile came over her face. "I knew you'd come," she said. "Don't ask me how, but I knew you'd come."

I didn't know where to begin. I had so many things to tell her and so many questions that I needed answered but I also realized how frail and sickly this woman was so I wasn't sure how much I should push.

Jackie waved from the doorway. "You have some things to talk about and don't need me hanging over ya. God bless you, it's the first time in ages that I've seen her smile."

I told Dorothy about Bob and Martha's death and how shocked I was to learn in a note that they weren't my real parents.

"I never met them," she said. "Bob and your dad were great friends and even though we fought about giving you away, he finally convinced me it was best. It broke my heart and I've thought about you every day since."

"Since you knew where I lived, and who was raising me, why didn't you come and see me or tell me the truth about my past?"

"Your father made me promise that I would never do that. Being a parent is providing the best opportunities for your children. You want them to have more than you did. Most importantly, if you love someone, you want to keep them safe."

"I appreciate that but,… even years down the road? What was it that you felt was so dangerous that you had to give me away?"

"Your father was involved in top secret programs most of which he couldn't even tell me about. He had served overseas and when he came back he was brought into a program called Blackout. He thought it was going to be something that he would enjoy and then, after he found out what was really going on, they wouldn't let him resign. It was about this time that we met. We dated for almost two years, got married, and four years later you were born."

Fey, who had been listening intently to the conversation, asked, "How did you wind up here? Jackie told us that you have been here for a long time."

Up to this point I hadn't introduced Fey to my mother - did I really just say that? - and I apologized to both of them.

"That's alright dear, I'm so happy to see you it doesn't matter. Now, to Fey's question. I'm afraid that I have always been sickly. Even as a child I always had some allergy, or sickness. Then, when I was married to your father, I was so worried, so scared, that I developed GAD or generalized anxiety disorder. He had me admitted here to help take care of me. He knew that if we were together there was the chance that they would catch up to him and so he had to stay on the run. He loves me so and knew this would be what's best for me."

I reached out and squeezed my mother's hand. It was trembling. "I'm sorry to hear that. Are you being treated for that here?"

"There's not much that can be done, I'm afraid. It's developed into a chronic illness and I suffer from panic disorder, nausea and I seem to always be so tired." A slight smile formed on her face. "I seem to be afraid of everything." She squeezed my hand back. "Maybe now that I've found you there can be one less thing to be afraid of."

Jackie appeared in the door and said, "I hate to break up this remarkable reunion but Dorothy needs to take some medication and get some rest."

I noted that her hand grip was becoming weaker and understood completely. "Okay," I said and got up from my chair.

"Before you go please tell me how you were able to find me."

"I told you that Bob and Martha put a note in a safety deposit box for me to read in case they died. Well, there was also another note, given to Bob years later… supposedly from my father, with a series of clues. It's too complicated to go into now but we deciphered it and it led us to you here at Whispering Pines."

"Oh my god," Dorothy said putting a hand over her mouth. Her voice was faint.

"What's the matter," I asked. "Are you alright?"

"I had totally forgotten about this until just now. Your father, when he dropped me off here years ago, gave me a note and said if Lonnie ever shows up see that he gets it. I remember telling him that there's no way he'll ever find me."

"Did he say anything else?"

"Yes. He said something like 'if he becomes as gifted as I expect, he'll figure it out.'"

CHAPTER 49

I LOOKED AT Fey and her face registered the same shock that I'm sure mine did.

"Here, let me get it for you. I've saved it all these years in a music box that my mother gave me when I was little." She wheeled her chair over to a night stand beside her bed. "It's still in the envelope that I was given. I've never opened it - never would."

She reached into the night stand's bottom drawer and removed a small wooden music box. When she lifted its cover a weak tinkling sound could be heard. Inside the box was a number ten envelope that had yellowed, but remained sealed. "I have no idea what's in it but I hope it helps." I noticed that her body was beginning to shake uncontrollably.

Jackie noticed it too and said, "Lonnie, say goodbye to your mother. Now that you know where she is you can come back and see her anytime." I took a piece of paper on her kitchen table and wrote my phone number on it and slid it under the salt shaker. I hugged her and kissed her on the forehead. "I'm so happy that I finally found you," I said. I felt tears welling in my eyes.

"You've made me a happy woman, Lonnie."

"We haven't talked about Dad. Is he alive?"

She stared off out of the window. "I have no idea. He dropped me off years ago and I haven't seen him since. Do you understand why I'm a nervous wreck? I've worried myself sick about both you and him - never seeing either of you, never knowing if you're alive."

"Why do you suppose he never came to visit you?" Fey said.

"He has spent his life trying to protect those that he loves. That's why he took Lonnie to be raised by the Cliffords. I'm sure that's why he hasn't come back. He is convinced that everyone's lives around him are in jeopardy. He felt so guilty when he realized that he was involved in evil government projects and found out that the people who oversaw these would stop at nothing to get what they wanted. There was talk about getting Lonnie involved at a very young age and your father wanted none of that."

"You mention that *he* wanted none of that. What about you, Mom?" I asked.

She looked deep into my eyes. "Of course, I didn't want that either but do you know how hard it is to give up your baby - to have you raised by someone else." Tears formed in her eyes.

I looked at Jackie who was making a get-moving motion, fingers pointed downward and waving back and forth. "This has been such a wonderful day," I said.

"Just seeing how good you look is wonderful," she replied. "Next time let's talk about you and what you and your girlfriend have planned."

I smiled awkwardly and noticed Fey was also smiling as she bent down to hug my mother. "I'm going to go back to New Orleans but I'll be back in a couple of days," I said.

"That will be wonderful. I'll look forward to it." She reached over to the music box which she had placed on her bed and lifted it haltingly. "Here, I want you to take this too. The letter has been inside it for years and it seems only fitting that you take it also."

"Oh, I couldn't take that. You said it belonged to your mother. It's a family heirloom."

A wan smile came to her lips. "That's all the more reason that you should have it. I insist. I have so little to give you."

I took the box from her, leaned down and kissed her on her forehead. "By finding you today you have given me more than you'll ever know. One last thing before I leave. I've never known what my real Dad's name is. Can you please tell me."

"It's Paul. Paul Rawlings."

CHAPTER 50

FEY AND I reached my car in the parking lot and I could tell by the bounce in her step that she was as ebullient as I was. She leaned over from her seat so that our shoulders were touching. "Hurry up. Open up that envelope," she said. "I can't wait to see what's inside."

I slid my fingers along the fold of the envelope and took out a piece of paper that had been folded in fourths. Sure enough, there was another drawing of a septagram and in three of the points - the three that were left blank in the first message that I received, there were numbers. The type of paper was the same as the first message and the hand writing was the same. If there was ever a doubt as to who the first message came from it could now be put to rest since, according to my mother, this was given to her by my father.

In the three points of the star were numbers: 20, 30 and _28 28_ We stared at the numbers for a couple of minutes and then realized that we weren't going to solve this mystery in the parking lot and needed to get home.

Fey was sitting forward in her seat rubbing her hands together. "What an incredible day."

"I certainly agree. Think about it, I found my mother I've never known, found out the name of my father, was given a family heirloom, got another series of clues, and... ," I looked over at Fey who was staring directly at me. "and if it wasn't for you, I would have left without having any of those things." I reached out and put my hand on her hand. "Thank you."

"A smile covered her face. "I'm so glad I came. I'm so glad I could help. I can't wait to try and solve the new clues." She leaned across her seat and threw her arms around my neck. I didn't reciprocate but didn't fight her either, we were both ecstatic.

As we were driving back to New Orleans I received a call from Antoine. "Hey Antoine, what's up?"

"Lonnie, I'm so sorry to be calling you but I'm afraid that I have a favor to ask. Where are you?"

"We're driving back home… and don't be absurd. You have been incredible. What do you need?"

"I have an after hours party tonight at the restaurant and I thought I had it covered but two people have called in sick. I should be okay for the evening shift but there are between 80 and 100 people coming in at 10:00 for a retirement party. Would that work for you and Fey?"

"Not a problem. We'll be home in plenty of time and will be glad to come in. And Antoine, guess what. I found my mother today, my biological mother. She's at a nursing home and I had a great visit."

"Oh Lonnie, that's terrific. I am so happy for you. You'll have to tell me all about it when you come in. Are you sure that tonight works for you?"

"Absolutely. See you tonight."

CHAPTER 51

I DROPPED FEY off at her apartment and went home to re-introduce myself to Sammi. Dalton had left a note before going to work saying that he had fed, watered and walked her and would see me later. I paused to reflect on the friends that I had and how fortunate I was.

When I arrived later at *Bon Vivant* I was inundated with workers coming up to me. Antoine had obviously told everyone that I had found my mother and the congratulations were effusive. Since most people knew I was not comfortable with personal contact, I got a lot of well wishes rather than hugs. When do you suppose the fist bump was invented?

It had been awhile since I'd last worked a shift but it wasn't long before I was in my stride. Since the retirement party was for a man retiring from a local insurance company after fifty years of employment, and the food would be served buffet style, Antoine had me take drink orders. He asked me if I minded if he told the party about my "special skill" - his words - and I thought it was the least that I could do for him.

It became a parlor game as I waited on several tables and Antoine encouraged special requests. Therefore, it wasn't just a Bloody Mary that was ordered but a Bloody Mary, extra spicy, three olives, no celery, and a dash of Worcestershire sauce. You get the idea. *No problem.*

"This is awesome," Fey said. "Plus, everyone is so happy to see you back here."

"It is kinda' fun," I admitted. "Plus, I'm glad that I'm able to help Antoine. He's been so patient with me with all of the time that I've missed."

"He likes you and it's not like you've been making up phony excuses."

I turned in my drink order to one of the three bartenders and then went back to help bus the many glasses that had accumulated on the tables. When I carried them into the dish room a middle-aged man wearing a white wife-beater was spraying hot water on a tray of glasses. He had close-cropped graying hair, steely blue eyes and the build of an NFL lineman. On his left bicep was a tattoo of a raven, it's head turned and mouth open. "You must be Lonnie," the man said. "My name is Bud." He dried his hands on a thin towel tucked into his waist and reached a hand toward me.

I set the tray of glasses down and shook his hand. His grip momentarily caught me off guard as it felt that my hand was trapped in a vice.

"I understand you've had an eventful last couple of weeks… finding your mother after losing what you thought were your parents."

"How do you know all that?" I asked

"You know, people talk about things in the work place and from what I'm told, you're a rock star around here."

"Well yes, it has been an unusual couple of weeks to say the least." I wondered who he had spoken to and what exactly had been said but I heard the bell signifying my order was up so I needed to break away. "Nice to meet you Bud." I paused before I left. "Say, that's quite a cool tattoo of a raven that you have on your arm. Is there significance behind it?"

"It's been nice to meet *you* Lonnie. Sometime when we have more time I'd like to speak with you about your good fortune, you know, get to know you a little bit and perhaps I'll tell you the story behind the tattoo."

I headed out of the dish room to pick up my drinks but not without thinking: Had Antoine spoken to him? Why would he want to speak with me?"

CHAPTER 52

FEY RETURNED TO her apartment took off her shoes and collapsed on her bed. It had been a busy night serving drinks and bussing tables but she felt it was more than that which had led to her exhaustion.

The last few days had been psychologically and emotionally draining for her as well as Lonnie and combined with the travel, she was glad that she didn't have to work the morning shift tomorrow. She reflected on the meeting with Dorothy and how Lonnie had solved the clues which resulted in his trip to Plain Dealing. It had been a worthwhile experience - for both of them.

Fey sat up, took her cell phone and tip money out of her pocket and placed it on her night stand. It had been a good night, as so many of them are at *Bon Vivant,* and when it's a late night gathering of drinkers, it's pretty much a sure thing.

After brushing her teeth she returned to her bedroom when her cell phone vibrated. She remembered that she had forgotten to take it off 'silent' when working. She recognized the number and answered. "Hello."

"We haven't spoken for awhile. About time you checked in isn't it?" said the voice on the other end.

"I just got home from work. I planned on calling you tomorrow. Until now I haven't had anything to report."

"What the hell are we paying you for then?"

"How quickly you forget. I told you about Wormwood and confirmed your belief that Lonnie was the super baby."

"That's all well and good but as the saying goes, what have you done for me lately?"

"We just got back from a nursing home in Plain Dealing, Louisiana called Whispering Pines. Lonnie's mother is living there."

"Can she help us?"

"No. Although she's not that old she's in horrible health. She requires around-the-clock care."

"What about the father? Do you know where he is?"

"No, he's not there and she has no idea where he is. In fact, she hasn't seen him since he dropped her off there years ago. What is significant though, is that she gave Lonnie a note from the father with more clues... the feeling is that if he solves these he'll be able to find him."

"If she hasn't seen him how did he give her a note with clues?"

"It was on a piece of paper inside a music box. She's had it since he dropped her off."

"If it's that old, how valuable can that information be?"

Fey hesitated. "It's too early to tell but knowing Lonnie he'll figure it out soon and then I can let you know what we find out."

"See that you do - the sooner the better." The phone was disconnected.

Fey sighed and placed the phone back on the stand. She climbed into bed. Sleep was difficult to come by that night.

CHAPTER 53

THE FOLLOWING MORNING I spent running errands and doing chores around the house. I hadn't been food shopping in weeks it seemed, but I hadn't been home much during that time either. To Dalton's credit, much of the cleaning, or at least picking up, was done by him. I was vacuuming the living room when my cell phone vibrated.

"Hello Lonnie, this is Jackie... you remember, from Whispering Pines. You left me your number."

One of the disadvantages of having a photographic or eidetic memory is that others don't and I'm constantly being asked if I remember things. Since they don't know that I remember everything and rather than be rude, or bother to explain, I play along. "Yes, I remember Jackie. What's up?"

"I'm afraid I have bad news. Your mom has had a heart attack. She's in intensive care at Parkview Memorial Hospital."

"Oh my God!" I said. "Is she going to live?"

"I don't know. As you saw, she's been in bad shape for awhile. I know how horrible the timing of this is since you just got re-connected. You may want to get here as soon as you can. I don't know if she's going to make it."

I was already headed out the door when I hung up. This is unbelievable, I thought. What possibly else could go wrong? My life, which had seemed so peaceful and placid for so long, was now one catastrophe after another.

I made the two hour drive to the hospital in ninety minutes and headed straight to the intensive care unit. I told the nurses who I was and was allowed admittance. When I walked in I was struck by how feeble, and yes old, my mother looked. She had an oxygen tube in her mouth and other tubes fastened to the back of her hand. Her eyes were closed. I sat down in a chair beside the bed and she opened her eyes. She removed the tube in her mouth. "Lonnie," she said weekly.

I got up and sat on the bed beside her. "Mom, how are you doing?"

"They said I had a heart attack so I guess I'm not doing all that well. How are you?"

I smiled. "I'm fine other than I'm worried about you. I'm sorry if my showing up unannounced caused you stress."

"Nonsense." She took my hand in hers. "You showing up is the best thing that's happened to me in years - maybe ever."

We sat for awhile without speaking. Occasionally her eyelids would flutter and a weak smile would cross her face. Rather than interfere with what seemed to be a sense of serenity, I merely sat and held her hand.

After several minutes she said, "Your Dad would have been so proud of you."

"I wish I could've met him. I've been told that he had many talents."

She turned her head to look at me. "He was a special man with many skills. Tell me, did you inherit any of his skills?"

Since I didn't like talking about myself, I didn't know what to say but this was a different circumstance. "I have an excellent memory," I said. "In fact, I remember everything that I've heard, seen, or read."

She smiled at hearing that. "I never had that, but your father did. He had so many strengths. He was especially skilled when it came to speaking foreign languages and knowing about other country's histories and customs. He loved studying those things. Anything else?"

"Well, I guess I have a pretty high IQ. Many things come easy to me."

A nurse came in to check vital signs. "Can I get you anything Dorothy," she asked. The frail woman shook her head wanly.

The nurse leaned down and whispered in my ear. "Can I speak with you for a minute outside?" We left the room and gently closed the door. 'Your mother has had a major myocardial infarction. There has been significant occlusion, a complete blockage, to her arteries. This is referred to as a STEMI."

I noted the seriousness of her tone. "What is the prognosis?"

"From what we have observed on the electrocardiogram there was a complete loss of blood flow in two coronary arteries. She is on thrombolytic drugs, clot busters, and needs to have major surgery or, at the very least, have stents put in. The problem is that she is not strong enough to go through this right now. We are monitoring her very closely."

"I appreciate your candor. What are the odds of her getting through an operation?"

"Truthfully, not particularly good. She has suffered major damage to her heart and, as I think you know, was not very strong to begin with."

"Can I talk with her a bit longer?"

"I'd limit it to a couple more minutes. She really needs to rest."

"Alright, and again, thank you for being so straight forward."

I walked back in and sat down. My mother did not turn but opened her eyes. "Is my chance of playing professional football out the window?"

I smiled. "I'm afraid so. Mom, I can't stay much longer. They want you to rest but I have another question that I've been wanting to ask you. Did I have a twin brother?"

"No, what makes you ask that?"

"I've been told that there were two of us that were so-called 'super babies' and were taken to be raised by foster families. I didn't know if the other baby was a brother or belonged to a different family. And I wondered why he wasn't raised by the Cliffords."

"The father of the other child was a work companion of your father's involved in the same government projects and the baby was about the same age as you, but Lonnie, they chose not to give their baby away. Your father talked about the dangers involved after we made the difficult decision to give you away but they decided to keep their baby and, in fact, tried to talk your father and I into staying involved. The other father was adamant about what they were doing and it became somewhat contentious between him and your father... and Lonnie it was a baby girl."

"Oh my god. I just assumed it was another boy. What happened to them?"

"I really don't know. The last I heard the mother had died and I believe the father was still in the program. Hard telling what happened to the baby."

"What are their names?"

"The father is named Miles Branson and his daughter's name was Sage. Miles was divorced shortly after Sage was born. I'm told that his wife saw how obsessed he was with his work that she left him. Around this time I became sick so I never really knew the mother."

"One last thing, Mom. Do the numbers 20 or 30 have any special meaning to you?" I purposely left out the last group of numbers with 28s and underscores.

She paused for just a few seconds. "Not that I can think of. Should they?"

"Not really, I was just curious." I could see my mother was getting weaker. Her speech pattern was stilted and her eyes were closing even as she spoke. I got up and kissed her on the forehead.

"Can you ever forgive me for having given you away," she whispered.

"I already have Mom, I already have. I love you."

I sat back down and contemplated my mother's condition. I was afraid that she wouldn't be able to recover and it wasn't long before I heard the tell-tale solid beeping sound of the electrocardiogram monitor. Nurses ran in but there was nothing they could do. My feelings were so ambivalent. I was sorry that I had lost my biological mother yet so happy that I had gotten a chance to meet her… to forgive her… to tell her that I loved her.

CHAPTER 54

IT WAS THREE days later that I once again made the trek to Plain Dealing. The staff at Whispering Pines was nice enough to have a short service for my Mom at their facility. She had told them that she would like to be cremated and have her ashes spread among the giant pines that bordered the property. Sadly, there have been many who have died there and it seems that that is what many others, who had no family, had done and it had become a sort of tradition.

I thought about how many people had attended my parents wake - I will always think of them as my parents - and how few were there for my mother. Death can be such a strange, and lonely, event.

They offered me the opportunity of taking her ashes in the urn provided but I told them that I would respect her wishes. I'm not sure what I would have done with the urn anyway. She had no connection that I knew of to New Orleans and I had our brief time together to remember her by.

I went back to working at *Bon Vivant* and was attempting to settle into my routine. Antoine had added me to the schedule and although I hadn't solved the most recent clues - I hadn't put much time into it - I just needed a little break so that some sense of normalcy could return to my life. I'm not sure that could ever be the case however, with what had recently transpired and what remained unsolved.

I was working the evening shift which was different since both Dalton and Fey were there as well. I had gone from having no contact with the wait staff to now having a pair of friends working beside me. I guess it's fair to call Fey a friend since we had been through a lot over the past couple of weeks.

It had been a rather quiet night, as nights in New Orleans go, and we were cleaning up shortly before midnight. Although we had busboys whose job it was to clean the tables at the end of the night, the wait staff would try to help so we could all get out of there at a "reasonable" time. I walked into the dish room with a tray of dirty dishes and saw Bud, who was stacking plates in a tray and sliding it into the industrial dishwasher.

"Hey Lonnie," he said looking up.

"Hi Bud. How are you doing tonight?"

"Absolutely great," he said wiping his hands on a rag. "Say, you got a minute?"

I looked at other waiters carrying items into the dish room and momentarily felt guilty but said, "Sure, what's up?"

"The last time we talked, when I met you actually, I told you that I'd like to get to know you better. I try to be friendly with all my co-workers and while I've spoken to several of them, you've been away much of the time since I was hired and I know you've been through a difficult time of late."

I was taken back a bit since I've never enjoyed engaging in social conversation which I felt was boring if not meaningless. "Thank you for your thoughts but I'm not sure you know what I've gone through lately nor do I really want to share my inner most thoughts."

"No, I don't pretend to know everything but I heard people here talking about you and what a tough time you've had losing what you thought were your parents and then finding your real mother, only to lose her too."

"They were my parents," I said.

"Yes, of course. I didn't mean any disrespect. I lost my parents when I was young and I thought you might like to talk about it with someone… you know, someone who's been through it. I certainly didn't mean anything by it."

His comments caused me to change my attitude. "Oh, I see. I'm sorry that I may have misunderstood your intentions and I'm sorry for your loss as well."

"No problem. It was a long time ago. How are you doing now? I know it hasn't been long."

"Okay, I guess. It *has* been a difficult couple of weeks and amazing really, how quickly one's life can change."

"How about your real father? Did your mother mention him? Have you had a chance to meet him?"

I wasn't about to go into my mother's story or the clues that I had been left. "No, sadly, I've never met him and don't know if he's alive or not. Of course we talked about him but she didn't know where he is or, if he's alive. I sure would like to find out something."

"Well, hopefully that will happen sometime in the future. Life can be amazing and, as you have seen recently, we never know what's coming next."

I figured I'd spent enough time away from cleaning up and I was now ready to move on. "You're right, we never know, take care, Bud."

"You too Lonnie. I'm always here to talk and maybe someday we can grab a beer. I'd be glad to tell you what I did to try and get over the losses in my life. And, more importantly, I'm a good listener. Sometimes it helps to share the pain in our lives." He reached out and patted me on my shoulder.

I wasn't sure what the proper protocol was for the moment so I just smiled and said, "Thanks Bud, I'll keep that in mind." I finished my cleaning and stacking chores and when we were done Dalton and I walked home. He tried to convince me to pop into the *Bourbon Cowboy* for a beer on the way and to "be my wingman while I scout out the scenery" - his words - but I told him that I was tired so I left him there 'flying solo.'"

I reached the condo in a few minutes and as I was preparing to punch in the daily pass code I noticed that the door was open. A wave of fear swept over me and I climbed the stairs cautiously listening for any sounds above. When I reached the top of the stairs I found the condo in total chaos. There were things thrown all over the floor, files and papers from my desk and drawers scattered across the room. In the corner of the living room was my black Lab Sammi. Her body was lying against the wall, neck twisted, eyes open, tongue extended. "NOOOOOOO," I screamed as I bent down and lifted her lifeless body into my arms.

It wasn't until I turned around that I saw a man sitting on my couch.

CHAPTER 55

"WHY DID YOU kill my dog?" I screamed, tears rolling down my cheeks.

Agent Montero got up off my couch and stepped toward me. "I'm really sorry about your dog Lonnie but I didn't do this to your place and I would never hurt an animal. I found it like this when I came here looking for you."

"How did you get in... and who the hell are you anyway?"

Once again Montero sat back down on the couch. "Please, come sit down and I'll tell you what I know. And you know who I am - Hector Montero."

"That's just it, I *don't* know who you are. You said you were an FBI agent yet Chief Bell in Leesville checked with his friend Wes Mathewson at Fort Polk and he said he'd never heard of you."

"Let me explain. I..."

I paced in front of him and thrust my index finger at him repeatedly. "Then, when I called the FBI field office here in New Orleans, they said there was no one by the name of Montero in their directory nor is there in any of the other six satellite offices in Louisiana."

He could see how upset I was and rather than escalate the one-sided attack he leaned forward on the couch. "Alright, I guess I owe you some answers. Please sit down and let me explain."

I sat down but was far from placated. "Why would you kill Sammi? Why did you trash my place - were you looking for those files that I told you that I had."

"First of all, let me make this perfectly clear, I did not do any of this to your condo. As I said, I came here looking for you and when I arrived the door was open. I hollered as I came up the stairs but there was no one here so I sat down and waited. The dog was already dead, the condo is as I found it."

"That doesn't answer the question about you being a phony FBI agent."

"Lonnie, I am not a phony agent. Because of protocol I have not told you exactly what it is that I am working on, or for. But I assure you that I am not a phony."

"Exactly? What is this exactly - you have told me nothing. And rest assured, until you tell me *exactly what you're up to,* there will be no further conversations with me. And I *am* going to call the cops to report this vandalism."

"I don't think that would be wise because, as I'm sure you realize, this wasn't done by some teenagers looking for weed. In order for them to get in it had to be a high tech program that overrode your security system. You told me earlier about the murder you witnessed and yet the police were totally unaware of it occurring. You said yourself that you couldn't understand that. Do you not suppose that this was done by the same people?" Montero stood long enough to take off his suit jacket, folded it and laid it over the back of the sofa. "Besides, how sick do you have to be to kill an innocent animal - a pet."

I walked over to a hall closet, removed a blanket and laid it over Sammi. "Before I talk about what I think, I want an explanation about your involvement in all of this."

He sat back down. "I told you that I'm an FBI agent which is not completely accurate but I was trying to keep it from being too complicated. Plus, there is this concept of confidentiality."

"That doesn't seem so complicated. Why the deception?"

"Here's where it gets a bit more convoluted. I'm part of what's called the Special Collection Service - SCS - which is code named F-6. This is a collaborative effort between the FBI and the CIA. Since this has never been acknowledged to exist by the U.S. government, you can see why I was reluctant, unable, to tell you this. It's easier to just say FBI."

"Especially since you were not expecting that I would try to reach out and get background info on you."

"Exactly, and I've not told anyone else about my affiliation or my assignment. This is highly classified but, since we need to work together on this, I need to share some information with you."

Montero now had my interest although I wasn't fully convinced that I could believe him. "What is your assignment?"

"I am only telling you this because of your involvement in this. I am part of a small task force created to investigate whether there is still clandestine experimentation being done. These activities were supposedly shut down by Congress years ago but we know that there may still be illicit projects being conducted by various covert groups."

"Where have you heard this?"

"I am not at liberty to say but suffice it to say that the NSA, which was formed by President Truman in 1952, has the most skilled technicians and extensive surveillance equipment in the world."

By now I was genuinely interested. "I don't pretend to know anything about this SCS that you mentioned but I thought the NSA dealt with collecting information from foreign countries and counter intelligence."

"It does that, but not exclusively. Federal laws prohibits many government agencies from listening in on others so the SCS assists these agencies through the collection of information. We also deal with domestic issues, especially if we have picked up information that lends credibility to our concerns."

"So, I'm to assume that you have heard something recently about these secretive projects."

"Yes, and that's where you come in. We want to know what you know about OPERATION: MIDNIGHT because we feel you may be the missing piece of the puzzle in all this."

CHAPTER 56

BEFORE THAT COMMENT could be addressed I heard the doorbell ring. The security camera showed Dalton leaning against the door. I buzzed him in.

Dalton stumbled up the stairs and it was easy to see the condition he was in. "Did you forget today's number code?" I asked, knowing full well the answer.

"Number code? I'm proud that I 'membered how to get home. He looked at the mess around the condo. "Looks like you dropped some things or d'you and Fey have a fight?"

Before I could respond he said, "I'm going to bed," and sloshed his way down the hall.

"I don't think he even noticed I was here," said Montero.

"No. It's a wonder he noticed the mess. Luckily he didn't see Sammi under the blanket. He will be devastated when he finds out in the morning. He'll be out cold in a minute. Let's get back to what we were talking about. Now that I know what your affiliation is, if I'm to believe you, who is it that broke into my place and what did they want?"

"I think you know the answer to that. You told me that you had files from Dr. Wormwood. Why don't you see if those are missing?"

I knew what the results would be but I looked in the drawer beside my desk. Although it had been locked, the drawer was open and it was empty. What he did not know was that I actually had put Wormwood's files in a security deposit box after making a few copies to give to Montero after our initial meeting. The files that were missing were those copies. "The files are missing, they were in my top drawer," I said.

Montero had followed me and said, "As I expected. I think that was a big part of what the break in was all about. It's a good thing you weren't home. It's hard telling what else they might have done."

What he said suddenly hit me and I once again realized the significance of what Wormwood was warning me about - and what happened to him. "One thing I guess I'm missing Agent Montero, is how you knew to come to my condo. How did you know about me? When you first came to my condo you told me that you got a call from a friend at Fort Polk yet now you tell me that you don't know either Chief Bell or Wes Mathewson."

Montero headed back toward the couch and sat down. "Lonnie, I haven't been totally forthright about that either. The truth is that we've been looking for, and then tailing, Wormwood ever since we overheard him telling a friend of his that he was quitting the government project he was working on."

"You've been tailing him?"

"Yes. Often times disgruntled employees are great sources of information. If you're upset enough to quit your job, you're probably willing to tell others what led to that dissatisfaction."

"Were you able to determine where he was working and what he and his team was working on?"

"No. While we can usually triangulate locations, the operation that he was involved in is highly sophisticated and had inherent system blockers. The one message that we obtained was sent from his apartment so we were able to ascertain that address."

"And he led you to me?"

"Eventually. It was not easy. This is a big country you know."

"And so you followed him every day… where he went, what he did. You knew that he was staying at *Le Pavillon?*"

"We did. We had a couple of agents from our task force assigned to him and they monitored his every movement." He stopped here and looked away for a moment before returning his look deep into my eyes. "But there's one more thing you should know - in the spirit of full disclosure. We didn't kill him, but we did remove his body from the hotel room."

CHAPTER 57

"YOU DID WHAT? You removed his dead body from the hotel room…
without telling anyone."

"Yes, think about what you're saying. Who were we going to tell…
certainly not the police."

I looked at him as if he had two heads. "Never in my wildest dreams
would I consider killing someone. And then, removing the body? Why
would you do that? Where's the body?"

"Lonnie, let me see if I can make this abundantly clear to you. As I told
you, we have been looking for, and then tracking, Gordon Wormwood for
a while now, ever since we obtained information that he had quit working
on highly classified government projects."

"How did you find out that he'd quit?"

"We overheard him on a phone conversation telling a friend, a former
government employee that worked with him for several years, that he had
had enough. He felt some of these projects were going too far and were
supposed to have been stopped years ago. You can see why it was important for us to find him and then speak to him about what was going on,
what experiments were now being conducted, and who was in charge."

"But you weren't able to find him?"

"That's right, at least in the beginning. After he quit he dropped off
the radar. He gave up the apartment he had been living in and, although
we had it watched for several weeks, we never saw him come back to it."

"There are obviously other ways to find someone."

"Of course, but he stopped using a cell phone, made no transactions with a credit card in his name and basically, just dropped out of sight."

I remembered him telling me that he didn't have a cell phone because they were just "tracking devices." "You eventually found him. How long ago was that?"

"A few weeks ago but we made the decision that rather than interrogate him right away we would follow him to see if he would lead us to the lab, the head of the program, or to one or both of the so-called 'super babies'. The government does this all the time. We'll look the other way at arresting a drug user or low level dealer because we want to get the distributor who's providing that stuff."

"And you think I'm one of those super babies?"

"I don't know. Are you?"

At this point I didn't know what to think. "According to Wormwood I'm one of those two but how would I know. I have a good memory but what is a super baby?"

"From what I've been told you don't have a good memory, you have a phenomenal memory. Science tells us that there is no such thing as a photographic memory, a perfect memory, but do you agree with that assessment?"

I felt it was time for me to open up to Montero, at least somewhat. He had shared some intel with me that he probably had no right to do so, I decided that I needed to be a little more trusting. "Agent Montero, forgive my unwillingness to open up but put yourself in my shoes. A few short weeks ago I was working as a waiter in a nice restaurant making a decent living and having a good time. Since then I found out my parents are not truly mine and then they are killed. I find my real mother, who also dies, and now I come home to find my dog dead and my condo vandalized. On top of that, I see a man get shot and am told by an FBI agent, who is not really an FBI agent, that I have been followed and may be a piece of a puzzle that is being investigated by a Congressionally-commissioned secret agency. I'd say that's pretty fucking unbelievable, wouldn't you?"

Montero nodded his understanding of how things have changed. "I can certainly see how your life has been turned upside down and why you don't want to trust anyone but let me assure you that I am on your side and you need to confide in me so that I can help you return your life to normal." He walked around the living room as if he wasn't sure what to say next. He stood in front of my bookshelf full of more trinkets and curios than books. "Ah, a Howard Miller clock. Nice," pointing to the mantel clock in the middle of the top shelf.

"A house warming gift from my parents." I took a long swig from my Pepsi. "Let me go back to your most recent question. I don't know about scientists belief concerning a 'perfect' memory. I've read all those articles also but all I know is how it relates to me because I know that if I see or hear something, I can remember it. Not partially, or vaguely, but verbatim. If I read a book five years ago I can see the words on each page in my mind's eye as if I am looking at that book today. It's nothing that I practice or I am proud of; it's just me."

"But that alone would not make you one of the super babies. There are reportedly a few hundred people in the world with eidetic memories, most of which are children, I've read. What other skills do you possess?"

"That's just it, I've never cared to examine or gauge the gifts that I have. Other people have tried to get me to be tested or challenged but I never cared to allow that. Wormwood timed me doing a Rubik's Cube and wanted to give me an IQ test to see if I am truly gifted but, quite frankly, I've never cared to find out. I can do intricate math problems in my head and games come very easily to me - I've never lost a game of chess for example - but understand, I don't need to be told that I'm smart any more than an inordinately tall person needs to be convinced that they are tall. You just know it."

Montero reached into his inside jacket pocket and removed a small notebook and pencil. "Okay, what is 412 times 78?"

"Thirty two thousand, one hundred and thirty six," I replied.

He looked down and nodded. "And what is the largest city in Botswana?"

"I have no idea, I must never have read that. What is it?"

"No freaking idea, I figured you would know."

"Christ, I'm not a computer. In order to remember something you first must have heard it or read it."

"Which gets me to the next question. Did you read all of Wormwood's files that were just stolen from you? If so, that could be a real problem because if they realize that, and are aware of your memory, you could be in danger."

"Yes. I did."

CHAPTER 58

I THOUGHT ABOUT what he'd just said and realized the potential seriousness of the situation. I wasn't sure what to say next.

Obviously Montero wasn't either. He got up, turned, and looked back at me. "Have you got something to drink? My throat's drier 'en a canyon cactus."

I walked over to the refrigerator. "I have beer, Pepsi and bottled water. What would you like?"

"I'll take a Pepsi."

I grabbed two and headed back into the living room. The clock read 2:45 but I was not ready to end our conversation and gathered, from looking at Montero, that he wasn't either. "Do you know who it was that broke into my condo?"

"Not specifically but, as I said earlier, my guess is that it was the same people who had been looking for Wormwood. They must have been searching for the files that were stolen from them. Wouldn't you agree with that?"

My mind was racing. "I assume so."

"The same people who had Wormwood killed."

"Which brings me back to the question; Why did you move the body?"

Montero rubbed his chin as if to determine whether he should go down this path. He made his decision. "We felt that if we had allowed Wormwood's murder to be investigated there could have been too much scrutiny put on by the police. My task force has put in too much time and money trying to determine who, what, and why these experiments are still going on despite Congressional committees having ordered them abolished.

We didn't need the spotlight being shined on this incident so it was decided that we should act and remove what could have been a huge distraction."

That comment annoyed me, it seemed so callous. "You're saying that the death of a renowned scientist was nothing more than a distraction?"

"That isn't what I meant. Certainly we didn't want him to be killed nor did we have anything to do with that. In fact, his murder was problematic because we never spoke with him. In retrospect, we probably should have done this differently."

"So, in essence, he died in vain."

"Hopefully not. He led us to you and it is our hope that you can provide us with the necessary information to find, and close down, the illegal and immoral experimentation that is being continued."

That's just it. I don't know anything about what's going on or where. I only know what Wormwood told me and what I read in his files. I couldn't really help you if I wanted to and frankly, I'm not sure if that's in my best interest."

Montero registered displeasure with that comment, his voice rising, "For Christ sake Lonnie, your parents were killed and your dog is lying here dead on the floor and you're not sure if it's in your best interest to help me. Realize the spot you're in."

His point was obviously a good one but I reverted back to my questioning. "What did you do with his body? What about his family?"

"He has no family. He was never married and has no siblings. We made sure to give him a proper burial."

I rolled my eyes. "I'm sure. "How did you get him out of there without anyone knowing about it?"

"Getting into the room was easy. We have lock pick sets that can get in anything. We had someone in there almost, as you were driving away, in fact. The men assigned to him put his body in a steamer trunk and took him on the bell cart right down the elevator into the parking garage."

"So, you've been following me too."

"Since the second time he went to Bon Vivant and then came back here to your condo."

I thought about what he'd said and found it both disturbing and somewhat terrifying. We all realize that 'Big Brother' is ubiquitous but we think of it in terms of others. When it's you that's under the microscope it takes on a very different meaning.

"Lonnie, do you have any idea who's in charge of these continuing experiments? Did Wormwood tell you? Earlier you mentioned a man named Spillbane, I believe."

"Yes, he told me that a man who goes by the name of Derek Spillbane is in charge. He was not sure if that is even his real name. He said that he's risen through the ranks and refuses to stop his experimentations. From what Wormwood said the man is obsessed."

"What else did he say?"

"That he operates out of a different location than what Wormwood did - in an underground lab somewhere around Asheville, North Carolina. He also said that because he knew he was working outside the law that he had plastic surgery performed and therefore, didn't know what the man looked like. I'm surprised with all the tools at your disposal that you've not been able to find him."

"This is a relatively new assignment for us. A couple of Senators had heard about it and stirred the cauldron. Plus, we felt that Wormwood would ultimately lead us to the lab or the man in charge. Obviously, that's not going to happen now. Is there anything else I should know?"

I paused and thought deeply. Should I bring my father into this and open up about the note that was given to my mother? "Agent Montero, there's one more thing but I'm not sure how it ties into your investigation. And, I'd rather not get into it tonight, or actually, this morning."

Montero looked down at his watch. "Understandable, I didn't realize it was this late. How about I come back this afternoon and we pick up from there? Oh, and Lonnie, if you'd like I will take Sammi's body to be buried. I know how difficult those things can be."

I went over, kneeled down, and kissed Sammi on the side of her face. I thought about all that we had been through when she was a puppy in Leesville; the long walks, car rides in Rusty and how she was always so eager to greet me when I came home. Once again tears welled in my eyes. "Thank you, I'd appreciate that."

"No problem. And one more thing. I appreciate the respect but if we're going to work together, you can call me Hector."

CHAPTER 59

I WASN'T SCHEDULED to work the next day until the night shift which was a good thing since I didn't wake up until almost eleven. I had picked up the mess that was strewn around the condo and a few minutes later was pouring myself a bowl of cereal when Dalton came into the kitchen. "Do you feel as bad as you look?" I asked.

"I don't know about that but I feel horrible. My head is killing me."

"I don't know why you do this to yourself."

"I kept buying drinks for this beautiful girl, a flight attendant from Akron, Ohio. Do you know the nickname for the city of Akron - it's the rubber city. Got it? I figured it was fate... you know, that I would need a rubber." He extended his arms palms up as if to say 'duh' and clarify any confusion I might have.

"Ya, I got it. So, what's the rest of the story?"

"So, I kept up with this blonde bombshell drink for drink and the next thing I know I'm hammered and she's off to her hotel with a co-worker. Ouch!"

"You never seem to learn, do you? You don't handle your liquor very well."

He reached into the fridge for a bottled water. "She was a flight attendant, I thought it was only pilots that had an ability to drink." His attempt to crack a joke was met with an eyes-raised look by me. "Say, where's Sammi?"

I knew this was coming. "Do you remember when you got home last night the condo was a mess with stuff thrown all over?"

"Vaguely."

"Well, someone broke in last night before I got home. They stole some of the files that I'd copied, threw things around," here I paused... "and they killed Sammi."

Dalton, who had been leaning on the counter, straightened up. "They what?"

"They strangled Sammi."

"Why in hell would they do that? That dog wouldn't hurt a soul."

"I'm sure it was a message to me. I'm not sure if it was saying: Keep your mouth shut or you're next or, was it just fortuitous that I wasn't home last night?"

"Jesus Christ, Lonnie, this is getting serious. Did you call the police?"

"Agent Montero was here when I got home and said I'm better off without them getting involved." I briefly explained to Dalton what had been discussed last night. "He's coming back this afternoon."

"Do you trust him?"

"I think so. I believe his story and, as scary as those people are, whoever they are, I need *somebody* on my side."

Dalton walked into the living room and a sense of sobriety swept over him. " Good God, my life might be in danger. I can't believe they killed Sammi. I didn't know her long but I loved that dog."

"She loved you too, Dalton. I could tell." I once again thought back to our days in Leesville. "She was a great buddy. There were many days that I came home from school after being picked on or made fun of and she was always there to pick me up. She'd run to greet me, her tail wagging and would lick my face when I bent over to pat her. I think my parents must have realized how important she could be in my life since I had virtually no friends." My mind went back to Dalton's fear about his life. "And yes, you want to be careful and vigilant."

Dalton took some aspirin from a jar in a cabinet beside the stove and headed back to his bedroom. "I need to go lie down." He stopped. "Careful and vigilant? Christ, I need a sign that says I'm NOT Lonnie Clifford. I'm stupid and can't remember a thing!"

As upset as I was about the loss of my first, and only, pet I couldn't help but smile.

A couple of hours later Montero returned. I had a chance to think prior to that time and had made up my mind to open up to him. There was no doubt now that whoever was behind the killing of Wormwood meant business. And, although the killing of Sammi couldn't be compared to the killing of a human, it was still incredibly painful to me.

I went over all that had transpired with Hector, as he now wanted to be called, and together we tried to make sense of it. The question that remained, and that no one had been able to answer, was what did they want from me. I posed that to the agent.

He thought for a moment before responding. "I've been thinking a great deal about that actually and it seems that it has to be one of two reasons. Either they want you to be part of their projects due to your amazing mental and memory abilities or they want you somehow removed because they view you as a threat."

"I have considered both of those options but what would they want with me in their program? And how could they possibly view me as a threat to them, I'm a waiter for crying out loud."

"Again, I see two potential answers to the first part. First, with your intellect, you could be invaluable in the study of whatever experimentation is being done. Every year the brightest of the bright coming out of M.I.T., Cal Tech or any other think tank are offered huge salaries to work in labs. You certainly fit that bill. Plus if, as you have been led to believe, you are the son of a product of their experimentation, there is the added incentive to study you and see just how and why you are gifted."

A smile crossed my face.

"Why are you smiling at what I said?"

"Your terminology is so flattering. I've never thought of myself before as a 'son of a product'."

"You know what I mean. The question that screams to be answered is: Are you naturally gifted, genetically gifted or, based on what might have been done to your father in a lab, chemically or scientifically gifted?"

"What about me could be considered a threat?"

Agent Montero took little time to respond to this question. "I don't know that you were until Wormwood came into your life. The fact that your father may have once been involved in this program makes it problematic. If they need to disavow any knowledge of the existence of their work anyone that knows anything about it is a threat."

I shook my head. "Think how ironic that is. The man comes to warn me that my life might be in danger thus putting my life in danger."

"Now that Wormwood's files have been stolen they might feel that that is no longer a concern. They may feel the danger has been allayed."

I decided that this was a good time to tell Montero the truth. "Actually Hector, the files that they stole were only a small portion of the entire package. You asked to see those files awhile ago and I made copies of just a few of them in the hopes of placating you. That was before I decided to trust and confide in you."

"Well, thank you for that. So that really doesn't eliminate the problem does it? It won't take long before they figure out that they don't have all of the files that went missing with Wormwood. Where did you put the originals?"

"I put them in my bank security deposit box. They would certainly want to get their hands on those. Plus, I read all of the files and therefore, have all of that information stored in my head. If they knew that, I certainly could be considered a threat if, as you suggested, they want to eliminate any loose ends."

Montero looked at me with incredulity. "You're telling me that you can remember everything that you read in those hundreds of pages of files?"

I nodded affirmation. "Just as if I was looking at the pages and reading the information to you."

"Unbelievable," he said. "No wonder they would want you. But, they still don't know about you having that ability. They don't realize yet that you are one of those so-called super babies."

"I can only hope they don't figure that out."

CHAPTER 60

THE MAN WHO went by the name of Spillbane put his feet up on his desk and continued to study the folder in his hands. A white lab coat covered his cashmere turtle neck and tight khaki trousers. His skin had a ghostly pallor as if he had spent his life underground, which indeed, he had. Much of it inside the cavernous caves of the Blue Ridge Mountains.

He was carefully leafing through the folder of a project he was working on when his cell phone rang. He looked down, recognized the name of the caller and answered. "What's up?"

"Boss, it's me."

"I know who it is Cricket. Otherwise I wouldn't have answered."

"Ya well, I did as you said. We broke into that kid's place and found the files related to the projects. My partner stayed outside on lookout while I went through the place. I got 'em."

"Were all the files there, all the ones that Wormwood stole from me?"

"I'm not sure. I took everything the kid had but it wasn't a very big pile, maybe 10-12 files all told. I didn't take the time to go through and read 'em but it didn't' seem to be anything related to the projects you may be working on now."

"Shit, I was afraid of that. That number is nowhere near the number that was taken and obviously the current files are the ones I want most. Are you sure you looked everywhere?"

"I went through that place like Grant took Richmond. I assure you that if he has more files they're not in that condo. Ya' want me to go back in and maybe rough up the kid a little til he tells me where the rest of them are?"

"No, not for now at least. Keep an eye on him and maybe he'll lead us to them. He must have either put them in a safe somewhere in that condo or he has them in another location. What I don't understand is why he wouldn't have them in one place. I don't need those floating around and I sure as hell don't need any more government interference."

"Why did Wormwood share his files with this kid boss? Couldn't have been a friend, with the age difference and all. Is he a relative?"

"Not sure, but I've got my ideas though. Oh and Cricket, did you do what else I asked?"

"Sure enough. I put bugs in both his office and the living room. They're not real high end but they should do the job at least in those main rooms. If he so much as sneezes there I'll know it. I haven't had a chance to listen to anything being said yet but it's all being taped so I'll keep you informed if there's anything being recorded that's important."

"Good job. That may get us some answers real soon. Did you put a tracker on his car?"

"No, he rarely uses it so I didn't feel the need. Oh, another thing. I strangled the kid's dog. He started to bark and you know how I hate dogs and besides, I thought I'd leave a little calling card, let 'em know that we're not fucking around."

"Christ, we don't want him panicking and pulling up stakes until we get all our files back and figure out what and who this kid is. Don't do anything stupid."

"You got it. Oh yeah, there's one more thing."

"What's that?"

"The guy I hired out west wound up getting killed in a shootout with the police. Both he and his brother actually."

"Can that come back on us?"

"Nah, I only met with the one guy. I paid him in cash like you said."

"But you know he got the job done?"

"Absolutely. I even checked in at the funeral to make sure."

"Sounds good, keep me updated on what you hear. I'm shocked the kid hasn't gone to the police."

"Will do boss, and don't worry, we got that covered too."

CHAPTER 61

MONTERO WAS STILL in my condo and was pushing me for more information but I told him that before he and I could continue discussing the events related to my circumstances I wanted to know what he and his task force were doing to solve the murder of Wormwood.

"As I told you, we had been following him for awhile. Of course we had no idea he was going to be killed but, because of our proximity, we were able to get into his room quickly after we saw you leaving the hotel."

"Did you try to solve the crime itself, who was responsible for the shooting?"

"Not immediately because our first priority was removing the body. But, the next day we were able to determine by the trajectory of the entry that the shot came from the roof of the office building across the street. We sent men up there but found no shell casings or other evidence. There is an air conditioning unit up there but there were no prints so I'm afraid that we have nothing to go on."

"It seems so unfair that this man, who leaves a governmental program that he feels is corrupt, gets shot and not only is the murderer not going to be caught, but the authorities aren't even aware that he was killed."

"It's my hope that with your help we can get to the bottom of this and perhaps even figure out who is responsible for his murder. Can we begin again?"

We spent most of the afternoon going over the events of the past few weeks. Since I told him that I had read all of the files, he grilled me on the various projects that were once in operation with an expressed interest in those that, according to Wormwood and his files, were being conducted currently by Spillbane. He then brought up the notes that had been given to me by my biological father. He held up the paper that had the first series which led me to my mother. Before we could continue Dalton came down the stairs. "Feeling better?" I asked.

"Yeah, the sleep helped. I'm working the dinner shift so I'd better get going. You guys look like you're having fun - making any progress?"

"Not sure yet," I said. "We're still trying to piece everything together. Tell everybody I say hi. I'm scheduled to work tomorrow beginning with the noon shift." Dalton nodded and headed down the stairs.

Montero picked up where we had left off. "Let me see if I have this right. You looked at the words arranged around this 7 pointed star - dolphin, Horton, Myrtle and Munin - and were able to decipher where your mother was living? To me that seems unbelievable."

I nodded. "Understand, it didn't just come to me. It took some research, a bit of deductive reasoning, and it took some time."

"Christ, it could have taken a team of cryptologists a year to solve that. In order to apply deductive reasoning you first had to arrive at some theories. I can't imagine how you came up with those."

I had no desire to either explain the process that I went through or bask in the accolades being given. "I think the biggest reason for my success was the statement made by my father on the note he delivered: 'If he becomes as gifted as I expect, he'll figure it out.'"

"What did that have to do with your being able to solve the clues?"

"It didn't help me solve the mystery but I love games, puzzles... you know, challenges. By reading that statement, I was not only challenged but I was led to believe there was a purpose to the words, that there would be a solution. It's a lot easier to solve a riddle if you know there's a logical conclusion."

"Then, when you finally found your mother, she gave you another set of clues. Is that right?"

"Yes. This time they are numbers in the spaces left blank in the Elven star from the first note." I laid the paper down in front of Montero in which the numbers 20, 30 and _28 28_ were arranged in the three quadrants."

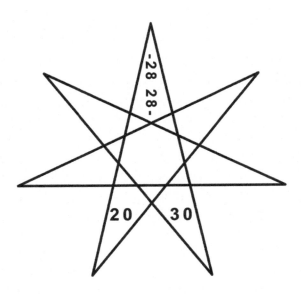

"Do you know what these numbers represent?"

"No. I haven't done a lot of thinking about them what with all that has gone on in my life the past few days. Solving the second part of the puzzle is my next objective."

"Do you think they tie in with the earlier clues that led you to find your mother?"

"I don't know but I doubt it. This note came from my mother so I am assuming that it is the next step in whatever journey my father wants me to take."

"But you think that these numbers are indeed clues?"

I didn't want to get too technical with the agent but since he was pushing I responded. "Hector, the word clue comes from the Middle English word *clew* which was a ball of thread. So yes, these numbers can hopefully help unravel the mystery just like in Greek mythology where a ball of string helped individuals out of the labyrinth."

Montero seemed a bit taken back by my response. "I can see that I'm definitely over my head here, but then, I am not a super baby or perhaps, better said, a super adult. Do you want to examine what the numbers mean?"

CHAPTER 62

I GOT UP and walked down the hall toward the TV room. I waved for Montero to follow me. When we both were inside the room I closed the door. "Before we begin working on my father's clues I want to take a look at the footage from the camera I have on my book shelf. I have my security cameras connected to the TV's in both the media room and in my bedroom."

Montero voiced amazement. "You have surveillance footage and you're just telling me that now. What, did you forget that you'd put them there?" His sarcasm was evident.

"Hardly. I've just had so much happen lately what with the loss of parents, the break-in and trying to figure out who you are and how you fit into this picture, that I hadn't figured out what to do about it. After deciding last night to put my trust in you, I figured we could look at the footage when you returned."

"You hooked the system up yourself? Isn't that difficult?"

"Not really. I just plugged the Internet protocol cameras into a Netcam Viewer Monitor and connected that to the TV HDMI port. Then I can switch the channel to see the video feeds. IP systems are relatively easy to install since there's only one cable to transmit the power data."

"Will the picture be clear enough to be able to see what is going on?"

"Oh yes. I installed an 8MP which is the highest resolution and can identify items or people up to 75 feet."

Montero sat down in one of the leather media chairs. "Are you sure it hasn't erased itself? Will it still be on the tape"

I grabbed the remote and turned on the television. "Absolutely. One of the advantages of using NVR is that it comes with options allowing you to customize the hard drive. While most recorders are set up for 3-7 days, the H.265 I installed is set up to only record motion and allows 40% more recording space. I can probably get up to two weeks."

"How many cameras did you install?"

"Four altogether. One outside in front of the condo and three inside. One in my bedroom, one in my office and one in the living room. The one in the living room is inside the Howard Miller clock you noticed earlier."

I changed the channel on the TV and rewound the recorder to the day before. After fast forwarding through the early part of the day a figure came on the screen first seen walking up the stairs of the condo. I set it to normal speed and the individual came into focus. It was a middle aged man who was short, stocky and bald. He stopped as he entered the living room to look around and it was then that I noticed the lengthy scar than ran over his left eye. He was carrying a small black satchel in one hand.

"This has got to be the guy that calls himself 'Cricket'," I said. "Wormwood told me that he does most of the dirty work for Spillbane and is very dangerous."

I watched in horror as Sammi came over to greet him. She was barking but her tail was wagging. He put both arms around her neck as if to hug her and then twisted. She fell to the floor, her lifeless body slumped against the living room wall.

Tears ran down my cheeks and I turned away from the screen. "Why would anyone want to kill a loving animal who wouldn't hurt a soul?"

"Lonnie, these people have done, and are doing, much worse to human beings - citizens of this country who have no idea what's in store for them. Let's keep watching."

I turned back and saw Cricket rifle through the drawers and cabinets in all three rooms obviously looking for the files pertaining to the projects they've conducted. He found the few that I had copied to give to Montero but was not content with those and continued to throw things all over the floor. He was not concerned about trying to search in a clandestine manner, but then, after having killed Sammi, it was a moot point."

"He certainly has no regard for someone else's property but why did he feel the need to make such a mess?"

Montero said, "At this point I think he's trying to make a statement. I'm sure he realizes that if there were other files they would be in the same location as the ones he found. It's for the same reason he killed a defenseless animal."

We continued to watch as Cricket reached into his black bag and removed several small items. He then went to the Dianne Parks painting, *Cathedral Plaza*, that I have hanging in the living room and removed it from the wall. He placed something behind it, secured it by pushing it into the corner of the frame and put the painting back on the wall.

"Those are listening devices. He's bugging your condo," Montero whispered. We watched him put a similar device under a lamp in my office. He then put the files from my drawer in his bag and walked out of the condo.

Montero spoke in a low voice. "I'll tell you one thing, it's a good thing we came down here. Now that we know where he put them and since there's nothing in this room, we can speak softly without them hearing what we're saying. Plus, they don't know, that we know, that they bugged your condo."

I sat in my chair in a state of shock. "My god, think of what this means," I said. "They know that it's Spillbane we're looking for, they know that I have Wormwood's other files, and they know that I'm supposedly the 'super baby' that they have been looking for. I really am in danger now. It's just as Wormwood predicted."

CHAPTER 63

I GOT UP from the leather media chair. "We need to get those bugs out of my condo," I said, my voice rising more than what was practical.

"Wait Lonnie. Maybe this is just what we need."

"What do you mean? I don't want them listening in on everything that I'm saying. That's creepy. Plus, if I'm able to decipher the newest clues then they'll know what I've discovered."

"That's just it. We can use it to our advantage. They can only hear what we say - or better said, what we want them to hear. We might be able to provide them with dis-information."

I thought about what he had just said. "That makes sense actually because, in addition to what I earlier mentioned, they already have my father's clues even if they don't know what they mean. Perhaps we can throw them off the trail if we *pretend* to solve the mystery."

And they now know that we removed Wormwood's body after they shot him. They were probably going to leave him there. I'll bet they were surprised that the death didn't make the news."

"Or maybe they just didn't care."

"That's probably true." Montero stood and rubbed his hands over his belly. "I don't know about you but I'm hungry. Should I order a couple of pizzas?"

"That works for me. Should we stay in here where they can't hear us?"

"We can work on the clues in here but we need to not let on that we know about the bugs so let me call from the living room. Do you have a preference?"

"My favorite is the Bourbon Special from *Vieux Carrie Pizza* on St.Louis. They have anything you'd want and they deliver."

"Let me guess, you know the number?"

"Of course." We walked down the hall into the living room. As he was placing the order my phone rang. I ducked into my office so as to not compete with Montero.

"Lonnie, it's Fey. I just heard about Sammi. I am *so* very sorry. Are you alright?"

I had tried to get my mind off of this. "I'm doing okay," I said, "but thanks for asking. As long as I stay busy and don't dwell on it I'm alright. I just can't get over the fact that those bastards killed a household pet."

"It's unbelievable. Sammi was such a sweet dog and I know how much you loved her. Listen, I'm working but I'm almost done and am going to stop over when I finish here. Do you need anything? I'll see you soon."

I didn't get a chance to respond before she'd hung up. Now that I know the place is bugged, I didn't want her to be here. Hell, I didn't want to be here. While waiting for the pizza to be delivered, I beckoned Montero back down to the media room and voiced my concern. "Hector, what's going to keep them from coming after me now that they know I could be the person they've been looking for?"

"What I'm going to do is assign a man to watch both you and the condo 24/7. That should keep you safe but what we need to do is try to smoke them out so we can get to the source. We need to find where Spillbane is working so we can put an end to it."

I understood what Montero was saying, and while it made sense, I wasn't too keen on being the "bait" to lure Cricket. "What do you have in mind?" I asked.

"Well, since they now know that you have more of their files stored in a safety deposit box, that they were unable to recover, it seems like that might be a good ploy to draw them out."

"You'd like me to 'announce' that I'm going to the bank and get those files?"

"Yes. I'll tell you that I want you to bring them to me knowing that they'll hear this and probably try to intercept you en route from the bank. We will be prepared for that and grab him when he surfaces."

"I guess 'surfaces' is a good verb choice for a Cricket - coming out of the shadows."

The pizza arrived and we spent the next few minutes devouring the pies and washing them down with Pepsis. "Wow, the crust on this pizza is outstanding," said Montero. "This city really does have exceptional food of all types and in all the various price ranges."

"Which reminds me. My friend Fey, and probably Dalton my room-mate, will be here soon. I think we should probably call it a day."

Montero wiped his mouth with a napkin. "Okay, let me work on assigning coverage for you and how we want to plant the seeds for grab-bing this Cricket character. Don't shy away from using your whole condo, but be careful what you say since you know they'll be listening."

I was vacuuming the condo when Fey arrived. She immediately walked up to me and wrapped her arms around me in a bear hug and laid her head on my shoulder. "I am so sorry for your loss," she said. "I know how much Sammi meant to you."

I found myself reaching my arms around her mid-section and pulling her tight. I'm not sure if it was an act of commiseration or because it just felt good. It lasted longer than any hug I had experienced since my Mom congratulated me after winning the 7th grade spelling bee. This one felt better. At last she straightened up. "How are you coming with solving the new clues? Have you made any progress?"

"Not really. I haven't put in any time on that yet. It seems like I've been awfully busy. I know that I've got to get going."

"Do you want to work on that now?"

I looked at the clock - the Howard Miller clock - and realized that it was getting late. I also realized that I didn't want to tell Fey about the condo being bugged. At least not yet. "I don't think so. It's been a long day and I think I'll wait until morning when I feel a little more refreshed."

"Understandable. Want to watch a movie?"

I knew she was just trying to get my mind off the break-in and the loss of Sammi,

Gbut it sounded good. "Sure," I said. "Any preference?" We walked down the hall into the media room.

"Not really. I just want to spend some time with you. I haven't seen you for quite awhile."

I sat down in the oversized leather chair and turned on the TV being sure to make sure I switched it to the proper channel away from the home security footage. Imagine my surprise when Fey came over and sat down in my chair beside me forcing me to slide over. I had never sat two in the chair and although it was oversized and there was room for two, it meant we were touching the entire length of our bodies. "This is more like it," she said.

More like what? I thought.

CHAPTER 64

CRICKET SAT IN his black Cadillac SUV with a notebook in front of him resting against the steering wheel. The tape recorder sat in the seat beside him as he diligently took notes. It had taken several hours to listen, re-play, and record the many pertinent comments that had come from the miniature devices he had planted in Lonnie's condo. He intended to bring the tapes to Spillbane but first wanted to share the highlights over the phone. No sense in wasting his time listening to the many mundane comments made throughout the day. He dialed the number to Spillbane's cell phone.

The man at the other end picked up on the fourth ring. "What's up Cricket? I'm awfully busy."

"Boss, you're not too busy to hear what I got to tell you. I just listened to the tapes from the bugs I put in that kid's condo and that has turned out to be a gold mine."

"Whatta ya got?"

"First of all, we now know why Wormwood shared the files with him. He IS the super baby that you've been wanting to find for years. His name is Lonnie Clifford."

Spillbane sat up in his office chair, his voice taking on a different level of attention. "Clifford huh... what makes you think that he's the individual that I've been looking for?" he asked.

"He's got an off-the-charts intellect, according to Montero, a photographic memory and, perhaps most importantly, both he and Montero acknowledged on tape that he was that individual. They even used the term 'super baby'."

"Hallelujah. I was beginning to doubt if we would ever find him. Maybe having those files stolen by Wormwood wasn't such a bad thing after all. Does Lonnie have the rest of the files?"

"I heard him tell Montero that he has them stored in a safe deposit box in his bank. I don't know which bank it is but I'm sure that we can get that info real soon."

"Good. I'm sure we can figure out a way to get those before he hands them over to the FBI or goes public with them." Cricket continued with his many revelations. "Sounds like having that condo bugged has proven to be valuable."

"For sure, and you'll want to know that Lonnie has been given a series of clues by his father."

"Really, clues to what? When could that have happened?"

"I don't know. I don't think he knows what they mean yet but he has a girl named Fey that hangs out with him and they have been working on trying to solve the mystery."

"A girlfriend huh. That's good to know."

"That's how they found his mother. The father gave him clues to that also. I heard Fey talking about it."

"That had to have happened a long time ago. We have to make sure that nothing like that happens again."

One other thing boss, they know about both you and me but they don't know either what you look like or where you're working." He continued, "Hell, I don't even know those things."

Spillbane was ready for the conversation to be over. "It's essential that we keep it that way. I appreciate what you do for me but you're going to have to watch your step. The less you know about any of this the better off you are."

"Of course. Do you want me to come back so you can hear the whole tape?"

"Not necessary, but you keep listening. I'm going to work on figuring out how to have you grab those files after he gets them from his bank… and Cricket, now that I think of it, there's one more thing I'd like you to do for me."

CHAPTER 65

LONNIE AWOKE AS he felt something shaking his shoulder. Startled, he looked up and saw Dalton leaning over him. He was even more startled when he realized that he was still in the plush media chair and that Fey was beside him, her head resting on his shoulder.

"Good morning sleepy heads," said Dalton. "Looks like the movie marathon got the best of you."

Lonnie sat upright which jostled Fey and caused her to wake also. "It was just one movie, *Don't Let Go,* and I guess we didn't even get all the way through that." He looked at the TV which was off.

Dalton saw him staring. "I shut it off when I came home last night. You two were dead to the world and downright cozy so I didn't want to wake you."

Fey sat up with a smile and stretched. "I can't speak for Lonnie but I got a great night's sleep."

Lonnie wasn't sure what to say so he stood up and said nothing.

"The only concern I have," said Fey, "is that now I'll never know how they solved that murder mystery."

Lonnie responded. "The smart phone makes a call to the future. It's all about time travel. I've seen the movie before."

Fey looked up at Lonnie, her eyes sparkling. "And you went along with my choice of movie even though you'd seen it before. That is so sweet."

Dalton looked at the embarrassment registering on Lonnie's face. "Okay, now that I got you two up I'm going to jump in the shower. When do you guys work today?"

"My schedule was switched so I work tonight," said Lonnie.

"I'm on the noon shift," said Fey, "so I've got a little time to work on your father's clues this morning if you want."

"I've got Montero coming over a little later but I could probably spend some time on that. I haven't made any progress." Lonnie thought about the listening devices in the condo and knew that he would have to either tell Fey about their presence or concoct an elaborate reason why they should work in the TV room when they had always been in his office or the living room. He decided that he wasn't yet ready to divulge the secret and grabbed two TV trays.

"I guess we can sit here for awhile," he said, closing the door to the room and then folding the wooden tables together.

Fey was surprised by his actions. "Aren't you going to want to use your office where you keep everything?"

"It's not necessary. I'll just bring my computer in here. I want to brainstorm and see if I,… we, can make any headway. He laid out the paper with the Elven star and the numbers 20, 30 and _28 28_ in their respective quadrants.

"Have you made any progress or arrived at any conclusions?"

Before Lonnie could reply Dalton, who also had not been appraised of the bugs, knocked on the door and then walked in. "Wow, first you sleep together and now you're having a closed door meeting. Your relationship has gone to a whole new level."

Lonnie, understanding the word play involved in Dalton's euphemism said, "We fell asleep in a chair, we didn't sleep together… and we don't have any type of relationship."

Dalton rolled his eyes. "*Whatever*," he said as he closed the door.

"I'm sorry if I've somehow embarrassed you," said Fey. " I don't think it's really that big of a deal."

"It's not - other than with Dalton, who is happiest when he's busting my chops. I'm going to use the bathroom and get a cup of coffee and a muffin. Are you interested?"

She ran her fingers through her hair. "In all of those actually," she said.

For two hours they worked on the numbers given to Lonnie as clues by his father but were unable to come to any solutions. Lonnie sat back with a sigh. "I think the toughest aspect of solving this mystery is that I'm not sure what I'm trying to solve."

"I understand that but is that really any different than the first series of clues? You didn't know what those words had in common or that by solving them they would lead you to your mother. Could these lead you to your father do you suppose?"

"I have no idea. I don't even know if he's alive. And, while those word clues were seemingly random, at least words have meaning. I just had to find the context. With numbers there is a sense of infinity. They could relate to virtually anything... the number of trees on the street or clouds in the sky."

"Possibly, but for him to leave numbers as clues, they must relate to *something.*"

Lonnie thought for a minute. "I'm sure that's true and I've decided that rather than try to guess what he's referencing, I'm going to examine them as I would words. I'm going to research their etymology."

"Sounds great but I've got to get going. I need to go home before I go to work. I'll see you later this afternoon at BV. And Lonnie, thanks for last night. I thought it was a lot of of fun."

I wasn't sure what to say so I just smiled.

Fey walked over toward me on the way out the door and leaned in to kiss me on the cheek. "Don't let Dalton get to you," she said. "He's just jealous." She turned and walked down the hall. I stared at her backside as she walked away and didn't feel the least bit guilty for doing so.

An hour later Montero arrived and with him were two agents that he explained were being assigned to provide security for me. He wanted me to meet them so that I knew who it was that was protecting me. He explained that they would split the day working twelve hour shifts. He guided us all down the hall into the media room before speaking softly. "Hopefully, with the subterfuge we are planning, we will grab Cricket quickly but until we do I want eyes on you 24/7."

Ben Evans was a dark-skinned man with a neck nearly as wide as his shoulders. He had a mouth full of white teeth and a hand shake that made me wince. His partner, Frank Irving, was not as wide as Evans but was a couple inches taller and no less imposing. Both wore dark suits and looked more like NFL linebackers than federal agents. As I looked at them stand-ing there in my media room the thought once again raced through my head: what in hell have I gotten myself into?

The agents left shortly thereafter assuring me that one of them would be stationed strategically outside my condo at all times but wouldn't be seen. While I wasn't thrilled at the prospects of that, it seemed preferential to the alternative.

Montero sat me down in the media room and explained his plan. "As I said earlier, we know that at some point Cricket is going to try and snatch those files from you so I suggest that we go into the living room and draw up a plan for you to pick them up at your bank. Since Cricket doesn't know, that we know, that your place is bugged, we will speak out loud to one another and establish a time when you will go and get them. What bank did you say the files are in?"

"Tulane Bank & Trust on South Liberty."

"How would you normally get there?"

"Because getting around the city can be difficult by car I generally walk most places that I need to go including to work. The bank is about a fifteen minute walk. It's not the closest bank but my parents always spoke highly of Tulane University so when I told them that I was moving to New Orleans they suggested that bank. It's a straight shot up Perido over to South Liberty."

"Got it. So it's right near the medical center. You must go right by Duncan Plaza if you go that way."

He was referring to a park the Downtown Development District had created. Designed for cultural activities and to showcase various monu-ments and statues, it had become a favorite for dog owners and sadly, hundreds of homeless, who hang out under the giant oaks. "Yes. Although I don't go to the bank very often, since I have direct deposit, when I do go I always cut through there on the way."

"That sounds like a place that Cricket might choose to waylay you if he knew that that was your normal pattern. What time does the bank close?"

"At 5:00 Monday through Friday."

"Okay, good. There should be less people in the park at that time. I know a lot of people use the Adirondack chairs and bistro style tables to eat lunch earlier in the day. We can have the park surrounded and kill two birds with one stone: catch him, which will alleviate your concern, and get him to tell us where Spillbane is working. Let's go have this conversation in the other room. What day are you available at that time to go to the bank?"

We headed out of the media room. "Tomorrow I'm off and the next day I work the morning shift," I said, thinking of all of the things that could go wrong. I'd seen too many movies where the best laid plans to catch the rat went awry and, as much as I'd like to see Cricket get caught, I still wasn't too eager to be used as bait.

We reached the living room and Montero sat down on the couch. I stopped at the refrigerator on my way. "I'm getting a Pepsi. Do you want anything?"

"Just a water please if you have one."

I grabbed a Kentwood Springs water for him and sat down opposite him in the chair. "So what is our next step?" I asked.

Montero played along, purposely leading the conversation so that it would be overheard by those listening. "You've told me about the other files that you are keeping in a safety deposit box. What bank are those in?"

I repeated where they were and went through an explanation of how I generally walk to the bank since it's such a short distance.

"You told me that you work tonight, are off tomorrow and then the day after next in the morning at *Bon Vivant*. Is that right? What time do you get out of work?"

"When I work the morning shift I go in early and will get off around eleven. Then, after helping to set up for the noon shift and putting together food that we donate to the food pantry, I'm generally home in early afternoon. Do you want me to go to the bank after work the day after tomorrow and grab those files?"

"I think that's a good idea. This will give me some time to plan so that I can be sure to orchestrate all of the contingencies involved. Also, now that I think about it, don't you think that you should go in your car? We know that Cricket might be watching you and we certainly don't want him to get his hands on those files. We're going to need those in order to shut down Spillbane and put an end to his clandestine projects."

"You're probably right but I don't want him, or anyone else, to change my lifestyle. I'm going to go about my affairs just as I normally would. He won't know when I'm going, or even that I'm intending to get them for you, so I should be fine."

"I guess you're right. As long as he doesn't know when you're going then there's no need to change your patterns." Montero gave me the thumbs up sign as he knew that everything we said was being recorded.

He left shortly after our orchestrated subterfuge which allowed me the opportunity to think about what this all could mean. I understood why they would want me to get the rest of the files and how my having those might flush out Cricket and whoever was working with him but it once again made it clear to me that I was putting myself in danger. As much as I would like to have Cricket caught and Spillbane's experimentations ended, I didn't like the inescapable fact that I was being used as bait.

✧

The phone call went to an answering machine so Cricket decided to leave a brief message. "As I expected, I got the info for you. Lonnie's files are in the Tulane Bank & Trust and he's going to get them the day after tomorrow to give to Montero. And get this, he's going to walk to the bank to pick up the files. I'll grab them and do that other thing real soon. Later."

✧

The night shift, as is often the case at *Bon Vivant*, went by quickly. When the place is packed, as it so often is, you hardly have time to worry about future events. Personally, I like it that way. I like the challenge of orders and numbers being thrown at me much like some people enjoy Sudoku challenges or crossword puzzles. Plus, I think the world of Antoine and enjoy the camaraderie of the waitstaff and others especially since Fey and Dalton had joined the team. And, even though it isn't my raison d'etre, the money isn't bad either. I used to think more about that but now that I received the inheritance from my parents I rarely do. I still haven't come to grips with that either.

CHAPTER 66

THE NEXT MORNING I made the decision that I was going to take advantage of not having to work and put in meaningful time to try and solve the numerical riddle left by my father. Since I was on hold regarding the files until I heard from Montero, I knew that I would have some uninterrupted time. Because I didn't want to have to worry about anything being recorded that I may inadvertently say, I took my computer into the media room and set up shop with a TV table.

I laid the Elven star with the numbers beside the computer and tried to determine if the numbers were in any particular order and if they should be examined as individual entities or were to be considered as a collective unit. It seemed to make more sense looking at each of them singularly and then, if I was able to discern the individual meaning, perhaps I could determine what the collective message was.

Since I didn't have any idea the meaning or order of these three numerical images and, since they weren't in numerical order, I decided that I would look at them from left to right, the way in which we read.

The first number was 20 and, not knowing where to begin, I googled it. My earlier thinking had been that the numbers might have represented some form of code much like the earlier message that allowed me to find my mother. I had examined the numbers as words and tried to dissect the letters themselves but had not been able to come up with any plausible possibilities. Now I was going to examine these as actual numbers and see if there was a pattern to be gleaned. My hope was to see if there was some historical meaning to these numbers.

I was surprised, not only by the number of references to the number 20 online, but also by the variety of sources. Since the beginning of time numbers have played a major role in society and had many religious implications. In fact, it was written that the number 20 was cited 117 times in the Bible alone. As always, I took copious notes and in addition to religion, I examined the references in various forms of numerology, symbolism, the examination of numbers in dreams and prophetic renderings among others. Most people are aware that 20 in Roman numerals is XX but fewer know that the Greek numeral for 20 is K. Could that be meaningful?

Although I didn't reach any definitive conclusion, I spent a couple of hours researching various possibilities before taking a break to grab a sandwich and a beer. I had grown fond of making Muffulettas at home. I know in other parts of the country they call them hoagies, grinders, sub sandwiches or Italians but this NOLA version has been made since the early 1900's when Lupo Salvatore, the owner of the Central Grocery, began combining all the ham and cheese ingredients and added his now-famous olive salad. I buy that and the other ingredients in his store and we often make our own Muffulettas at home.

After putting a couple more hours in examining the number 30, my phone rang and it was Fey who said she had just finished her shift and was going to stop over. I told her that I was fine with that and that I had been researching numbers all day and wanted to bounce a couple of ideas off of her. It seemed that I was not only getting more use to her companionship, but was actually beginning to like it.

She asked what I'd found but I was cognizant of the listening devices in my condo and told her I'd tell her when she got here.

When Fey came up the stairs a few minutes later I handed her an Abita Amber and she chuckled, her white teeth lighting up her smile. "You've come a long way, Lonnie. The first time I came here I had to beg for a glass of water and now you meet me with a cold beer as I walk in. I knew you were teachable."

She wrapped her arms around me in one of her patented hugs. I gently, awkwardly, hugged her back and then headed toward the media room knowing that she would follow. I didn't want her to begin asking me questions in the living room for fear that my silence or non-answers would be both awkward to her and telling to those who were listening so I offered a bit of banal conversation. "How's everything going at BV? What's new over there?"

"Not much different than last time you were there," she replied. "We were busy as usual. You know, I had always heard that 'Breakfast at Brennan's' was a big thing but we do well in the morning also."

"It never used to be like that when I started there," I said, "but it continues to grow." We had reached the end of the hall.

"Oh, I meant to tell you, Bud talked with me the last time I worked at night. He seems like such a nice man and he asked me all about my family and such. He asked me a lot about you as well. I hope you don't mind but I told him a bit of what you've been going through including your trying to solve the numerical clues. He was fascinated by that. I don't know if it's because he lives on his own and is lonely but he seems to really care."

I wasn't happy about her sharing my problems with a relative stranger. "I wish you hadn't done that," I said. "Although he seems like a nice man, I'd rather not have my issues discussed with anyone." I stepped in and closed the door softly behind me.

"So, you feel that you've made some progress today?"

"I'm not sure if it's progress but I have some ideas. I'm still not convinced though that there's going to be a clear-cut solution to this riddle."

She waited for me to pick one of the leather chairs and then sat in the next one over. Thank god, I thought, she's not going to squeeze in beside me again.

"Let me look at the clue page before you begin discussing your thoughts," she said. I handed her the photo copied sheet. After a glance at the page she leaned back in her chair. "Okay, go ahead."

I began. "Understand, these are not considered to be definite conclusions but are talking points and I'll give you my reasons for arriving at my beliefs."

"Okay, I'm listening."

I held the sheet up. "I don't know what my father was trying to tell me by leaving these numbers but remember, this was given to my mother several years ago just like the original clues that were mysteriously left at my home in Leesville. So, in both cases, I was in my teens and everything was very different. There's no way he could have predicted what happened with Bob and Martha, when I would get the notes or, what the hell's going on in my life."

"No, but that makes it even more significant."

"He left me a note that gave me clues to find my mother. He couldn't have known if I could solve the clues, or if I could find where she was living or, even if I would get them before she died."

"So, if he guided you to find your mother, it's only reasonable to believe that this second set of clues are an attempt to guide you toward someone or something else."

"Perhaps. Or is he trying to steer me away from someone or something? Knowing a bit of his story and the lengths he went to to keep me safe, I feel that might be his goal. To warn me about someone."

"You say that the clues were left several years ago at a time in your life when things were very different. But why didn't your father leave you more up-to-date clues. Or, better yet, you're a grown man, why not come speak with you and either warn you in person or become part of your life?"

"I've thought about that non-stop since I found out that Bob and Martha aren't my real parents. The only explanation that I can come up with is the one I didn't want to accept... he must have died."

CHAPTER 67

"I AM BEGINNING with the number 20 only because it's on the left and that is the direction in which we read. I researched over a dozen different potentialities and have considered whether the number is to be symbolic, like so many passages alluded to, or whether it is tangible. Even trying to solve this minor dilemma creates a myriad of possibilities."

Fey turned in her chair and stared directly into my eyes. "Tell me your thoughts."

"There are many aspects of numerology and one of these, Biblical numerology, symbolizes the cycles of completeness and often is connected to a perfect period of waiting, labor or suffering. In this vain there are references to Jacob, Solomon, and the children of Israel. The number is also tied in with one who is a team worker and diplomat and expresses a comprehensive point of view. I don't see either of these fitting into my situation or personality, do you?"

"No, I don't. You are more of a loner than a diplomat. I hope that doesn't hurt your feelings."

"Not at all. I just want to get to the bottom of this."

"So what comes next?"

"Then I went to Tarot cards which presents a very different view of the number twenty. As you may know, cartomancy, using playing cards to predict the future, has been done since the mid 15th century and while many feel it is related to the occult, it has been believed to have esoteric links to ancient Egypt, the Kabbalah, Indian Tantra and the I Ching. The concept of divination, which is to foretell or predict, ties in with God being divine, and goes back much earlier than that and, since my father wouldn't have known when, or if, I was going to discover his clues, he would had to have had great faith in divine or prophetic beliefs."

"And a belief that you would be gifted enough to both work with his clues and ultimately decipher them," said Fey.

I nodded in agreement. "Which brings me back to my thinking. The number 20 Tarot card is referred to as the 'Judgement' card and calls for truth. It encourages one to make a life-changing decision requiring the use of both intuition and intellect. The expectation is that one is at a crossroad and your decision will have life-long implications. This decision comes after a lengthy period of confusion or misunderstanding when the pieces of the puzzle of your life are finally coming together. The belief is that by examining your life lessons and past you will be prepared to trust your judgement and move forward on the right path. In a nutshell, I'm being told to not be afraid of what appears to be major changes in my life, accept these and move on."

Fey sat forward in her chair, excitement in her voice. "That sounds exactly what you're going through - a period of confusion or misunderstanding."

"My thoughts exactly. My whole life has turned out to be a period of confusion or misunderstanding. And how about this, it follows the 'Sun' card - get it? - (Son), which is symbolized by masculinity and courage and other qualities such as happiness, honor and success. Now I realize that these are such general terms that many people could ascribe such qualities to themselves and as for the Sun-Son reference I may be reading too much into this but remember, these are clues and I am supposed to be 'gifted enough to figure it out.'"

"What about the next number - 30?"

"Again, I spent a great deal of time examining all of the possibilities and according to numerology it is supposed to symbolize creative self-expression, socializing, tolerance and imagination."

Fey chuckled, "I'm not buying it."

"Ha, neither was I so I moved on. Thirty is listed as the number of the cycle or circle which is the geometric expression of absolute completion or infinity. There are thirty days in the month, it plays a major role in our clocks and time overall and there are 30 upright stones in Stonehenge.

"Fascinating but I don't see the connection."

"No, but I believe I could see it when I turned to the Bible. The most commonly recognized reference to the number 30, and that number is mentioned 87 times in the book, is the number of silver coins Judas accepted for betraying Jesus. This proverb is so widely believed that it is written in hundreds of languages and the number carries negativity much like that of 666."

"And how does this number tie into your situation?"

"Don't you see?" I found myself raising my voice and despite the door being closed I didn't want any of this conversation being picked up on the listening device. "If my father is trying to warn me about something or someone what better analogy is there to compare a person to Judas, the first and greatest traitor of all."

"I think I see where you're going with this. You feel that your father is trying to make you aware of… or better yet, beware of…"

"Yes, Derek Spillbane."

CHAPTER 68

"IT MAKES SENSE, doesn't it," I said to Fey. "These two messages are telling me that what I thought was my life was not real. Understandably it was based on confusion and misunderstanding which only recently came to light. There's no way I could be expected to know any of the history of my parents."

"And now that you have been enlightened, according to your father's clues, you are ready to make life-changing decisions while being aware of an individual - Spillbane - who is analogous to Judas."

"Exactly. But I see Spillbane acting as Judas toward my father rather than me because they were involved together as brothers-in-arms in the government projects. From what my mother said, my father tried to extricate himself from the government project he was involved with and when he was unable to do that my parents tried to convince the father of the other child, Miles Branson, to take the baby somewhere for safekeeping. You may remember my mother saying that not only did Branson not want to do that, but he tried to convince my father to stay involved."

"So, do you think that Derek Spillbane is really Miles Branson?"

"It seems like it would make sense doesn't it. Wormwood said that Spillbane began in the program about twenty years ago, the same time that my father became involved, and that he had become so protective of it that it was considered by some to be an obsession. We all have seen movies and read books about the mad scientist working in his laboratory who has been derailed from society and reality in order to protect whatever evil thing he's working on."

"Yes, but what we've seen and read is fiction. How could something like this be occurring under the noses of, or auspices of, the United States government?"

"I know it sounds bizarre but think about all of those files that we read with all of those heinous experiments being conducted on our own soldiers or civilians. Also, don't forget that my father's clues were delivered inside of a septagram or an Elven Star which is said to 'defend secrets from the outside world.' I'm convinced that all of the clues that were left me were well thought out and significant."

"Which leads us back to the third part of the clue. The one that is different than the others since it is not simply a number but includes other marks. Are those underscores?"

"It looks like that's what those are."

"Why do you suppose he would include underscores along with numbers?"

"Those were originally called under strikes or under bars and go back to the use of typewriters when someone wanted to underline something for emphasis."

Fey shook her head and looked at me quizzically. "How would you know that?"

"We went over that in high school in keyboarding class. Didn't you take that?"

"I did but I don't remember any of those terms. But anyway, that doesn't fit here because they are not underlining anything."

"I agree. The other use could be to fill visual space indicating that something is missing. It seems to me that my father wanted me to realize that something is missing both in front of, and behind, the number 28."

"Do you have any ideas what those missing numbers could be? I'm assuming they would be numbers since all the rest of the clues in this note are numeric."

"No, I haven't figured out what they are but I agree with you that it would make sense that they're numbers."

I heard Dalton coming down the hall and figured this might be a good time to quit since I'd been working on the clues most of the day.

There was a light knock on the door and Fey and I just looked at one another as if to say 'we know what's coming next.' "Come in Dalton."

He opened the door gently a couple of inches and poked his face in as if to catch us in a compromising position. He then stepped into the room. "I was trying to be polite, you know, and not walk in on anything."

I decided that I wanted to put an end to this type of conversation and let both of them in on what was occurring in the condo. I stood and once again closed the door. They looked at me suspiciously. "Okay, it's time that I told you the reason for my shutting the door and working in the media room rather than at my desk which I typically do." I spent the next few minutes explaining what Montero and I had learned about the listening devices and how we were trying to use our knowledge to help trap Cricket which could help lead to Spillbane's location.

"Oh my god," said Fey in a voice slightly above a whisper. "I can't believe they've been able to hear everything we've been saying. That's so creepy."

Dalton of course agreed. "Why didn't you tell us this sooner?"

"Because we didn't want to alert them that we knew about the devices. I was afraid that if I told you, you would speak and act differently and we would lose the advantage we now have."

"What's the plan?" asked Fey.

"As you both know the files that we read, those that were stolen by Wormwood, are critical to all involved. We need to get those to the powers that be in order to show that heinous testing and experimentation is still going on and obviously, they want to get their hands on them so as to destroy them and eliminate what could be incriminating evidence. Montero wants me to take the files out of my safety deposit box and lure Cricket into a trap."

"That sounds dangerous to me," said Dalton.

"Me too," said Fey. She stood and shook her head as in disbelief. "It's really incredible - one day you're waiting on tables minding your own business and the next day you're in the middle of clandestine government experimentation."

"I know. All I've wanted is to have a quiet peaceful life in my own place in a beautiful city. Do you suppose that I'll ever get that chance again?"

"I sure hope so, Lonnie. When do you intend to get the files?" asked Fey.

"I believe the plan is to go tomorrow afternoon after I get off work. He wants me to go through Duncan Plaza where he thinks Cricket will try to intercept me. Montero feels that he can capture him there and because of the surroundings and time of day there will be less chance of anyone getting hurt or there being collateral damage."

Dalton put both hands on his head in a display of concern. "I'm working that shift but I'll be a mess just thinking about it."

Fey agreed. "I'm not working then but I'm already a nervous wreck. I can't imagine what I'll feel like tomorrow afternoon."

I glanced back and forth at both of them. "So you can imagine how I feel."

CHAPTER 69

FEY HEADED BACK to her apartment. It was about a fifteen minute walk which gave her plenty of time to think about the intended confrontation tomorrow afternoon between Lonnie, Montero and Cricket. She had so many thoughts racing through her head and although she had no idea how the following day's actions would turn out she was worried.

With this in mind she decided to call home. It had been awhile since she checked in and hoped it would take her mind off her concerns. She took out her phone and dialed the number as she walked east along the city streets. Her mother picked up on the first ring,

"Hey Darling, I was hoping to hear from you soon. How's everything?"

"Pretty good Mom, just awfully busy and I'm a little tired."

"Are you doing too much? Do you need to cut back your hours at the restaurant?"

"No, it's not that. It's just that I have an awful lot on my plate right now."

"Is that an inside wait-staff joke, honey?"

"Ha, no. I just have a great deal on my mind, that's all."

"I just an concerned about you. That's what mothers do,"

"That's just like you to worry about me. More importantly, how are you doing? Is there anything new with your situation?"

"No, nothing new. I'm doing okay for now. It's tough but I'll be alright. Sure would like to see you sometime soon. I miss you."

"I miss you too, Mom. Say, did you get the money I sent you?"

"I did, but honey, you shouldn't be sending me that. And where did you get that kind of money?"

"Oh, I just had a little bit extra and wanted you to have it. I know how much you can use it. You deserve it, Mom. I'm going to run but will hopefully call again soon. Love ya."

"That's very thoughtful of you Fey, and I love you too. Don't work too hard."

Fey hung up and thought how much her mother meant to her. As she continued to walk she realized how hungry she was, She hadn't eaten since she left *Bon Vivant*. She stopped at one of the street vendors which are ubiquitous and legendary in the city and offer a multitude of choices. Fey saw many items that attracted her attention including the meat pie that she purchased. What she didn't see was the dark sedan that had followed her walk home.

CHAPTER 70

AS THE MORNING wore on so, too, did my anxiety. I had a hard time concentrating on my orders as I was preoccupied with what to say, what to do, and how to act when confronted by Cricket. This was, to the best of my knowledge, the man who shot Wormwood and the man who had violently killed Sammi for no reason at all.

Montero had informed me that he would call me in the early part of the afternoon after I had completed my work and had dropped off the food at the food pantry. I busied myself doing something that I felt was necessary in my garage downstairs and after completing that project I was in the kitchen when my phone rang.

"Lonnie, it's Hector. You ready to get the job done?"

"I'm not sure what it is that I'm supposed to have done to get ready, but if you're asking me if I'm done my work and have my brief case, then yes."

"I mean, are you mentally prepared? What you are about to do, ensnare Cricket and ultimately bring an end to the evil experimentation, is a valuable and selfless act that will help our nation."

He concluded his pep talk and switched to the particulars as to when, where and how I was to proceed after picking up the files at the bank. "It's now 1:15. Plan to be at the bank at 4:00. There will be less people in the park at that time with plenty of light. Now, walk into your living room. After you hang up the phone go into the media room and I'll call again with further directions."

I did as I was told and then held the phone away from my ear so it could be heard by anyone listening. But, to be sure, I repeated my directions. "Okay, I'll head out towards the Tulane Bank & Trust around 3:45 and should be there by 4:00. After I pick up the files I'll head down Gravier and through the Plaza. Are you going to meet me at the condo so I can turn the files over to you?"

"I sure will. Don't say a word to anyone in the meantime and I'll see you later. No one knows what you're doing so you should be fine."

As earlier directed, I walked back into the media room and my phone rang almost immediately. Montero wasted no time. "You will be coming down South Liberty, taking a left onto Gravier and then heading southeast into Duncan Plaza. We have no idea where Cricket might attempt to attack you but because the park has a large berm on each side of the center walkway which prohibits cars or people on either street to see the middle, then my guess is that it will be when you have reached that point."

"What shall I do when he comes towards me?"

"By all means just give him your briefcase with the files in it. At that point it becomes my responsibility to step in. Obviously we want to take him with there being no chance of anyone getting hurt so hopefully he'll see that he has no options and will surrender quietly. After you give him the files you just keep walking toward the other end of the pathway and go home. I'll get back to you later and let you know how it all went down."

I hung up the phone for the second time, took a deep breath and turned on the television. Now I had to find a way to kill the next two hours without driving myself crazy.

CHAPTER 71

LIKE SO MANY of the days in New Orleans, it was sunny and warm as I made my way up to the Tulane Bank & Trust. Although I didn't consider myself an ideal candidate for wearing shorts due to my un-athletic, un-masculine physique, I learned early on that they were the most comfortable option, along with a tee shirt, especially when walking any distance.

I had with me the briefcase that had belonged to Dr. Wormwood knowing that it would carry that which I intended to put in it. The airtight leather case had a locking system but I felt no need to adjust the numbers and lock it. Since I didn't know the code, I left it as it was so it could be easily opened by just pressing my thumbs against the metal clasps on each side.

There were more people on the street than I anticipated but with a population of over 1.2 million and an annual daily average of almost one hundred and fifty thousand visitors, I guess it could be expected. I passed a variety of establishments, most of which were designed to separate the tourists from their disposable income.

As a waiter interacting with customers from all over the world, we are encouraged to learn as much about the history, culture, attractions and cuisine as we possibly can and I find that more of an enjoyment than a chore. New Orleans is so different than any other city in America and although I appreciate its charm most days, today I just wanted to get this over with and hope that my life could return to some degree of normalcy.

As I walked down South Liberty Street toward the bank I stopped to look around to see if there was anything or anyone that might be deemed suspicious. While Montero assumed that Cricket would wait until I got near Duncan Plaza to confront me, we had no idea if this was his plan.

I entered the bank and went up to the vault teller who had me sign my access card, recorded my time-in and then followed me over to my box with her guard key. We both inserted our keys at the same time which is required to open the box and then, after I removed it, she returned to her window. My box, number 3317, which costs me $125.00 per year is 10x10x23 inches, the largest they offer and plenty big enough for what I needed. I carried the box into a viewing room to take care of my business. These used to be called "coupon booths" because patrons would go inside these to cut the coupons off of their government bonds. I returned the box to its location, was again met by the necessary teller and was clocked out.

I exited the bank, looked around once again and began the slow walk toward the park. I was just about to turn left onto Gravier when I saw an attractive blonde woman walking toward me from straight ahead. She had on tiny, tight white shorts, a mint green top and open-toed sandals. Sunglasses covered her face. I took a few more steps and then realized it was Fey, her usual big smile radiating her face. I stopped short and caught her off guard by yelling, "Fey, what the Hell are you doing here? Are you nuts?"

She didn't expect that reaction so the smile disappeared from her face. She removed her glasses, stepped in closer and put a hand on each of my shoulders looking deep into my eyes. "I'm here to support you, Lonnie. I know how nervous you've been thinking about this and I wanted to be here for you."

"Fey, this isn't some game we're playing. These people are serious. You could get killed."

"I'm not going to get killed. *We're* not going to get killed. Montero and his men will deal with him and besides, Cricket doesn't know that we know what he's doing." She started to walk. "C'mon."

I shook my head. I couldn't believe that she would do this and thought about walking away but I didn't want to create a scene and I also knew that she wouldn't be dissuaded. We took the turn onto Gravier and crossed the street so that the park would be on our right. The traffic on this street, like many in this city, is one way and in this case, heading towards us. Also, like many streets, there is very little curbside parking. I made sure to walk on the inside, the briefcase in my right hand. It was only three or four blocks to the Plaza but it seemed interminably slow as we looked around us with every step that we took.

The Plaza itself covers over 4.5 acres and is surrounded by such notable buildings as City Hall and the Louisiana Supreme Court Building. It was intended as green space for visitors and local artisans when it was first designed in the 1950's but after Hurricane Katrina it was used as a disaster relief encampment for those displaced and now, years later, it has become a housing haven and hangout for the homeless. On any given day dozens of them have set up small pup tents or have dragged in a mattress to lay on the grass. Sadly, the accompanying trash is a constant public blight and cause of continual civic debate and embarrassment.

We crossed over Loyola and were now twenty yards from the entrance to the park. I could see the multi-colored tents amidst the towering oaks and food trucks parked on the side of the street but there was no sign of either Cricket or Montero and what I assumed would be his cadre of agents.

The Plaza is bisected down the middle by a fifteen foot wide brick walkway that runs all the way from Gravier to Perido. A thatched pavilion sits midway between the two streets in the center of the Plaza and is used for a multitude of community events most recently as a makeshift food provider. The City Hall rises above the park at the opposite end, it's 36,000 square feet of office space a monolithic testament to a bygone era. Built in 1957 it too, because of its perennial state of disrepair, is a cause of much consternation and debate.

Fey put her hand in mine and held on tight as we entered the park on the curved concrete trail several yards before the brick path. A man of indeterminable age in torn clothing with streaks of dirt across his face approached holding a torn piece of cardboard that read, "Please help." I noticed several others watching from a few yards away including a man with a faded jean jacket and an orange beanie cap pulled down low on his head. I was afraid that if I stopped to donate I would be overrun by the others waiting nearby in a like condition so I whispered "sorry" and kept walking.

After taking several more steps we stopped to look around. I was trying to determine whether to continue walking through the park. I decided instead to sit on one of the benches beside the brick path. We had no sooner sat down then we felt the presence of a man who had come up behind us. I didn't see him approach so I assumed that he came from inside one of the many tents.

A gun was leveled between our shoulders at the height of our faces. "Don't do anything stupid and nobody will get hurt," he snarled. Just keep looking straight ahead." He reached down, took the briefcase out from under my arm, lifted it up over the back of the bench and said, "You won't be needing this, Lonnie my boy."

Neither of us turned to look at our assailant but we both knew it was Cricket. I had been told by Montero not to engage him in any way nor make any comments that might provoke him. I had no inclination to do either and kept staring straight ahead. I felt Fey's hand tighten in mine. "One last thing," he said, "and then I'll be out of your hair." Once again he laid the gun over the park bench so that we were able to see it. "I think I'll take this little sweetheart with me if you don't mind."

He took a step left, grabbed Fey's left arm by the upper part of her bicep and lifted her to her feet. I saw the smile on his face and fear on Fey's as he pulled her in close to his body, the gun and briefcase in his right hand. I had no idea what to do and froze in my seat. As he started to move away, I looked beyond him to the side of the street and saw a black SUV beside the curb that I hadn't seen before.

Fey was more being dragged than walking toward the vehicle when I heard someone behind the berm in back of me shout and then saw one of the homeless men in tattered clothing kneeling down behind a large flower pot. It was the man in the jean jacket and orange cap. In his hand was a gun pointed at Cricket. "Drop the gun or I'll shoot," he shouted. Cricket was as surprised as I was but he immediately turned Fey so that her body was between himself and the homeless man. He walked backwards with one arm around her neck dragging her towards the SUV. Behind him a large man dressed in black got out of the vehicle on the driver's side and fired a series of shots at the man in the berm. He was speaking to Cricket and was shooting as if to cover him while he dragged Fey to the vehicle. - It was Montero!

People throughout the Plaza began to scream and run helter-skelter in the opposite direction. I dropped to the ground beside the park bench and watched as Montero walked up beside Cricket, his back to the SUV, and opened both doors on the passenger side. He slapped Fey and then violently shoved her into the backseat. He placed the briefcase on the floor of the front seat.

Montero turned to exchange fire again with the homeless man and as he attempted to move laterally away from the Cadillac he was hit in the face, his head virtually exploding. His body dropped onto the concrete, blood pooling on the white surface, his extremities extended ungainly. Cricket stepped over the body, fired a round of shots at the berm and then hustled around into the driver's seat. He peeled out into traffic sideswiping a Honda Accord in the near lane. The racing engine and burning tires could be heard as the SUV disappeared down Gravier Street. The screaming and wailing continued from people in the park who had witnessed the horrific incident and were panicking, unsure what would happen next.

Still in shock at what I had just seen, I stood up and saw the homeless man scrambling towards me. As he got close he removed his orange hat and threw it on the ground. It was Bud!

CHAPTER 72

"BUD, WHAT IN hell is going on? Who are you and what just happened?"

He walked over and looked down at the body lying awkwardly with blood and particles of brain splattered on the concrete. He removed his Jean jacket and laid it over Montero's head. He removed an FBI badge from his pocket and waved it in front of the handful of spectators that had gathered around the body, many of whom were still screaming and crying.

"Let's go," he said, moving toward Lasalle Street. My car is parked over here and we need to get going if we're going to save Fey. I'll try to answer your questions while we're driving."

"What are you doing with Montero? Are you just going to leave him there?" I was running alongside him now and looked back at the crowd gathering around the body.

"We don't have time to deal with him now. The police should be there soon and I'll call it in also."

"Call it in? What does that mean?" We reached a metallic blue Ford Explorer on the street and he directed me to "get in and buckle up."

Bud reached for his cell phone in a dash cradle as he pulled out into traffic. A male voice came on the other end but I could only hear what Bud was saying on his end of the conversation. "Hey Chris, it's JP. Listen I've got to be quick but I've got a couple of issues you need to deal with. The first is Montero at the Plaza. You'll need to get a couple of uniforms down there ASAP and take care of that."

"Yeah, he's dead. I didn't stop to deal with him but I placed my jacket over his head."

"No, I didn't get House. He grabbed Fey and held her in front of him so I couldn't get a shot off. He escaped with her so that's where I'm headed."

"Yeah... ,I'm headed to the motel where he's been staying... the Crescent City about fifteen miles from here. I'm hoping he goes back there before he takes off."

"Lonnie's with me. I wanted to get him out of there... no, House doesn't know that I have him. In fact, I don't believe that he knows what hit 'em. I'm sure that he and Montero thought this was going to be an easy 'grab and go'... no, he got a few shots off but never hit anything and never really got a good look at me..."

"Okay, send some backup, including an under cover over to The Crescent City Motel out on St. Bernard's by Lake Pontchartrain... and Chris, send a couple of units over to Lonnie's condo will ya' and pick up Montero's two associates, Evans and Irving, or whatever their real names are. I'm sure that Montero expected Lonnie would be back there soon and had them wait at his condo. Great... Thanks."

I listened intently to the one-sided conversation I was hearing and, although I was able to somewhat figure out what 'Chris' on the other end of the phone was saying, I had no idea what I was involved in. I looked at Bud who placed his cell phone in the console of the Explorer.

He looked at me and said, "I know you must have a million questions but let me first assure you that I am on your side and am working to help you get back the life you want to lead. Most importantly, I have been a friend of your father's for many years and I am also a federal agent."

"Oh great," I said, "another federal agent. That's just what I want to hear. I've heard all that from Montero... and speaking of him, what the hell was the deal with him. Who is - was - he?"

"Montero was an accomplice of Franklin House, the man you know as Cricket. He was assigned to ingratiate himself in your life and gain your confidence."

"I can't believe that he would do that. He helped me set up a ruse with Cricket and told me things about him that I wouldn't think he would want known... like with the death of Dr. Wormwood and removing his body and all."

That was all part of an elaborate scheme, a long-con if you will. Once they knew that you had had contact with Wormwood it was all designed to get back their files and nothing was going to get in their way. Montero told you that he removed the body from the hotel, right? What he didn't tell you is that he was the one who pulled the trigger."

I thought for a moment of what he had just said. "That's unbelievable. I knew there had to be someone else involved because I saw a short guy going toward the room when I was leaving but I didn't know the shooting was done by Montero. I didn't trust him in the beginning - I thought his story was kinda' fishy - but he was convincing."

Bud was driving much faster than the posted speed limits but obviously wasn't afraid of being pulled over. "Where are we going," I asked.

"We just recently found out that House has been staying in a motel outside of the city and I'm guessing that he will return there to get his things before he heads out. Now that Montero is dead he may assume that his other two associates are compromised and will be picked up outside of your condo. I'm sure he'll try to contact them and then I'm expecting that he's going to go back to North Carolina which is his home base."

"What does he want with Fey?"

"That's just it. He doesn't want anything with her. He grabbed her simply for protection and that's why I'm afraid for her life. He has a few minutes on us but I'm hoping that I can get to his motel room before he leaves for good... or decides that he doesn't want to deal with her and gets rid of her. Now that he got their files back he has no reason to want to hang around."

I felt the fear of Fey being killed permeating my body but knew it was time to tell Bud the truth. "Actually, he didn't get their files back."

"What are you saying? I saw him take your briefcase and place it in the front seat."

"Oh, he has the briefcase. It's just that I never felt that the plan Montero designed was going to work. Since I knew it was the only leverage I had, I never took the files out of my safety deposit box. Cricket has a briefcase filled with blank pieces of paper."

CHAPTER 73

BUD LOOKED AT me with incredulity. "You filled your briefcase with nothing but blank pages?"

"Yes, I included a couple of previously copied files on the outside but the predominance of the papers are blank sheets from a ream I bought earlier at Staples."

"Amazing. Weren't you afraid that he would look inside in your presence?"

"Absolutely, but something about this entire plan never sat well with me. If Montero simply wanted to examine the files and turn those over to his superiors, which I can understand, he could have taken me to the bank at any point to retrieve those. I can't imagine that any agent would be willing to put a citizen in jeopardy for that. His proposed plan of catching Cricket in the act of robbing me seemed foolhardy if not disingenuous."

"Did you suspect Montero of working with House all along?"

"Not really. I thought at first it was fishy but then he did and said a lot that appeared to be helping me. I figured if his plan did work then Cricket would be killed or captured. Then I would explain my subterfuge and go and get the actual files. No harm, no foul, so to speak... and if it was all a set-up then I took other precautions."

Bud had pulled off the highway and took a turn down a side street at a dangerous speed. The Explorer rocked onto one side. "Hang on, time is of the essence if we're going to have a chance to catch House and save Fey. We're just a couple miles out now. You said 'other precautions', what are you saying?"

Before I could answer my cell phone rang. I looked before answering - it was Fey's number. But the voice on the other end was not that of Fey.

"Hey smartass, I'll bet you think you're pretty fucking smart with your plain pages and your powder. Well let me make something clear to you right now. I'm done fucking around with you"..cough. "I've got your pretty little girl friend tied up in the other room and I'm going to give you exactly one hour to produce those files - *the real files* - and if I don't get those by that time her pretty little face will be carved like a Halloween pumpkin. You got that? I will call you in exactly forty minutes and tell you where to bring the files... and one more thing smart boy".. cough,cough, "make sure you come alone."

He hung up before I could say anything although I'm not sure what I would've said anyway. I had put him on speaker phone so Bud heard the entire threat. "Let's hope that I guessed right and that he and Fey are at the Crescent City Motel. We're almost there. I'm not sure what we'll do if he took her somewhere else."

'We'll need to get the real files." The thought of Fey being cut or worse presented pictures in my mind that I didn't want to think about. Why did she have to get involved anyway?

Bud brought me out of my horrific thoughts by asking again, "you mentioned that you took other precautions. What were you referring to?" He slowed to take another corner with a mother and small boy midway across the street.

I looked at him and raised my eyes as if to share the thought that I'm not sure if what I'd done was the right thing... or if it would work.

My pausing alerted Bud that something was up. "Lonnie, what the hell did you do?" he asked again.

"Well, you know how I told you that I had this suspicion that something wasn't right or that Montero's plan wouldn't work. I'm sure you heard Cricket coughing. In addition to putting blank pages in the briefcase, I also put in a container of ricin."

CHAPTER 74

"YOU DID WHAT?" Bud fairly screamed at me.

"I put in a small container of ricin powder that I mixed up. I made sure the cover was on very loose so the assumption is that when Cricket - or House as you call him - opens the briefcase, he will be exposed. Montero tossed the case in the front seat when he was escaping so I've got to imagine that he loosened the cover on the container and it spilled onto the pages. I was very careful not to jiggle it when I was carrying the case and if things had gone smoothly, I would have told Montero before he opened it."

"My god, that stuff is dangerous. Where did you get it?"

"I mixed it up myself yesterday. When Wormwood told me awhile back that my life might be in danger I purchased some castor beans and, as you may know, ricin can be produced by processing the castor beans into castor oil. I knew those beans might come in handy at some point and I figured, what better time than now to use it."

"Where did you learn all this? Christ, that stuff is deadly. A speck of that the size of a grain of salt if ingested is enough to kill a human. How did you handle it so you weren't compromised?"

"I, of course, am aware of everything you just said and was extremely careful using a mask, rubber gloves, tongs and a tiny funnel to put it in an empty plastic pill container that I had. I removed the shorts and tee shirt I was wearing and put everything I'd used in a plastic bag. I then burned everything in my garage. As to where did I learn this, we discussed this in Biology class back when *Breaking Bad* was all the rage. It wasn't difficult."

"This changes things going forward. First of all let's hope that Fey was not in proximity to House when he opened the briefcase."

"I'm thinking she wasn't because when he called me he said he had her 'tied up in the other room'. He wouldn't have opened the briefcase until he had her under control."

"As you could hear on that call, he was coughing with regularity. What else do you remember about the effects of ricin?"

"It's much more deadly if it's ingested but in either case the symptoms won't be immediate. Since we can assume that he inhaled some he should have trouble breathing, shortness of breath and coughing, as we heard. Over the next few hours he will experience more severe respiratory problems and fluid beginning to fill his lungs. We don't know how much he inhaled but there was enough in that pill bottle to cause great harm. It won't be pretty."

I could see the Crescent City Motel sign up ahead on the right. Bud pulled over in a vacant parking lot a couple of hundred yards from the entrance and came to a stop. He took out his cell phone and placed a call. This time he put it on speaker.

"Hey Chris, it's me again. Listen, we've got a different set of rules to play by now. I've got you on speaker and as I told you earlier, Lonnie's with me. Because he put blank paper in the briefcase instead of the files that Wormwood stole, he received a call from House saying he was going to kill the girl if he didn't get the real files in an hour... yeah, that was about a half hour ago. He said he would call Lonnie back in forty minutes and give instructions as where to meet."

The man's voice came through loud and clear. "Obviously he's not going to get the files so what's your play? I have men on the way, in fact, they should be there any minute, and a SWAT team coming also."

"Good, but what else I didn't tell you is that Lonnie put a small bottle of ricin in the briefcase House snatched and we're pretty sure that he's inhaled it. We have to make sure that he stays away from Fey or else her life could be at risk also."

"That does change things. Thoughts?"

"We'll need a hazmat team for one thing. I've parked a couple of hundred yards west of the motel in the parking lot of a vacant store that was once a Blockbuster. Contact everyone en route and have them meet me there... and Chris, we've only got a few minutes so tell them to hurry but come in 2 1/2." Bud hung up the phone.

"What does that mean," I asked.

"Arrive quietly. For a state or city cop it would mean no lights or sirens. We don't know which room he's staying in although I would assume that he'd want a discreet room out back somewhere. We don't want to alert him to our presence. Right now we have an advantage since he doesn't know, that we know, where he's staying. He also doesn't know that you're with me."

"What do we do now?"

"We wait. We wait until you get a call back from House and we wait until the men assigned here show up. I have a plan."

CHAPTER 75

THE CRESCENT CITY Motel is a 120 unit establishment on the outskirts of the city that serves a myriad of truckers and countless tourists who wish to enjoy the splendor of New Orleans without paying the premium rate many of the top hotels charge. Unfortunately, like many of the less-successful motels that attempt to promote a sense of charm and allure of the area without providing the sophistication, they resorted to gaudy fripperies.

The owners attempted to recreate the lavish architectural style showcasing the French tradition of the 1800's with Fleur-de-lis wallpaper, stucco walls and "Briquette enter poteaux" or bricks between posts. They had running dog style wrought iron gates surrounding the property both on the ground level and on the second floor balcony railings. A garish neon sign and chipped exterior paint contrasted the intended elegance.

The motel was configured in a horseshoe design with two levels of rooms on three sides. In the middle was a good size parking lot with broken, tattered asphalt and vehicle lines that had long since eroded.

We sat in the parking lot as two city police cars, an unmarked sedan and an armored SWAT vehicle pulled in behind us. Where we were parked we could see nothing of the motel except the neon sign perpendicular to the building out front but, as Bud explained it, 'House can't see anything that we're doing either which is more important."

"What's your plan?" I asked.

He turned in his seat to look directly at me. "I don't have time to explain it all now because I need to go out and orchestrate this to all of the factions involved, but here's what's important to you… and to Fey. Because of his inhalation of the ricin we don't want him to go anywhere and take her with him. The fact is that we don't want him even going near her."

I understood clearly what he was saying. "How can we guarantee that?"

"We can't, but what we've got to do is buy some time. I need you to stall him a little bit so I can get my people clued in and in position to do what I hope will work."

"How should I stall him?"

"When he calls, as he should in a couple of minutes, you need to tell him that you haven't got the files yet. You had to walk home from the park and get your car and you're almost to the bank now. We don't want him going anywhere yet to meet you because obviously he'll want to take Fey with him and, as I said, I don't want him going in to get her, untie her, or anything else. If you can stall him it will allow us to do what is necessary. My challenge is to get him to come out of his room without Fey."

"How much time do I have to stall?"

"Fifteen minutes should be enough. Tell him that you'll absolutely get the files and that you'll drive towards him. We don't want him to feel that he needs to leave early to get someplace convenient and we don't want him to think that we know where he is. Tell him that you'll call him on Fey's phone after you have obtained the files and are back in your car. That should keep him in the room until we can get ready. Can you do this?"

"I think so… I certainly hope so. I don't want anything to happen to Fey."

"Nothing's going to happen to her." He opened the car door. "I've got to put this plan in motion, I'll check back in a bit."

A couple of minutes later my phone rang and, as expected, it was Cricket.

"Ya' got my files smart boy, the real files?"

I went through the explanation that Bud had laid out for me and attempted to be both calm and reassuring. I'm not sure I was either but, in any event, he seemed to buy it. But not without leaving me the same threat that he had earlier.

"This is your last chance Lonnie, or maybe I should say it's your pretty little girlfriend's last chance. Don't try to be a hero, just do what I fucking say"... cough, "Oh, and one more thing. I'm not sure what the powder is but you'll pay for puttin' it in the bag."

I assured him that I would do as he said and told him that I would call him on Fey's phone as soon as I had the files which shouldn't be long. My hands were shaking as I hung up my phone and I thought about how Fey must be feeling right about now.

Bud was speaking to his gathering in a small circle and after a brief discussion they broke up and returned to their vehicles. He opened the door to the Explorer and leaned in. "Were you able to get us a few more minutes?" he asked.

"Yes, he threatened me again, of course, but there didn't seem to be a problem. As you suggested, I told him that I would call him after I had the files."

'Terrific." He paused. "Now Lonnie, what we're about to do is dangerous so I want you to stay in the car. I know you're worried about Fey but I assure you there's nothing you can do and I don't want you to get hurt."

"Can you at least tell me what you're trying to do," I said.

"I'm sure you saw that we have a couple members of the SWAT team here. I'm hoping that we can draw him outside his motel room and let one of those boys do their thing. He's a dangerous man who has done a lot more than you know about so we need to get him off the street."

I watched as he headed for the motel office along with the two snipers. One of the plain clothes officers was wearing jeans and put a Kevlar vest on underneath a New Orleans Saints tee shirt; seemingly another tourist in town to enjoy the good life. He added a baseball cap that he put on backwards and took a red Solo cup out of the cab. His partner gave a thumbs up as he drove the nondescript sedan into the motel parking lot. All systems were hopefully go.

CHAPTER 76

BUD WENT DIRECTLY to the front desk and fortunately the person behind it was also the owner eliminating any need for going through an intermediary. His name was Anthony Quinn and he looked like anyone but the old time movie actor. In fact, he looked more like a tourist on Miami's South Beach. He wore a Hawaiian shirt, teal shorts with an elastic waist band fighting to hold back his stomach and flip flops. He had a complexion that hinted at an enjoyment of alcohol and thin black stringy hair.

After he had been shown the necessary FBI credentials and had the situation explained to him he became apoplectic. "You have no right to bother my guests. This could damage my reputation and ruin my business to say nuthin' 'bout damage to my property."

"We have no desire to ruin your business or reputation," said Bud, "but this is a man who has killed several people and harmed many more so we will be doing this with or without your cooperation Mr. Quinn."

After being told that the government would cover the expense of any damage "You can call me Tony," was the response. He was shown the picture of Franklin House and asked if he remembered what room he was staying in. "That ain't the name he registered in… t'was Joe Bennington, but hell yes, I remember. Hard forgettin' a small bald man with a scar across his face. He's in room 72, the Bayou Suite, up above us kinda' in the middle."

"What's the Bayou Suite consist of?"

"Living area with TV, little kitchenette and a back bedroom with king size bed. It's very nice."

"I'm sure it is. How long's he been here?"

"Been a week. Paid upfront with cash. I thought he was weird lookin' but he ain't been no trouble."

"How many other guests do you have staying here?"

Tony went to his registration book and took a brief look. "Only seven last night but it changes night to night. Most of 'em stay for only one night... you know, truckers and all. There'll be more showin' up soon."

"Any idea how many would be in their rooms now, because we need to keep them out of harm's way. How about cleaning staff or other workers?"

He went over to look out the window facing the parking lot. There were only four vehicles including a U-Haul truck and a black SUV with a large dent on the passenger side. "It 'pears there's only one other here sides Bennington or whatever, 'cause the Mustang convertible is mine. I don't recognize the gray Buick. He looked down at his book. That's a Dominic Capello with the UHaul. He signed in this mornin' said he'd been drivin' all night from Pennsylvania He's in room 3."

Bud said, "The Buick is one of ours so don't worry about that one but I need to get Mr. Capello out of here. How much did he pay for the room?"

"Countin' tax came to $60."

Bud reached into his wallet took out three twenty dollar bills and said to the officer who had just come in from the Buick, "Go give this to Capello in room 3 and get him out of there."

"You said that House was in room 72 in the middle so what I need are the keys to two rooms on the other side of the driveway with a view to room 72, preferably in the corners."

"You can see all of the rooms on one side from all of the rooms on the other," he said. "If you want corner rooms then probably 101 and 120 are the ones you want. He took the keys off the hooks behind him and handed them to Bud who in turn gave them to the two members of the SWAT team.

"Are there stairs on that side of the motel so they can go up without attracting a lot of attention?"

"Yes, on both ends. So they can go up the stairs and then just turn the corner and those rooms will be the first ones they come to." Tony realized what might be occurring. "They're not going to destroy my property are they?"

" We certainly hope not. These men are highly trained professionals." He waved to the two to head to their locations. "Now, Tony, you have phones in every room, right, here's what I want you to do."

CHAPTER 77

CRICKET SAT IN a tired cloth recliner in room 72 pretending to watch TV. He was becoming more irritable by the minute. "What the fuck is that kid waiting for? Surely he must have got those files by now." He looked in on Fey who was bound and gagged on the bed and then stepped back into the main room and looked out the window as he heard the piercing sound of a car alarm going off from somewhere in the parking lot. Just then the phone in his room rang.

"Hello, is this Mr. Bennington?"

"Ya, what do you want?"

The voice was shrill and hurried. "This is Tony from the front desk. I don't mean to bother you but there's a drunk guy out in the parking lot and he's throwing rocks through car windows. I'm trying to warn my guests then I'm going to call the cops. I just thought…"

Cricket hung up the phone and looked out in the parking lot. A guy in a baseball cap, jeans and Saints tee shirt was rocking back and forth barely able to keep his balance, obviously under the influence of alcohol. He watched as the man picked up a loose hunk of asphalt from a hole in the center of the lot, stumbled back and heaved it into the passenger's side window of the Buick parked three spots to the right of his SUV.

Another series of car alarms screeched and the drunk, who had momentarily leaned against the Buick, lost his footing and slid down onto the pavement. Cricket watched him struggle to get to his feet, look at the black SUV, and smile. He headed back to the center of the lot, picked up a good size chunk and slowly bounced toward the vehicle. Cricket opened the door to his room, raised his gun, and fired a shot at the man. It just missed him and caromed off the pavement into a room on the other side of the motel. He lifted his gun again and yelled, "don't even think about it pal or I'll..."

Cricket was unable to finish his threat as two .338 Lapua Magnum cartridges fired from the SWAT team member's Remington 700s tore into his chest. He was dead on contact and his body recoiled from the impact and fell over the wrought iron railing onto the pavement below.

I watched as a modified fire truck with the words HAZMAT RESPONSE on its side pulled into the driveway of the motel. I had heard the shots but decided to wait until Bud came and got me. Not only did I not want to be in danger but I also didn't want to get in the way.

The car alarms were finally shut off and an eerie silence permeated the area. Traffic cops in their blue and white vehicles had shut off traffic in both directions on St. Bernard's Avenue so there was no activity until an ambulance arrived on the scene several minutes later.

It was almost an hour later that Bud came walking toward me with his arm around Fey. She had tears coming down her face and looked wan and bedraggled. I jumped out of the car, ran towards her and threw my arms around her. She fell into my arms and gripped me tightly, her body wracked with sobs.

"We checked her out very carefully and there is no worry," said Bud. "She told me that he never came in the bedroom other than to tie her up and gag her before he opened up your briefcase. The hazmat team wrapped her up to get her out of the room."

I looked up at him over Fey's shoulder. "Is he dead?"

"Yes, you probably heard the shots. House will never hurt anyone again. Listen, it's going to take me awhile longer to wrap things up here so I'm going to have a patrol officer give you a ride back. Are you two going to be okay?"

"I think so," I said as Fey nodded agreement into my chest.

Bud gently put his arms around both of us. "You guys have been through a lot. Go home and get some rest. And Lonnie, I'll give you a call tomorrow so we can discuss some things. I know we have a lot to talk about."

We were dropped off at my condo and for the first time in a long while I felt relaxed knowing that I didn't have to worry about Cricket. I also felt relieved that I didn't need to determine Montero's role in the deception or be concerned with what proved to be the two bogus security guards assigned to "protect" me. One of the first things that I did was remove the bugging devices that Cricket had planted in my living room and office. I couldn't be sure if there was anyone else listening in or involved in the unscrupulousness but I knew that Spillbane, the architect of the clandestine affairs, was still out there. Either way, I didn't want to think about it now. Nor did Fey.

She was still trembling from her experience. "Do you mind if I stay here tonight Lonnie?" she asked. "I don't want to be alone."

While I hadn't gone through nearly the same trauma as she had, I understood how difficult it must have been. I offered no resistance when she took my hand and led me into my bedroom. We removed our shoes and laid down, our arms wrapped around one another in a union of comfort and security. When she placed her lips against mine I let her lead and tried to imitate her actions. Although it was a novel experience, somehow it just felt right. Later, we removed more of our clothing and climbed in under the covers.

CHAPTER 78

I WOKE UP early when Fey was climbing out of bed.

"I've got to work the morning and afternoon shifts today so I need to get going. When do you work again?"

"I'm down for this evening but I think I need to talk with Antoine again. As happy as I am with not having to deal with Montero, or worry about Cricket, I still want to find my father. Bud is supposed to call me later today and hopefully he'll be able to provide some answers.

"What's the deal with him?" A big smile came onto her face. "He's had us fooled all along. He's certainly not your average dish washer."

I sat up, my back against the headboard. "Ha, I guess not. I don't have any answers for you because we went right from the Plaza to the motel. I plan on asking him a lot of questions. Also, I need to try and solve the third clue so I intend to put some time into that today."

A serious look came over Fey's face as she sat back down beside me on the bed. "Lonnie, I can't tell you how much I appreciate you being there for me yesterday. I didn't want to go back to my place and be by myself." She paused and grew somber. "Plus... , I have something that I need to talk to you about but I don't have the time right now."

"I wasn't sure what it was she was thanking me for or needed to say but for once I felt I should speak what was on my mind rather than what I was supposed to say or what social norms would dictate how I respond. "Fey, I was really worried about you when Cricket grabbed you. I'm glad you stayed here last night... for a lot of reasons."

She leaned in and we kissed yet again. It felt natural and was unforced.

Her hand went to the side of my face and then behind my head pulling me in. "You're getting pretty good at this," she said as she stood up and headed out. "But there's still room for improvement. We may need to practice a bit more later."

Several hours later Dalton came downstairs and I caught him up on all that had transpired in the last 24 hours. Needless to say, he was flabbergasted and immensely relieved. "Thank god, maybe now I'll be able to sleep."

I glanced at the Howard Miller clock which read 9:45. "Yeah, it seems to have been a real problem," I said. "What time did you get home?"

"Sometime after midnight, I really don't remember. Your door was closed so you were fast asleep. Listen, I'm off today so I'm going to go play golf. Do you want to join me," he asked, knowing full well my reply.

I smiled. "I'll take a rain check, but thanks for asking." I finished picking up around the condo and went to my desk to re-examine the clues I'd been left. I was glad that I no longer had to play that silly game of using the media room so I wouldn't be overheard.

I laid the note with the Elven star out and looked at the third series of numbers beside the other two. I was not sure if I had accurately arrived upon the meaning of the first two - 20 and 30 - but I felt my theories were viable considering the originator of the clues and how they had tied in with the first series. The words Munin and dolphin, once solved, led to the next two, Horton and Myrtle, which allowed me to find my mother. In other words, there was a direct correlation of clues leading to a direction or destination.

Could the last series of numbers; _28 28_ be clues leading to a destination? If the first two are encouraging me to be prepared for life changes and warning me to be aware of Judas, ie. Spillbane, then the last series may be trying to provide direction once again - in this case to help me find my real father?

I was enthused by the direction of my thinking but again came to the realization that these numerical clues had been dropped off many years ago and might have no actual relevance to today. I decided that I would not let that type of negative thinking interfere with any progress that I might make.

I suddenly had an idea... an idea of what, or where, the clues might be pointing me and went on my computer to research my theory. It seemed that the blanks, or underscores, were the most telling aspect of the numbers and perhaps, I hadn't put enough time in on them. I had tried filling in various possibilities earlier but was not led to any conclusion. I went to a particular site and found what I was looking for. "I'll be a sonovabitch," I said out loud to no one but myself. "That makes too much sense. I don't know why I didn't think of that sooner." I read further in hopes that it would take me from the general to the specific but before I could reach a solution my phone rang.

"Hey Lonnie, this is Bud. How are you and Fey doing!"

"Pretty well I guess. She's gone to work and I'm doing some work on my computer. I can't believe all that happened yesterday. It was unbelievable... and speaking of that, I think you have a lot of explaining to do. I still don't understand who or what you are."

Bud chuckled. "I understand why you would feel that way but I'm afraid that this isn't the time to do that. While I'm happy that we were able to get House, Montero, and the others off the street, I'm afraid there is a bit more to do so I need to take a ride. I'll be gone a couple of days and then I promise I'll explain everything."

"Are you going to Asheville?"

There was a lengthy pause at the other end of the phone and then a hesitant reply. "Why... yes. What makes you ask that?"

"I want to go with you."

"Lonnie, I can't let you go with me. It's much too dangerous."

"Bud, I know you're going to Asheville to confront a guy by the name of Derek Spillbane. Wormwood told me all about him. He also said that he was an obsessed scientist but not a dangerous person. That's why he used Cricket - House - to do his dirty work."

"I wasn't aware how much you knew about all of this. I obviously knew that Wormwood had contacted you but I didn't know what he told you before he died."

"Listen, as much as I would like to see Spillbane captured and shut down, that's not why I want to go to Asheville. Ever since the couple, who I thought were my parents, were killed, I tried to find my mother, which I did. Now, I want to find my father, my real father, and I believe he's there."

There was no response for several seconds. Finally, I spoke again. "Did you hear what I said?"

"Yes, I heard what you said… it's against my better judgment but throw some things together. I'll be over in an hour to pick you up… and Lonnie, you may want to let Dalton and Fey know where you're going."

"I will and I need to speak to Antoine also because I'm down to work tonight. He's golfing now but I'm sure Dalton will pick up that shift for me." This time it was me that paused before speaking. "Thank you, Bud, I appreciate you letting me come."

CHAPTER 79

ONCE AGAIN, I called Antoine to ask to be replaced on the schedule for a couple of days. Once again, Antoine couldn't have been more understanding. I am hoping this trip to North Carolina will provide some answers and then allow me to return to normalcy and that which makes me happy.

After interrupting Dalton on the course and getting his agreement to pick up my shifts, I called Fey and told her where I was headed. She took it much the way I expected, "I am so excited for you... I know this is what you have been working for, but is it going to be dangerous?"

"I don't think so. Remember me telling you that Spillbane let Cricket take care of all the dirty work. I'm hoping that's true. Are you okay? I know yesterday was a hard day - for all of us."

"I'm fine. Working has been a good thing since it's kept my mind off yesterday. As always, everybody here has been supportive. You should know though that Antoine is going in to get test results later today. He hasn't been well and I heard a couple of the other wait staff talking about it. We're all concerned."

"That doesn't sound good. I just called to tell him that I wouldn't be in tonight but he didn't mention it."

"That doesn't surprise me. Listen, I've got to go, my order is up but I hope you find what you're looking for. Please be careful... and Lonnie, I'll be waiting for you when you get back."

I hung up the phone with a smile on my face. It seems that my smiling has been happening a lot lately when I'm around Fey. I never imagined that I'd develop feelings for a girl but that certainly seems to be the case.

I threw some things in an overnight bag and was ready when Bud beeped from outside the condo. I put my bag in the backseat and climbed in front. I had no idea what the consequence of this trip would be or how long I'd be gone but I could only hope that it would provide the last pieces of my life's puzzle.

Bud was dressed in jeans and a navy blue polo shirt with what appeared to be LL Bean loafers. He looked more like he was going to a ball game or cruise rather than confronting an individual engaged in illegal experimentation.

He noticed my look of confusion. "I thought I might as well be comfortable. From here to Asheville is well over six hundred miles. It'll take over ten hours although I can probably cut some of that off by calling ahead."

I assumed what he meant was reaching out to state police authorities along the way but recognizing that we would be going through Mississippi, Alabama and Georgia, before we got to North Carolina, I was intrigued by what type of authority he possessed.

"Does an FBI badge give you carte blanche freedom to drive how you want?"

He smiled at the question. "Pretty much, but I don't want to take advantage of it. I only produce it when I feel it's essential."

"And is it essential that we get to Asheville in record time?"

He grew serious. "The Federal government, with mandates from Congressional hearings, has been trying to shut down all forms of improper and illegal experimentation for years now. The fact that House and Montero are dead is a start but, as you know, they were only the arms of the operation. The man you call Spillbane is the head of the operation, the mastermind behind all of the activities. I'm afraid if he doesn't hear from House in a reasonable amount of time he'll assume the worst and may try to close down shop. I want to get there before he does that. It's important and, quite frankly, it's personal to me, so that's why the need for speed."

I understood his rationale as it related to the sense of timeliness but wasn't sure what he meant by the issue being personal. I also wasn't sure that I'd get a response but asked anyway. "You said that it was personal. What did you mean by that?"

"I'm not sure that I want to go into that... at least not yet. Let me ask you a couple of questions."

"Okay." I reached to the side of my seat and pushed the lever that guided the seat backwards giving me more leg room.

"You said that you wanted to go with me to Asheville in order to try and find your father. What makes you think that he's there?"

I knew this question was coming at some point and figured with the ride being this long we'd have time to get to the heart of all that has transpired and I hoped to accomplish. "If you don't mind, I need to give you a bit of the back story before I directly answer your question."

"No, I don't mind. In fact, I'd like to hear it."

I began with Wormwood's initial visit, explained the death of Bob and Martha, the death of Wormwood and the files that he stole from his work which I subsequently took. I then described the note that was found in the deposit box in Leesville and the clues that led me to find my mother.

Bud listened with interest. "Tell me the clues that were left and how you were able to discover what they meant."

I didn't know how specific he wanted me to be but as I went through the four initial clues and broke down the thought process involved in arriving at a solution he encouraged me to go into more details. I did that and he asked me questions as I went along.

"This is fascinating," he said. "What's next?"

I looked out the window of the Explorer as the trees of rural Mississippi passed by on route 650. I glanced at the speedometer and saw that it registered 85.

Bud saw that I was glancing at the speed. At that point we had been riding for about ninety minutes. "Are you alright? Do you need to stop for a piss break or get something to eat?"

"No thanks. I'm good for awhile longer."

"Okay, let me know when you need something. Now, tell me about your mother. How did that go?"

I thought back to the brief amount of time I was able to spend with Dorothy. "She was a wonderful lady. She was frail and not in good health but she had a twinkle in her eye and a good sense of humor. She broke down when she brought up how tough it was to give me away. I told her that I forgave her."

"I'll bet that meant a lot to her."

"It did. I only wish I could have known her longer, spent more time with her."

"I'm sure she did what she felt was right... for you. Sounds like she was a special lady."

"I think she was Bud, I think she was. Now you can see why it's so important for me to find my father."

Bud nodded his understanding. "So what's the next step then?"

My mother gave me another set of clues that she told me was given to her by my father. She'd kept it in a music box for years. I've been working on trying to solve these clues for awhile but I think I've finally come to some degree of finality."

"What were these clues?" Bud asked.

"This time they were numbers." I went over both 20 and 30 and how I felt they were related to both potential danger and a change in my life and how I was to beware of a man analogous to Judas who I took to be Spillbane."

"That's pretty intricate. It must have taken you a long time to reach a solution."

"Yeah, but I don't know that it's the solution. It's more of a possible solution. While it seems like the earlier word clues were designed to be specific - in order to find my mother - it seems that these number clues are more general. Kind of a guide warning me what's next."

"What about the third number?"

"It's actually a set of numbers with an underscore both before and after the number 28."

"And what do you think that means?"

"I keep needing to remind myself that these clues, the numbers on a piece of paper, were given to my mother many years ago. Obviously a great deal has, or could have, changed since my father wrote these down.

We are on our way to Asheville due to whatever information your agency has gathered. For me it's because Wormwood told me not long ago that that's where Spillbane is now conducting his experiments.

Bud realized where I was going with this. "So you're saying that what now may seem easily recognizable was much less so years back."

"Exactly."

"How does that tie in with the numbers 28 and the underscores?"

"I believe that my father was extending or clarifying his warning to me. In addition to telling me that my life was in danger and I should be prepared to have it change due to the threat of a man named Spillbane, he was telling me where that danger was located."

Bud pulled the Explorer into a rest area off the highway and turned the vehicle off. "Fascinating. Where did you deduct that danger was located?"

I hadn't had time to share my theory with anyone but felt this was as good of a time as any. "I feel that the underscores are the keys to the last series of numbers. Because there was a space between underscore 28 and 28 underscore, I took that to mean that both numbers were actually three digit numbers. When I tried filling in each of the possible options I got nowhere until I tried using the same digit in both spaces."

"What did that get you?"

"By putting the digit 8 in each of the two blanks it made the numbers 828 and 288."

"And the relevance of that is?"

"The relevance of that is that it pinpoints the city of Asheville. Our lives are governed by the technology that we use and the federally pre-scribed differentiations. The number 828 relates to the zone improvement plan - more commonly known as postal 'zip' codes. Virtually everyone of them assigned to the city of Asheville begins with the numbers 828."

"And 288?"

I watched as a car pulled in beside us at the rest area and a couple climbed out. "The only telephone area code that is used in the city of Asheville, North Carolina is 288. Don't you see how telling that is. Certainly that can't be coincidental that my father would use the only numbers ascribed to that city without it being meaningful to the warning he was giving. And this message was given years before I knew anything about Wormwood, Spillbane, Cricket, or anything else pertaining to illegal experimentation." I felt like a courthouse lawyer concluding his final arguments and waited for confirmation.

Bud paused and then spoke softly. "You know Lonnie, it is really quite remarkable what and how you were able to arrive at this many salient solutions." But, and he paused again, "if you were as gifted as I expected you'd be, I knew you'd figure them out."

CHAPTER 80

I SNAPPED MY head from looking out the windshield to stare at him. I realized that my mouth was open. "What did you just say?" my voice trembling.

"I said that if you became as gifted as I thought you'd be then you would figure it out."

I absolutely froze in my seat and still wasn't sure what I had just heard. "Are you... are you telling me that you... you are my father?" My voice trailed off with uncertainty.

"Yes, that's exactly what I'm telling you." He reached across the seat, took me in his arms and hugged me. I squeezed him as if my life depended on it and felt tears pouring down my face. I was embarrassed for just a second until I felt those on my cheeks that were falling from his eyes. It didn't matter. Neither of us wanted to let go.

After what seemed like a lifetime, for in many ways it had been, we separated and returned to our previous positions. "How long have you known that I was your son?" I asked.

"I've known for a long time. Remember, it was me that gave you to Bob and Martha to raise. It was the toughest decision that Dot and I ever had to make - and I've had to make some tough ones. Listen, I need to use the rest room. Let's do that and then we can get back on the road and I can catch you up on things and answer your questions - I'm guessing you've got a few." A smile overtook his face.

"Just a couple," I chuckled. I walked to the building with a smile that wouldn't leave my face. THIS IS MY DAD, I kept saying to myself.

I wasn't one to use profanity, especially gratuitously, but I felt this called for it - this was unfucking believable.

After using the facilities we returned to the Explorer and while there were a plethora of questions I wanted to ask the one most pressing was: "Why did you wait so long before telling me this? I've been driving myself crazy trying to find out if you were even alive. And why didn't you visit my mother. She loved you so much and was sick with worry about you - and me."

"Lonnie, everything I've done - in some cases we've done - was with one thing in mind and that's to keep you safe. I've made decisions and done things that I'm not proud of but I promise you it was with you, and also your mother, in mind."

Tears came to his eyes as he thought of his wife. "Dorothy was a good woman and would have been a great mother if given the chance but sadly, with my involvement in the service and later government projects, she was never given the opportunity. She was never very healthy but all of the worry I put her through made it much worse. I'll regret that til the day I die. Especially seeing what a wonderful young man you've become."

"How did you get involved in all of that... and why didn't you just walk away?"

"That's a long story but I'll try to give you a condensed version. Although I always found that schoolwork came easily to me I never had an interest in going on to college after graduating from high school. Plus, I always wanted to be a Green Beret so I decided to join the Army Special Forces."

"That must have been quite a challenge," I said.

"Absolutely, but very rewarding. So, after all of the preliminary training, I entered SFQC which is the Special Forces Qualification Course. This is a fifty-three week program that's broken into six phases.

After doing all of the orientation, tactical and collective training, etc. we did what is called the Language and Culture phase which lasts twenty-five weeks. This immersed us in a variety of languages including the basics such as French and Spanish plus others such as Arabic, Chinese-Mandarin, Korean, Persian, Russian and Tagalog. Because I found learning these very easy, and could do it very quickly, I finished at the head of the class, so to speak. My memorization skills are pretty advanced, which I know, is also inherent in you."

I smiled at this comment since it further solidified in my mind that this truly was my father. "Yes," I said, "and I sometimes don't know if it's a blessing or a curse but I obviously inherited that ability from you." The miles were piling up behind us but I was eager to hear more. "Go on."

I then served two tours in Afghanistan, the latter as an intelligent sergeant dealing with digital intelligence systems and biometrics for a 12-man ODA, or Operational Detachment Alpha, where incidentally, is where I met Bob Clifford."

"He told me that you saved his life," I said.

"I was fortunate enough to be in the right place at the right time but I just did what was expected. He would have done the same for me." His voice trailed off. "We were brothers and after that became very close. He was the first person I thought of when I wanted to have someone raise you. He was a damn good soldier - and an even better man."

"I then did one tour of duty in Iraq and wound up using some of the weapons created by DARPA including the ADS or Active Denial System which is an invisible heat beam. This was nicknamed the 'pain ray' and the Pentagon denies having used it but I know better and that came back to bite me later."

"After I returned stateside I was asked to take a battery of other tests of all varieties and according to later reports I aced all of those. This drew the attention of the higher-ups who were looking to conduct specialized experimentation in the creation and development of advanced soldier training and tactics. I was encouraged, or perhaps convinced, to become part of a new program known as Blackout - what is now referred to as OPERATION: MIDNIGHT. This was where I was introduced to a scientist by the name of Miles Branson."

"The man that I know as Derek Spillbane."

"Exactly. I don't know why he changed his name but I've been told that he's also had plastic surgery in order to disguise his looks from those that know him or worked with him."

"How did that program come about? What did you hope to accomplish?"

"When I first was selected to join DARPA I was thrilled because I was one of the few involved that was not a scientist. I was identified as a genius based on my testing but I believe it was because of my memory that I was invited. It originated as a research and development agency with a reaction to Russia's launching of Sputnik under Eisenhower but quickly led to the study of infrared sensing, radar and gamma ray detection and ultimately to the ARPANET which was a network system that resulted in the creation of the Internet. They also developed what was called the Aspen Movie Map which was the precursor of what is now known as virtual reality."

"None of that sounds evil. In fact, they're positive contributions to society."

"No question about that and much of what DARPA is working on is beneficial, but the work that Branson does is off the grid and has gone too far. That's why he went off on his own, changed the name internally to OPERATION MIDNIGHT, and that's why he needs to be shut down."

"When did you meet him?"

"We met years ago and from the beginning I had an overriding fear that he was a loose cannon but initially he wasn't in a position to manage agency direction. As time went on he ascended and quite frankly, I think he has become more demented."

"I can see why you would feel that he was dangerous but I still don't understand why you felt the need to give me away?" I knew this question would be the hardest to answer but is the answer that I most needed to hear.

He put both hands on the steering well and paused before answering. "This was by far the hardest part of my experience. When you were born I was new to the program and as I told you, I was one of the only participants not a scientist and one of only a few members of the military involved. Most everyone else was a civilian."

"So basically you were at the bottom of the hierarchy in this program."

"Exactly... other than a few Army grunts. Although this was a non-military assignment in a Federal agency, I was still a member of the service and was given orders to adhere to whatever orders I was given in this program. When I agreed to be part of this I thought I was going to be part of the administration of the operation due to my role and involvement on my ODA team. I soon learned that this wasn't the case and by then I had no options since I was contractually obligated."

I could see the frustration that he was feeling in the remembrance of the events. "I'm sorry to rekindle negative memories. What did they make you do?"

"Much of their work through the years has been evolved around creating the 'super soldier.' The feeling has always been that through genetic engineering and pharmaceutical involvement there can be huge upgrades in natural skills. By enlisting me into the program, someone who they felt was of superior intellect and abilities, they hoped to exponentially advance their experimentation and understanding."

"How were they going to do that?"

"Much of what they have been working on was of the chimera nature which is the creation of an organism by combining the genetic material from two or more sources. This term comes from Greek mythology which describes a creature that was part lion, part goat and part snake."

I was having trouble wrapping my head around this concept. "What's the purpose or value in this?"

Many scientists believe that this may ultimately save lives through the creation of organs for transplants but most people, including many congressmen, believe it is ethically immoral. In 2005 Senator Brownback of Kansas introduced the Human Chimera Prohibition Act but it didn't succeed in stopping the practice. At any rate it is controversial.

"Were you involved in this?"

"Unfortunately, yes. They injected some of my brain cells into various animals to determine if these animals would then obtain human memories or thought consciousness. The hope was that by using me, due to my superior memory, it would strengthen the intelligence and understanding of the animal test subjects."

"Did it?"

"I believe it's too early to tell and frankly, I wasn't privy to their findings, just their experimentation. There have been human-monkey chimera embryos successfully created and to a lesser extent human-pig embryos. What to me is even more disturbing is the intent to put non-human stem cells into human embryos. The US has banned funding for this and in Canada it is a criminal offense."

"I had no idea this type of research or experimentation was being done, supposedly all under the umbrella of modern science."

"Yes, in Branson's mind any type of experimentation is for the good of mankind regardless of the misery or deaths that result. This research falls under the title of GOF or gain-of-function and is done extensively in China where there are virtually no restrictions. Another aspect of their research is altering pathogens to make them more deadly. It is there that Middle East respiratory syndrome (MERS), severe acute respiratory syndrome (SARS) and probably the research into bat coronaviruses at the Wuhan Institute was conducted. What is most troubling is that much of the work being done in those laboratories is being funded by the United States."

"Amazing. Just like all of the heinous experimentation done in the 1950's and beyond that I read in Wormwood's files. All being done without the knowledge of the American people. What else did Blackout do?"

"They immersed me in virtual reality situations whereby I was subjected to the gruesome killings of my men and I. They also subjected me to atrocities that were committed by me and my troops. These were horrific in nature and way beyond what would be allowed by Article 3 of the Geneva Convention. There were multiple incidents of killing and mutilation of civilians."

I shuddered to think of such actions and how disturbing it must be to have to not only commit such acts but also to view them. "What did they do to you after forcing you to see that?"

"They then injected me with a beta blocker called propranolol. This was supposed to erase all of the terrifying memories that soldiers are subjected to during wartime action. The hope is that if they can eliminate the psychological effects of war that they can create an army of soldiers who can return to civilization with no remorse or guilt. They felt that this would eliminate Post-Traumatic Stress Disorder (PTSD) but one of their concerns was they didn't know what other memories might be blocked."

"This sounds horrible - in both instances. Did it work? How did it effect you?"

He looked upward and shook his head side to side. "Not very well I'm afraid. The first few times they administered it I not only could remember the atrocities, but I had countless nights of reoccurring nightmares. As for whether it blocked other memories, I really don't know. You can't discuss or evaluate what you can't remember."

"That makes sense. Were they doing this type of experimentation on the other soldiers in the program also?"

"Much more and, in many cases in my estimation, much worse. In the other servicemen they tried to genetically modify human fat into pure energy by rewiring the metabolic switch which would create soldiers that required less food. They experimented with withdrawing blood from soldiers and then replacing it with transfusions of artificial blood which led to heart attacks and death in some instances. Then they utilized transcranial magnetic stimulation (TMS) on all of us. The intent was to increase mental processing by using magnetic fields. This was supposed to promote advanced reasoning and enhance fighting capabilities. This began by strapping electrodes to us in a chair and escalated to our being forced to wear a type of helmet fastened to the head. Supposedly a soldier would have not only his technical expertise expanded but also increase his ability as a marksman. We went through dozens of training exercises utilizing various forms of TMS."

"I tried to imagine the wearing of such a headpiece. "Did it hurt using the helmet? Did it work?"

"Again, we never knew the results of all of these exercises but what we did know was the tremendous headaches that we had as a result of wearing them. It felt like a knife was being embedded behind my eyes."

He stopped, took a deep breath and began again. "Lonnie, do you understand why I had to get you, and later your mother, out of that environment? It's one thing for me to have to go through it, I signed up for it, but there was no way that I wanted you to have to be subjected to any of that."

CHAPTER 81

I BELIEVED THAT I had a much better understanding of what my father had gone through and why he felt the need to take me away from that environment. "You said earlier that you have tested as a genius. I was told by Wormwood that I was a 'super baby'. How could that be determined at such an early age and what did they intend to do with me?"

"It's really quite subjective. Although there are many different tests designed to measure one's intelligence quotient there is no definitive quantifier. The toughest test is called the Mega Test. Only one in a million people can pass this test and Marilyn von Savant is reportedly the only individual to record a perfect score of 185."

"The Mensa club is limited to the smartest two percent of the population. So, there are many very bright people, but for the sake of understanding the term 'genius' it is simpler to understand that such a person has the ability to think and learn better and faster than others."

"That's all well and good for adults but what categorizes a super baby. What made you or others think that I was gifted at such an early age?"

Here he looked over at me and smiled as if he was taken back to a much earlier time. "There is of course no way to test the IQ of an infant but there are several indicators all of which pointed to you being highly advanced."

"Typically babies vocalize at 4-5 months, repeat their first words at twelve months and form their own words around eighteen months. You were forming sentences at fourteen months as well as understanding instructions and following verbal directions. That is considered to be exceptionally advanced. Other indicators were how early you held eye contact, associated the creation of sounds by head movements, your ability to focus and match shapes and colors at ten months and… oh yeah, the fact that you required virtually no sleep."

"This led you to believe that I was, or would turn out to be, more intelligent than others."

"More significantly, it led others around us to recognize that you had a chance to be special. Branson was constantly trying to gauge your level of advancement and when he continually asked to run tests on you we decided that it was time to get you out of there. We wanted you to have a normal upbringing and knew that as long as I was contracted to serve that wouldn't be the case. After many tearful nights I took you to Bob and Martha's house and never told anyone where you were."

This brought me back to what I was originally told. "Wormwood told me that that were actually two super babies, that Branson himself had a child about the same time and that you tried to convince him to get the baby away from Blackout for its own good. I assumed it was a boy until Dorothy… my mother, told me differently."

"Yes, this is all true. He named her Sage and when I saw what he was putting that baby through, all of the measurements, tests, and experiments, I tried to make him see the light. Not only did he refuse to give the little girl away but he masterminded, monitored and manipulated her throughout her childhood. She was not a child to him, she was a project, something to be pushed and probed. She is just a couple of months younger than you and from what I understand, is still working with him in his experimentations."

"Branson wanted very badly to find you and bring you back into his program. Not only did he want to run a myriad of tests comparing you to his daughter but I believe in his demented mind he would like to have the two of you produce a child or children. In his mind they would be superior beings capable of achieving extraordinary things."

"My god, he is a sick bastard."

"You see why I didn't contact you or visit my wife these past few years. I knew that he had House looking for you and was afraid if he found Dot he might harm her even if she didn't know where you were. He didn't know that she didn't know and, as poor as her health was, it would have killed her much sooner. I fulfilled my military contract just a short while ago and after doing some investigatory work I was able find you. That's when I became a dishwasher by the name of Bud." A smile filled his face.

I thought about all that he had said. "You know," I said, "there's a hell of a lot of restaurants in New Orleans but I'll bet *Bon Vivant* is the only one with an FBI Green Beret genius as a dishwasher.'

His laughter filled the vehicle. "Ha, it just shows you that if you work hard and put your mind to it, you can accomplish anything."

"Which leads to the next question. What are we hoping to accomplish by going to Asheville?"

"This is where my becoming a federal agent comes into play. A couple of years ago, when I knew what the date was that I would have fulfilled my military obligation, I went to a Senator, whose son had served with me in Afghanistan, and told him the types and extent of the experimentation being done by Branson. At first he didn't believe me but after I was able to convince him that what I said was true, he pulled some strings with a congressional committee and I was given special clearance through the FBI to put an end to his operation."

"Lonnie, I fully intend to bring in the agency, expose his horrific deeds to both the government and the public, and shut down, once and for all, Miles Branson. But, before I do that, I plan to look that man in the eye and tell him exactly what my plans are. That man robbed me of years of happiness that I could... should, have had with both you and Dot. I know how much his program, his operation, means to him so while exposing him can't replace the years that I lost, it will still give me great pleasure."

We drove several more hours and then decided that we should find a motel and get some sleep before embarking on the mission in the morning. Since he had done most of the talking to this point, he asked many questions of what it was like growing up in Leesville and of my many memories of Bob and Martha. I found it odd now to talk about my childhood but I told him how wonderful they had been as parents.

He listened intently and nodded understanding. "I knew they would be," he said. "I didn't know Martha that well but I knew Bob to be a warm, caring individual."

I told him about being bullied, how I didn't really like school or feel the need for it, how I learned to drive by going around the farm roads in Rusty and how I had never had a lot of friends or a girlfriend.

He smiled. "I wouldn't worry about that. I've always been a kind of a loner myself. I think most people with high IQ's tend to be. As for a girlfriend, unless I'm mistaken, I would say that Fey thinks a great deal of you." We pulled into a Holiday Inn Express and as he climbed out of the Explorer said, "I'm going to get us a room. Why don't you give her a call while I'm inside. I'll bet she'd be thrilled to hear from you and perhaps you have something to share with her." Once again huge smiles filled both our faces.

I couldn't wait to speak with her but only wished that I could have told her in person. She picked up on the first ring. "Hey Lonnie, I was hoping you'd call."

"Fey, you have no idea what I'm about to tell you. I found my father - Bud is really my father. BUD IS MY FREAKING FATHER."

"Oh my word. What are you saying?"

"I'm saying that the man we know as Bud, the man who has worked as a dishwasher, is really a Green Beret, a specially assigned FBI agent and, most importantly... my father." I went on to explain how I came to find this out, why he sent me to live with Bob and Martha and how we shared reminisces of live experiences.

I could hear her sobbing at the other end. "Oh Lonnie, I'm so happy for you. I can't imagine how happy you must be."

"I'm thrilled. I am so excited and have so much more to tell you but I want to wait to tell you in person." We talked for a few minutes until my father returned to the car. Later, as I laid my head on my pillow, I thought to myself: *Is it really possible that I'm sleeping in a room with my father and I might actually have a girlfriend?*

CHAPTER 82

MORNING SUNLIGHT WAS peeking through the curtains of our room when I woke. My father handed me a cup of coffee and a chocolate donut. He said he had been up for a couple of hours attempting to determine exactly where Miles Branson was in the mountains outside of Asheville.

"Don't you know exactly where he is? Didn't you work with him for several years?"

I worked in conjunction with Blackout but after the early years none of us ever were in direct contact with Branson himself."

I nodded. "That's what Wormwood told me also. He said there were two or three different labs built in the caves of the Blue Ridge Mountains but he never knew exactly where he was. This could be almost impossible then couldn't it? I'm assuming there are a lot of caves and lord knows the mountains are huge."

"I guess so," he said emphatically. "They're almost 600 miles from north to south, a total of 35,000 square miles and includes two major national parks and eight national forests. I'm guessing that Branson converted an old mining tunnel into a lab since mining has been huge in North Carolina for centuries. There's over 800 of those alone. My expectation is that he is running his operation in one lab as kind of a command central while the actual subjects and experimentation is taking place elsewhere."

I lifted my arms at the enormity of the task. "So how do we find him?" I asked.

I have a couple of items that should come in handy that I got before I left New Orleans. One of which is an infrared camera when we get close."

"How are we going to know when we get close?"

He reached into his pocket and removed a cell phone . "The miracle of modern science," he said. "This is House's cell phone and I picked it up after I had the hazmat team make sure it was safe. Since I'm sure that he was in contact with Branson, and there was only one number that he called in western North Carolina, I have had technicians working to triangulate the position of that phone."

"Will that work even in the mountains?"

"Not as precisely as it will in an urban setting, because there are less towers but the process is the same. This is an analog process that measures the signal strength and the time lag for signals to reach each tower which then determines the approximate position of the phone. The process is called multilateration or MLAT for short."

"How accurate is this system?"

"Typically within one hundred feet but to be sure we also used the 'pinging' system. This is a digital system derived from Sonar and echolocation where a phone is sent sound waves and that phone determines its latitude and longitude and sends its coordinates back via the SMS system. This can be even more accurate than triangulation."

"So you have a good idea of where he is?"

"I think we can certainly get close. Get up and get dressed, I want to get going."

I jumped in the shower, got dressed and we were on our way. He told me that we were about an hour outside of Asheville and we were going to head north from there for perhaps another hour. "Have you notified other agents where we're going to be? What if Branson becomes enraged. Could it become dangerous?"

"Ha, you ask a lot of questions... but, they're all good ones. My hope is to surprise him. That's why I want to get there early. Branson is a lifelong scientist and as such is not prone to violence. That's why he hired people, like House and Montero to commit the crimes."

"The agency has an idea of where we'll be, after-all, they found his location. I thought I'd call after we locate the lab. That way I'll have some time to confront him alone with backup coming when needed."

"What do you expect to find in the lab where Branson is located? From what you've said that's not where the actual experimentation has taken place."

"You're right. Since supposedly no one has been in his lab, with the exception of Sage perhaps, I have no idea what we'll find. I would assume that there is an inordinate amount of research material and paperwork. As a scientist he has no doubt been recording results for years. He's in contact with other scientists and lab assistants via emails, all of whom have pledged fidelity to him. That's the beauty of email and the internet, you don't need a physical presence."

"Has Congress been aware of these others? Why haven't they been shut down?"

"Yes and no. Most members of Congress have no idea what's going on. Obviously, through my involvement and the agreement that I made with that one select intelligence committee, there has been some information exchanged but they wanted to wait until we could find Branson before pulling the plug. He is the mastermind behind all of this and the fear is that if we shut down the satellite labs he will just find other researchers or scientists to continue his work."

I thought back to Wormwood's assertion that there were two super babies and that Branson was looking for them both. I voiced this question to my father.

"Wormwood was wrong in this instance - not that there aren't two of you, there is - but Branson wasn't looking for the other one. She's been with him all the time and I assume is working with him in his lab. I only knew her when she was an infant and, like you, she was very advanced. He's probably kept her cloistered underground."

We stopped for gas in Asheville and then continued our drive. After a few minutes on Route 40 east we got on 221 and headed north. "I've never been up here, the scenery is beautiful."

"It certainly is. You can see Mt. Mitchell there in the north which is the highest point east of the Mississippi River. Notice the blue tint. They believe these mountains may be one billion years old. They call this region 'Land of Sky' with 125 mountains over 5000 feet high."

"Is it always blue like this or is it just foggy today?"

"It's a kind of a fog but a healthy fog. It comes from the trees releasing what's referred to as VOCS or volatile organic compounds. It's from isoprene in the air and gives us that piney smell that you get in a forest."

"Or in candles," I joked.

"Exactly," he chuckled.

My cell phone rang and when I answered it I was surprised to hear that It was the realtor I was working with in Leesburg. I put him on speaker phone.

"Good morning Lonnie, it's Dan Sargent. I hope I didn't call too early."

"Hey Dan. Not a problem. I've been up awhile and am on the road in North Carolina. What can I help you with?"

"Actually, I hope it's me helping you. As you know we put your property on the market for $349,000 and we have what I think is a clean offer. They offered $330,000 with 20% down and no contingencies. They have been pre-approved, are willing to waive an inspection, and are hoping to close in 30 days. What do you think?"

"Wow, that sounds great. What do they intend to do with the property?"

"It's a middle aged couple. He is stationed at Fort Polk and is up for retirement later this month. He hopes to become, in his words, a 'gentleman farmer.'"

"Dan, this sounds terrific. I am thrilled they want to keep it as a farm. Draw up the paperwork and I'll sign it."

"Will do Lonnie. I'll send it to you to docu-sign. Congratulations, this sounds like a win-win for both parties."

"Thanks for everything Dan, you did a real good job." I hung up the phone and explained to my father what had just occurred which prompted me to follow up. "When I went to the bank following the death of Bob and Martha the manager Bill Donovan transferred money from their account into mine" I turned to look at him. "There was over

$300,000 in that account and Bill said he was given much of that money by you… why did you do that?"

"Wow, that's incredible. I gave him $250,000 so he must have invested some."

"He said he did but that doesn't answer my question."

His tone became serious. "As you may imagine I've made good money for quite awhile and frankly had nothing to spend it on other than Dot's care. I've never had to make house or car payments, pay for insurance or buy food. With the nature of my government involvement I never knew if I would make it out alive and, as is the case with every parent, we just want what's best for our children. My intent was to help you with your college expenses."

I looked at this man, who despite having had virtually no interactions with me, has made every decision with me in mind. I felt an overwhelming sense of guilt. "Do you mind if I ask you a tough question?"

"Of course not. You can ask me anything you want."

"As you know, I never did go to college. In fact, I never even finished high school. I took some of that money, that you set aside for my education, and bought a condo. I feel like you've made any number of sacrifices for me and I've been selfish." I felt tears welling in my eyes but didn't want him to see that so I looked down at my feet.

"Lonnie, I'm going to interrupt you before you even ask your question. If you think that I'm upset because you didn't finish high school or go to college you're very wrong. Some day I hope you are blessed to have children. All you'll want for them, just like me, is to be safe, healthy and happy. I'm glad that I was able to help a little bit and after getting to know you for a short while I can see that you don't make frivolous decisions. I love you Lonnie."

I wiped the moisture on my cheeks and said, "I love you too. And I know you've been calling yourself Bud but I heard you on the phone call yourself JP and Dorothy said your name was Paul. I'm not sure what to call you."

"Legally it's Joseph Paul. I tend to go by my initials but Dot always called me by my middle name." Here he paused and looked me square in the eyes…"but how about you call me Dad."

CHAPTER 83

WE DROVE ANOTHER hour and went through the town of Marion, the home of Linville Caverns, according to the signs: "The Only Show Cavern in North Carolina" and saw the signs for Grandfather Mountain a few miles ahead. "Is that where we're headed?" I asked.

"The triangulation tells us that it's in that mountain but it's beyond the roads used by all of the tourists. Obviously Branson wouldn't want to be near them nor in a place where hikers might accidentally stumble upon him. It's a beautiful mountain originally called *Tanawha* or 'fabulous eagle' by the Cherokee. There's a suspension bridge on the mountain that draws a lot of people but we're going beyond that."

We eventually arrived at a dirt road off Route 221 several miles after we passed a parking area at mile 299 and the Blue Ridge Parkway veered northeast. The road

ran for a couple of hundred yards and then branched off in several directions each of which looked undeveloped.

We came to an opening, parked the Explorer and got out.

My father took some items from out of the back including a gun. Since I am not familiar with types of weapons I asked him about it. "This is a Glock 22," he said holding it up. "Most police officers and FBI agents use these. It holds fifteen rounds and has three safety features. It is a beautiful piece." He began walking, "It looks like we may be on foot the rest of the way."

"Do you know where we're headed?" I asked.

"The technology tells me that we need to use this path," he said pointing to the one going straight ahead. It can't be far from here since Branson would had to have access to the road system."

"How can we get any signal here in the mountains?"

He pointed upward as we walked under a canopy of tree branches. "We caught a break because the University of North Carolina has a cell tower on top of Grandfather Mountain. The signal is pretty good actually."

We spotted various animal tracks on the narrow path, followed them for a short while and then came to a clearing. We could see a small stream higher up that disappeared in the rocky terrain with areas of erosion and my father pointed to that. "We're near now. See where that stream disappears. That is a karst line indicating there is a void in a type of soluble rock like limestone. This could be the cave we're looking for."

I looked at the terrain and saw the stream trickling down the elevation but wasn't sure what my father saw. The wind had picked up in intensity. "How will we be able to determine if it is?"

He took the case from off his back and removed an infrared camera. "If we get a little higher we'll be able to determine if there is a cave here. The temperature in a cave is almost always the average temperature of the area around it. For example, the nearby Linville Caverns, that we saw the signs for, stays a consistent fifty-two degrees all year since that is the area's year-long average and, if this is the cave we're looking for, it will be about the same. Since it's quite a bit warmer than that outside now we should know soon."

Sure enough the camera, using infrared thermography, recorded the difference in temperature gradients. I looked at the blue, green and purple color palettes emitted from where the stream disappeared into the rock and could see the difference from the heat radiated elsewhere.

My father was elated. "We now know that's a cave, we have the triangulation coordinates indicating that this is the location and now we just need to find the entrance inside. Our concern is that underground caverns often have multiple chambers or rooms so although we might be on top of the cave the entrance could be anywhere."

I thought about what he had said. "It seems to me that if Branson has made a lab out of this cave then at some point he had to have had trucks deliver all of his supplies and equipment. While that was awhile ago, and the landscape would certainly have grown up after being damaged by the deliveries, it had to have been accessible to the trucks. Therefore, it still should be."

"That certainly makes sense," he replied.

I continued. "I suggest we go back to the original clearing where we parked and continue to the right. There might be another entrance higher up but that wouldn't be for daily use or deliveries."

"He would have to have an escape exit as you suggest, you always need one of those in any bunker, but I'm not sure he's coming and going on a daily basis. I'll bet he's hunkered down, perhaps with his daughter, and come out very rarely. This is probably as much a survival shelter as it is a laboratory."

I considered this. "When we do find the entrance how will we get in? I can't imagine that he would allow easy access as secretive as he's been with everything."

"No, I agree. There may be some form of security or, because he's so far off the beaten path, he might believe that hiding away is enough. I think it's safe to assume," he chuckled, "that there won't be a neon sign out front."

We got back in the vehicle and continued along the worn pathway barely wide enough for one vehicle. Branches from the tree growth on either side brushed the side of the Explorer. We could see some sporadic ruts where tires had traversed in rainy conditions and then dried.

After a slow drive of several hundred feet we were met with another moderate clearing. The mountain rose above us to our left as far as the eye could see, the wind whipping down the hill. In front of the elevation were two scrub pines about fifteen feet apart standing about six feet tall. Neither was particularly full. To our right and ahead a thick growth of beech, oak and sugar maple trees filled our vision. Many of these rose hundreds of feet in the air and had been residents of the area for generations.

He turned the SUV around in the clearing so that it was heading out and then we exited the vehicle. "It seems like we're at an impasse," he said. He turned completely around. "There could be an entrance up the mountain but, as you suggested, that wouldn't solve the issue of delivery access. There would also have to be intake and exhaust vents. We may need to head in another direction." He headed back to the vehicle.

I paused. "Before we leave take a last look around. Do you notice anything that seems out of place here?"

"I'm not sure what you're referring to," he said.

"Look at those two pine trees. Do they not look out of place to you? On the other side and in front of us the trees are on top of one another in dense thickets yet those two in front of the mountain are not only isolated but they have dirt underneath them with no underbrush either." I looked around raising my arm. "Why would they be so different than all of these others?"

My father followed my actions and walked over between the two trees, the dirt swirling steadily. "I see what you're saying." He dropped to one knee and swiped at the ground with his hand. The loose dirt moved easily and after several handfuls were pushed aside we could see there was something just inches below the ground level that appeared to be metallic.

I joined him in his efforts and after a couple of minutes of work we could see what we had unearthed. It was a wide slab of black metal with hinges high and low on the left side and a thin handle midway on the right. Was it the entrance we were searching for?

CHAPTER 84

MY FATHER SLID across in front of me, brushed the dirt from around the handle, and reached down to see if it would open. "This looks like a door to a bulkhead someone might have to their basement, only much bigger."

"It would have to be if he was going to move furniture or lab equipment inside and if this is indeed the cave that we've been looking for."

"According to the coordinates it certainly could be. Let's see if we can lift it up."

"Interesting that he has it hidden under ground. Do you suppose that there's another entrance and he comes back here to fill the dirt in around the trees for camouflage?"

"I'm sure there's another way to get in, probably just big enough for a human to climb in, but as strong and swirling as the winds are here near the mountain the door probably gets covered over on its own. Notice, too, that the dirt here is loose and easily moved. He may have had some delivered to assist in his efforts."

What he said made sense as we could see some of the dirt blowing back onto the door that we had already cleared. "How did he get here? There's no vehicle anyway near."

"He wouldn't want to leave a vehicle to alert any hikers that there's something here so my guess is that he uses a motorcycle. That way he could just take it inside and no one would be the wiser. C'mon give me a hand with this."

We stood facing the side of the door. Because of its length and width the opener itself was longer than most and it allowed us to both get our hands inside the handle. There was no clasp or latch since, as with many bulkhead handles, one only needed to lift the door to enter. "Together on three," he said. "One... two... three."

The door hesitated at first and then, primarily due to my father's strength, it released its tension. The dirt around the hinges created a bit of resistance but we each walked around an end and gently laid the door down on the ground.

Beneath where the door had been were several wide steps going downward and then what appeared to be a ramp heading upward toward the mountain. We could not see more than a few feet of it but it appeared to be both wide and smooth.

"Take out your cell phone and turn the flashlight mode on. Let's see what's at the end of this ramp."

"Are you sure you don't want to wait for reinforcements or at least backup?"

"I've waited a long time for the chance to confront him face to face. I lost men under my command and... more importantly, years that I could have spent with you and your mother. I'm not going to miss out on this chance to look that son of a bitch in the eye and tell him that he's getting shut down once and for all."

I understood the passion that burned inside him. "What do you suppose they'll do to him?" I asked.

"I don't know and frankly I don't give a damn. I just want him to understand that his time, his fiefdom, has come to an end. C'mon let's see what we've found."

We climbed down the stairs which were deep enough so we could now stand and headed up the ramp. The footing was dirt with a crushed stone layer on top creating a smooth surface. In order to create a tunnel passage the ground had been excavated and the temperature inside was noticeably cooler, the air damper. Our phones only allowed us to see a short distance ahead so we purposely remained quiet not knowing what, or where, the tunnel ended.

We went a few more feet and could see a door in front of us that had been built into a wider opening with steel plates on each side. Once again, the width of this entrance was considerably more than a normal door and it appeared to be about eight feet in height. When we got close enough we shone our flashlights on the door handle and saw that it was a keyless door lock. "Shit. I was afraid of this," he said. "This lock requires a code and, unlike the simple numerical version, this model has an alphabetical component."

"What's the difference?"

"It has the potential to be much more difficult since there's 26 options instead of just 10. The combinations are nearly endless. Furthermore, we don't know if it's a three-letter code or a ten-letter code or anything in between. I can't imagine our being able to figure it out and lord knows we can't just knock on the door and expect to be welcomed in."

I noticed that he was speaking in a voice slightly above a whisper so I did as well. "Actually, while I of course don't know the code, I think it may be easier."

He looked at me quizzically. "What makes you say that?"

"Simply this, with numbers they could be in any order or format. They could be in a pattern or could be completely random. But, with the alphabet, people would select a designated order. By that I mean a word. No one would simply select a random order of complex letters. Can you imagine a code being XKQWZPV for example. You and I might be able to remember that but most people couldn't. For that reason, we need to think of a word that Branson might have chosen."

My father nodded. "That makes sense, but before I try I am going to go back out and get in touch with my supervisor so he knows where we are. He told me to contact him as soon as I had found the lab and, although we're not positive it's Branson's, I can't imagine there being a keyless lock otherwise. There's no service inside here so I'll be just a minute."

He returned a short while later. "Now, let's see what we can come up with. I'll try the most obvious Branson names first." He punched in his name, former wife's name, and Sage, his daughter's name, none successful.

I tried Spillbane and DARPA and MIDNIGHT but had no success either. He then tried Linville, then Grandfather and then mountain with no luck. "I'm afraid that we're out of luck and we sure can't break in." He rubbed his hand along the surface. "That door is carbon steel."

"No, but you've given me an idea. Let me try one more option." I punched in the seven letters that I had in mind and there was a whirring sound. The door was unlocked.

"Oh my God, what did you punch in?"

"I used the name 'Tanawha'. You told me about the Cherokee word for the mountain and I thought he might relate his mission to the fabulous eagle of Cherokee tradition."

"Great idea." My father took the doorknob in his hand. "You stay behind me. I don't expect him to be violent but it's hard telling what he might do if threatened."

CHAPTER 85

MY FATHER STEPPED inside the cave with me one step behind. I was immediately taken by the lighting, whirring of equipment and air purification system that enabled the breathing to be so much different than in the tunnel outside.

We looked around and noted that the ceilings were all covered in corrugated tin with the walls a wainscoting of the same material. The floor was hard with what looked like a composite surface.

What caught my attention most of all was the amount of scientific equipment which covered virtually every inch of the lab's perimeter. My only experience with science labs was high school Biology class back in Leesville but that was nothing like this. There was the usual amount of microscopes, test tubes, Bunsen burners and flasks that most labs would offer but more impressively was the amount of apparatus that I was not familiar with.

My father moved slowly through the lab not concerned with what was present for equipment but rather on edge as to what or who could be behind it. He had removed his Glock and held it in front of him. He waved to me with his other hand to follow him.

We went deeper in the cave past a series of sinks, freezers and refrigerators and could see up ahead that there were two openings off the main corridor, one on each side and a closed door straight ahead. The room on the right had a light on, the other, across from it, was dark. Although there was no sound from either one we approached cautiously staying as close to the wall as possible.

When he was one step from the door on the right my father stopped, put a finger to his lips, and held the gun straight up. I leaned back against the wall careful not to make a sound. After a momentary pause he crouched down and took a giant step into the doorway the Glock pointed straight ahead.

I was directly behind him but could see over his right shoulder. There in the room sitting behind a metal desk and looking straight toward us was a man in a white lab coat, an assortment of papers and Manila folders on the desk in front of him. To his left, also in a lab coat, was a young woman standing in front of a television monitor.

"Why am I not surprised to see you here Captain Rawlings, although figuring out the code couldn't have been easy." The man leaned back in his chair. "I figured when I didn't hear from either House or Montero in the last couple of days that something must have gone wrong. What happened to them?"

"I'm afraid they made some poor decisions and neither of them will hurt anybody ever again. The other two that were working with Montero have been arrested. Do you suppose they'll implicate you in the death of Wormwood and whoever else you had killed?"

The man nodded. "I have no idea what you're talking about but you can put your weapon away. I assure you that neither of us are armed."

My father lowered his gun but held it at his side. He took one step inside allowing me to come into the room beside him. "We meet again, Miles. At least I assume that you're Miles Branson since you certainly don't look like the Miles Branson that I worked with in the past."

The man sitting in front of us was bald on the top of his head with tufts of gray hair on both sides running to his ears. His face was full with a double chin and puffy cheeks. He wore horn rim glasses and had a thick gray mustache under a bulbous nose. He appeared to be in his seventies.

He smiled. "It's amazing what they can do… a few shots of Botox, some hair implants and plastic surgery and I'm a new man… or perhaps," he chuckled, "an old man. I go by the name Derek Spillbane now, however, I thought I'd make a new start."

He pointed to the young woman standing beside him. "I'm sure you remember Sage," he said, "and am I to assume this is Lonnie?" The woman was strikingly attractive with straight raven-colored hair to her shoulders and what looked like green eyes. She was both pale and thin.

I was surprised at the tone of my father's response. "Yes Miles this is Lonnie. The child that I gave up to protect from you… from your heinous experiments and malevolence."

"Why Paul… may I call you Paul? As I remember that was what your wife called you. You still don't get it do you?" He pointed to an entire wall opposite his desk where dozens of television screens each showed an animal or individual in some form. Some were in cots, some were on exam tables and many were in what looked like cages. "It's not that I'm malicious, it's that I'm ahead of my time. What I'm working on will revolutionize both warfare and mankind in general."

"At what cost? How many people have to bleed, suffer or die before you're happy? Where are these people being held anyway?"

"Where they are is not important, they're not in this cave." He stood up and walked over in front of the monitors. "For Christ sake Rawlings, wake up. This is cutting edge stuff that will take the U.S. into the 22nd century."

My father scoffed. "Like the cutting edge zoonosis experimentation done in China with bats which resulted in the death of half a million people?"

"So what. Most of them were on death's door anyway. There's going to be some glitches but the chimeral studies will prove beneficial in the long run. Take a look here." He pointed to a pair of screens in the right corner. In these cages are monkeys who have had human microcephalin genes inserted into their hippocampus. I am studying neurological disorders in them." He walked laterally his arm extended showing us multiple screens of pigs, bats and mice. "All of these have been injected with human genes and the hope is to grow human organs for transplants. Scientists in China have cloned monkeys with human genes that actually scored higher on memory tests involving pictures and colors than those of like-aged human children."

"This genetic engineering has got to stop. There is no place, no need, for the creation of human-animal hybrids and bioethics must be respected." My father stepped toward the monitors on the left of where

Branson was standing. He looked closer at several of the screens. "What the hell is going on - these are humans!"

"You're every bit as bright as I remember you," said Branson sarcastically.

My father put his face up against a screen. "Wait a minute... that's John Stewart. I remember him from back when I was in the program... and that's Rufus White. They were two of the other servicemen brought in. They both look not only emaciated but in great pain. What are you doing with them?"

Branson seemed to beam at the thought of his response. "They are involved in important studies in blood transfusions both between races and in the use of artificial blood. Do you know hundreds of years ago scientists experimented with using water, urine and even wine in transfusions?"

My father shook his head in disgust. On the next screen was what looked like a middle-aged man sitting on the floor of a cage with an open mouth and dark circles around hollow eyes. "What are you doing to this person?"

"He is part of a vital program currently studying the impact of deprivation. He has gone through both food and water deprivation and is now involved in a sleep depriving study. It has been over 80 hours since he's been allowed to sleep with our current goal being 120 hours."

"That's just wrong," said my father. He moved to his left and looked into another dozen monitors and Branson came up beside him as way of explanation.

"Those subjects are part of vital programs studying the reaction to and impact of pain, as well as psychological and pharmacological experimentation and the resultant studies of various injections and implants into subjects."

He went screen to screen. "This subject has received testicles from a goat. The intent is to increase one's sex drive. This type of xenotransplantation was first done by John Brinkley years ago and there have been several hundred instances where slices from monkey testicles were inserted in humans."

"Can you not see the beauty in the science? This subject has been standing at attention for 48 hours. This one has had over 300 sessions of electric shock therapy." He paused in his movement. "Do you want me to go on?"

"Where are you finding these 'subjects' that you are experimenting on? I can't imagine that you have received their consent or they know what's being imposed upon them."

"We pick up homeless people from some of the major cities and offer them a roof over their heads and three squares. You'd be amazed at how many of these people are excited to take us up on that." A smile came across his face. "The North Korean government picks up people in a black van they call 'The Crow' to experiment on. I'm no different. The way I see it we're doing a public service. It's a win-win."

My father was not buying any of Branson's argument. "Do they feel that way when they're in a cage, having their genitals removed, or having their bodies pumped full of chemicals? I don't care that you think this is acceptable in the name of science and neither does our society. What you're doing - and have been doing for years - is not ethical."

"Who are you to decide what is or isn't ethical?"

My father pointed a finger toward Branson's face. "I'll tell you who I am. I'm the person who's going to shut down your operation."

Branson's attitude, perhaps because he recognized the situation he was in, changed dramatically. "Paul, think about how much time, how much of my life I've put into my work." He looked at his daughter. "I have Sage working with me and there is so much more that I can do - so much more that we can do. Now that you and Lonnie are here, why don't you join us. Imagine what the four of us could accomplish working together."

"Neither Lonnie nor I have any interest in working on your projects. As you know, I've done everything I could to keep him away from Blackout, OPERATION: MIDNIGHT... away from you."

"As you know, I've had people looking for Lonnie for awhile. I assure you that I have never wanted, nor intended, to hurt him. In fact, it's quite the opposite. I've been told that he turned out as gifted as we thought he might... as gifted as my daughter. My plan right from the beginning was to have these two work in harmony." Branson looked at me and then back at his daughter. "Can you imagine what might be possible if these two were to have children."

Hearing that, I felt it was time for me to speak up. I had let my father do the talking since we arrived in the cave but now it was getting personal to me. "Dr Branson, or Spillane, or whomever, I appreciate the fact that you recognize my talents and potential and I surely mean no disrespect to your daughter, but you have no right to make plans for my life."

"What… is she not attractive enough for you? Have you noticed how beautiful her eyes are? Like Mengele before me, I have long been fascinated by the colors of one's eyes and have made great inroads in the science. He wanted to cure heterochromia, which I see that you suffer from, by injecting adrenaline directly into the eyes. Instead, I have been injecting her eyes with a beautiful green dye for years now and feel it has been highly successful." Sage turned so that we could better see her eyes.

I was aghast at the thought of this. "Why would you do this? How could you possibly risk your daughter's vision, or even life, for something so trivial, and frankly I don't feel that I'm suffering from having different colored eyes."

Branson scoffed at my comment. "Your comment is both petulant and immature. That's the problem with so many young people today, it's all about themselves. How about thinking outside your myopic box and looking at the big picture. Think of how your children, brilliant children, might be able to help mankind."

I felt the frustration mounting. "You need to understand that each of us deserves the right to do what makes us happy as long as - unlike you - it doesn't hurt others. I enjoy working as a waiter, living in New Orleans and being able to choose my friends and hopefully, a mate with whom to have children. Doesn't Sage deserve that same opportunity?"

He wanted no part of my argument. "Bullshit. It's up to parents to make decisions for their children because they do not have the experience to do so. We mandate them eating vegetables, going to bed on time and what to watch or read because if left to their judgement children would make improper decisions. I will decide when, and with whom, Sage procreates."

My father had heard enough. He looked at his watch and said, "Miles,

I have no idea what the authorities intend to do with you. As you know, that's up to the Department of Justice. You've been involved in illegal experimentation for years now to say nothing about any others whose death you are responsible for. There is an FBI team arriving now to take you into custody."

"Do you understand what you're doing Rawlings? This is my life's work." He swept his arms in a wide arc. "This will be the salvation for countless people for generations to come."

"Oh, I understand exactly what I'm doing and only wish that I'd done it years ago."

Branson looked resigned as he got up from behind his desk. "Can Sage and I at least take some files with us. I have so much data that is both indispensable and irreplaceable. Let me take a handful of the most recent cases."

"Sorry Branson but I can't let you do that. Furthermore, I have no idea what the government authorities will do with those or any of your other equipment when they arrive. Again, that will be the DOJ, not the FBI, that makes that decision. Grab what you need for personal items and let's go outside."

"You'll regret this, Rawlings. You and everyone else in your short-sighted agency. I have life-altering data, ground breaking results from so many projects that could… that will, change the world."

My father headed out of the TV monitor room. "Be that as it may, I believe you are not only evil but insane. Let's go," he said with increased emphasis.

"I cannot believe you're doing this to me." He beckoned to Sage.

My father and I walked behind the two while we exited the lab and walked through the tunnel into the clearing. He had once again removed his Glock and was keeping it trained on Branson - just in case. As we approached the Explorer three FBI vehicles pulled into the clearing one of which was an armored SWAT vehicle. "I wasn't sure what we were going to find when we got here so I requested some heavy metal," he said.

The agents parked their dark sedans beside my father's SUV leaving space for the SWAT vehicle up front, closest to the tunnel entrance. My father removed a pair of handcuffs from the back of his Explorer and placed them on the two Bransons with one cuff on each of their wrists. When the agents saw that my father had the pair under control they gathered around. I stepped away so as not to intrude but I could hear their plans as could the Branson's.

The intent was for one team to take Branson and his daughter to Quantico for an interrogation while the others would remove files from the cave.

The agents huddled to finalize plans and after a couple of minutes of conversation the discussion broke up and my father came over beside me. Branson and his daughter had been left standing in the clearing and neither had moved during that time.

As the team of agents assigned to take the pair back to Virginia walked toward them Branson called out to my father. "Hey Rawlings, if you think for a minute that you're taking Sage and I back to some military prison to be poked, prodded and studied then you've got another think coming."

I watched as he reached with his one free hand into the pocket of his lab coat and removed something which he then placed in his daughter's mouth and then his own. My father screamed "Stop, Stop him!" He raced across toward the scientist and grabbed at his face squeezing his cheeks. Branson turned his head away freeing himself from my fathers grasp. He lost his balance and fell to his knees dragging his daughter down with him.

I watched as Sage fell unconscious and a minute later so, too, did Miles. "God damn it," my father shouted looking up at the mountain. I wanted that sunovabitch to stand trial and answer to all of the crimes he's committed and illegal experimentation he's done.

I stepped closer to the bodies lying on the ground, "What did they take?" I asked.

"I'm assuming it was something like cyanide pills," he said. "They have the capacity to work quickly, especially on her since she's much lighter."

One of the other agents kneeled down checking for a pulse in Branson and found none. After a time in which everyone involved voiced annoyance and displeasure at what had happened, an agent, whom I had heard my father call Chet, said, "I'll take the bodies to Quantico to be autopsied. Let's get in there and grab all of the files and records he kept. There's nothing more that can be done out here. JP, why don't you and Lonnie hit the road. We can finish up."

My father nodded his agreement. "Thanks Chet, if you're sure you're okay then that's what we'll do. It's been a tough couple of days. I just want to make one more trip inside."

My father took a couple of minutes to speak with the men on site and then walked back down into the tunnel. A few minutes later he returned to the Explorer where I was waiting. "I went back into the lab to take some pictures and see if there was anything that I felt compelled to take. I'll need to weigh in on this entire experience when I file my report and wanted to get one last look. There's nothing more that I can do now. Whatta ya' say we head back to the Big Easy."

"Sounds good to me," I said, but I could tell that he was having trouble fathoming what had occurred.

"Can you believe that, rather than answer for his work, he killed himself."

"I find it even more staggering that he allowed his daughter, someone who had her whole life in front of her, to die also... and why would she go along with that?"

"I'm sure that he had convinced her long ago that this would be their exit strategy if they were ever caught. This was not a spontaneous act. Here she was, a brilliant young lady who could have done so much for society, and instead she follows her father to an ignominious death. Do you see why I was desperate to get you away from him and his insanity?"

"I absolutely understand now. Thank you."

CHAPTER 86

WE HEADED BACK home and before long my father pulled off the road to make a call to his superiors in the FBI headquarters and one other to the Senator who chaired the committee originally authorizing him to search for Branson. He apologized for stepping outside and walking a distance away but I understood. While it was alright for him to tell me who he was going to call, it was not permissible for me to hear all that was said.

It was now late in the afternoon and as the sun was just beginning to set over the mountain my phone rang. It was Fey.

"Lonnie, it's Fey. Are you alright?"

"We're both okay but I can't say the same for Branson and his daughter. They committed suicide before they could be taken away." I spent the next ten minutes describing the days events without going into too much detail.

I pictured her blonde hair, beautiful smile and curvy body and wished that I was holding her in my arms. "How are you doing, how's Dalton and everyone at *Bon Vivant?*"

"I called Dalton a little while ago to ask if he'd heard anything from you. He said he hadn't but he and I are doing fine. But, I'm afraid I have some bad news. Antoine got the results from a biopsy that he had done recently and… it isn't good Lonnie. He doesn't want to talk about it but I heard him on the phone telling someone that he had stage 4 pancreatic cancer. I don't know what that means in terms of treatment or time but I know it isn't good. We all feel so bad."

"Oh my god, that's horrible news. He's such a great guy." I paused and had tears fill my eyes as I thought how kind and patient he had been with me throughout my ordeal. "Is he still coming in to work?"

"He comes in every morning but then leaves. I don't know how long he will, or can, do that."

"Fey, please tell him that I am praying for him and will be back soon - hopefully tomorrow. And tell him that I will take as many shifts as he needs me to so that he doesn't need to worry... and tell him that I will call him on the way home." I realized that I was rambling but I was sure that Fey understood what my feelings were. "Will you do that for me?" I asked.

"Of course I will, I'd be glad to."

"... and one more thing."

"Yeah."

"I really miss you Fey and every time I think of you a smile comes to my face. I can't wait until I can have you in my arms again," I paused because on one hand I couldn't believe I had just said those words but on the other it just seemed right.

"I miss you too Lonnie and I feel the exact same way but as I told you the last time that we were together, there's some things I've got to tell you. Be safe and hurry home."

We drove a couple more hours and then decided to stop at a restaurant outside of Atlanta. I had a fried chicken dinner, which was edible but couldn't compare to that of Willie Mae's Scotch House back home in NOLA. I thought of Montero earlier commenting on how exquisite and varied the food choices were in New Orleans.

As we finished our meal my father said, "I know you've anxious to get back, as am I, but would you mind if we found a motel and stopped for the night?"

I thought about offering to drive the last leg but understood this wasn't the time and said, "Sure, no problem."

I looked at him and realized how hard he had worked the past couple of days and how much he had been through both emotionally and psychologically. I had been thinking of how much my life had changed but realized, especially after today, that so had his.

CHAPTER 87

THE NEXT MORNING I felt a sense of relief and satisfaction I hadn't felt in years. I couldn't wait to get back to New Orleans to see Fey, Dalton, and a return to normalcy. Until my daily existence had been turned upside down by Wormwood's intrusion and the resultant complications, I hadn't realized how much I craved regimen in my life. I also was anxious to share my father with those close to me and to explore what having him in my life meant to me.

"What'll happen to all of the scientists and subjects that we saw on those screens now that he's gone?" I asked.

"I will file my report accompanied by several of the photos I took on my phone along with the actual files that you still have and I'm sure there will be a comprehensive effort to find those other labs. So many Congressmen and women have chosen to put their heads in the sand and refuse to believe that this type of experimentation was still being done but that should no longer be the case."

"I'm just glad that it's finally over - and more importantly, I'm glad to have finally have found out the truth and have you in my life."

"I'm glad of that, too, and glad that I no longer need to be a dish-washer," he joked.

I laughed at his comment but then was reminded of something he had promised to tell me long ago - before I knew he was my Dad. "You told me awhile ago that you would tell me the story of your tattoo. - of the raven, or perhaps you have others."

"Ah yes, I did say that didn't I. I have just the one tattoo but it means a great deal to me. I chose the raven because it best symbolizes the father of the Gods - Odin.

As you recognized in solving one of the early clues, Odin used two ravens to gain knowledge."

"Hugin and Munin: thought and memory."

"Yes, and in his search for ultimate wisdom, a higher state of consciousness, he was willing to sacrifice an eye and hanged himself for nine days."

I listened and felt that I could see where he was going. "You made a similar sacrifice."

He became solemn. "Absolutely. I feel that I made a huge sacrifice, not in hanging, but in giving up the two people in my life who meant the most to me. Hence, the tie in with Odin and the raven. Every morning when I wake up I rub that patch of ink, think of what I've done, and vow to make every day a meaningful one - now with you in my life."

He continued. "Speaking of dishwashing, I need to call Antoine and give him my notice. I won't leave him in the lurch but he'll need to hire someone else."

"If you don't mind I was going to call him this morning anyway and tell him that we're coming back. I hear he is not doing well but he's usually at the restaurant in the morning." My father nodded and I dialed the number.

Antoine picked up on the second ring.

"Hello Antoine, this is Lonnie. I'm here with my Dad, and I'm going to put you on speaker. We're heading back now to New Orleans."

"Oh Lonnie, I am so thrilled to hear what has happened. You have been through so much and I can't even imagine how happy you must be to have finally found your father."

I noticed his voice was both raspy and weak. "I am Antoine, but how about you. I understand that you've been given some difficult news."

There was a pause on the other end of the line and then a slight cough. "Yes, it's true. I'm afraid that I have been diagnosed with both pancreatic and lung cancer. I'm told that I have not been given much time to live and I was going to wait until I saw you in person to ask you this but now that you're on the phone I'll ask you now. Then you can think about it and talk it over with your father. Is that okay?"

I wasn't sure what he was asking but of course said, "Absolutely, what would you like?"

"What I would like… is for you… or you and your father, to take over *Bon Vivant.*"

I was staggered by the depth of that question and struggled to respond. "I guess I don't know what you mean by that, Antoine."

"I mean that I would very much like for you to have my restaurant… to own it and run it like I have for the past thirty-seven years."

My father and I looked at each other with a sense of disbelief. "I could never do that… and furthermore, you may live a lot longer than the doctors think. And besides, what about family?"

Antoine chuckled which led to another cough. "Lonnie, I know that you realize the definition of *Bon Vivant* relates to good food and dining but it also refers to a good life and that is what it has given me, For all of these years I have been privileged to not only make a good living, but also to meet many outstanding people." He began to wheeze and paused.

"In the five years that you have worked with me - not for me, but with me - I have grown to consider you my son - the son that I never had. Now that you've found your real father I am thrilled to hand you off to him." He chuckled again.

"As for family, I have one brother. Francois lives in Baton Rouge and has no interest in owning a restaurant. Hell, he's only been in *Bon Vivant* twice since I've owned it. I haven't even seen him in over three years. But, because blood is blood, I'm going to leave the money I've saved to him. Ha, but he's going to have to come here to get it… see me one more time."

"Lonnie, you would be doing me a favor. I don't want to sell it and I don't want it to wind up in some New Yorker's hands with newfangled ideas." He once again paused to catch his breath.

I was still somewhat in shock. "Antoine, you've taken me completely by surprise. I really don't know what to say."

"It would mean the world to me if you would say 'yes'."

I again looked at my Dad who was solemnly nodding his head in what I took to mean, 'accept this kind offer from someone who you would make extremely happy'.

"Antoine," I said, "If you're sure that this is what you want, then I would love to take you up on your incredibly kind offer. I would like nothing more than to own and manage - hopefully with my father - *Bon Vivant.*"

"I hope you know that you've just made an old, sick man very happy. And Lonnie," he said with a chuckle, "I might know where you can get a couple of pretty good waitstaff."

After hanging up my father and I spent the next couple of hours discussing that turn of events, what it meant for both of us, and how my life had suddenly become so propitious, at least financially. After all, owning a restaurant, condo and bank account couldn't make up for the loss of Bob, Martha, my mother, Sammi or the years without my Dad.

We drove on and I smiled as once again the speed limits were considered suggestions not ultimatums.

CHAPTER 88

THE NEXT MORNING I was awakened by my phone ringing and when I looked at the clock I saw that it was after 9:00. We hadn't arrived until 2:00 so I wasn't surprised that I had slept in. I looked at the phone and saw that it was Fey who was calling.

"Hey Fey, Good morning,"

"Good morning. I'm glad you're back. You been up long?"

"Only since the phone rang," I said. "But it's time I got up. What are you doing today."

"I work both the afternoon and evening shifts so I'm off this morning. Are you going to be home for awhile, I'd like to come over?"

"Yeah, I'm going to be here. I think Dalton's working and I need to clean the condo."

About an hour later Fey showed up and unlike her normal arrival where she bounces up the stairs, she was walking slowly and I could tell something was bothering her. She walked directly into the living room and sat down on the couch. Tears were rolling down her face. "Fey, what's the matter?" I sat down beside her and put my arm around her shoulders.

She put her head down and sobbed into her hands.I waited allowing her to gain her composure. Finally, she looked up and turned towards me. "You know how I told you after I spent the night that I had something I wanted to talk with you about?"

"Yes, you didn't have time at that point, you said."

"Lonnie, I feel awful because I've done something horrible." Her body was wracked with crying. "But please know, I never meant to hurt you."

I asked softly, "What are you talking about? What did you do?"

"First of all, I lied to you. When we were coming back from Leesville I told you that I hadn't spoken with my mother and have had no contact but that isn't true. The truth is that I have a good relationship with my mother and we speak a couple of times a week."

"Why did you feel the need to -"

"Please... let me finish. I've held this in for too long and need to get it out." I nodded.

"What I told you about my step father was all true. He was a total dick and was the biggest reason I moved to New Orleans. My mother on the other hand is so sweet and caring. The problem is that she recently had a house fire - Joe was smoking and fell asleep - and she didn't have enough insurance to cover the repairs. Rather than help with a solution, he left her. Mom was devastated emotionally, psychologically, and even financially because, as big a jerk as he is, he has a good job and made many of the payments. She's staying in a rundown motel." She began to cry once again.

I pulled her into my body. We hugged for a long minute and then I asked, "Are you sure you want to keep going? I'm so sorry that this has happened."

"I do... and Lonnie, it's me that's sorry. You haven't heard what I did. I took money for reporting on Wormwood... and later... on you." She stopped again.

"What did you report... to whom... what for?" I found myself at a loss for words and stuttering.

"After Wormwood was seen coming to *Bon Vivant* the first time I was confronted by a man who offered me money if I would call every time I saw him. Then, after he came to the condo, and it was determined that you were the super baby, I was offered more money to report on your findings... they wanted to know if and when you found your mother and your father."

"Who was it that you were dealing with? Who was paying you for this information?"

"Two men actually, a Ben Evans and Frank Irving who identified themselves as FBI agents. They followed me one night when I was walking home and made me an offer. They swore me to secrecy and assured me that no one would get hurt. They said I would actually be doing a public service. Oh Lonnie, I feel so bad but I knew my mother needed the money so I sent it to her - $5,000 in all. I would never do anything to hurt you." Her eyes once again filled with tears.

I could see how genuinely upset she was and my heart steered my direction. I pulled her into me and hugged her with all my might. She reciprocated and then pulled back her head to kiss me. "I love you," she said when we finished kissing.

"Fey, I want you to know that I forgive you. After what I've gone through trying to find my parents, I completely understand why you would want to help your mother. And there was one more thing that I was going to say but I seem to have forgotten."

She looked at me with a quizzical look.

"Oh yes," I continued, "now I remember... I love you too."

She rolled her eyes and smiled.

CHAPTER 89

THREE WEEKS HAD passed since the events in Asheville and behind the scenes Antoine had made good on his phone declaration on the ride home. The restaurant was now in my name. I had tried to have my father's name added as well but he was having none of that. "Lonnie, thank you for wanting to have my name on the paperwork but that is not necessary. Antoine wants you to own it, and besides, I will be here to help you manage it. Not that you'll need me to."

We were gathered at *Bon Vivant* on a Saturday morning. We intend to host a grand re-opening party but that will take place later. This was for the current employees of the restaurant and anyone who had worked there in the past. We chose a morning to host this because we wanted Antoine to be there. He was growing weaker by the day and, although he now used a wheel chair to get around, he assured us that he would make it.

Fey, Dalton and several others of the waitstaff had put up balloons and signs thanking Antoine for his many years of ownership and kindness. Word of mouth advertising had been incredibly successful and the entire restaurant was full of people - all wanting to thank the man who had been their boss and, most knowing of his health condition, to pay their respects.

I had arranged with the management of Brennan's to have this break-fast party catered because I didn't want any of the current employees to have to work and when I told them the reason for the party they told me that there would be no charge. "There's been no one nicer or more professional in our business and our city," was what I was told.

When I told him that I was taking over ownership he said "maybe when I retire in 25-30 years you can repay the favor, if you can remember this conversation." His laughter on the other end of the phone indicated that he had at some point heard of me. "It's a deal," I replied.

Fey, Dalton, my Dad and I arrived a couple of hours ahead of everyone else along with one other person. She was recently hired to be the hostess at *Bon Vivant* and we all felt Marcia Chadwick, Fey's mom, would do a great job. Needless to say, Fey was thrilled.

It was now the time that we'd told Antoine to arrive. He was carried inside and then placed in his wheel chair by his brother Francois.

Many were surprised to see how many people were in attendance and, as all of the employees new and old came up to say hello or shake his hand, they were saddened to see how frail he had become.

We had a small microphone and speaker set up and I gave everyone who wanted to speak a chance to come up. It was slow at first as no one knew just what to say but soon there was a line and the expressions of love and gratitude permeated the room.

Finally, as I saw that Antoine was starting to get tired, I took the mic and handed it to him and asked if there was anything he'd like to say.

He started to thank everyone and as he did tears poured down his cheeks. "I never could have imagined this day or how many friends I have made simply by running a restaurant. I know that I am not well and may not have much longer to enjoy this great city."

He paused to collect his thoughts and catch his breath. "But I want you to know how happy I am that Lonnie Clifford is taking over *Bon Vivant*. I have no doubts that he'll do a fabulous job. And Lonnie, before I leave I have one request. I'd like you to tell the gathering here today when you started working here and what you were wearing. He handed the microphone back to me.

This caught me totally off guard and I hated to speak in front of crowds but felt I owed him the answer to his question. "It was on a Tuesday, April 8th, five years ago. It was cloudy and overcast when I arrived at 7:52 - eight minutes before our scheduled meeting. I had on a pair of khaki trousers that were a bit too long and a light green polo shirt…"

Antoine took the mic away from me. "And that, ladies and gentlemen, is why we believe he is truly *gifted*."

ABOUT THE AUTHOR

RICK SIMONDS HAS spent a lifetime sharpening his craft as a writer and spent many years teaching creative writing to high school students. In addition to having written columns for two newspapers in Maine, he has served as both a columnist and feature writer for national trade magazines. He is the author of Blood Code and Blood Sport, both highly acclaimed murder mysteries. He continues to live and write in Maine.

Ricksimonds.net

OTHER WORK BY RICK SIMONDS

BLOOD CODE

"Very few things scare me, this book did."

STEVE WEBSTER,
Detective Sergeant and
author of One Promise Kept.

*"Edgy and Tense, the suspense kept me
turning pages well into the night."*

JOE LOUGHLIN,
Asst. Chief of Police (ret.) and
author of Finding Amy.

BLOOD SPORT

"A terrifying tale loaded with suspense, action and police procedure."

BILL BUSHNELL,
Kennebec Journal

"Simonds has an exciting and entertaining hit mystery here."

WATERVILLE MORNING SENTINEL